WORRYBIRD

WORRYBIRD

The Life Story of a WWII Bomber
and the Crew Who Flew Her

RODERICK STANLEY

Published in the United States by Flying Horsemen Publishing LLC
Appomattox, Virginia.
2nd Printing

Jacket design: Jason Stanley

Front jacket photo: National Archives. USAF 51982AC. Waves of Consolidated B-24 Liberators of the 15th Air Force Fly Over the Target Area, Concordia Vega Oil Refinery, Ploesti, Rumania, 31, May 1944

Back jacket photos: National Archives. USAF 62053AC. Bombing of Hatvan, Hungary, by Consolidated B-24 "Liberators" of the 15th Air Force, on 20, September 1944.

Author photograph: Jane Stanley

Library of Congress Control Number: 2024903813
Hardcover ISBN 9798989630905
Paperback ISBN 9798989630912
eBook ISBN 9798989630929

Flying Horsemen Publishing LLC
PO Box 306 Appomattox, Virginia 24522
Worrybird449@gmail.com

1st Lieutenant William G. Stanley

1923 - 2019

Contents

PREFACE

"WARS PRODUCE MANY STORIES OF FICTION," Ulysses S. Grant wrote in his memoirs concerning the immediate post-surrender rumor of meeting with Confederate General Robert E. Lee under an apple tree, much to the detriment of the innocent tree and the truth. I hope the truth didn't suffer from the abuse of my pen in the writing of this story.[1]

"What's going to happen to my diary?" my father, Bill Stanley, known as "Stan" by his *Worrybird* crewmates, asked me a year before his passing. Judging by the expressionless look on his face when he heard my recommendation of donating it to a military archive such as the Army's Heritage and Education Center, I knew he envisioned something else. Unfortunately, I didn't press the matter, and he was soon gone from us. Too late to ask the many questions I have since thought asking of him.

As my brothers, sister, and I went through Dad's personal belongings, I was deemed the depository of most things historically related to our family. As I perused through the documents that now occupied the full length of

---

1. Grant, Ulysses S., *The Personal Memoirs of Ulysses S. Grant, 2 vols.* New York: Charles L. Webster, 1885, p. 488. Small pieces of the unfortunate tree, carved into a soldier's Civil War memorabilia keepsake, are viewable at the American Civil War Museum-Appomattox, Virginia.

a folding table, I came across a box full of files labeled: "Discharge Forms," "Bombardiering Records," "Army Records," and the one pertaining to this story, "Diaries." There I found his original war diary covering his time as a crewmember of the B-24 Liberator heavy bomber, the *Worrybird*, along with transcribed versions of the war diaries of *Worrybird*'s pilot, Norman "Pop" Blomgren, and another by her navigator, Robert "Bob" Simmons.

I had seen them years before when Dad began to open up more concerning his time as the bombardier on the *Worrybird*. He even wrote about some of the episodes detailed in his diary into a thin spiralbound booklet for his family entitled; *The War Years 1942–1945 William G. Stanley*.

And yet, he wanted more. Staring at the three diaries a few days after his celebration of life service, with his memory still so strongly imprinted upon my mind, I remembered something he had said a few years earlier about those diaries now held in my hands. "Those diaries would make a great book!" he said, holding his hands up and shaking them to emphasize the point, as he often did when telling a story.

A story. Not just a dry publication of the many, now yellowing pages, but a story combining the experiences of three of the *Worrybird*'s officers. But what kind of story? There have been many excellent, primary source historical books and novels written concerning an individual's World War II exploits, accomplishments, sufferings, and ultimate triumphs. What could I add? Like many of life's questions, the answer came in the most unusual of circumstances.

It was while I was reading to my three-year-old grandson, Henry, when the idea literally appeared on the pages in front of me. "Gramps, don't stop!" Henry exclaimed as I stopped reading while I pondered the possibility. For I was reading an illustrated children's construction site book in which the trucks, excavators, dozers, and even cranes were conversing with one another. They had consciousness. They were "alive."

Why not? It had been done before, a book about a war seen not through the eyes of the human participant, but through the eyes and the perspective of one of the participant's tools of war. *Traveller,* authored by

Richard Adams, recounts another war, the American Civil War, through the eyes of the aforementioned General Robert E. Lee's horse, Traveller.

While Traveller was alive, he had feelings, possessed empathy for others, and could communicate, albeit not through the spoken word. An aircraft, Jeep, or a GMC deuce-and-a-half truck is a whole new ballgame. Or is it?

How many times have you talked to an inanimate object as if it were alive? A car, truck, boat, or ship? Spoken to affectionately when it does well by you, or calling it every cussed name ever conceived when it does you wrong. Be careful, for he, she, or they may have feelings.

From her "birth" to her ultimate "death," this is the story of World War II's air war over Europe through the *Worrybird*'s perspective, through her eyes. She also shares the seldom told struggles crossing the United States to meet her crew for the first time and their harrowing transatlantic crossing.

The stories *Worrybird* relates all occurred. The names of the planes, of the aircrews, the nuances of the missions, and the results, occurred mostly as written. The three diaries supply not only the real- time inner thoughts of the authors, but also details of the mundane life between missions. The diaries are exceptional in their similarities. It's not hard to imagine Stan, Pop, and Bob, sitting at their small individual tables under flickering kerosene lamp light, putting down on paper their thoughts of the day, each with only a slightly different take on the transpired events. I have no record that Harry Bursten, the co-pilot, kept a diary, though I am sure his take and details of events were given, incorporated and welcomed.

Backing this up were the six books of reminisces and research written by members of the 449th Bomb Group Association. The *Worrybird* was one of the sixty-four planes composing the 449th Bomb Group. Some of the mission and life-in-camp details were supplemented by these memories. These records were also invaluable in discerning the actual names of the planes, beyond their unique, individual combat number, giving each the aura of individualism, of being alive.

"Ground truthing" all of the above were the individual mission files of the 449th Bomb Group kept at the Air Force Historical Research Agency

(AFHRA), Maxwell Air Force Base, Montgomery, Alabama. The Army scrutinized, reported, documented, and copied everything. And none of it was thrown away. While the sterile data, such as takeoff, bombing, and landing times of every plane was in itself useful, it was the after-mission interrogation reports that shed light on an individual plane's mission experience. These gave the aircrew the opportunity to not only document their observations, but also a chance to vent their true, immediate thoughts and emotions concerning the mission without fear of reprisal. This stuff never gets in the books. It does in these pages.

Flying under the Golden Gate Bridge, the near lethal encounter with a "hurricane," singing onstage with Jack Teagarden's band, and narrowly becoming lost over the Atlantic, are recollections I have of my dad telling my siblings and me his wartime stories, at least the ones he wanted us to hear. These stories were not described in the diaries of the men, for all three began April 3, 1944, the day they arrived at the base they would call home for the next five months.

The only "stories of fiction" which occur in the book are twofold. First, there was no one to archive *Worrybird*'s travel from her Dallas, Texas, birthplace, to her Novato, California, destination. While her leapfrogging across various Army Air Corps airfields is mostly correct, the true to life pilots, aircrews and servicemen mentioned mostly were not. Their names are included to individually honor them and their actual WWII service.

Secondly, the dialog is how I interpret it given the circumstances. The tone, the sentiment, and the fear, are based upon what Stan, Pop, or Bob expressed that night in their diary entries, or as documented in the after-action interrogation reports. And of course, there was no one there to record the aircraft's interplane dialog, or *Worrybird*'s most inner thoughts. There, I believe, the truth indeed was "stretched."

The author
Appomattox, Virginia

PROLOGUE

Stanley farm east of Cunningham, Kansas, Christmas night, 1933

*"D*ICK HAD A LATE LUNCH *at Stony Springs and started the return flight home, richer by thirty dollars for the morning trip."*

"Thirty dollars! Holy smokes, just for flying a few hours in the morning," exclaimed Rut, a young lad of eight years.

"Quiet, and stay on your side of the rope! You know this bed isn't big enough for the both of us as it is," demanded Rut's older brother Bill, known as "Billy" to everyone, who at the mature age of ten was a much more worldly lad, already tall and lanky. "Now let me finish this chapter before Mom yells at us to put out the lamp and go to sleep."

"He was cruising blissfully toward home, less than twenty miles from their own airport, when a spatter of oil struck the front of the cabin and blurred the glass. His attention instantly focused on the engine, Dick's eyes detected a thin stream of oil shooting from under the cowling. He looked at the oil pressure. It was dropping fast. An oil line had broken."

"Golly Ned! I think I'd pee in my pants if that happened to me," interrupted Rut. A quick look of a stern, furrowed brow from his brother quieted him for the last time.

"The home field was still a good eighteen miles away and there was only one thing to do; land and try and repair the broken feed line. The oil was

spurting out in sharp jets, spattering over the front windows and making vision difficult. He would have to get down fast and with this realization Dick looked for an adequate landing field. The only level ground of any extent nearby appeared to be a clover field slightly to his right and he nosed the Robin that way. There was a low rim of willows on the near side of the field but getting over them safely was a chance Dick would have to take."

"He tried opening one of the front windows but a spatter of hot oil seared his face and he closed it promptly. He was losing oil rapidly and to keep the motor from burning up he snapped off the ignition. It would be a 'dead-stick' landing."

"There was a last spurt of oil from the motor that blanketed the front windows with a dark film and Dick's view of the fast-approaching ground was limited to what he could see from the side windows. It was going to be hard to judge the distance. Then he caught sight of the willows which bordered the side of the field he was approaching. They were low but so was the Robin. The motor was dead and Dick sensed, too late, that he was going to crash." [1]

A loud squeak from the bottom stair step gave early warning that the young Stanley brothers' story time was about to come to a quick, unscheduled conclusion. "Billy! Rut! You douse that light and go to sleep. Morning is going to come early enough, along with your chores," said their mother in a soft but definitely firm voice.

"Yes, Mom," the boys dutifully replied in unison.

"Sure am glad you won that book," said Rut in a hushed tone.

---

1. Patton, Harris. *Wings of the North. The Young Eagles Series.* Chicago, Illinois: The Goldsmith Publishing Company, 1932, pp. 44–45. Billy received this book as a Christmas present from his Sunday School teacher. The inside cover is signed "Billy Stanley, Gr. 5. 10 years old. Got it December 25, 1933." This book put into the young Stanley brothers' heads the dream to fly one day. The fact that my father kept the book for over 80 years signifies its sentimental value. In author's possession.

"Won nothing," Billy exclaimed indignantly, "I earned that book by not missing a single Sunday school class this year."

The ensuing silence was finally broken when Rut wistfully asked, "Billy, do you think you could be as brave as Dick was if your motor died and you knew you were going to crash?"

"Well, sure," said Billy with the swaggering confidence of an older brother. "It's just a matter of doing what you practiced, remembering your training and not getting excited, that's all."

"I don't know," said Rut. "I think I would still pee in my pants."

After a few quiet moments, Rut pensively asked, "Billy, do you think we'll ever learn to fly and have our very own plane?"

"Oh, I'm sure of it, both of us," softly replied Billy with a faraway look in his hazel eyes. "Now put out the lamp."

With his cupped hand cradling the back of the lamp's chimney opening, Rut blew softly across the opening, sending curling smoke streamers into the waxing moonlit night of their frosty bedroom.

PART ONE

From little towns in a far land we came,
To save our honour and a world aflame.
By little towns in a far land we sleep;
And trust that world we won for you to keep!

Rudyard Kipling, 1919

1

BIRTH

NORTH AMERICAN AVIATION ASSEMBLY PLANT, DALLAS, TEXAS, JANUARY 1944

In a foggy and dreamlike awareness, interrupted by a cacophony of clanging sounds of metal assaulting other metal, another B-24 Liberator heavy bomber slowly came to the realization that not only did it exist, but that it was conscious. And as with all other sentient organisms with consciousness came the myriad questions of existence: what am I, who am I, what am I doing here, where is here, why do I exist, just what is my purpose? And like most other living beings, many of the answers to those questions wouldn't be divulged until the very end of their life's journey.

The first abstract thought of the B-24, now known solely as 42-78173, was that it didn't like noise. This just wasn't any noise, but a noise that filled and overwhelmed every silent thought. BRRRRP. HISSSS. BR-RRRRRRP. Twanggg, Blam, Blam, Blam.

Noise, noise, NOISE! Hammers, mallets, grinders, metal cutoff saws, chains, air compressors, and the pneumatic rivet gun and bucking bar combo of thousands of workers simultaneously working on over thirty B-24s as quickly as humanly possible. And the workers, ranging from 16 to 60 years of age, were mostly White, Black, and Hispanic women working side by side. Sometimes there were over ten of them on a single plane, jabbering away at high volume to help pass the time away. It was at this moment that 42-78173 realized that these creatures, which had two dangling, gawky appendages and possessed bipedal locomotion on two long, lanky stalks, could talk out loud, while it could not. No matter how hard it tried, 42-78173 could not convey to these creatures to stop making their infernal racket.

Ziing. Rat-a-tat-tat. "Yeow! What the Sam Hill was that?! And who the hell is Sam Hill?" Zing, rat-a-tat-tat. "Will you stop it for Pete's sake! Now where did that come from? I am sooo confused," 42-78173 thought with the raspy sound of desperation in its voice. "If you don't stop, I'm going to roll myself right out of here as soon as the monstrosity in front of me gets out of my way. Do you hear me!?"

"Whoa, partner, that wasn't very neighborly of you calling me a monstrosity like that now, was it?" exclaimed another Liberator a scant five feet in front and above it.

"Who said that, and where are you?" 42-78173 cried out.

"Why, right in front of you, kid. You know, that so called monstrosity," said the nearby Liberator, the sarcasm barely hidden in its Texas drawl.

Ziing. Rat-a-tat-tat. "Will you stop doing that!" it bellowed. "What in the blazes are those things doing to me?"

"Why, they're making the rest of you. If you hadn't noticed, you aren't exactly all put together yet," said the other Liberator. "And that zing you feel? Get used to it. Those are called rivets, and there's over 360,000 of them in you. Just be glad you were still asleep when most of them were drilled and hammered into you. And those 'things' are people, and you might as well get used to them 'cause they're going to be all over and in you like flies on a cow pie."[1]

"Why is it you know so much, or at least pretend to?" 42-78173 said suspiciously.

"Why, that's because I'm older than you, kid. You stick with me and keep your ears open, maybe you'll learn as much as I know," the front plane said smugly.

"If you know so much, then just what are we? And if I'm not complete yet, then what will I be when they're done working on me?" it asked.

"Why, that's simple, you'll be a Liberator just like the rest of us in here," replied the older ship.

"A Lib, Libby, Libbyrater, you said?" it stuttered, still trying to master the nuances of verbal speech.

"Jeesh, no, a Liberator," said the front plane in an exasperated voice. "I heard a person who was installing my de-icer bladders say that's what we are. Someone in a place called England said that we're going to help liberate millions of these people who are under Hitler's yoke. And before you ask, no, I don't know where England is or who Hitler is. He must be some sort of tyrant, though, to have that many people under a yoke. And that must be one gargantuan yoke; nothing like the two in front of those seats in our cockpits.[2]

"Say, I think I'll call you *Libby* if you don't mind. It sure beats kid."

"Nah, I don't mind," said *Libby* with a little more self confidence in her voice now that she had an idea of who and what she was. "So, if I'm *Libby*, what are you called?"

"Well, of course they call me *Texican* since I was born here in Texas," he boasted. "That's where we are, a land they call Texas where everything

---

1. Baine, A.J. *The Arsenal of Democracy*, p. 162. Boston: Mariner Books, 2014.

2. Ambrose, Stephen E. *The Wild Blue*, p. 22. New York, NY: Simon and Schuster, 2001.

is big. Where else would they build something like us, I ask you? They say us Liberators are the biggest planes being built anywhere."

Looking out her front turret, all *Libby* could see was the shiny thin aluminum skin of dozens of other Liberators extending beyond her vision. Looking out her upper turret, all that was seen were steel girders, metal ducting, fans, and bright, dazzling lights. Oh, so many lights, dangling fifty feet above her. Out her back turret, she was shocked to see another Liberator slightly below her and oh-so-close. Close enough, she thought, she could reach out and touch it with the two dark, ominous pipes sticking out of her back end.

"Say, *Texican*, what are these two pipes sticking out of us in the back?" asked *Libby*. "Wait! There are some of them sticking out my front and on top too."

"Those are what they call Browning .50 caliber machine guns. We're supposed to get two more sticking out below us and two more sticking out our sides," informed *Texican*. "Not sure what we're going to use them for, though. Maybe they'll stick and sting someone who gets too close, like them thorns on prickly pear or mesquite trees. Golly, nothing hurts as bad as getting poked by those fellas. They'll put a hole right through our thin skin, don't you know?" he said in a painful tone.

Again looking out the back turret at the Liberator behind her, *Libby* noticed four huge, bizarre-looking, oval pods hanging onto what she sensed were its wings, two on each side. Looking out her front and top turrets she noticed she also had these strangely shaped pods hanging off her, as did every other Liberator she could see. "Now what in the heck are these things and what do they do?" she pondered. At first glance, she thought they looked like tits on a boar. Something just wasn't right, and they seemed to be missing something. What, she had no idea.

"Hey *Texican*, what are these weird-shaped pods dangling off our wings?" queried *Libby*.

"Why those are our engines. Pratt and Whitney Twin Wasps, they're called. From what I hear we'll use them to move around instead of being pulled along by this big ol' chain under us. And get a load of this. Those four engines are as powerful as 4,800 Texas mustangs! Can you imagine that? We are one invincible machine that no one will want to tangle with, don't you know?" *Texican* said with pride.

"I don't see how they're going to move us along. They don't even reach the ground. Is there something missing?" asked *Libby*.

"You sure are one inquisitive bird, aren't you?" exclaimed *Texican*. "But you're right, they're missing their propellers. I saw them on some Liberators outside this here building when they opened up the big doors. They remind me of huge prairie nymph flowers. You know, the one's with three petals, except they're as long as two of those people standing on top of each other."

"I'm just not sure what to make of all of this," muttered *Libby* in a shaky, unsure voice.

Just then she noticed that the ten people who had been poking, prodding, banging, riveting, and making a general nuisance of themselves were exiting through her body or coming down off her wings on ladders. And except for their insistent gabbing, it was getting awful quiet. All of the people were leaving. Moving in a line in marching order, they sort of reminded her of a line of fire ants heading solemnly in a single direction to some unknown destination. Just as potentially painful, too, she thought. "Man, now I'm sounding like *Texican*. Oh, this is more like it though. I could get used to this quiet," *Libby* cooed.

But it wasn't totally quiet now that she listened. From somewhere, everywhere—no, from overhead, she could hear people's voices and other mesmerizing sounds permeating the air. But unlike the incessant jabbering of those who worked on her, this was a pleasant sound. A sound with... oh, what's the word, she pondered. Rhythm, that's it. And that voice, it's actually soothing to my senses, unlike the high-pitched whine of the people working on her. I could listen to this all day. And what's that they're saying? No, wait, that's what they call singing, isn't it, she realized. How, she didn't know.

Listening to the words set to a mystical tone, she was mesmerized. There was something about the lyrics that seemed to strike a chord with her. Exactly what? She wasn't sure. She'd have to think about that.

"And that was, of course, The Song Spinners, with *'Comin' in on a Wing and a Prayer'* here on KSKY, found at 660 on your radio dial," announced a tinny voice on the overhead speakers.

"Don't get too used to it," warned *Texican*, breaking *Libby's* much needed musical reverie. "Another passel of these people will be coming in to replace the ones that just left. And they'll keep doing it over and over again, never giving us a moment of peace."

And as good as his word, within a few moments, a whole new gaggle of people were streaming in like fire ants to the different ships inhabiting the plant. Some disappeared into the bowels of those ships, while others entered rooms only to reappear a minute later carrying a dizzying array of items of all descriptions, which were but a few of the 1,225,000 parts in a B-24. These included wiring and cables of all lengths, sizes, and colors, 1,700 tubes, again of all sizes and lengths, some joined with blue and red unions looking like Christmas decorations. Then there were bottles, aluminum sheets, ribs, levers, and even cast-iron seats with no padding. Padding which could soothe the aching posteriors of the pilots who would soon be inhabiting them for up to eleven hours on end.[3] And as always, a metal box, of varying sizes, shapes, and colors, was carried by everyone, which hid an assortment of tools that would have been just as appropriate in a Spanish Inquisition torture chamber thought *Libby.*

As soon as that thought passed through her, a whole new group of people began pouring into her, setting down their tools of torture and carrying what seemed like armloads of different pieces and parts of every description. Some clambered their way to her very front nose turret, an-

---

3. Bowman, Constance & Allen, Clara Marie. *Slacks and Calluses*, p. 95. Washington, DC: Smithsonian Institution Press, 1999.

other two onto the flight deck, while another splayed out below her nose into a compartment that she heard called the bombardier's station. A whole handful stayed in her belly doing who knows what. But the most disconcerting was the smallest of these people, who they called Clara, wriggling her way actually inside one of her wings.

"Now, I wonder what this Clara is doing inside my wing?" *Libby* puzzled.

"Oh, get used to that!" exclaimed *Texican*. "Clara is what they call a woman. And since they're smaller than the other people they call men, women get to slither their way into our wings to install gas line tubing, and not just that, but to sometimes drive some of those nasty rivets into us. But what's worse is when they cram what they call 'black stuff' around our rubber gas tanks. Boy, that stuff sure stinks."[4]

"What's that you say? Rubber gas tanks, stinky black stuff?" inquired *Libby*.

"I just learned about those myself," said *Texican*. "I don't quite understand it all, but those tanks hold 2,794 gallons of what they call 100-octane high-test gasoline. Our engines feed on it to propel us. They're made out of special rubber that can seal up, so none of that gasoline leaks out. It must be special stuff for them to not want it to leak out so bad. But if it does leak out, that stinky black stuff is going to soak it up like rain in the West Texas sand."[5]

"Golly, whatever they're doing in my belly sure tickles," giggled *Libby*. "Why, they're pulling wire up and down my belly all the way up front and then back to my tail," she realized.

"That's something else you'll want to get used to. There's supposed to be over five miles of that stuff in us," informed *Texican*.

---

4. Ibid., p. 105.

5. AAF, Manual No. 50-12, B-24 Pilot Training Manual, Rev. May 1, 1945, p. 135.

"That sounds like a lot. But what's a mile?" queried *Libby*.

Texican thought about that for a second, trying to figure out how best to describe distance to someone who's only seen the limited inside dimensions of a factory building, one with no view of the outside world due to there being absolutely no windows. "That's it," he thought with a proud smirk. "Alright, can you see the far end of our building in front of you? Use your top turret to look."

"Yea, though it's pretty far away," squinted *Libby*.

"OK, now use your tail turret to look behind you to see the back end," instructed *Texican*. "One mile is four of our buildings laid together, so, let me do some rithmatick here, five miles would be, ah, twenty of our buildings in a row," he proudly stated, quite impressed with his rithmatick skills.

"That sure is a lot of wire," an astonished *Libby* replied.

"Well, if that wasn't enough to impress you, we also have almost one mile of tubing in us carrying that high-test gasoline, oil for our engines, hydraulic fluid, fire extinguishing fluid, de-icer fluid, and oxygen all throughout us. It takes a lot to get us Liberators going and keep us up in the air, don't you know?"[6]

Ruminating for a moment over what *Texican* had just described, *Libby* had a sudden flash of understanding, of comprehension as to why she, *Texican,* and the rest of the Liberators were being built. And it had been divulged in of all things, a song.

"*Texican*, I've got it! I know what we are, what we supposed to be, what we supposed to DO!" exclaimed *Libby*, almost tripping over the words as she spit them out in a staccato litany.

---

6. Ambrose, Steven E. *The Wild Blue*. p. 164. New York, NY: Simon and Schuster, 2001.

"Slow down, *Libby*. What's that you say? You know why we're being built?" asked *Texican* with more than a bit of skepticism in his voice. "And just how did this revelation come to pass?"

"They explained it in that song coming from up in the rafters. Don't you ever listen to them when you can?" an incredulous *Libby* asked, wondering how anyone could ignore something so mesmerizing to the soul.

"Why no," replied *Texican* sheepishly. "That's just more noise to me, with their voices flowing up and down that way. It reminds me of squeaky windmills complaining in the wind. I just can't follow it or join in, and when I do, it just sounds something awful."

"Well, if you had been listening during that last shift change, you would have heard the words in a song they call '*Comin' in on a Wing and a Prayer*,' said *Libby*. "We have wings. And they mentioned they had a motor gone. We have motors, though I'm not sure where their motor went to. They said something about their radios were humming and waiting for the word. We have a radio set. How do you think we talk to each other? And they really had a fight and they really clobbered the target. Don't you get it?" asked *Libby*. "You had said they call us Liberators 'cause we're going to liberate a bunch of people from some tyrant named Hitler. Well, that's what we're being built for. We're going to fight and hit our targets from up in the air. We're going to fight that Hitler fella. He's our target. They said they actually sing as they limp home, maybe since one of their motors was gone."

"So you think you have all the answers?" questioned a skeptical *Texican*.

"Heck no, there're some things I don't understand at all. Like, what's a prayer? I understand comin' in on a wing, but a prayer? Not sure I've seen them put one of those on us yet. And they said we put our trust in the Lord. I trust you, *Texican*. I even trust those people who are putting us together, but I'm not sure I can trust something I haven't seen. And of course I have no idea how we're going to hit our target if we're up in the air. Those .50 caliber Brownings aren't long enough to sting 'em."

"You know, I may have just the answer to that," responded *Texican*. "I've been piecing together some of the jabbering those people have been making in my belly. They keep mentioning they're working in a bomb bay and complaining about having to straddle a nine-inch-wide bomb bay catwalk. And then there are the men who built a couple of what they called bomb racks in there. They were mightily impressed that they could hold 8,000 pounds of bombs. That's like six of our engines, don't you know?"

"Say, you might be on to something there," said *Libby*. "The lads that were putting my bomb racks in said they could be arranged to hold all types and sizes of bombs. Things called fragmentation or incendiary, and what they called general purpose ones from 100 pounds up to 1,000 pounds. You know it makes me feel kind of bloated thinking of carrying all of that in me."

"Don't you know it," agreed *Texican*. "They say we weigh 36,000 pounds with nothing in us but can weigh up to 65,000 pounds when we're loaded to the gills. Makes me sweat to think about it. Say, do you remember they call that small compartment under our nose the bombardier station? I wonder if that's where they control all those so-called bombs?"

"Could be. Makes as much sense as anything else," replied *Libby*. "That bombardier is going to have to be awfully good at his job if he plans to smash someone with those bombs from up in the air. Say, *Texican*, do you think Clara could be one of those bombardiers? I mean there's more of them women working on us than men, so why not?" puzzled *Libby*.

"I don't rightly see why not," replied *Texican*. "I don't think they'll be at those controls in the flight deck flying us though. We're mighty big, and those women seem awfully small to try and control something like us."

"Don't know 'bout that," *Libby* argued. "Didn't you listen to that last song heard overhead? Oh, that's right, you don't pay any attention to that noise, as you call it. Well, if you had listened to the words of '*Pistol Packin' Mama*,' which I think you would have liked right off, Bing Crosby and those Andrews sisters sang about some Texas women who I think could handle us."

"What's that about Texas women being able to handle us? Well, of course they could handle us, being Texan and all," replied an incredulous *Texican*.

"I can't remember the words exactly, but it told the story of three tough gals from deep in Texas that you just wouldn't want to fool with. They had no problem toting a pistol around and they knew how to use it according to some poor guy who had been carousing in the bars at night."

"Wooee!" exclaimed *Texican*. "Now, that I like. Maybe you're right about Clara after all," Texican exclaimed pondering an image of Clara behind his controls.

Nearing the end of their construction line, only one more station was required for *Texican* and *Libby* to become truly complete. It was one they had been dreading since they first noticed the poor Liberators in front of them leaving that final station with their wings appearing to droop. For up to now, a point of pride of all the ships, no matter at what stage of completion they were in, was their bright, metallic aluminum skin. As reflective as crystal, *Libby* could see a mirror image of herself on the ship in the line next to her. Looking out her top turret to the back of the shop, the overhead lights were duplicated by the thousands on the brilliantly bright skin of her sister ships. It just made her proud to be called a Liberator, but not after the next station.

"*Texican*, I really don't want to go on ahead," she worried.

"*Libby*, I have come to the realization that it really doesn't matter what we want, for we aren't the ones in control. They are," *Texican* stated as he stared at the worker finishing the Liberator ahead in line. The man's right arm made a final graceful, swiping motion as a spray of paint covered the last vestige of its gleaming aluminum.

This wasn't just any color of paint. The color of this paint seemed to hide—no, it robbed—the ship of anything beautiful, thought *Texican*. It was a dull, pallid green that seemed to actually absorb not only light but life itself. The only thing that made him smile, though a small one at that, was the large white star in a circular field of dark blue in the middle of the fuselage. "Well, at least they're proud of the fact that we were made here in the Lone Star state," a resigned though mistaken *Texican* mumbled to no one but himself.

[*Courtesy of 454th Bomb Group Association*]

Unbeknownst to both *Libby* and *Texican*, seventeen ships behind *Libby*, about halfway down the production line, the first ship to be left in its polished, bright aluminum skin was slowly coming into consciousness. Its crew would name it the *Problem Child*.[7] Her nose art would be that of a standing, raven-haired beauty holding up an extremely short black dress exposing quite a bit of bare thigh, well contrasted against the bright aluminum. The Army Air Corps had determined that the extra cost, time, and weight of that drab olive-green paint was not worth the minimal camouflage it purported to give the ship. Furthermore, testing had shown that without paint, flying in its polished aluminum skin, an aircraft had an eight mph increase in top speed, and a large bomber had a weight reduction close to 300 pounds.[8]

This speed increase and weight reduction would be crucial to these ships in a few months' time over the killing skies of Europe, or the islands

---

7. http://www.454thbombgroup.it/b24camo.htm . She would be lost over the skies of Ploesti, Rumania, 24 June 1944.

8. http://www.defensemedianetwork.com/stories/the-u-s-army-air-forces-stri ps-its-planes-of-paint/

of the Pacific and mainland Asia. It could mean the difference between life and death, between being able to get up in the morning to do it all over again, or to be mourned by your brothers in arms. Many a plane would be coming home on a wing and a prayer having run out of fuel, the ship having been pushed past its range and durability limits. A few hundred pounds could make a difference.

Libby and *Texican* were just two of the 18,482 B-24s to come out of America's "Arsenal of Democracy" during World War II.[9] This was President Franklin Roosevelt's term for the United States' ability to reinvent itself from a nation producing goods and merchandise for pleasure and comfort to one of producing war materials for not only our own, but the entire free world's very existence.

In a hastily announced joint session of Congress in May of 1940, President Roosevelt had called for "50,000 military and naval airplanes to meet the threat of modern war." There were then just 5,563 planes in the entire Army Air Force and Navy, most of them obsolete.[10] Critics and skeptics were quick to howl, from within our shores and abroad. Adolf Hitler commented of the United States, "*What is America but beauty queens, millionaires, stupid records, and Hollywood?*"[11] By the end of the war, the United States would produce and deliver 158,880 planes to the Army Air Force, plus an additional 73,711 to the Navy, and 59,654 to our allies, mainly Britain, the USSR, and China.[12] Nobody should mess with the United States of America.

---

9. Baine, A. J. *The Arsenal of Democracy*, p. 286. Boston: Mariner Books, 2014.

10. *The Wichita Beacon*, May 16, 1944, pp. 1, 11

11. Herman, Arthur, *Freedom's Forge: How American Business Produced Victory in World War II*, p. 13. New York, NY: Random House, 2012.

12. USAF Statistical Digest World War II, Office of Statistical Control, AAF, December, p. 127

Liberators would be built at five locations throughout the continental United States by four different manufacturers. Consolidated Vultee Aircraft Corporation in San Diego, California designed and built the aircraft. It was also built at Consolidated's plant in Fort Worth, Texas, as well as in Ypsilanti, Michigan, at Ford Motor Company's massive Willow Run plant; Douglas Aircraft in Tulsa, Oklahoma; and North American Aviation in Dallas, Texas.

It was the most produced military aircraft the United States has ever made, then and now, surpassing the other, more commonly known World War II four-engine heavy bomber, the B-17, by over 5,500 ships. It could fly faster, farther, and carry a larger bomb load due to its innovative high-mounted Davis wing and roll-up bomb doors, like a tambour door of a rolltop desk. But behind this roll-up door, something far more lethal than paper would be found.

Unfortunately, that aeronautical and bombing efficiency came at a great cost in personnel. The Davis wing had a very high wing load, making it vulnerable to a well-placed piece of enemy flak, cannon shell, or machine-gun fire. Many B-24s were seen death-spiraling to earth with one or both wings folded up like an inverted umbrella with the internal wing tanks on fire. And while the wing gave the Liberator a loaded combat range of 1,700 miles, its maximum ceiling height (how high the plane could fly) was a full 7,000 feet lower than the B-17's. The B-17 could easily fly well above the 26,250-foot maximum ceiling height of the Germans' most popular antiaircraft gun, the 8.8cm *Flugzeugabwehrkanone* (Flak) model 36/37, though the larger 10.5 and 12.8cm guns could both reach and exceed the 35,000-foot B-17 ceiling.[13] The B-24 would struggle to reach the former, lesser height.

---

13. Lepage, Jean-Denis. *The Illustrated Handbook of FLAK, German Anti-Aircraft Defenses 1935 - 1945* pp. 102–106. Gloucestershire: Spellmount, 2012.

Also, due to that high-mounted wing, the roll-up doors, a slab-sided fuselage, and a twin rudder tail assembly, the Liberator could hardly be called a graceful looking aircraft. Many derogatory labels would be given to the plane: flying boxcar, spam can in the sky, or the flying brick, to name just a few.

However, it was built for one purpose and one purpose only: to carry and drop up to four tons of high explosives on the German Nazi and Imperial Japanese war machines. It didn't care what it was scornfully called as long as it got the job done and came back to do it all over again for however long it took.

But first, it had to learn how to soar like an eagle.

B-24s on North American Aviation assembly line in Dallas, Texas, awaiting propellers and possible paint. Two .50 caliber Brownings can be seen menacingly protruding from the front and top turrets. [Courtesy of Vintage Aviation News]

2

SPREADING THEIR WINGS

FLIGHT APRON OF THE NORTH AMERICAN AVIATION PLANT, FEBRUARY 4, 1944

"I WONDER WHERE THAT *TEXICAN* has gone off to?" queried a concerned *Libby*. It had been four days since they were rolled out of the large hangar doors of the assembly plant, emerging like long-legged, unsteady, newborn calves, according to *Texican*. The emergence from the confines of the assembly plant was beyond her comprehension. Three variables compounded her immediate confusion: light, a feeling of dread, and the seemingly limitless blue sky stretching above.

The hundreds upon hundreds of brilliant, individual, domed lights inside the plant just couldn't compare to the brilliancy of the single globular point of light currently hanging precariously in the sky, even though it wasn't much higher than the plant's rooftop. It hurt to look at it, and *Libby* prognosticated that she wouldn't be able to see anyone or anything coming out of it. If she only knew how prophetic her notion was.

Trepidation. That was the best way to describe the way *Libby* was feeling at the moment. An uneasy, constant queasiness felt in the pit of her sub-frame. It had to do with boundaries, or more exactly, the absolute lack of them. In the confines of the assembly plant, the boundaries felt safe. She knew those around her, her place in the scheme of things, that her goal was to become whole, to mature. But now? Even though she was surrounded by other Liberators, she felt alone for the first time. So alone.

And then there was that sky. To say it was limitless was to almost belittle the vastness of it. While other aircraft, including Liberators, appeared to be floating high in the sky, *Libby* was having a hard time getting any sort of distance perspective. This was unsettling to her since she always considered herself as having an excellent depth of field perception by using her vision simultaneously out of all her gun turrets. All she knew was that some of them were awfully high up there, and she wondered when she would get the chance, like *Texican* apparently did. But then again, "*Texican* got the chance, left me, and hasn't returned. What happened to him?" Nothing bad, she hoped.

"I sure don't like this unknowing part," she lamented.

As if to answer *Libby*'s complaint, four people, bundled up as if it was cold, appeared to be approaching her from behind. "Strange, it's as warm here as it ever was inside the plant," the perplexed plane thought.

With a slight tug, *Libby* felt the covers over her pitot tubes removed while someone opened her bomb bay doors. The unrelenting chatter of the four heavily clothed men began as soon as they entered her, with two occupying the pilot seats on her flight deck, one standing behind them, and one crawling up past the pilots, eventually taking a seat at the navigator's table found between the front turret and the pilots.

"OK, what do we have here?" asked Louis Voris, a tall, broad-shouldered man of wide berth, sitting in the left-hand pilot's seat staring down at the Army Air Corps B-24 acceptance checklist. He was known as "Judy" to everyone. No one dared to ask him why.

"Ship 42-78173," replied John Worland, a slightly built, much shorter, handsome young man of twenty-four with dark hair and blue eyes sitting in the right co-pilot's seat. Whenever he flew with Judy, anyone who saw them walking down the flight line together almost always called out, "There goes Laurel and Hardy," with a stupid smirk on their face. "Put it where the sun don't shine," would be John's thought as he ignored the ignoramus.

"Let's put this bird through her paces. We've got another Lib to do and I also have at least two P-51s and an AT-6 waiting for me also," said Judy.

Standing behind them, Wilbur Brown, the flight engineer, announced that he had turned on the four fuel selector switches and that the load gauges indicated 1,200 gallons on board.

Judy adjusted the seat to its furthest back setting, set the parking brake, and then adjusted the rudder pedal position. John made the same pedal adjustments, though made at the other extreme range.

"Hey Wilbur, get yourself out of the emergency escape hatch and check my control movements, will ya?" called Judy.

With Wilbur standing with half his body out of the top of *Libby* and looking aft, he watched as Judy put the steering yoke through all its paces, causing the left and right tail-mounted elevators and wing-mounted ailerons to flutter up and down. Judy stepped on the rudder pedals, with their absurdly long travel, while Wilbur watched the left and right tail rudders adjacent the twin rear vertical stabilizers pivot right, then left. With that accomplished, Wilbur departed the ship the way he had arrived.

"Ignition switches one through four off," John yelled out his side window down to Wilbur, who was now standing next to engine number three with a large-wheeled fire extinguisher at the ready. With that, he started the slow process of hand turning the propellers through two complete revolutions, a process he repeated with the other three engines.

After Judy turned off the generator switches, one for each of the four engine-powered generators, Wilbur started up the small, onboard gasoline-powered engine auxiliary power unit.

With the power unit supplying electricity to the onboard circuits, *Libby* smelt a whiff of ozone, and felt a sudden surge of tingling course through her, a sensation she had never felt before, something akin to what she had heard some of the female workers call sex. Even though those female workers were whispering to themselves in quiet, hushed tones, with *Libby*'s keen senses, she had heard and understood it all. *Libby* determined that she would like sex most of all.

"Alright, let's run through the checklist and get these engines running," Judy commanded. "One through four ignition switches and master switch on."

"Check," replied John.

"Auxiliary hydraulic pump on?"

"Auxiliary hydraulic pump on," replied Wilbur.

"AC power for instruments?"

"Check," said John.

"Auto flight controller is off," stated Judy.

"De-icer off?"

"De-icer off," John replied after checking.

"Intercooler switches are open," John said.

"Cowl flaps are fully open," he added, after waiting thirty seconds for them to completely open.

"Props are set to high rpm and superchargers are set to off," Judy said.

"Setting mixture controls to idle cut-off position," Judy said as his hands flittered along the control panel, which consisted of a myriad 27 separate gauges and 12 engine control levers.

"Fire extinguishing valves in the ready," commented John as he also checked out his window to make sure Wilbur was clear of the number three engine.

"Fuel booster pumps on engines one through four, reading eight pounds pressure," John informed Judy.

It would take two sets of hands simultaneously moving amongst the throttle, starter energizing switch, priming switch, and eventually pressing and holding the starter mesh switch to bring *Libby*'s first engine to life.[1]

It was with the long energizing of her number three engine's starter that *Libby* knew something was about to happen to her, something new, something powerful, an awakening. With the pressing of the starter mesh switch, her propeller started to turn with a high-pitched, loud whine.

One agonizingly slow revolution, two, three, four. "Come on, babe," whispered *Libby*. Five, six, and then, a sputter, cough, and with a belch of black and blue smoke, as if in final protest, the engine caught and roared like 1,200 newborn children. As Judy set the mixture control to auto lean, the engine settled down to a smooth, throbbing rhythm of one thousand revolutions per minute. A steady, but reassuring vibration cascaded down through her metal bones. It was a reassuring purr to her.

"Oil pressure: 45 pounds; rpm's: 1,000. Number three fuel booster is off," shouted John.

"Let's begin the starting sequence for number four," yelled Judy as the engine and prop noise from the engine immediately outside John's open window attempted to drown out his words.

Repeating the entire process, John's outside engine, number four, also coughed and slowly sputtered to life. Soon, engine number two, the inboard engine on Judy's side, roared to life, and finally, followed by the outboard number one, bringing *Libby* to full life.

She could feel the pull of those four props even though they were only idling to warm themselves up, a slight forward pressure on her wheel chocks and a desire to release her brake shoes which were pressing against the drums of her wheels. "Patience, patience. Freedom will come," *Libby* reminded herself.

---

1. Consolidated Vultee Aircraft Corporation. Pilots Amplified Check-Off List, B-24D, E & G Airplanes. 1944.

"What are the engine readings?" Judy asked after a few minutes of idling.

"Oil pressure: 45,50,45, and 50 pounds. Oil temp: 50,45,45,50 degrees C. Head temps: 160, 170, 160, and 165C. Fuel pressure: 14 pounds, 1,000 rpm across the board. Manifold pressure 15 inches," replied John as he finished scanning the instrument gauges.

"Vacuum pumps, check, reading four inches, and brake accumulator pressure reads 975 pounds," said Judy.

"Wilbur, check the tail de-icer boots for inflation, will ya?" asked John.

With that, John threw the de-icer lever to the right, sending alternating pressure and vacuum to the rubber boots on the leading edges of the main wings, observed by John, and to the leading edge of the tail wing assembly, which Wilbur observed inflating and deflating.

"Tail wing de-icer boots, check," replied Wilbur. "I'm heading out to retrieve the wheel chocks."

"OK, while you're there, check for de-icer fluid propeller runoff," said John. With that, he turned the anti-icer control rheostat to six gallons per hour, sending a small stream of antifreeze to the props, which Wilbur acknowledged.

After pulling out the wheel chocks and stowing them in the bomb bay, Wilbur climbed in and operated the manual bomb bay door lever, closing them. He then made his way back up to behind the flight deck and climbed halfway out of the escape hatch, peering forward beyond *Libby*'s nose out onto the taxi apron. *Libby* would need a traffic monitor to make sure she safely made it to the runway.

Upon observing Wilbur enter the flight engineer station, Judy released the parking brake and, after setting the props for full high rpm, increased speed to the outside, left engine to turn them onto the taxi strip.

"Finally, I get to fly like the rest of the guys. It sure took long enough," exclaimed *Libby* with slight exasperation in her voice. But no sooner had she said that than Judy retarded the engines, brought her to a stop, and re-set the parking brake right at the beginning of the runway. Oh, so tantalizingly close.

No sooner had *Libby* exclaimed her dissatisfaction at stopping when she heard and felt all four of her engines increase in speed, and her props changing pitch through their entire range. Then she could feel the ailerons being moved to neutral, her elevators move and held ever so slightly tail heavy, and her rudders set at about two degrees right. "I sure hope they know what they're doing," thought a concerned *Libby*. "I feel a little out of kilter."

"Let's run up number four," instructed Judy, as he increased the rpm's to 2,000, the highest yet, sending a surging pulse through *Libby*.

Having flown in the co-pilot seat many times with Judy, John knew what to expect next, and had already put the mixture into auto rich, turned on the booster switches, and double-checked that the de-icer was off. He then checked the all-important ignition magnetos on number four. You wouldn't want to lose those in flight. There was a reason to have a redundant pair on each engine.

With an affirmation on the magnetos, Judy slowly opened the throttle wide open, observing the manifold pressure at 37 inches. With the super-charger turned on, John noticed the manifold pressure jump to 49 inches, right on cue.

At 2,700 rpm, *Libby* noticed the wind tunnel effect that the rapidly rotating twelve-foot prop had on the dust and sand on the runway. "I sure would hate to be sitting in line behind me. That must be what one of those dust devils that *Texican* described to me looks like," she lamented after remembering her friend.

With a lowering of the number four engine speed to a soothing 1,000 rpm, the process was started all over again for the number three engine. After a quick check of the engine vitals, it too was run-up for its magnetos check, manifold pressures, and final increase to 2,700 rpm, sending yet another central Texas horizontal dust devil along its way. With number three purring at a now steady 1,000 rpm, John extended the wing flaps to their take-off position of ten degrees down. This was only possible after number three was running, for it ran the only hydraulic pump for some of *Libby*'s vital functions. This not only included the wing flaps, but the landing gears, bomb bay doors, the auto pilot, some of the machine gun turrets, and the all-too-important brakes. If one was to lose an engine in flight, you hoped it wasn't number three. Of course, there was a small electrical auxiliary hydraulic pump in the bomb bay. And if that wasn't enough assurance of maintaining hydraulic pressure, there was always the hand pump next to the co-pilot's seat. Hydraulic pressure was important.

"Certainly, three independent hydraulic systems would be enough to keep me in the air," thought *Libby* over the throbbing noise of all four engines.

Following a repeat run-up procedure for engines two, and lastly number one, *Libby* felt an electrical surge course through her as John turned on all four generators, while each was checked for their 50-amp output. At the same time, she felt her engine cowl flaps slowly close until only partially open. "Sure hope they remember to open those back up, or my engines are going to soon be feeling a tad bit on the warm side," a concerned *Libby* mused.

"Hensley tower, flight NAA 173 requesting altimeter check and take off permission, over," *Libby* heard over her radio circuit. "Well, that's a bit distracting," she thought. "Someone's putting words into my mouth, and I feel like I'm talking in tongues. I wonder if they'll keep doing that." And to answer her was the tower reply.

"Flight NAA 173, altimeter is four niner one, winds twelve out of the south, permission granted."

"Great, let's just have anybody jump in. A regular tower of babble I am," a frustrated *Libby* said to no one.

Her frustration was soon a thing of the past as she felt her parking brake released and all four engine throttles put to their stops. There are numerous ways of describing it, but none can convey the adrenaline rush of absolute power *Libby* felt, smelled, and heard cascading through her like nothing before. She was propelled faster and faster down the runway, totally out of her control, with engines at full power sending not a dust devil behind her but four full-blown tornadoes launching anything on the ground wildly into the wind. And yet, she didn't mind. The hands holding her throttles wide open felt strong, secure. But they couldn't compare to the hands on her pilot's steering yoke. Huge, rough, calloused, but oh so confident. This confidence was exuded into *Libby* herself, and she felt like she could do anything, including fly like the wind.

Her ground speed seemed reckless, for she didn't feel firmly planted to the ground. *Libby* felt herself becoming lighter and lighter the faster she went. And then when she heard John yell out 110 mph, she felt Judy begin to pull back on her yoke ever so slightly, causing the attached cable to pull on the rear elevator flaps on her tail. Like many of her control systems, the elevator control cables and pulleys would make Rube Goldberg proud. Consisting of over 240 feet of cable, sixteen pulleys, four chain sprockets, and a handful of cranks and levers, it was amazing that it worked. But work it did, because that's when the magic happened.[2]

Libby's first inclination that she was flying was when she no longer felt and heard the low rumble of her nose gear contacting the concrete runway. Within seconds, this was followed by the complete absence of noise and vibration from her two main wing-mounted landing gears as they too left terra firma.

"So many new and indescribable sensations," thought *Libby*, both visual and tactile. And then the runway disappeared from view and was replaced by something entirely new: water, the smooth, calm waters of the 2,700-acre Mountain Creek Lake. With a bit more speed, *Libby* felt herself become even more slippery when all three of her landing gears were brought up and stowed within her. After she reached 150 mph and her wing flaps were raised, she felt like an arrow. Higher and higher she

---

2. Consolidated Aircraft, Flight Manual, B24D Airplane, p. 7. 1942.

went, and when she looked down, a momentary wave of nausea and panic gripped her, though quickly quelled by the feel of Judy and John's reassuring hands on her yoke and throttles.

Then came the "tests." For the first time *Libby* felt her belly turret lowered from her body and swiveled in all directions, her bomb bay doors were opened and closed, and the incessant chatter of tongues tested the radios in all corners of her.

And then she started to lose her engines. Judy had reached above the windshield and purposely feathered the number four engine, bringing it to a nerve-racking stop before turning the prop back into the wind, thus restarting the engine. This was then repeated on the remaining three engines.

"You could have warned me you know!" scolded an irritated, but relieved *Libby*.

She then felt hands flittering amongst most of her controls: the props, throttles, mixture controls, cowl flaps, turbocharger controls, and she really felt the sensation of power and speed. Higher and faster she climbed. Judy, John, and Wilbur covered their faces with strange-looking masks with only their alert eyes visible. A strange new sensation was felt as a new fluid—no, gas—was surging through a previously unused system into those strange masks. *Libby* realized it was her oxygen system, and the men appeared to be using it. "Strange, I wonder if they all need that when I'm up here higher than the birds?" pondered *Libby*. "Leveling off at 25,000 feet, 290 mph," announced Judy over the radio. "Head and oil temps look good on all four," replied John.

"Alright, I'm bringing her back down to 10,000 feet. We'll cruise at 165 mph on our way back to Hensley," Judy announced to all.

After a pleasant, mesmerizing time akin to floating in the heavens, it ended all too soon. *Libby* sensed the ground getting closer and closer. She also felt her speed decrease as Judy's and John's hands again darted across the control panels, slowly throwing levers, flicking toggle switches, and turning controls, all culminating in *Libby*'s three landing gears slowly lowering themselves to an open, locked position.

With slow, gut-wrenching comprehension, *Libby* realized she was getting into position to land. "I guess what goes up must come down, at least that's what they say," she murmured with a slight quiver in her voice.

With John extending the flaps 20 degrees down, *Libby* could feel the 140 mph wind buffet against them, slowing her further. The landing strip was up ahead now that she had finished her turn. With a further lowering of the flaps to 40 degrees, it felt like someone was physically holding her back. "I'm over the runway!" exclaimed *Libby* as she heard, more than felt, her throttles pulled all the way back. "I'm just floating on air, why doesn't Judy let me down now?"

But Judy didn't. He'd landed too many Liberators to know that you just don't slap them down onto the runway. With *Libby*'s nose a little high, she was held off the runway as long as possible, letting the main landing gears touch first, ever so slightly, before letting the nose wheel settle slowly and kiss the ground. With toe pressure applied to the brake pedals, wing flaps retracted, and cowl flaps fully opened, *Libby* felt herself slow to what felt like a crawl. She was then taxied back to North American's apron in front of what *Libby* considered home: the manufacturing facility building.

With the mixture controls placed in idle cut-off and the ignition switches all turned to off, the four Pratt and Whitneys fell quiet; all too quiet. The only sound *Libby* heard was the metallic crackling and pinging coming from the engines as they cooled down.

Libby's reverie was broken by Judy, John, and Wilbur's movements as they secured her in her parking spot in amongst the other Liberators. After the three had left her and closed the bomb bay doors, she felt one of Judy's calloused hands gently pat her on her fuselage. Quietly, she heard him whisper, "Welcome to the Army Air Corps, girl." After all, in truth, he was a teddy bear of a man.

Deep in thought, *Libby* didn't notice the ladders being propped up against both of the vertical stabilizers on her tail. There, eighteen feet above the ground, a pair of ground crewmen painted, in white numerals, 2-78173. *Libby* was official.[3]

A sudden flash of roaring, dark green wings and fuselage appeared and just as quickly disappeared high above, breaking *Libby* out of her daydream. "Did I really just do what I think I did? Was that really me up there?" She started to break out in a warm sweat as her metal skin, still cold after the minus 20-degree temperature she'd endured at 25,000 feet, condensed the moisture found in the warm and humid air at ground level. She remembered the anxiety of both takeoff and landing, and the rush of power and exhilaration she felt climbing to 25,000 feet with her engines at full military power. Then there were the maneuvers that Judy had put her through, testing the endurance of her airframe. "I swore I was going to break apart like a prairie chicken when he put me in that 60-degree bank and when he dove pushing me well past 300 mph," she thought, her sweat now dripping onto the cement apron.

However, if someone knew where to look, they would have noticed a broad grin slowly spreading out onto her slab-sided fuselage below each of the pilots' side windows.

"But hot damn, that had to have been better than sex!" she whooped.

---

3. The first digit of *Libby*'s serial number, 4, was left off for space considerations, as it was done for all military aircraft.

3

REUNION AND FIRST LOOK AT DEATH

LOVE FIELD, DALLAS, TEXAS, FEBRUARY 6, 1944

"JEEZ, DO YOU CALL that a flight, guys?" asked an incredulous *Libby* of the crew who were departing through the bomb bay. It had been a sojourn of less than five minutes, including takeoff, early in the morning, with the sun barely over the horizon, landing ten miles northeast of Hensley Field at the Army Air Corps' Love Field, Dallas.

It had been a hectic, confusing few days following her maiden flight. Ground personnel had crawled all through her, like those damn fire ants, adjusting joints and knobs, replacing a few small parts, and changing her engine oil. That was no small amount of oil. Each of her fourteen-cylinder engines held 132 quarts. The largest Detroit automotive engine built before the war, the mammoth 431-cubic-inch Cadillac V16, held nine. For an air-cooled engine such as the Liberator's Pratt and Whitney, oil was its life blood. Lose oil pressure, it's bad. Run for more than a few minutes at 212 degrees F at full military power, it's worse. Those engines were made to perform flawlessly at 100-degree temperatures during a summer day in Libya, as well at the 40 degrees below zero found at 25,000 feet during a European winter. A ship would need a good—no, a great—ground crew and chief to keep it flying.

After the irritating ground crew had finished with *Libby*, she was humiliatingly towed to the far side of the parking apron, where 50 yards in front and behind her were what appeared to be low but wide bunkers made of sandbags. A large, dark opening beckoned in the center of each.

"Now what's going to happen?" a perplexed *Libby* asked herself. "It's bad enough you tow me over here like I couldn't do it myself. I'm not helpless, you know!" she shouted at the ground crewman as he hooked her up to a portable power unit. He then scampered into her bomb bay and turned on the auxiliary hydraulic unit.

"Well, they're fixin' to have me do something with all of that power," she stated. *Libby* hadn't seen anything yet, as far as what she was truly capable of when she had power.

"Now what's he doing?" she pondered. The ground crewman had dropped out of her and scampered over to the tow vehicle. He grimaced as he picked up two large, green metal boxes, one in each hand. They were both the same color she was, *Libby* noticed. He should have picked up just one, she thought, for he dropped one of the boxes, spilling its contents.

"Ooh, sparklies," cooed *Libby*, as her eyes caught the flash of afternoon sunlight reflecting off a hundred linked, bright brass cartridges and copper-jacketed bullets for her .50 caliber machine guns. Each was as long as a man's hand.

Within a few minutes, *Libby* was literally shaken out of her reverie by the sudden staccato explosion of the firing of the twin machine guns in her tail turret. Firing at twenty-six rounds per second, the short, three-second burst into the firing test bunker shook *Libby* to her bones. And the noise! She couldn't hear herself as she yelled at the person to stop. But stop it did, only to be repeated from her top turret guns, followed by the guns in her nose turret.

"At least they can't test my belly turret, being parked here on the ground," said *Libby* triumphantly.

Following the pickup of a few hundred expelled, empty cartridges, and losing her power as she was shut down, she again was humiliated in front of all the other airplanes by being towed back to her spot on the parking apron.

Left alone to her thoughts, she went over what had transpired the last few days, trying to make some sense of it.

"There's absolutely no doubt in my mind that I was made for some higher purpose than just sitting around here," figured *Libby*. "It's obvious from Judy and John bringing me up so high, and testing those bomb bay doors, that I'll be dropping bombs from high up. Higher than the clouds. And that sign I saw being towed out of the plant, *Leading The Invasion With The Bombers You Build,* I bet that has to do with fighting this Hitler fella that *Texican* mentioned," she reflected. "And those Browning .50 cals in my turrets, they're going to hurt him a lot more than mesquite thorns, let me tell you!"

Now, one day later, sitting on the taxi apron of Love Field, *Libby* wondered if the Army Air Corps' motto wasn't "hurry up and wait."

Before the sun could rise a few degrees higher, an Army Jeep, in the same drab olive-green paint as everything else seen around the field, pulled up to *Libby*. Pouring out of the overstuffed transport, four individuals gathered their belongings and proceeded to the open bomb bay door.

Libby noticed that they were dressed the same as Judy, John, and Wilbur had been yesterday, but there the similarities ended, for they were women.

Dressed in the same, but baggier fitting, khaki flight coveralls and dark brown, fleece-lined flight jackets, they could easily have been mistaken for a male flight crew except for their hair and diminutive sizes. All four wore their hair at the shoulders, with varying degrees of curl. While they were all slim and fit, and two were tall enough to have been labeled "a tall drink of water" by *Texican*, it was the other two that stood out. Or rather, didn't.

And it came as a complete shock when those two took their positions in the pilot and copilot seats.

"I'd rather fly any other plane than the Liberator," commented Yvonne Stafford, as she adjusted the pilot's seat far forward. "Can you reach those rudder pedals, Belle?" she asked with a twinkle in her dark eyes.

"Oh, that's so funny," replied Isabel Steiner, known as Belle to her friends, as she adjusted her copilot's seat to its frontmost stop. It was rumored that she had stood on her tiptoes when her height was measured during the WASP medical examination. Five foot two inches was the minimum height requirement for the women to serve.

"Let's get this girl in the air," announced Yvonne over the interphone channel of her headset.

Libby noticed with interest that this aircrew was no different in their procedures to get her to the taxi apron than with Judy, John, and Wilbur on her maiden flight, or with the short flight to Love Field this morning.

As she raced down the runway gaining speed and feeling weightless, an intoxicating sensation she didn't think she would ever get tired of, *Libby* felt the same kind of confidence emanating from the hands gripping her yoke as well as the ones holding her throttles wide open. But the hands were so different, not a callous on them. Small, almost delicate, but holding onto that yoke like a bronco buster's grip on a saddle horn. "There I go thinking like *Texican* again," mused *Libby*.

As she settled into an easy cruising speed of 165mph at a low 8,000 feet, *Libby* couldn't help but think back to the day she and *Texican* had debated if women could fly a Liberator such as themselves. "Well, I guess this sure proves that women can handle something like us. These must be some of them tough gals, from deep-down Texas, way they sang about in *Pistol Packin' Mama*," declared *Libby*.

She was right, but then she was also wrong.

Yvonne and Isabel were just two of the 1,102 women members of the civilian-run Women Airforce Service Pilots organization. Derived from two preexisting women's aircraft ferrying organizations, WASP was created in the fall of 1943 to help alleviate the critical shortage of male combat pilots. By replacing the men who had been testing and ferrying airplanes between manufacturers, modification centers, and points of departure from the United States, these women freed men to use their valuable talents in combat.

Trained in all aspects of flying, from obvious flight control to navigation, radio, and flight engineering aspects, WASP pilots flew every type of military aircraft available during the war. That included everything from PT-13 Stearman biplane trainers to the mammoth B-29 Superfortress bomber. Thirty-eight of the 1,102 would give their lives for something they didn't have to do but did because they loved it.

Based at the Army Air Corps' Love Field, the 5th Ferrying Group consisted of 88 WASP pilots, including Yvonne and Isabel. While they were currently "Texicans," they, like most of the others, couldn't call it home.[1]

"Belle, you're from California, aren't you?" queried Yvonne.

"Born in Oregon actually, but my folks moved to northern California when I was a kid. Heck, the biggest town to us wasn't even in California. It was Reno, Nevada," replied Belle.

"Just wondering. Most of the planes we bring to Tucson eventually end up at Hamilton Field outside of San Francisco," stated Yvonne.

Belle turned her head toward Yvonne and nodded in recognition. "Been there. Used to fly into it when I was in the Stanford Flying Club at school. If the wind was coming out of the south, you'd better watch those drafts from the Sonoma Mountains when you circle around. And if you took off to the north, you had about five miles to gain 1,200 feet in the Navato Valley or you'd plaster yourself against those mountains. No thanks in a Liberator."

"Is that where you earned your license?" asked Yvonne.

---

1. https://texashistory.unt.edu/ark:/67531/metapth1077853/m1/1/

"Yeah, myself, Dale Adams, and seventeen boys," grinned Belle.[2]

"Sounds like my story," replied Yvonne as she adjusted the rudder trim. "You know these 24s fly alright, once you trim them out proper. Sure would hate to fly these in tight formation though, your legs would definitely get a workout with these rudder pedals."

"It was myself, Mildred Iles, and eighteen boys in our class," Yvonne continued. "I was in a Civilian Pilot Training program at Southwest Louisiana Institute in Lafayette. Mildred didn't graduate, though. She was in it as a hobby. You can't be in it part time. It has to be your first love to be able to compete. Got my nursing degree, and I was hoping I could combine my flying ability with my medical skills somehow. But what do they say: the best laid plans of mice and men? Ha!"[3]

Belle nodded in agreement as she quickly scanned the engine gauges for anything amiss, though the engines were purring along in a dull but mesmerizing monotone.

"Pilot to nav, can you give me a course correction status?" Yvonne asked over the interphone.

"Nav to pilot, continue at heading 265, altitude 8,000. We're 400 miles out, flight time two and a half hours to Biggs Field," replied the navigator.

"I haven't been to El Paso as a fuel stop. Mostly Midland or Big Spring," commented Belle.

"Biggs isn't too bad. Good long runway, Franklin mountains to the west, pretty consistent west-southwest wind. Can't say much for the accommodations at Fort Bliss though. I like to get most of Texas behind me. Makes the route tomorrow seem not so long, it's only 250 more miles to Tucson from there," Yvonne replied.

With the mention of a destination, *Libby*'s auditory senses perked to life. "What's that about Texas being mostly behind us? Do you mean to tell

---

2. Stanford University 1937 Yearbook, p. 192

3. *The Daily Advertiser*, Lafayette, November 19, 1940, p. 3.

me that we've been flying for an hour, and we've got two and a half more to fly, and we still won't be out of Texas?" asked an astonished *Libby*. "Boy, *Texican* sure was right when he said Texas was big. I wonder, though, what this Too-sun is all about?" she pondered.

Following an uneventful landing at Biggs Field, *Libby* was refueled and gone over by the ground crew before spending a lonely, miserable night on the airfield's apron. During the night she had experienced something new, and she didn't like it in the least. Not by a long shot.

As the crimson sun had been setting in the southwest, sending golden red-light streamers into the evening twilight, a more sinister sporadic, blue-white light had illuminated the hidden northwestern horizon. The flat anvil tops of the towering cumulonimbus clouds were first to appear over the lofty 6,500-foot Franklin Mountains of Ellenburger dolomite, six miles in the distance. Soaring higher than *Libby* could ever fly, these clouds looked alive. They were roiling and angry, alternating white then menacingly black, briefly exposed by white, jagged flashes of lightning. Then she had heard it. Thor's Hammer. And it was coming for her.

She first felt the low rumbling in her landing gears, before the deep, rolling thunder arrived. "This must be what a stampede of longhorns sounds like," uttered an awed and terrified *Libby*. The mountains had long been obscured by dark blue bands of heavy rain when undulating curtains of white appeared, racing eastward. Then the wind hit.

"My gosh, I wish they had strapped me down," said *Libby* as a super-charged, cold wall of wind hit her head on. "If my flaps were down, I do believe I'd be flying right now," she had shouted into the gale as her wings began to flutter. Then the hail hit.

"Yow, that felt like someone drove a rivet into my wing!" *Libby* had scowled as the first of many hail pellets pinged off her wings like errant popcorn seeds. Within seconds, she couldn't hear herself scream as thousands of pellets assaulted her aluminum skin. Fortunately for her, they were only pea-sized, therefore they did not damage her canvas ailerons, elevators, and rudders. It still hurt, though. Then the rain hit.[4]

"I can't see a darn thing," *Libby* commented, as sheets of cold rain pummeled her, though without the sting of the hail. As quickly as it began, however, it ended, as if someone had turned off a spigot.

The following morning, as Yvonne, Belle, and the others were performing their pre-flight checks, *Libby* was contemplating the previous evening's storm. It had shaken her to her core, both mentally and figuratively.

"I can handle the physical pain of the thing," she ruminated. "But that storm came from the sky, the heavens. And that's where I belong, not that." With a sudden realization, *Libby* now understood that there were things and events out there that could hurt her. Or worse. In a few hours, she would see just how bad.

Minutes later, with the gentle but firm grip of Yvonne's and Belle's hands on her controls, *Libby* felt more like herself as she slowly climbed to 8,000 feet in a blue sky, with scattered white, fluffy, unmenacing clouds.

Circling to the southwest to skirt the Franklins, Yvonne asked the navigator for a heading to Tucson, their final destination.

"Nav to pilot. Come to a heading of 277, maintain 8,000, 165mph. We're 238 miles out, one hour 45-minute flight time," responded the navigator.

After a slight course correction, Yvonne pointed out her front left windshield and beckoned to Belle, "We need to be mindful of updrafts from Chiricahua peak over yonder. And once we clear this range, we need to watch ourselves over Rincon Mountain east of Tucson."

---

4. Famme, J.H., "Design Analysis of Consolidated B-24 Liberator." *Aviation.* July 1945, vol. 77, number 7.

Cocking her head toward Yvonne, Belle responded, "Yeah, sure thing. Are you OK, you seem preoccupied," she asked, concerned with Yvonne's blank stare.

After a moment's hesitation, Yvonne replied pensively, "These mountains around here have always put me on edge. Last fall a crew of nine slammed their Liberator into the side of Rincon. They said it was just a routine training flight. Don't they know there's no such thing as routine?" She continued with rising passion in her voice, "And then there's what we heard last night. That's what's really bothering me," she said, her voice feathering into a whisper."[5]

"What are you talking about? I didn't hear anything that would put me in such, well, consternation," a confused and concerned Belle replied.

"Oh, that's right, you didn't join us in the mess with those guys from Consolidated," said Yvonne. With what seemed like reluctance imprinted upon her youthful, 23-year-young face, she told Belle what she had learned the previous evening.

"They had flown in from Tucson yesterday morning. They're headed to the North American plant in Dallas." Clearing her throat, she continued, "It appears a B-24 took off from the Consolidated Modification Center Wednesday and didn't gain enough altitude. It hit some power transmission lines and went down."[6]

"Oh, sweet Jesus," whispered Belle. "Survivors?"

With a trembling voice, Yvonne responded, "Yeah, the four officers and four of the non-coms."

The unasked question floated heavily, laden with trepidation in the air between them, with nothing but the steady drumming of *Libby*'s engines filling the void. Ten was the normal crew size of a B-24.

---

5. *Tucson Daily Citizen*, August 2, 1943. p. 14.

6. *Tucson Daily Citizen*, February 3, 1944. p. 2.

In a breathless, hushed voice, Yvonne finally confirmed what Belle had reluctantly deduced. "Two of the non-coms couldn't get out of the plane as it burned."

Except for what was needed to guide *Libby* toward Tucson and to land at the modification center, no further words were spoken between them.

Staff Sergeant Thomas Irving, 24, of Plains, Pennsylvania, and Sergeant Howard Thompson, 26, of Pulaski, Virginia, both leaving behind young brides, were just two of the 14,903 young men who died in the 52,651 training or ferrying accidents that occurred within the continental United States during World War II, destroying 21,583 aircraft, including 1,989 B-17 and B-24 bombers. There was indeed no such thing as routine.[7]

As Yvonne banked *Libby* into the wind, low over Tucson, lining up her approach, the bright aluminum remnants of the unmistakable twin tail assembly of a B-24 reflected brightly in the Arizona sun, contrasted against the black, burned, skeletal remains of creosote bushes. Its four Pratt and Whitney engines hung loosely from their wing spars, all of the aluminum sheeting having been melted off, or incinerated, by the hellish inferno created with the burning of over 2,700 gallons of gasoline.

Comprehension crept slowly over *Libby* as she came upon the grotesque scene before her. Bulkheads, stringers, spars, and engines were openly displayed, as if a monstrous, crude autopsy had been performed. It meant only one thing.

Death. Death was a possibility for her. She had never considered it. Was she any different than that poor SOB she just flew over? As her wheels touched the cement runway, she now understood that anything could happen, either while trying to reach the sky or trying to return to the safety of the earth. As *Libby* was taxied up to the apron and parked amongst

---

7. United States Air Force Statistical Digest World War II, Office of Statistical Control, AAF, December 1945, pp. 185, 309. https://apps.dtic.mil/dtic/tr /fulltext/u2/a542518.pdf

dozens of her fellow Liberators, she felt so vulnerable and unsure of herself. "Even among others, parked safely on the ground, death could visit me in the form of a storm, and there is nothing I could do to stop it. Not that I could do anything if I was going to crash. It's all in their hands," lamented *Libby*, glancing at the WASP flight crew as they walked away from her without so much as a goodbye.

Feeling sorry for herself, *Libby* hadn't taken time to take stock of her present situation and surroundings. Now, sitting with dozens of her siblings, she hadn't noticed the three huge hangars, all laid abreast, beyond them. The wide doors, all open, seeming to beckon her, were each 250 feet wide and forty feet tall. Within each, brightly profiled by the overhead lighting, she slowly made out the gleaming bodies of twenty-four Liberators like her.

"I'd swear I'm back home in Texas," an astonished *Libby* murmured.

And then she finally paid attention to what someone was blathering in the background, over her radio channel. It had a familiar tone and frequency. Twang.

"I tell y'all, I felt lower than quail shit in a wagon rut," she heard.

"*Texican?*"

Inside one of the three hangars at the Tucson Consolidated Modification Center. [Courtesy of Pima Air & Space Museum]

4

Loaded for Bear

Consolidated Aircraft Modification Center, Tucson, February 23, 1944

"IT'S ABOUT TIME I bugged out of this place. I swear, moss is beginning to grow under my flaps," *Texican* drawled to no one in particular. It had been over two weeks since he had landed at the hastily constructed modification center, with a single runway strip tucked right up to the imposing hangars, now situated behind him.[1]

Overseas, it hadn't taken long in the battlefields of the skies to reveal offensive as well as defensive design deficiencies in most, if not all, of the aircraft built for the United States armed forces. Our enemies were constantly changing air tactics and finding vulnerable points in each type of combat aircraft. Our returning crewmen—those that did return—were

---

1. Air Force Historical Research Agency (AFHRA). Maxwell AFB. Reel ACR-68. Aircraft Record Card 42-78172. Also see Historical Research Frustration Addendum.

quick to point out these deficiencies in their post-mission debriefings. Usually in blunt, no uncertain terms.

Also, because of the global nature of the conflict, identical aircraft were operating in highly varied conditions, from the frozen Aleutians to the hot, humid tropics of the south Pacific to the deserts of northern Africa. Each of these theatres of operation demanded specific requirements for the aircraft operating there.[2]

Constantly inserting the latest design change or an individual service requirement within the assembly line process of the manufacturers was both impractical and inefficient. Those lines had to keep cranking out planes as quickly as possible to keep up with demand and to replace the ever-increasing losses. Ergo, 21 aircraft modification centers were built across the United States. Aircraft would be flown directly from their place of manufacture to a center dealing with that specific aircraft, hopefully along its path of departure from the United States to its designated combat theatre. Tucson had been built for B-24s.

"Hey *Libby*, maybe I'll see you down the road sometime," *Texican* said into his radio, as his engines were going through their startup process.

Approaching the end of her "zipper line" of twelve Liberators in the middle hangar, *Libby* was a few days behind *Texican*, each in their own apparently never-ending Greek Odyssey. "Sure thing, *Texican*, down the road," *Libby*'s voice trailed off to a whisper. She knew in her heart that that would be most unlikely.

"Maybe it's a good thing we're being separated," *Libby* contemplated. "I'm not sure how I'd react to seeing *Texican* as a burnt-up hulk or smashed to smithereens against a mountaintop. Though it sure has been fun the last few weeks. I do say I feel downright fine. As fine as dollar cotton, as my good friend would say."

---

2. http://www.warbirdsandairshows.com/Aircraft%20manufacturing/modific ationcenterswwii.htm

During the previous two weeks *Libby* and *Texican* had bantered back and forth, like a couple getting ready for a big date, getting decked out in their finest. In a way, they were. For they were getting fitted out with the latest upgrades, from more firepower in the form of two additional Browning .50 cals in their waist windows to more armor plating for their key components, the crew. The most formidable addition to them, however, was the integration of the Sperry S-1 bombsight and its companion A-5 autopilot. The International Business Machines Corporation had built them at their converted typewriter plant in Endicott, New York. It was just a small part of the "arsenal of democracy" in action. Technologically more advanced than its better known counterpart, the Norden bombsight, it turned them all into the world's most accurate harbinger of destruction from the heavens.[3] That is, with good weather, no cloud cover, and with no dense, opaque smokescreens. And not being knocked about by 58-pound German Flak projectiles disintegrating before their eyes upon the detonation of seven and a half pounds of Amatol high-explosive.[4]

The one thing that didn't change was their drab, olive green skin. Some of the other ships were being repainted in a dual-tone blue, much more pleasing to the eyes. To *Texican*'s mortification, others were having their large blue and white star unceremoniously removed, to be replaced with a roundel, composed of a concentric circle of red, white, blue, and yellow. To an observant eye, and one in the know, an individual could at least have a notion of what theatre of war they were going to end up in. But soldiers and aircraft weren't in the need to know. For now, *Texican*'s and *Libby*'s color and markings stayed the same. Olive drab green, a large lone star on each side, and, to them, the most important marking of all,

---

3. Searle, Loyd. "The Bombsight War: Norden vs. Sperry." *IEEE Spectrum*, September 1989.

4. German Explosive Ordnance, Dept. of the Army and the Air Force. Washington, DC, 1953, pp. 482, 483.

their individual identifications, 2-78172 and 2-78173, still proudly and prominently displayed on their respective tails. For now, they would have to keep guessing as to their eventual destination.

Two days later, *Libby* was in the air to places unknown to her, and also unknown to her ferrying flight crew. For there was a storm brewing. A big one, right in their path. The day before, a storm described as the "worst rainstorm to visit the district in years" had hit southern California, and it was heading east. Three inches of hail stones had covered downtown Los Angeles, turning it into a winter wonderland. *Texican* had made it only to Phoenix, ninety miles to the northwest, before his journey was prudently halted.[5]

"I think I'd make better time if I were to hopscotch my way to wherever I'm going," a disgusted *Libby* lamented as she was being taxied to a spot among a multitude of her siblings perched on the tarmac. It had been a flight of less than an hour before her wheels touched the runway at the Air Corps' William Field outside of Phoenix. Due to the large number of aircraft massing at the field to wait out the storm, *Libby* didn't notice, or hear, *Texican* parked nearest the taxiway.

Texican's stay ended when he attempted to depart the following morning. He only got as far as the air base in Blythe, California, 170 miles to the west, before again being forced down by the relentless storm.[6]

"Well, for once I'm glad I didn't go anywhere and just sat here on my haunches the last couple of days," said *Libby* as she watched the sun begin its torpid rise into a cloudless but cool morning. There had been tarmac activity all night as ground crews, barked at by demanding crew chiefs, had prepped planes for the next day's departure. They had to get the aircraft

---

5. *Topanga Journal* and *Malibu Monitor*, February 25, 1944, p. 1. *Arizona Daily Star*, February 25, 1944, p. 11.

6. AFHRA, Maxwell AFB. Reel ACR-68, Aircraft Record Card 42-78172. Also see Historical Research Frustration Addendum.

out of there. After all, the war machine required its continual feeding. Now flight crews were emerging from the low metal headquarters building, like the ubiquitous fire ants, to their designated aircraft.

Once in the air, *Libby* realized she was continuing a northwesterly course over the same desolate, rocky, scrubby terrain she'd been traversing ever since leaving Dallas. This changed like a season once she cleared some rocky, barren mountains at 10,000 feet. Before her, splayed out like a never-ending patch quilt, was a valley composed of quadrilaterals clothed in the entire color palette of greens and browns. She'd never seen anything like it. "Now, why didn't the Air Corps pick one of those greens to paint us in?" she wondered. For an hour and a half, she was dazzled by the spectacle and thought nothing could be more impressive. She then banked west.

Skimming the earth at a low 1,000 feet, after passing round, tree covered hills, she came upon a sight which almost caused all four of her engines to sputter. There before her were the vast, blue-green waters of the San Pablo and San Francisco bays. "Well, this sure makes Mountain Creek Lake seem like a drop in the proverbial bucket," an astonished *Libby* exclaimed.

Following a flyby and circling of an airfield, *Libby* felt her flaps being extended, as well as her landing gear being deployed. "Well, I guess here's another meaningless stopover in my journey without end," she lamented.

Oh, but she was so wrong. For it was here, at Hamilton Field, across the bay from San Francisco, that *Libby* would assume a new identity and become complete, becoming part of an inseparable family, a family composed of a band of ten brothers.

5

A Nom de Guerre and Family

Hamilton Army Air Force Field, Novato, California, February 28, 1944

*L*IBBY HADN'T SEEN SO MANY military aircraft since she left Love Field. And there were many she had never seen before but only heard about from some of her gossipy siblings. There were sleek B-17G bombers that she appreciated with a jealous eye, parked adjacent to dozens of more boxy Liberators. What astonished her most was the fact that they were gleaming in the California sun in their virgin silver aluminum skin. "What makes them so special?" she wondered. Then there were the dozens of single engine P-40 Warhawk and P-39 Airacobra fighters that reminded her of the P-51s and AT-6s made beside her in Dallas. "Buzzy little things. What was it *Texican* had said? Oh yeah, 'like flies menacing a paddocked horse'," she remembered with a slight grin concealed behind her front turret.

But the aircraft that really caught her eye were the twin-engined and twin-boomed P-38 Lightning fighters. The dual rudder design of its tail kind of reminded her of herself, which sure didn't hurt her impression. Being built 350 miles to the south, in Burbank, California, *Libby* would soon appreciate these "fork-tailed devils" for far more than their good looks.[1]

While staring approvingly at all the aircraft circling overhead and surrounding her on the ground, *Libby* had paid scant attention to the ten men sauntering up to her port side.

A fast, flickering hand motion observed peripherally out of her nose turret finally caught her attention. There, ten young men of the Army Air Corps were gesticulating with their arms, hands, and even heads, as they pondered something centered on her fuselage below the pilot's window. "Am I drooling out of my pitot tube or something?" *Libby* wondered. She then observed the tallest one, in an officer's dress coat, holding up something at arm's length.

Sighting along his arm and squinting with one eye closed, the officer held something in his outstretched left hand, seemingly aiming at a spot above her front landing gear.

The more she looked the less she was sure what it was. "Jumpin' Jehoshaphat, what the heck is that thing?" a perplexed *Libby* wondered. She saw flashes of yellow, red, and brown, on an object smaller than the smallest of one of her dash gauges. "Does that thing have a beak? Like a bird? I swear it has big white googly eyes. That brown. Is that a pinecone? What the bloody hell is that thing? And more importantly, what does it have to do with me?" a now anxious *Libby* pondered.

The ten men appeared to come to some sort of conclusion, ascertained by the nodding of their heads. With that they opened her bomb bay doors and proceeded to enter and fan out to all her crew positions.

---

1. Tillman, Barrett. *Forgotten Fifteenth*, p. 18. Washington, DC: Regnery History, 2014.

"Well, just come on in and make yourselves comfortable like it's home, why don't you?" scowled *Libby*. She noticed the tall one put the strange object in his pocket and crawl into the bombardier station.

"Hey, Pop, I wonder which targets will cross this bombsight's cross hairs, Japanese or German?" asked the bombardier, Second Lieutenant William Stanley, known as "Stan" to the crew. At twenty years old, he was the youngest officer. The oldest son of a central Kansas farmer, he had been a sophomore in college when the war caught up to him in February of 1943.

"Well, if in a few days our orders state to fly to Hickam Field, Hawaii, I think it will be pretty clear," replied Pop as he adjusted the pilot's seat. At twenty-six years old, Second Lieutenant Norman Blomgren of McHenry County, Illinois earned the moniker "Pop" by being the oldest of the crew. Montgomery Ward lost a Chicago headquarters manager when the war caught up to Norman in April of 1942.

"How's the view out of that co-pilot's seat, Harry?" asked Pop.

"Right now the view is great. I'm just wondering what it'll be in a few weeks," answered Second Lieutenant Harry Bursten. A son of Russian immigrants, Harry had been trying his hand at becoming a baker in Kansas City.

"Speaking of views, take a look at Bob there," Harry mentioned, pointing out the windshield to a head spinning like a whirligig in the small, plexiglass dome, known as the "astrodome" located along the nose of the ship, below the pilots. "Are you tracking Messerschmitts or Zeros there, Bob?" Harry yelled down, with a smirk on his face, to the navigator, Second Lieutenant Robert Simmons.

"Here's hoping I won't have to," Bob replied. A twenty-four-year-old civil servant, working at a Middletown, Pennsylvania airfield, Bob was initially rejected by the Army Air Corps due to his rail-thin frame. He must have hit the feeding trough.

Checking out the front nose turret's twin guns in front of Bob, Sergeant Cecil Yeates declared that Bob didn't have anything to worry about. Not as long as he was behind those guns. Doubtless a typical, cocky response from an untested twenty-year-old. Cecil had been driving a grocery delivery truck through the piney woods of east Texas before he enlisted.

Standing behind Pop and Harry, twenty-three-year-old Sergeant Bill Blankenship studied the fuel transfer switches, gauges, pumps, and assorted valves. As flight engineer, he had the critical job of keeping the 17,000 pounds of gasoline evenly distributed among the 18 different fuel cells located in the wings and overhead. And at critical times over enemy territory, he would man the top turret guns. A far cry from the responsibilities of an Asheville, North Carolina railroad porter.

Swinging the .50 caliber Brownings out of the storage harnesses into their waist window opening positions, Corporal Charley Debord and Sergeant Jim Reed, standing back-to-back, took aim at imaginary foes. Twenty-four-year-old Charley had been helping his dad on their Sulphur Springs, Texas farm when he enlisted. At nineteen years old, Jim was the youngest on the plane. Working at a sawmill in Vermont's Green Mountains before enlistment, it was arguable which was louder, the whine of a four-foot-diameter sawblade or the angry bark of the Browning.

A few feet fore of Jim and Charley, Private First Class Joseph Windham examined his future confines. Joseph pondered how he ever got through the slender hatch opening of the belly ball turret in training. It appeared as small as his hometown of Roscoe, Texas. At five foot nine, he knew he was on the tall side to fit, fetal style, in this lethal fishbowl. Not only could he not wear his parachute, he couldn't even wear the smaller reserve chute on his chest.

Sixty-six feet aft of Stan, who was currently toggling non-existent bombs from the bombardier's station, Sergeant Joseph Fox settled himself into the relatively spacious tail turret with its twin Brownings. With almost unobscured above, side, and rearward views, the rest of the gunners would rely heavily on Fox to announce the presence of any approaching threat.

"I haven't had so many people in me since I was on the Dallas assembly line," *Libby* quipped. "And they sure took me at my word and are making themselves comfortable. I do think they intend on staying with me awhile. Must admit, I do like the feel of, oh, what was his name? Pop! Yeah, I like the feel of those hands on my yoke. Not as calloused as Judy's were but just as firm and confident."

And confident they all are. But anxious too, with a bit of youthful self-doubt creeping into them because of the unknown. Unknown, as in how each of them will respond at a critical moment.

They had been training together as a crew at Tonapah, Nevada, for the last three months. Initially, they were geographically scattered individuals from all walks of life: occupationally, economically, educationally, and spiritually. Now they were one. There was no animosity. No bickering. The Army wouldn't have allowed it. And as airplane commander, Pop wouldn't have allowed it either. In that way only are they unlike a band of biological brothers.

They each knew how to mechanically perform their particular job, albeit in a training center, safe in the States. But how about accomplishing it when bullets, explosive cannon shells, or jagged, lethal, sizzling chunks of hot steel are ripping through the plane's paper-thin skin? Or when the concussion of exploding Flak shells is suddenly lifting the plane like it hit a thermal? Or when the adrenalin is pumping through you faster than the blood coursing through your veins? Or the fact that sweat is pouring down your gloves, yet your eyelids are frozen open due to the thirty degrees below zero air whipping through the plane's open windows? The self-doubt is understandable. After all, they are but citizen soldiers.

IN THE EARLY MORNING dawn in a sleepy fog, *Libby* felt the gentle, feathery stroking of her fuselage. Right where she liked it, below and behind her chin. As she came out of her morning stupor, she realized there was someone standing on a short ladder leaned up against her, below the pilot's window. That someone was a man older than any of the ones who had been in her yesterday, and he was holding a small paintbrush, glistening with glossy black paint.

"Now what is he painting on me?" *Libby* wondered as recognition slowly dawned on her. "It's probably not more numbers, since all the ones I've seen on any other plane are white. Well, all except the black ones on those arrogant, silver B-17Gs," she groused as she glanced at the Flying Fortress parked next to her.

That's when she noticed a reflection of herself on the bright aluminum skin of her B-17 companion. Transcending the entire day, *Libby* watched in fascination as a shape slowly emerged. With splashes of glossy black, white, red, and bright yellow, an image came into being. One that she had seen before.

"My gosh, that's the strange pinecone bird that Stan was holding up, and it's riding a large bomb through the air. Must be at least a 500-pounder.

"I don't know about this," a disturbed *Libby* mumbled.

Then the man came down off the ladder and moved to the left of the bizarre bird caricature. Standing on the pavement, he began to infill the black outlined lettering in the same bright yellow paint he had used on the long beaked bird. Having difficulty deciphering the mirror image, it revealed itself to her slowly:

"W....O....R....R....Y"

"Worry?"

"B....I....R....D"

"Bird?" she asked in a squeamish uptalk tone.

"*WORRYBIRD?!*" she screamed, loud enough to be heard by all who were monitoring the proper radio frequency. "Is that what those guys really think of me? Some anxious, nail-biting, laughable cartoon character?" an anguished *Libby* whispered breathlessly.

With a final flourish, the artist then added three dots followed by a long dash below the now completed nose art.

"Hey *Libby*. Oh, wait. I mean, hey *Worrybird*, nice likeness you have painted there," commented a taxiing B-24G in a mocking tone as it found a spot amongst the Liberators crammed on the apron.

Libby swiveled her turret to get a better look at her verbal antagonist. The vision that awaited her would have stopped her if she had been on a full military power takeoff.

While this mocking B-24G also had a figure depicted riding a bomb earthward, this figurine was not a stunted, pinecone-bodied bird. No, this one was a long-legged, blond beauty, stretched out straddling the bomb with her chest poised up, supported by her outstretched arms. And there wasn't a stitch of clothing to be found. Above this Esquire-ish magazine cover beauty, was somewhat questionably painted the words "Valiant Vi rgin-ia."[2]

"Well, I'm not sure what to say about that," a dumbfounded *Libby* mumbled.

"Hey, wait a minute. How do you know my name?"

"Well, that's easy," *Valiant* said as her props wound down.

"Nobody who was in Dallas a few weeks ago, doesn't know yours or *Texican's* names. Nobody could get a word in edgewise over the radio the way you two were blathering. I was at the head of the line when you came to and started asking all those questions. Questions that we all had by the way," *Valiant* stated, like a parent giving advice to an innocent child.

"Anyway, it's good to see you, and I hope to run into you again somewhere down the road, *Worrybird*," *Valiant* said as a fuel truck pulled up to top off her tanks, for it was her turn to depart to destinations unknown. Unbeknownst to both of them, *Valiant* would get her wish. Both of them would meet again, side by side, high above enemy territory.

---

2. https://449th.com/42-78158/

The next morning, the entire crew of the newly christened B-24G Liberator, the *Worrybird,* stood arms akimbo, while they admired the cartoon-like artwork.

"This is great! Perfect! The best twenty-five bucks we ever spent!" an enthusiastic Bob Simmons bellowed.

"Oh, I know what that bird is thinking right now," Harry stated with a mischievous grin on his face. "Yeah. It's screaming, 'Stan, you moron! You were supposed to drop the bomb AFTER I got off!'" Harry bent over in gut wrenching laughter, and of course the rest of the crew joined in. Except one.

"Sure. Go ahead. Laugh, you idiots," Stan said in a mock, pissed-off tone. Trying to change the subject, he pointed to the slash of paint comprising the three dots and dash. "I wonder how many people besides a radio operator will recognize the V for Victory in morse code?"

"I'm wondering how many guys who don't have your musical appreciation will recognize that as the opening to Beethoven's Fifth Symphony?" Pop responded, after regaining his composure.[3]

"Well, that's their loss. It's a beautiful piece of work. And I'm talking about the Fifth *and* the bird," added Stan.

As Bob had stated, the crew had paid twenty-five dollars to an otherwise unemployed artist to paint the nose art. An artist who, until recently had been working for the Walt Disney animation studios. For the rest of their time together, the crew will affectionately call their ship *"Bird."*

The *Worrybird's* nose art caricature was fashioned after a popular 49-cent good luck charm. The sales description stated: *"Take care of all your worries—turn them over to the Worrybird."*[4] It depicted the flightless

---

3. For those not familiar with the classical music genre, it is also the beginning and ending sequence of Electric Light Orchestra's rendition of Chuck Berry's "Roll Over Beethoven."

4. Sears, Roebuck and Co., Chicago, Illinois. 1942 Christmas Catalogue, p. 8.

Kiwi Bird, which, according to popular culture, doesn't care where it's going, only where it's been. For one already knows what has transpired, where you've been. There's no second guessing as to what has happened. But what about where you're going? What will befall you then? There are nothing but unanswerable questions.

Where this crew was going, it would take more than proficiency in their combined, respective abilities in order to return. It would also take luck. Luck that a Worrybird might bring.

Stan's Worrybird good luck charm, much the worse for wear. This was the model for the Worrybird's nose art. Though not a superstitious person, Stan would carry his Worrybird in his flight suit on all missions. Purchased in San Francisco, one was given to each crew member and to the artist.
[Author's possession]

"Band of Ten Brothers" in the snow, Tonapah, Nevada, February 1944. Front row, L-R: William "Bill" Blankenship, Joseph Windham, Cecil Yeates, Joseph Fox, Charley Debord, James Reed. Back row, L-R: William "Stan" Stanley, Norman "Pop" Blomgren, Harry Bursten, Robert "Bob" Simmons. [Author's Personal Collection]

B-24G Liberator Worrybird. Serial number 42-78173. Photo location un-known, though before she flew any missions. Cecil Yeates' front turret with twin 50 caliber Brownings. Stan's bombardier station in armored plexi-glass underneath. Bob Simmons' navigational "astrodome" behind turret. Unknown ground crewman. [Author's Personal Collection]

6

DEATH CAN COME IN SO MANY WAYS

HAMILTON ARMY AIR FORCE FIELD, NOVATO, CALIFORNIA, FEBRUARY 28, 1944

DEPARTURE FROM SAN PABLO BAY came quickly for *Worrybird*. Others who had come before, and immediately after, would languish for another one or two weeks before their eventual departure. But they will catch up to her in this quartermaster game of leapfrog across the chessboard of U.S. Army airfields.

"Drat, I hate rain," *Worrybird* scowled as Pop and Harry ran up her engines as they sat on the taxiway. A light mist had slickened the airstrip during the early morning hours, while dark, ominous clouds coming off the ocean threatened. A 500-foot cloud deck covered the upper half of the surrounding and potentially life-threatening mountaintops.

"Good thing the wind is out of the south so we can take off out over the bay. I don't like the idea of taking off into those mountains hiding behind us," Harry mentioned to Pop as he set the wing flaps to their takeoff position.

"I'm just glad the rain stopped. I don't like the idea of my head hanging out the side window during takeoff. I feel like a slobbering hound dog with its head out a car window, just so I can see the strip," a relieved Pop commented. A B-24 didn't have windshield wipers.

"Bill, can you check out the radio? I'm getting some static from the tower," Pop asked the flight engineer, who had double duty as the radio operator, and was currently standing right behind Pop's right shoulder. His normal station was presently occupied by Stan, Bob, and Cecil, stuffed like sardines in the cramped cubicle. Pop didn't want them in their normal stations in the nose during takeoff. The last thing you wanted was a nose-heavy bomber when trying to get into the air. Balance was critical. The remaining gunners were sitting with their backs against the bomb bay bulkhead in the waist.

"Strange having all the guys bunched together like this," thought *Worrybird*. "Of course, I haven't had this many in me during a takeoff. I wonder if this is normal?" she mused as Pop and Harry pushed and held the throttles to their stops while simultaneously releasing the parking brake.

Instead of Texas dust devils erupting from the backside of the throbbing engines, a whirlwind of prop driven mist cascaded behind *Worrybird* as she picked up speed down the runway.

Once airborne she quickly passed over marshland that was soon replaced by the waters of San Pablo Bay. Skimming below the grey steel cloud deck, she soon found herself banking to the south into San Francisco Bay.

"Hey Stan!" Pop yelled over his shoulder into the flight deck.

"Yeah, Pop?" Stan replied, after squeezing his way past Bob, Bill, and Cecil, sticking his head into the cockpit.

"Go tell the guys in back to get to the waist windows. They're going to witness something in a few minutes that they'll never see again and will want to tell their grandkids about one day. And then get your butt back up here," Pop commanded.

"Sure thing," Stan replied before heading down the crawl space passageway to relay Pop's message. What Pop meant was known only to himself and Harry.

After a few minutes *Worrybird* felt her right wing dip ever so slightly as she banked to a more westerly heading. She was also losing altitude, not that she had much to lose in the first place. Unlike any other takeoff, where she would have immediately started gaining altitude, they had leveled off at only three hundred feet above the waters.

"Now what the heck is this guy doing?" *Worrybird* wondered, dropping the pilot's affectionate nickname.

As she was finishing her westerly turn, an apparition slowly appeared in front of her that defied her ingrained aeronautical logic. Two large, Poseidon-inspired towers, seemingly rising out of the waters with their tops obscured by the low hanging clouds, were directly in her flightpath. Connected by what appeared to be a steel ribbon, hanging from a cluster of thin cables, like strands of kelp, it seemed to glow a golden-orange. Even in the sunless sky.

The Golden Gate Bridge.

And with sudden comprehension, she knew they were all going to die, for this crazy fool of a pilot was going to fly under it.

"Altimeter?" asked Pop to Harry, not wanting to take his eyes off the quickly approaching bridge.

"One hundred," Harry replied after leaning over to check the gauge.

"That'll do," replied Pop with confidence in his voice.

"Any lower and I'll be doing a belly landing on the water!" *Worrybird* yelped as they approached the bridge, now filling the entire view in her windshield.

She grimaced and wished she could duck her twin tail as the bridge passed exactly one hundred feet above her while threading the needle at 165mph. Full military power was then felt by everyone. And when Pop and Harry pulled sharply back on the yoke, sending her into a heavenward hyperbola above the dark blue waters of the Pacific, the whole crew broke out in a rambunctious whoop and holler. Pop just grinned.

Worrybird wasn't grinning though. She was wondering what the hell she had gotten herself into. She knew what she was capable of, and more importantly, not. But as she had learned, it wasn't in her control. It was in his. The one they called Pop. Did he have what it took to get them all through this? She knew one thing for sure: he was going to have to prove himself to her, and so far he hadn't. Far from it.

To reach their final destination, Pop would have 10,595 miles of flying to prove himself. On one of their impending sixteen legs of flight, he'd get his chance, sooner than any of them thought.

One thing the crew now knew for sure, and that was which enemy would appear under Stan's bombsight crosshairs. For Pop had put the *Worrybird* into a graceful bank to the southeast, back over coastal California. They were heading back east. It wouldn't be the Imperial Japanese.

Pop had received their orders to report to the Caribbean Wing Command at Morrison Field in West Palm Beach, Florida, 2,800 miles across the country.

"I know that runway," said *Worrybird* later that afternoon with recognition in her voice, as Pop banked into an approach to William Field outside of Phoenix for the second time.

"I don't get to stay long enough anywhere to make friends, or even an acquaintance," she mumbled, as first thing the following morning she was off again, heading southeast over familiar terrain. "I do believe I know where we're heading for once." A scant two hours later, *Worrybird* and her crew were landing at Biggs Field, El Paso, a first for the men, but not for the experienced *Worrybird*.

"I don't like this place. Nothing but bad memories," the consternated plane thought as remembrance of a raging West Texas storm flashed through her like the ragged lightning and hail of a month ago.

Fortunately for *Worrybird*'s frame of mind, this stay was also brief. Within a few hours she was back in the air continuing her southeasterly course. This took her over the Edwards Limestone escarpments of the Texas Hill Country, deep into the heart of Texas. "Sure wish I was flying with *Texican* alongside me. I bet he would be spouting me some yarn about what we were flying over," *Worrybird* thought wistfully.

As *Worrybird* entered a memory-induced brain fog, the largest Army airfield she had yet encountered was emerging on the horizon. Kelly Field was six miles southwest of the Alamo, whose defenders *Texican* had constantly serialized. With its five runways and large maintenance and supply depots, it was more a mammoth industrial complex than an airfield.

At least here she and her crew got needed rest, fuel, food, and a maintenance checkup. They'd need it. Their next leg was to be the longest yet, a thousand miles to Jacksonville, Florida. But then again, the best laid plans...

SOMETHING JUST AS LETHAL and threatening as enemy flak and tracer-laced machine-gun bullets had been following *Worrybird* since leaving California, and it was quickly catching up to them, like a menacing specter hovering over their shoulder. And it would be getting stronger as it marched east toward the Gulf coast.

Weather. *Worrybird* had lived through it. But it would be a new, frightening experience for the untested crew.

"All right, guys, listen up," Pop announced tersely over the interphone headset.

"Bob, give me a course to the nearest airstrip that can handle us."

"Bill, go check the *Bird*'s rudder rigging, it's feeling awfully sluggish."

"Cecil, as assistant radio operator, get up there and wait for Bob's nav report on the closest field and contact them."

"What am I asking them?" questioned Cecil with nervousness flittering in his response.

"Asking nothing. You will tell them we are declaring a flight emergency and are landing," instructed Pop in a calm but firm voice.

Swirling, groping, black and grey hands of the specter had caught up to them, engulfed them, and wasn't going to let go. An easterly marching Pacific storm front had met, merged with, and was feeding on the northward progressing Gulf tropical moisture. The *Worrybird* had flown into what would be termed a March "baby hurricane."[1]

"Nav to pilot," asserted Bob in a no-nonsense voice. It was no time for familiarity. Training had taken over.

"Go ahead, nav."

"Closest airfield is the Pensacola Municipal, eight miles at a heading of ninety-five degrees. The Naval Air Station is twelve miles at a 170-degree heading."

"Pilot to radio."

"Radio here."

"Contact Pensacola Municipal. Tell them we're coming in and request wind vector."

At that moment, Bill returned after an examination of the exposed rudder controls and reported that the labyrinthine cable and pulley system looked fine. Pop was actually hoping Bill would have found something wrong. As flight engineer Bill could have fixed it. He knew more about how the *Bird* flew, and more importantly, how to keep her in the air than anyone aboard.

"Harry, I think that hail took out more than the front turret's canvas shrouding. It must have shredded our rudders too. Our ailerons and elevator surfaces should be fine at least. I'm going to need your help with what's left of the rudders," Pop said matter-of-factly.

"Sure thing. At least the engines all look fine," replied Harry after a quick scan of the myriad of engine gauges.

It had not been the rain, the lightning, nor the gusty wind that had blown them around like a ping pong ball in vertiginous swells that put

---

1. *Pensacola News Journal.* March 12, 1944, p. 6.

them in this predicament. It had been the hail. This hadn't been like the pea-sized hail in El Paso. No, this had been a truly inescapable curtain of hailstones that had fallen upon them, with the added benefit of the *Bird* crashing into it headlong at 165mph.

Any vulnerable canvas surface had been shredded, including the front turret shrouding seam. With this gone, a gale was tearing through the turret and making Bob's adjacent navigation station a living hell. It was also obvious that the canvas-covered rudders had at least major holes and tears in them, giving Pop major concern about steerage ability.

"Radio to pilot."

"Pilot, go ahead."

"Pensacola gives permission. North-south runway number one. Be advised winds at twenty-five, gusting to forty out of the southwest, though they are turning westerly. Altimeter, one hundred twenty."

"Thanks, Radio."

Within a few minutes after turning into the proper heading, the airport came into view, aided by its bright runway and installation lighting, a blessing in the faltering evening twilight. But of course, it wouldn't remain so easy. After a single flash of a bolt of cloud-to-ground lightning, the airport lighting went out as quickly as a snuffed candle.

"Oh, sweet Mother of God, help us sinners now!" exclaimed a hurting, absolutely terrified *Worrybird*. "How the heck is Pop going to land me now? He can't see the airport, let alone the runway!"

Whether from an answer to *Worrybird*'s repeating an oft overheard prayer or just random chance, assistance came in the most unusual form.

Lightning.

The single bolt that had shrouded the airport in darkness was just a precursor to an absolutely wild, strobe light effect lightning show, revealing the runway for Pop's and Harry's capable hands.[2]

Before *Worrybird* could utter her thanks, she felt herself floating crablike above the runway as her pilots fought a significant westerly crosswind gust. As her wheels touched the sweet earth and she turned to the parking apron, she vowed she would never doubt the skill and ability of Pop as airplane commander again. He had more than proven himself.

The *Worrybird* was not the only aircraft to be affected by the storm. Fifty miles to the west an Army Air Corps transport plane carrying Bob Hope and his contingent from California to Miami had been forced down in Mobile, Alabama. Fortunately for all on board they landed safely. Such was not the case for two other Air Corps planes, one in central Alabama and another in southern Arkansas. Those planes and their entire flight crews were lost.[3] No flight is just routine.

2. *Pensacola News Journal.* March 12, 1944. "Pilot Lands By Lightning," p. 4. While the article does not name the pilot of the Army Air Corps bomber for security reasons, timing of the storm with the March 3rd California departure of *Worrybird* suggests the possibility that it was "Pop" and the *Worrybird*.

3. *Birmingham News.* March 12, 1944. p. 1; *Sun Herald*. Biloxi, Mississippi. March 13, 1944, p. 3.

7

ARE WE THERE YET?

OVER THE SKIES OF EASTERN FLORIDA, MARCH 24, 1944

"As time goes by ... " Stan softly crooned as he took a deep breath to yet again serenade *Worrybird's* captivated crew.

"Pilot to Stan," Pop spoke up over the interphone, interrupting Stan's solo performance for the crew.

"Go ahead, Pop."

"How about we enjoy the view in quiet solitude for a while?" Pop asked as he glanced at Harry, who was rolling his eyes.

"Oh. Sure thing," a much-chagrined Stan responded, as he slinked further into the backless seat of the bombardier's station under *Worrybird's* nose. He had been enjoying the unimpeded panorama of Florida's white beaches against the blue-green waters of the Atlantic rushing by. Passing the time in song. This won't be the last time they overhear Stan singing through the headsets. Though it will be the last time they hear it in such a serene, benign setting.

"Hey, wait a minute. You didn't ask *me* if I wanted Stan to stop," *Worrybird* protested. "Do you mean to tell me no one else appreciates that fine tenor voice?" she asked, dumbfounded.

It wasn't that the crew didn't appreciate Stan's fine voice; he certainly had one. Coming from a strong musical family, he had been the tenor in his college quartet, the Stinkpots, a parody of the then-wildly popular jazz group, the Inkspots. It's just that ever since that night in Pensacola, they had heard him sing *Old Black Magic* and *As Time Goes By* ad nauseam.

Having landed in Pensacola, a pure Naval port city where a B-24G was as rare as hen's teeth, it took time to find the needed parts after the storm, and the expertise to install them. As in almost two weeks' time.

So, what do four young, innocent, good-looking, bachelor Army Air Corps officers do in a port city? They spit shine their shoes, put on their officers' dress uniforms (known as "pinks and greens,") all adorned with silver wings above their left breast pockets, and hit the clubs. Clubs filled with Navy men.

While they sauntered along the streets of downtown Pensacola, they had more than a few swabbies give them a double take and a glancing stink eye. They didn't think anything of it until they entered the club for which they had been searching.

For they had entered a sea of white. As in a blizzard. A blizzard composed of over a hundred men dressed in white. Their Naval dress whites, enlisted men and officers alike. Self-consciously, the four Army airmen in contrasting dark green found an empty table, sat down, and soon found it was hard to get a drink. But they were there for a reason, and that was to listen to Jack Teagarden and his band.

It had been said of Jack that he was the best American jazz trombonist, and perhaps singer, in the jazz music scene, playing and singing with other greats such as Armstrong, Goodman, and Miller.

Following a long set, and needing to rest his chords, Teagarden asked if anyone in the sea of white would like to come up and try out their vocals with the band. Either no one in white had the talent or they were too petrified to embarrass themselves in front of their shipmates. Not so with one in green.

"Stan, get up there. You've been regaling us in song anywhere you can, including the showers," Bob goaded, as he elbowed Stan in the side.

"Sure, why not? Doubt I'll ever have the chance again in my life. Nothing ventured, you know," Stan said, accepting the challenge, perhaps aided by liquid courage.

After perusing the available sheet music, Stan came up with the two that he knew well: *As Time Goes By*, made famous in the recent movie *Casablanca*, and of course his favorite, *That Old Black Magic*, which Judy Garland had released the year before. Her rendition was sultry, perhaps because she knew it had been written about her.

Stan's performance, while not sultry, was impressive enough that they didn't have to pay for another drink that long night.

ONCE REPAIRED, AND AFTER landing at Morrison Field outside of West Palm Beach, the crew received their new, much anticipated orders. However, they couldn't open the envelope, marked secret, until they were airborne. All they were told was to set a course for the thousand-mile leg to Borinquen Field, Puerto Rico the next morning, flying the B-24G with serial number 42-78173.

The next morning, once the *Worrybird* had leveled off at 6,000 feet in a southeasterly heading over the Bahamas, Pop asked Harry to open the orders and read them aloud to all, with everyone donning their interphone headsets.

"All right guys, the moment of truth," Harry declared as he anxiously opened the envelope with perspiring hands and quickly scanned the sheet of paper for the pertinent information.

"OK, '*Under authority contained*, blah, blah, blah, *the following named officers and enlisted men*,' yeah, OK, '*in aircraft as indicated.*' Hold on, here it is: '*from Morrison Field, West Palm Beach, Florida, via the South Atlantic Route to El Aouina, Tunisia, reporting upon arrival thereat to the responsible agency of the Fifteenth Air Force for assignment to the Fifteenth Air Force. Persons will use APO 12859,'* etcetera, etcetera. You can read the rest," Harry finished as he slowly slid the orders back in their envelope.[1]

With the steady droning of *Worrybird*'s engines, each man was temporarily in the throes of their own thoughts, asking themselves questions. As with most of life's adventures, however, answering one question opened up a limitless supply of others. A personal Pandora's Box of possibilities. And not even the Army Air Corps knew the answers to some of them. Those answers would come, one by one, piggybacked with *Worrybird*'s life journey.

The South Atlantic Route, along with the alternate North Atlantic Route, had been devised and built before the United States declared war on December 8th, 1941. In order to supply Great Britain, Free France, and Russia with needed war materials under our Lend-Lease agreements, air transport corridors and bases needed to be established for cross-Atlantic air shipments. Once the United States entered the war, those routes became vital to the Army Air Corps in transferring America's air might to the battlefronts.

The *Worrybird* would fly into and out of many of the recently constructed airbases as it progressed southward: Borinquen Field, Puerto Rico; Waller Field, Trinidad; Atkinson Field, British Guiana; Val de Caes Field, Belém, Brazil (where each of the crew became a "Son of Neptune" for crossing the equator); São Luís Field, São Luís, Brazil; and finally, their debarkation point from the west, Parnamirin Field, Natal, Brazil.

Exotic places for boys from Texas, Kansas, Missouri, or Illinois. Next stop: Dakar, Senegal.

---

1. Headquarters Station #11 Caribbean Wing, ATC. Morrison Field, Operations Order # 892. West Palm Beach, Florida, 24 March 1944. Author's Collection.

"DON'T WORRY, THE *BIRD* is in great shape, she'll do just fine," Bill responded to Pop's query about her fitness after four hours of flight. "With the current rate of fuel consumption, we'll have about four hundred gallons left," he added to further alleviate Pop's concerns.

As airplane commander, responsible for ten lives including his own, Pop doesn't want to leave anything to chance. At 1,876 miles and over eleven hours of flight time, this was the longest leg of any for the *Worrybird*. And it's not like there were any airfields, or even a barren piece of dirt to land on, if the need arose. Just the unending, rolling surface of the Atlantic Ocean. Being a "Son of Neptune" wouldn't help. And *Worrybird* never learned to swim.

"Nav to Radio, anything yet, Bill?" Bob queried eight hours into the monotonous flight.

"That's a negative, Bob. We probably have another hour to hour and a half of flight time to go before we pick it up," replied Bill, who was as anxious as Bob. Almost.

For the past 1,400 miles, Bob had been navigating their way across the Atlantic by dead reckoning. With constant recording of their true heading, airspeed, drift, and time, Bob had a fair idea of where they were and where they were heading. Of course, being off by just two degrees meant a sixty-five-mile navigational error death warrant. To help guide the Dakar-bound aircraft home during the final stages of their trip, they listened for the "beam": a powerful but narrow radio signal that was broadcast directly from Dakar toward Natal, Brazil. It was usually picked up by approaching aircraft within three to four hundred miles of the African coast. It was a simple matter of the aircraft staying centered on the beam, with the help of the navigator and radioman, thus bringing them home.

Having long become mesmerized by the constant droning of her engines never changing speed or pitch, *Worrybird* at first didn't notice the new sound: a high-frequency, alternating hum coursing through her. But commotion on the flight deck made her very aware.

"Whoa, Bill's acting like he has a bee in his bonnet. I wonder if it's that high hum on the radio. Hadn't heard that before. Looks like Bob is getting in on the action now, too," *Worrybird* exclaimed, noticing Bob grabbing charts, paper, pencil, and his Keuffel & Esser slide rule. She soon felt herself ever so slightly change course.

"Glad we have that beam. We would have missed Dakar by ninety miles," Bob said disgustedly to Stan after giving Pop a course correction of three degrees. "These clouds are making this night sky black as ink. We would have flown right past it. Right out into the Sahara," he said with emotion, wildly jerking a thumb over his left shoulder. Bob's navigation table faced aft.

"Quit knocking yourself out. You're doing this over a faceless ocean. There're no pilotage points for reference, and this weather front is playing with the wind direction and speed, therefore drift," Stan said convincingly. As bombardier, Stan was also the assistant navigator.

"I know. But I'm better than this, and I just feel like I let Pop down. That's what burns me," Bob said, shaking his head while engrossing himself with his charts, thus cutting off any further discussion.

Worrybird had gotten used to the steady hum of the beam coursing through her, like a constant companion, comfortably snuggled up to her. So, when it suddenly disappeared, it came as a shock. No warning, just gone.

"Radio to Nav, we've got a problem. I lost the beam," Bill informed.

"What do you mean you lost the beam? Did you adjust the antenna?" Bob quizzed.

"Yes, I did. Dakar is just not transmitting."

"Well shee-it," Bob spat, glancing at Stan. "Here's hoping I remember my star checks from nav school."

"Nav to pilot."

"Go ahead," Pop responded, expecting the call. He had been listening in on Bill and Bob's conversation.

"We lost the beam, so I need to perform celestial observations. Can you take us above the cloud tops? And once we're in the clear, maintain a course of forty-two degrees and keep the *Bird* at 165mph steady."

"Will do. Everyone, don and check your oxygen masks. We may have to go above 10,000. Stan, perform a mask check on everyone. Bob, how long do you think we need to remain above?" Pop asked as he put *Worrybird* into a gentle climb through the clouds masked by the dark of night.

"We're about 275 miles out. I'll need to take several observations to decrease the acceleration error, so let's stay above until I tell you to take her down for the approach," Bob replied confidently. Let's hope it's for an airfield approach and not for the search of a city, he thought to himself.

After that, it was all business for Bob. Taking the sextant out of its olive-green case, he began "shooting the stars" through the plexiglass astrodome. He fancied himself an 18th-century mariner circumventing the globe with the tools he was using. There was no difference except for the diminutive size of his chronometer.

Picking the first of the three needed stars was easy. Prominent in the western sky was his favorite constellation, Orion, the hunter. And blazing bright red on the hunter's right shoulder was Betelgeuse.

"The hunter. Is that us or you, *Bird*?"

Next was the star Regulus, high overhead in Leo.

"Leo the lion. Are we ready to pounce or will we be pounced upon?" Bob wondered as he checked the altitude reading on the sextant's scale.

Staring out toward the front of *Worrybird*, directly in her path, was Spica. Like a Christmas star guiding them east.

"Virgo the virgin. Perfect. I sure wish you could stay that way, *Bird*. But I'm afraid not," Bob lamented as he read the final star position.

"You'd think I was Captain James Cook and it's 1779. Crazy," Bob mumbled as he shouted readings and times to Stan who sat at the navigation table, pencil at the ready. Fortunately, they had broken through the clouds at 9,000 feet and the crew had gladly taken off the foul, stale-smelling and tasting oxygen masks.

After a few slight course corrections during the last hour and a half, Bob radioed Pop and told him to bring the *Bird* down below the cloud deck. Leaving the fading stars in the early morning twilight behind them in a shallow dive, Pop took them all into the murky, veiled darkness of clouds.

"Well, hot damn," Harry exclaimed after what had seemed an eternity in blackness. As *Worrybird* slowly came out of the bottom cloud deck, pinpoints of light began to appear through her windshield. These were not the pinpoint lights of stars but the sprinkling of landing lights at Dakar Field. She was almost perfectly lined up for a landing.

It was Bob's turn to grin. A big cheesy one.

8

SEARCHING FOR RICK'S

OVER THE DESERTS OF THE WESTERN SAHARA, MARCH 31, 1944

"AND I THOUGHT KANSAS WAS DRY," Stan commented as he watched the apparently endless, brown-pigmented sand and rock of the western Sahara pass underneath. It was harsher than Stan's recent Kansas dust bowl memories.

Sometimes life is composed of congruent extremes. Nothing was more obvious than contrasting the *Worrybird*'s last two legs of her seemingly endless journey. Beforehand, nothing but water could be seen. Monotonous blue, broken only by an occasional foamy whitecap. On the current leg, more than 1,300 miles of lifeless sand and rock. The only water to be found would have been at the oasis of Tindouf, Algeria, almost a thousand miles into the journey and one of only five visual pilotage points for Bob's navigation.[1] They were trying to get to Marrakech, Morocco. But first they had to cross the Atlas Mountains.

Their biggest impediment yet encountered, soaring above 13,500 feet, the Atlas range separated the seemingly inhospitable Sahara from the thin ribbon of North African civilization, desperately hugging the Mediterranean Sea coastline. And they had been instructed to fly through it.

The two hundred miles of flying through the twisting, undulating gorges, staying below and away from the denuded, potentially deadly mountain peaks, was an extreme test of *Worrybird*'s pilots and navigator. They were never so glad to see an airstrip, looming ahead in the green oasis of Marrakech.

Others attempting to navigate the Atlas Mountains on their way to establish the 15th Air Force had not been as fortunate. The previous December, the B-24H *Pudgy II*, flown by Captain David Council, flew into one of the cloud-shrouded peaks. The plane was carrying the entire officer and 14-man NCO staff of the nascent 719th Squadron of the 449th Bombardment Group. One week later, severe icing caused Lt. William Thieme, Jr., also of the 719th, to order the crew of his B-24H, the *Battlin' Betty Ann*, to bail out. The parachute of Operations Officer Captain Hiero F. Hays failed to open.

These were not the first planes of the 719th to be lost. On the first leg of their journey overseas, Lieutenants Sheldon Zimmerman and Paul Lahr, piloting the B-24H *Hassen the Assassin*, skimmed a mountain peak while attempting to land at Borinquen Airfield, Puerto Rico. Unbeknownst to *Worrybird* and her crew, they too will soon become members of the seemingly snakebit 719th Squadron.[2]

---

1. Currier, Donald. *50 Mission Crush*, pp. 35–36. New York, NY: Pocket Books, 1993.

2. Shepherd, William D. *Of Men and Wings*, p. 17. Panama City, FL: Norfield Publishing, 1996.

After an overnight stay, a quick one-hour flight brought the *Worry-bird*'s crew to a much-anticipated destination: Casablanca. For Americans of that period, nothing conjured up more exotic images of style and intrigue.

Roaming the streets filled with French-influenced neo-Moorish architecture, the "boys" were in search of Rick's, the nightclub made famous in the movie. Who knew, maybe they'd run into Humphrey Bogart and Ingrid Bergman in a smoke-filled room? Maybe Stan could sing *As Time Goes By* accompanied by Sam on a Kohler & Campbell upright piano.

But they never did run into Bogart or Bergman, let alone find Rick's. But they knew that all along. The movie had been shot at a Warner Brothers studio in Burbank, California, next to Lockheed's P-38 fighter production plant. Heck, there never was a Rick's Cafe. Nor did the "real" story take place in Casablanca. It occurred in Tangier, two hundred miles to the north.

But they all knew this was the last chance to postpone the inevitable. One more round before the bar closed. For tomorrow they would fly a thousand miles east to Tunis, Tunisia, and receive their final orders. Sometimes a temporary self-delusion is better than stark reality.

The inevitable was ugly, mankind seen at its worst. As they flew east along that thin band of human civilization along the Mediterranean coast, the *Worrybird*'s crew got its first glimpse of just how ugly and uncivilized mankind could behave. Battle scars and debris from U.S. General George S. Patton and British General Bernard Montgomery's pincer movement against Germany's "Desert Fox" Erwin Rommel littered their route. Blackened carcasses of tanks, troop carriers, and airplanes of all makes and nationalities were visible, even at 3,000 feet. From that elevation, the actual devastation was somewhat sanitized. You couldn't reach out and touch it and feel dirty. Ten months' time had also cleansed the oily smoke and acrid taste that had once permeated the air.

From her elevated perch, *Worrybird* was also taking note of the devastation. Among the battle's debris were occasional remains of a B-24, painted in the same color as the entombing sand, or the bleached skeletal body of a B-17. But it was the numerous black, ugly craters with emanating rock and debris-scattered star fields that held her attention. Were they the result of bombs dropped from those B-24s and B-17s? Did they portend the destructive power that she too would soon be carrying in her belly? In disarming contrast, they also made her recollect a memory of beauty, of wonder.

"Those craters remind me of what Stan taught me over the Atlantic a few nights ago," *Worrybird* remembered. Stan had borrowed Bob's sextant and cast an appreciative eye toward the moon's craters through the magnified eyepiece. Rattling off names of major craters that he remembered from his astronomy class of another lifetime ago, *Worrybird* had intently listened and learned. For she wasn't much different than a two-year-old child, listening, learning, mimicking. Not only in what was said, but how it was said. By studying the tone, the inflection, the dripping of perspiration, the rhythmic relaxation and tightening of their grip, *Worrybird* knew more about how a crew member privately felt than they themselves.

Coming in low over the previously German-held El Aouina Field north of Tunis, *Worrybird* realized there was something different almost immediately, even before her wheels touched. War had visited this place. Lining the sides of the airfield, like high tide flotsam, were the remains of over two hundred military aircraft of all imaginable types and markings.[3]

"I'd recognize that beautiful lone star anywhere," she exclaimed, glimpsing a few American P-40s and P-38s amongst the detritus of war. "And that's the same red, white, blue, and yellow circle I saw painted on planes back in Tucson," as a few British RAF Spitfires and Hurricanes were observed in the carnage. "But those markings I've never seen before, and

---

3. deZeng IV, Henry L. *Luftwaffe Airfields 1935–1945. Tunisia*, 2016. https://www.ww2.dk/Airfields%20-%20Tunisia.pdf

there's absolutely nothing to like," she whispered, and shuddered as her wheels touched the pierced steel plank runway.

For the majority of the junkyard mélange possessed markings of lifeless black. Either in the form of a black cross sometimes outlined in white, or more menacingly, high up on the tail fin of most planes, what could best be described as a canted symbol of a four-legged spider. These were the undeniable cross and swastika markings of Nazi Germany's air force, the Luftwaffe. *Worrybird* had met her enemy for the first time, though from the lack of interplane radio chatter, she knew they were lifeless, without souls.

The majority of the aircraft were German Junker 52s, the infamous tri-motor transport; the Italian SM-82 transport; and a few Messerschmitt 323s, the gigantic six-engine transports capable of carrying 130 equipped men. For Germany, the El Aouina airfield had been about bringing in much needed gasoline and ammunition for Field Marshal Rommel's be-leaguered army.

But for *Worrybird* and her crew a much more intimidating aircraft stood out amongst the rest: sleek and long-nosed, with the pilot's canopy melding into the fuselage, the Messerschmitt 109 fighter. Sitting lifeless, it still exuded danger, fear, pure evil. With its nose cannon shooting 20 or 30mm exploding or incendiary shells, the agitated interphone shout of "109s, twelve o'clock high!" sent instant, sweat-chilled shivers down the spines of any Allied bomber crew. It took only three or four well-placed 30mm shells to take down a four-engine heavy bomber.

Upon opening and reading their "Secret" marked orders at the fol-lowing day's morning briefing, the men of the *Worrybird* had just one question: "What the hell is a Grottaglie?"

The slow, easterly grinding slog of the Allies across North Africa, Sicily, and eventually into the "toe and heel" of southern Italy by the fall of 1943 had secured the foothold needed to fully establish and expand the 15th Army Air Force.

While the 8th Army Air Force, based in Britain, had been relentlessly pounding northern and central Germany's industrial complexes since September of 1942, they could not reach into southern Germany or Austria. Nor, more importantly, could they reach the oil rich regions of the Balkans, specifically Rumania, which supplied Germany with 58% of its imported oil. [4] It would take the 15th Air Force, located in southern Italy, to reach these vital targets. The targeting of oil production and refining, railroad marshaling yards, and aircraft manufacturing complexes, as well as support for the scheduled August 1944 invasion of southern France were its primary goals.

They would accomplish and exceed these goals by flying out of twenty-four recently bombed and eventually captured German and Italian airfields in southern Italy. Grottaglie was one of these, located on the instep of Italy's heel, 450 miles northeast of Tunis.

Navigating a little more than an hour by dead reckoning over the agitated waters of the Mediterranean, Bob was anticipating the airfield at Farello, Sicily as a pilotage point. "Nav to pilot, Farello dead ahead, come to a heading of thirty-six degrees for Grottaglie," Bob instructed Pop.

Most of the men aboard knew of the friendly fire tragedy that had occurred during the Sicily invasion of last summer. The headlines had reluctantly hit the newsstands and eventually become public knowledge while they were in Pensacola, over eight months after the in-air tragedy. A 2,400-year-old quote by the tragedian playwright, Aeschylus, was never more appropriate: "*In war, the first casualty is truth.*" However, none realized it had occurred immediately below them and in the same exact airspace they were currently occupying. They should have just asked *Worrybird*.

---

4. Rumania is an older English derivative of Romania. It was used throughout all three diaries and in official Air Corps mission orders during the war, and will be used within this text where applicable.

"What's that? Farello?" asked a bewildered *Worrybird*. With a scrutinizing eye, it didn't take her long to discern the scattered, burned skeletons of planes in the fields and orchards surrounding the airfield. She had seen those planes before. They were American C-47 transports. And she swore she could hear, still wafting breathlessly on the air, the ghostly cry of those planes as their skin was ripped by shell. With a sudden realization, she now knew that what that tired old, unstrung C-47, otherwise known as a "Gooney Bird," had told her on the flight apron of Natal, Brazil was true.

"I tell you, *Worrybird*, our own Navy shot us down when we got over Farello, like we were flying fish in a barrel," *Gooney* stammered as she was being loaded with supplies. Natal was a staging point for C-46s, C-47s, and converted B-24s to be loaded for the long trip to India, over the Himalayas, and into China to supply its hard-pressed army. "Flying the Hump," it was called, and *Gooney* had been pressed into service after the Sicily invasion. *Worrybird* passed it off as old lady scuttlebutt. "We wouldn't shoot ourselves down. That's just crazy talk," she had scoffed.

But it hadn't been crazy. On the night of July 11, 1943, 2,304 paratroopers in 144 C-47 transports, which had taken off from Tunisia, were to reinforce a beachhead American and British troops had established two days earlier at Farello. Just before their arrival the Luftwaffe had launched a bombing raid on the naval invasion force. The onboard Navy and land-based Army anti-aircraft gunners' nerves were justifiably frayed.

Flying at only 1,000 feet, the lumbering inbound C-47s were sitting ducks. An itchy-fingered gunner did not use the established Wing, Engine, Fuselage, Tail aircraft recognition system, better known as WEFT. He indiscriminately opened fire, believing the transports to be another attack wave of the Luftwaffe. This was followed by the fire of almost every available anti-aircraft gun on land and sea. The entire harbor and shoreline became ablaze with muzzle blasts. Twenty-three planes were shot down and thirty-seven heavily damaged. There were 319 casualties.

In this case, a more appropriate definition of WEFT would have been Wrong-Every-Fucking-Time.[5]

"Just how many ways are there to die!?" *Worrybird* shouted with anguish into the mute wind as her journey's final leg continued unabated. "Mountains, power lines, crazy pilots, hail, clouds, ice, becoming lost. And now, our own side shooting us down!"

As her wheels touched the single, muddy, crushed-stone runway of the 15th Air Force's Grottaglie Airfield, *Worrybird* questioned if her nose art caricature—known for good luck—contained enough mojo to see her through what was coming next.

---

5. Conner, Joseph. "How a Friendly Fire Tragedy in Sicily Transformed Airborne Warfare." *WWII Magazine*. February 2021, vol. 35. no. 5, pp. 28–37. This most egregious of the many possible vulgar expressions will be found sparingly in the forthcoming pages when defining the many colorful, commonly used military acronyms. As well as when found in the applicable Air Corps' historical records.

PART TWO

"Through our great good fortune, in our youth our hearts were touched with fire. It was given to us to learn at the outset that life is a profound and passionate thing."

Oliver Wendell Holmes, Jr., Memorial Day, 1884

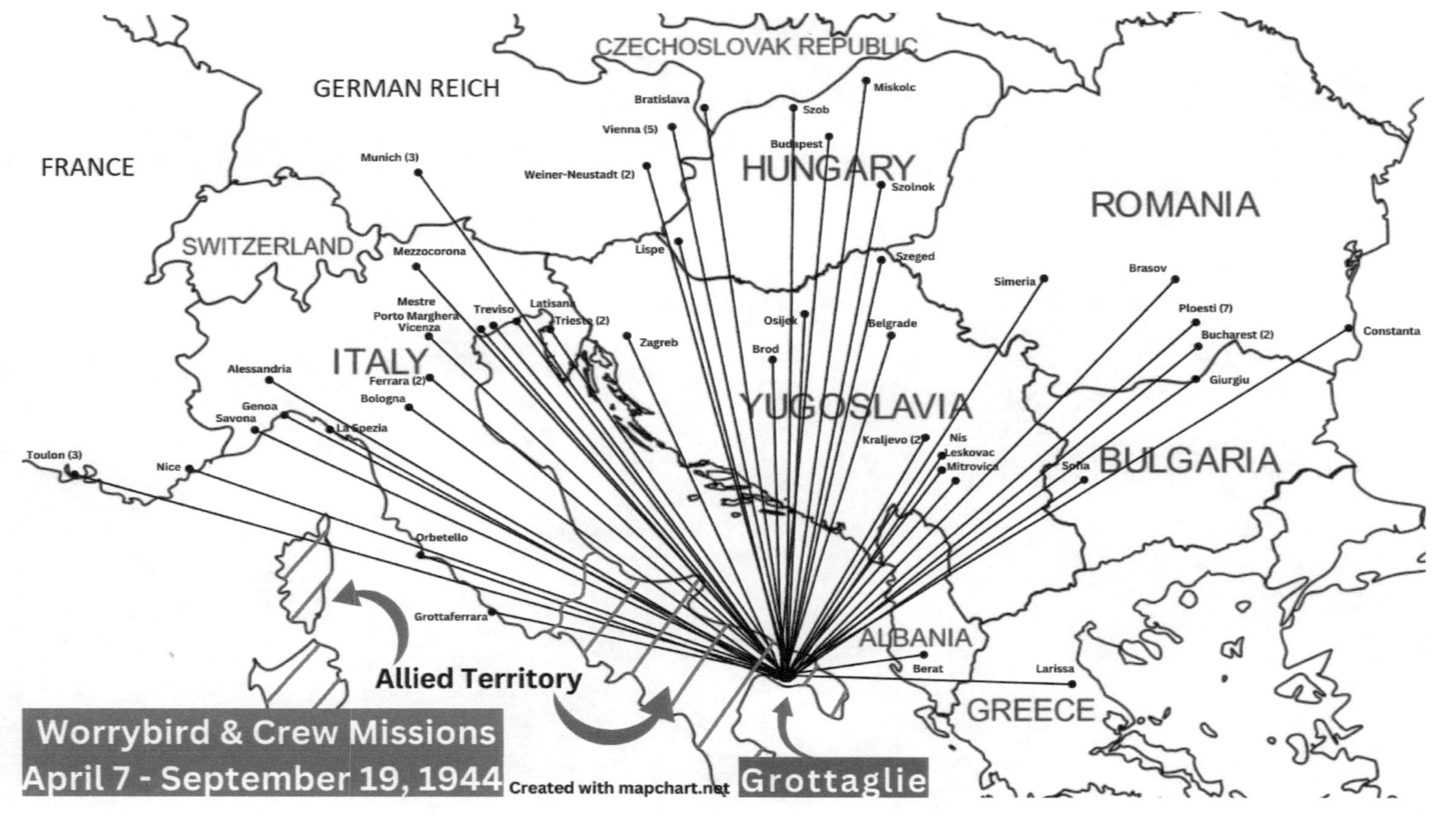

FRANCE
GERMAN REICH
CZECHOSLOVAK REPUBLIC
SWITZERLAND
HUNGARY
ROMANIA
YUGOSLAVIA
ITALY
BULGARIA
ALBANIA
GREECE
Bratislava
Miskolc
Szob
Vienna (5)
Budapest
Munich (3)
Weiner-Neustadt (2)
Szolnok
Mezzocorona
Lispe
Szeged
Simeria
Brasov
Mestre
Porto Marghera
Vicenza
Treviso
Latisana
Trieste (2)
Osijek
Belgrade
Ploesti (7)
Bucharest (2)
Constanta
Zagreb
Alessandria
Ferrara (2)
Brod
Giurgiu
Bologna
Genoa
Savona
La Spezia
Kraljevo (2)
Nis
Leskovac
Mitrovica
Sofia
Toulon (3)
Nice
Orbetello
Grottaferrara
ALBANIA
Berat
Larissa
Allied Territory
Worrybird & Crew Missions
April 7 - September 19, 1944
Created with mapchart.net
Grottaglie

9

I'M A LITTLE CONFUSED

GROTTAGLIE, ITALY, US ARMY AIR FORCE FIELD, APRIL 3, 1944, 16:00 HRS.

"I'M SURPRISED BILL didn't take a gander at my engine props. The air sure has that sweet smell of prop antifreeze wafting through it. Funny though, I don't feel the ticklish dripping down the blades," *Worrybird* pondered as she was left alone with her thoughts, parked among a few other B-24s immediately after landing on another strange airfield.

Upon landing, Pop taxied *Worrybird* over to a group of other drab-green B-24s parked on the dirt and grass on the east side of the short and potholed, north-south-oriented gravel runway. A truck had soon arrived, upon which the crew had thrown themselves and their luggage and driven off in the direction of a low, rather decrepit brick building at the other end of the field. What had really caught *Worrybird*'s eye, however, were the two, mammoth skeletal structures that dominated not only the airfield, but the entire skyline.

Grottaglie Airfield, known as Marcello Arlotta Field to its previous German and Italian occupants, had been built in 1915 to support semi-rigid airships (dirigibles) and small aircraft. The semi-rigid airship *Roma* had been housed in one of the newly constructed hangars. The pride of Italy, it was 410 feet long and 92 feet tall when built in 1921, necessitating the tremendous dimensions of the hangars. But they were now just remnants of their majestic past after the 12th US Army Air Force had paid them a visit from Tunisia during the summer of 1943.[1]

The bomb racks in the belly of a B-24 could handle many types of aerial bombs, depending on the target. For structurally substantive targets such as railroad bridges, submarine pens, or railroad marshaling yards, the tremendous concussive effect from 500- or 1,000-pound general purpose bombs would be appropriate. A wooden-structured aircraft factory's destruction would be vulnerable to 100-pound incendiary bombs.

For an airfield or airdrome, a different approach would be required if the intention was to use the airfield after capture, as was the case for Grottaglie and all the other German-held airfields in southern Italy. Why pummel an airfield with 1,000-pound bombs, leaving hundreds of fifteen-foot-deep craters that would need filling?

Enter the 20-pound fragmentation bomb. It was designed to rip through an aircraft's thin aluminum skin but do only minor damage to the runways. The June 4, 1943 bombing of Grottaglie by twenty-three B-24s would have dropped between 2,300 and 4,600 of these lethal pomegranates. By the September 8 capture of the airfield, forty-eight German and Italian aircraft had been destroyed, fifty-nine airmen killed, and the thin,

---

1. Purchased by the U.S. Army Air Service, the *Roma* crashed February 21, 1922 in Norfolk, Virginia, killing 34 airmen. Its original engines are on display at the USAF Museum in Dayton, Ohio.

corrugated steel coverings of the airship hangars blown off like wheat chaff in the wind.[2]

As *Worrybird* stared at the denuded hangars she noticed a Jeep raising dust as it drove toward her like a bat out of hell down the white caliche-covered headquarters road. As it was pulling up next to her, she could feel the vehicle's headlights giving her an uncomfortable, appraising once-over.

"Corporal, the Sergeant and I will find our own way back," said a tall, brown-haired individual, unfolding himself from the front passenger seat after it had ground to a halt beside *Worrybird*. He wore a dark leather jacket and a flight cap with one gold bar pinned to it.

"Sure thing, Lieutenant," the Jeep's driver responded, and with a quick, sloppy salute, he popped the clutch, sending a rooster tail of dust and gravel into the air as the Jeep gave *Worrybird* a final flippant, over-the-back glance.

"Sir, are you going to let him get away with that?" asked the disgusted Sergeant as he wiped dust off his leather flight jacket.

"Oh, Art, I'm too tired from yesterday's mission to get bent out of shape because some corporal wants to get back to camp. And besides, I've got tomorrow's mission to look forward to," the officer said with an ironic smirk. "Let's get this plane over to the squadron."

"Hey, it's nice to see these replacement ships. They aren't covered in aluminum patches, and the nose art is still bright and shiny," commented Art VanArkel, Second Lieutenant Charles Lynch's flight engineer. "*Worrybird*, that's a little different," Art said after noticing the nose art as they climbed into the bomb bay.

"This is Lieutenant Blomgren's plane. I graduated with him at flight school in San Angelo. Boy, that sure seems like ages ago," said Lt. Lynch

---

2. deZeng IV, Henry L. *Luftwaffe Airfields 1935–1945: Italy, Sicily and Sardinia,* 2015. https://www.ww2.dk/Airfields%20-%20Italy%20Sicily%20and%20Sardinia.pdf

as he climbed into the pilot's seat, though he usually occupied the right co-pilot's seat during missions.

"Looks like these guys are taxiing me over to that group of planes over there," said *Worrybird* as she sniffed the air. Glancing to her left she passed by hundreds, if not thousands, of gnarly trees budding out in yellowish white blossoms. "I bet you that's what I'm smelling. Huh, the trees remind me of Texas live oaks. Boy, that sure seems like ages ago," she whispered with a nostalgic tone.

"We'll put her next to my ship over there," Lt. Lynch said as he pointed to the closest of three available spots. Until five days ago that spot had been occupied by the B-24 known as *Sunshine*. She had been knocked down by Flak during the March 29 mission over the railroad marshaling yard in Bolzano. But through a bizarre navigational twist of providence, *Sunshine* would soon fly again, though with a German Luftwaffe crew.

With two engines shot out, there was no way *Sunshine* could make it back to Grottaglie. Switzerland, however, was a mere 75 miles to the west, and she had enough altitude to make it. Thirty minutes later, the virgin navigator, who was on his first mission, told the pilot, Lt. Gifford Hemphill, to land the plane at a fast-approaching airfield, thinking that they were in Switzerland. Switzerland was actually eight miles farther north. *Sunshine* instead landed in German-held northern Italy where she along with the crew were captured and held as POWs.

After repairs the Germans made use of *Sunshine* through war propaganda films, including one purporting to show the crew being "captured" in a re-creation of the unfortunate events of two weeks prior.

It's doubtful, however, if the Germans ever used that particular film as war propaganda for her citizenry. The nose gunner, Malcolm Harper, refused to stop giving the V for Victory sign made popular by British Prime Minister Winston Churchill. In take after take, this hard-nosed, utterly defiant Okie would not give the Germans the satisfaction of appearing defeated. You can take the man out of the Country, but you can't take the Country out of the man.

"Art, go ahead and get back to camp. We're on for tomorrow's mission so it'll be an early rise. I'll close things up here," Lt. Lynch instructed as he placed the mixture controls in idle cut-off and turned all the ignition switches to the off position, bringing *Worrybird*'s props to a standstill.

"Hey, thanks, Lieutenant. See you after the briefing," Art replied as he turned off the fuel valves and departed the flight deck, leaving Charles Lynch to ponder about tomorrow in a hard to come by, quiet, solitary setting.

"Well, *Bird*, welcome to the 719th Squadron of the 449th Bomb Group, better known as the 'Flying Horsemen'. Hope you don't mind me calling you *Bird*. That's what Norman, er, I mean Pop, called you," Charles softly spoke to no one in particular. Except *Worrybird* was listening intently.

"No, I don't mind," she responded. "It seems my name is always changing. At first, I was known just as a number, 42-78173. Talk about dehumanizing. Then a good friend of mine named me *Libby*, which deep down I'll always be. But then my crew decided to rename me *Worrybird*. That took some getting used to, I must admit. But if everyone wants to shorten that to *Bird*, well, that's just fine too," she said, though she knew the Lieutenant occupying the pilot's seat couldn't hear her. Then again, with the way he was talking, almost in a whisper, and his moments of silence while she answered, he sure made it seem like he did.

It was the slow, rhythmic, but tense gripping of her yoke that alerted *Bird* to the fact that this young man, who until two years ago had been cashiering in his small Idaho hometown on the Snake River, was troubled.

"*Bird*, I just can't get the sight of those three B-24s from yesterday out of my mind," Charles said. Other than his voice, the only sound heard was the slow metallic ticking of *Bird*'s cooling engines and an occasional distant aircraft's engines being warmed.

"We hit a ball bearing plant up at Steyr, Austria. They told us that one plant produced ten percent of the total German ball bearing production.

No ball bearings, no engines for their Luftwaffe. So I know it was important, like all of the missions. But Jesus," Charles rasped.

"Twenty minutes before the bomb run about seventy German aircraft jumped us. Me-109s, FW-190s, Ju-88s, you name it they flew it at us. Our P-38 escorts had left us minutes before, leaving us to fend for ourselves. Not that I blame them, they just didn't have the range to stick around for long," Charles continued, still massaging her yoke.

"The Jerries really became aggressive over the target, even through their own Flak. In one case ten came in all abreast on our six and fired rockets. You'd see flames erupt from under their wings with a long white smoke trail marking their path. Reminded me of our engine contrails at high altitude. Can't imagine what Harry, our tail gunner, thought watching those things approaching us. I think I'd be frozen in place. But you know, out of all of that, we got off lucky with just a few holes in us and our radio antenna knocked off."

With the mention of his ship losing its antenna, *Bird* self-consciously looked with her top turret to make sure hers was still there. It was.

"Somehow, even through all of the Flak concussions, rockets flying by with their contrails, Me-109s coming within 100 feet firing their cannons, and machine-gun tracers zipping at them, those damn bombardiers kept their cool and plastered the place. Remarkable," Charles said, shaking his head with admiration.

"You know, *Bird*, after dropping the load, getting off the damn bomb run and turning for home, you think that you've dodged death again. It's a euphoric feeling. It really is. But not this time," Charles whispered.

"Out of nowhere, one of those infernal rockets hit a ship in the six-plane box right in front of us. I know this is all new to you, but you'll soon be learning how to fly in a tight-packed group of five or six planes from your squadron. And when I say tight, I mean so tight that there's no way a fighter could get between us. Wing tip to wing tip," Charles continued.

With the mention of flying wing tip to wing tip, all *Bird* could think of was her memory of being knocked all over the sky in that terrifying hailstorm. "What if there had been another plane just a few feet from me," she pondered. On cue, Charles gave her the answer.

"I don't know if the pilot was killed, or if the concussion threw the plane sideways, but it hit the tail of the plane in front of it. The nose of their plane was ripped off right behind the pilots. I saw them oh so briefly still strapped in their seats. The plane in front lost its tail and then the wings just folded up and fluttered behind it. Of course, all of this debris has to go somewhere," Charles said, spasmodically gripping and releasing the yoke as if he was kneading bread.

"Grip that yoke any harder and he's going to twist it right off the column," *Bird* thought. "Wow, these memories are really disturbing him, and now they're starting to get to me," she realized, as her warming skin dripped with condensation.

"The plane behind them ran right into what was left of their ships, and its wings also buckled up and then it broke in half at the waist windows. Broke like snapping a sun-dried twig. Thirty-one men and three ships gone in less time than I just spoke about it. Funny thing, though, I can picture it like it was in a slow-motion movie being shown over and over and over. Like it was on a continuous movie reel. Hey, pass the popcorn, will ya?" Charles said, the words dripping with sarcasm as he slowly climbed out of the seat.

Unknown to Charles at the time, the final scene of the big screen drama of the ships *Peerless Clipper*, *Superstitious-Al-O-Ysius*, and *Miss Behavin*, had yet to be written. There had been a miraculous survivor from the mid-air collision.

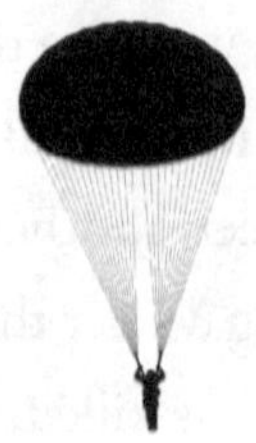

"FIGHTERS AT 11 O'CLOCK!" came in hurried and frantic, though loud and clear, through twenty-one-year-old Sergeant Mark Schneider's interphone headset. Swinging *Miss Behavin*'s ball turret to face the incoming onslaught, he suddenly found himself in a violent spin as his plane disintegrated around him at an altitude of 21,500 feet. He was totally unaware that a German rocket had found its mark, and that *Miss Behavin* had collided with *Superstitious-Al-O-Ysius*, and both of them caused the chain reaction destruction of Lt. Jacob Kury's ship, the *Peerless Clipper*. The *Peerless* had been paid for by the employees of the Peerless Woolen Mills of Chattanooga, Tennessee. All $308,471 of its cost.

Training took over, and somehow, without electrical or hydraulic power assistance, Mark was able to rotate the turret such that his one and only means of escape, the entrance/exit hatch, opened into the wildly spinning back half remains of *Miss Behavin*. Extracting himself from the turret, his search for his previously stashed parachute was futile, for it had been flung out the ripped-open fuselage as it spun at over 60 revolutions per minute. The spin induced a crushing g-force, and a lack of bottled oxygen quickly caused Mark to lose consciousness.

Three and a half hours later, Mark woke to the sensation of the bone-penetrating, arctic cold of the Austrian Alps.

Opening his eyes to crimson, crystalline sunlight, he was at an absolute loss as to his whereabouts and just what the hell had happened. Through blood-filled eyes, he finally realized he had survived, was indeed alive, and was buried in four feet of snow.

Strewn about him for 100 feet in all directions, was what once had been *Miss Behavin*, the largest piece being the mid-section tail assembly that he had previously occupied. Somehow, and to his dying days, he would ponder why he alone of the thirty-one men involved, had survived a freefall from 21,500 feet without a parachute.[3]

An Austrian ski patrol would find him and ultimately transport him to a Linz, Austria hospital where he would spend five weeks recuperating. He would spend the remainder of the war at Germany's Stalag Lufts No. 4 and No. 1, where on May 1, 1945, he would wake up with tears streaming down his face, gazing at a makeshift, hand-sewn flag, composed of 48 stars and 13 stripes on the compound's flagpole, which until the day before had flown a Nazi swastika.[4]

AFTER CLOSING THE BOMB BAY doors, Charles Lynch stood eyeing the adjacent Liberator, his ship, named *Born To Lose,* which was currently adorned with a bright green shamrock for nose art. "I wonder if that crew chief will ever get around to repainting it? I much prefer *Hoosier Honey,*" Charles stated before walking off toward the 719th's officers' tent area situated amongst the adjacent grove of fragrant, flowering olive trees.

Born To Lose had been a replacement ship flown in from the 451st Bomb Group located at Gioia, thirty miles up the Italian "boot" from Grottaglie in early February. Wanting to personalize their new ship, the crew decided to rename it *Hoosier Honey* for their pilot, twen-

---

3. Mark Schneider's complete harrowing story can be found in the 42-52086 MACR, pages 1-16. MACR stands for Missing Air Crew Reports. These reports provide detailed witnessed testimony to the loss of U.S. aircraft and their crews. The complete MACR records can be found at https://www.fold3.com/ This is a subscription service.

4. https://www.nationalww2museum.org/liberation-stalag-luft

ty-one-year-old 1st Lt. John McCormick, who was from the city of Gary, Indiana. The war had found him sweating in front of the blast furnaces of U.S. Steel on the shores of Lake Michigan.

"Hey there, *Bird*, did Lt. Lynch fill you in on things goin' on around here?" was suddenly heard over the high-frequency band of *Bird's* radio, interrupting the contemplation of what she had just learned.

"Whoa, who goes there?" *Bird* exclaimed with surprise.

"Right next to ya, starboard side. Call me *Hoosier*, though I'm from Dee-troit," replied the adjacent Liberator, which had its plexiglass covered in canvas, all in the ubiquitous olive green.

"Got'cha," replied *Bird*, looking through her top turret. "I'm from Texas," she added, with only a slight touch of humility. "I heard the Lieutenant talking about your name change. What's with the drapes?"

"Drapes, yeah, right," *Hoosier* scornfully chortled. "The ground crews cover our windows 'cause on a sunny day it gets as hot as a steel blast furnace in here," he said, repeating something he had heard Lt. McCormick mutter.

"Were you eavesdropping on us a while ago? 'Cause I think those were Lt. Lynch's private affairs, and he didn't want to share them with nobody," said *Bird* defensively.

"No, couldn't help it. He must have left the power to the radio on if I heard him talking. Don't worry, though, it's nothing I didn't already know, 'cause remember, I was there too," replied *Hoosier*, just as defensively and with a touch of indignation.

With sudden realization, *Bird* knew she had been a real ass. Of course *Hoosier* knew about Charles' demons; he had to have them too after witnessing that calamity. "Sorry 'bout that *Hoosier*. I wasn't thinking, and my mouth got away from me. I can't afford to not make friends here. I think I'm going to be needing them," *Bird* said sheepishly.

"Oh, that's alright, *Bird*. You're new, fresh fish and all. And, hey, look, you're learning already 'cause you're right about making friends down here. It's the only way we have a chance to survive this. Make good, tight friends on the ground and make it tighter up there when we're flying 'in the box' that Lt. Lynch described to you."

"That's something I don't understand, *Hoosier*. Both you and Lt. Lynch say that we have to fly almost wingtip to wingtip in this box, but isn't that what caused those three Libs to crash into one another?" asked a confused *Bird* as she peered down her starboard wing and tried to imagine another ship between herself and *Hoosier*. The thought caused a welling surge of nausea deep in her bomb bay, just like the feeling immediately after hitting a thermal.

"Well, in this case you're right again," *Hoosier* acknowledged. "But that's the only way we can keep those Germans out of us. Plus, each of our gunners can help the other gunners on the planes next to you, something they call saturated field of fire. No one in their right mind would want to get in between two planes with twenty of those Brownings chattering away. Those German flyers are good, and they aren't crazy."

"Of course, nothing is for certain, that's for sure. Sometimes no matter how tight we fly, well, let me just say a few of us don't come back. Sixty-two of us left the States in December bound for Grottaglie to make up the 449th. There's only thirty-two of them left. Half of them gone just like that. Good thing replacements like you are coming in to take their place," *Hoosier* said matter-of-factly.

"*Hoosier*, this is all moving too fast for me. All that I have to do and learn, and for what? Just to be shot down or knocked out of the sky to become a burning heap of aluminum on the ground?" asked *Bird* with alarm in her voice. The nightmarish memory of the burned, skeletal Liberator remains she'd seen in Tucson was still fresh in her mind. She wished she was anywhere but here. Tunis, Dakar, Pensacola, San Francisco, Tucson, or Dallas with *Texican*. "Oh, *Texican*, I sure could use you next to me right now," she whispered, recalling in contrast a pleasant, comforting memory.

"Listen kid, you'll learn pretty quick that you don't do this for yourself. It's all about going up there day after day to protect the plane that's next to you, in front of you, above you, and below you. They're more than your friends. They're your family too. You're going up there and getting so close to them that you'll be sucking in most of their engine exhaust. And when the bombardier takes over your flight controls on the bomb run, you're not going to flinch so much as an inch, no matter how much the Flak is trying to push you around. You are going to learn how to maintain a flat, level, constant flight for ten, fifteen, twenty minutes, knowing you're on a collision course with a storm front of angry, broiling black Flak clouds that are staring you in the face."

"And you're doing it for those ten men aboard you. By now I suppose you consider them part of your family, just like we are going to be," *Hoosier* said, pointing to the rest of the planes in the squadron around them.

"And you do it 'cause you're pissed off. Lt. Lynch told you what he saw, not what he heard, like what I heard. Not only did I watch in horror as those planes were ripped apart, but I had to listen to them. Listen as they cried out," *Hoosier* exclaimed.

"And you know what the strangest thing is? They didn't cry out in pain. No. They cried out that they were sorry they caused each other's demise. Can you imagine that? They were sorry," he said with wonderment. "*Miss Behavin* crying out to *Superstitious* she was sorry to have torn off her tail. *Superstitious* screaming as *Miss Behavin's* nose was ripped off. And both of them screaming to *Peerless Clipper* to get the hell out of the way even as they were disintegrating before their very own eyes," *Hoosier* continued, as engine oil began dripping from his engine cowlings.

"To top it all off, I had to listen to the cries and pleadings of the poor souls who had crewed those planes. And I'm not just talking about when they collided, but when they were flailing in the air as they fell with no chutes. Or their chutes were on fire. Or as they rode their airplane remnant down, trapped by centrifugal force in what would certainly be their aerial coffin." *Hoosier* spat.

"No!"

"Aaaaah!"

"Mother!"

"Get out!"

"Lucy, Antonia!"

"Mom!"

"...Love you...!"

"Ed, dive!"

"Tom, your chute!"

"John, what the hell!"

"My God, Jacob, pull up!"

"Jesus!"

"God!"

"A lot of God was screamed, their voices feathering upon the slip-stream as they fell away," *Hoosier* finished in a murmur, repeating something he had heard after he landed and his crew knelt beside him with their heads bowed. The only sounds heard for long afterwards was the muffled roar of distant full-throttle takeoffs.

"Oh, *Hoosier*," *Bird* stammered softly. "What can I possibly say?"

After a moment to ponder the question, *Hoosier* replied, "Not much, *Bird*. But I've often wondered, whose name would be my last if I was spiraling down, out of control? Something to think about."

In the ensuing moment of silence, *Bird* reflected on just that. But she didn't have to think long, nor hard as to the answer. For there really was only one for whom she cared enough about, such that it would be the last name on her mind as she fell to earth: *Texican*.

"But, hey, let me introduce you to the other guys," *Hoosier* quickly blurted to change topics, scattering *Bird*'s gloomy thoughts like confetti in the wind.

"Port side of you is lucky #13, *Dixie Belle*. She's also from Dee-troit."

"Let's see, in front of you is #16, *Consolidated Mess*. He came into the 719th same day as I did."

"Whoa, wait a minute," *Bird* exclaimed, catching up to *Hoosier*'s rapid-firing litany. "Was it named that to make fun of Consolidated Aircraft? You know, the ones that created us! Or maybe make fun of us Liberators?" she exclaimed, as her voice rose in pitch and volume.

"Calm down there. Boy, all of you from Texas are quick to jump, let me tell you," said *Hoosier*. "And no, it was already named that when we got him, and from what I hear, it's somehow making fun of the mess hall food the previous crew had to eat. Now, can I continue?"

The *Bird* thought it best just not to say anything.

"Off your tail is #8, *Paper Doll*. She's one of the few Dee-troit originals that came over here in December."

"Say, *Hoosier*, all of these planes have numbers painted on their rudders. Will I be getting one?" *Bird* asked, feeling a little left out.

"Sure will," replied *Hoosier*. "Everyone gets one. They call that your combat number. I'm the second #11."

"What do you mean the second?" *Bird* questioned uneasily.

"The first #11 was *Battlin Betty Ann*. She never made it here. From what I heard, the poor girl iced up over those Atlas Mountains on the way over and went down. When a replacement comes in, it takes up the lost plane's number," *Hoosier* stated as if it were a natural, everyday occurrence.

"So, what lost ship number will I be getting?" *Bird* asked morosely.

"Well, let me think here for a sec." Pondering the 719th's recent losses, *Hoosier* finally deduced what indeed would be *Bird*'s combat number. "Probably #3. Yeah, we've been waiting since early February to replace the last #3. That was *Los Lobos*."

"I'm afraid to ask, but what happened to him?" *Bird* asked reluctantly.

"Oh, I remember that day for sure 'cause that's the day I arrived," *Hoosier* recalled. "We were coming in over the field for our landing when I saw a crumpled Liberator leaning against the earthen drainage dike at the beginning of the runway. Some introduction to Grottaglie, huh? It was *Los Lobos*."

"Apparently the pilot, Lt. Zimmerman, had gotten him airborne for that day's mission when *Los Lobos* came back and made a downwind landing. I certainly wouldn't want to try a downwind landing, no siree.

And here they were attempting that with full tanks and a full bomb load!" *Hoosier* exclaimed incredulously. "Not sure what Zimmerman was thinking."

"You know, in my short time being in the air, I've already come to realize there're more ways to meet one's end than being a target of Germany. I've seen it and have survived some of those very possibilities," *Bird* pointed out.

"No doubt you have, but let me continue the intros," *Hoosier* continued after the interruption, unimpressed. "So next to *Consolidated Mess* is #6, *Sky Bandit*, from Tulsa. He got here a few days before me, just like #4 over yonder, *Buzzer*. He's from San Diego."

"I can only see the tail fins of the rest of the squadron," *Hoosier* said as he looked in all directions from his numerous turrets. "Let me think now, there's *Sweet Mother, Patches, Lonesome, Our Baby, Dragon Lady,* and of course *Two Ton Tessie.* You can't miss her with that nose art," *Hoosier* finished.

"Well, all I can say is I'm glad to meet y'all, and I hope I live up to those that have come and gone before me," *Bird* stated solemnly. "So do I fill out the rest of the squadron?"

"No, not completely. We're still missing a new #2, 5, and 9 to bring us up to our full strength of sixteen. It's been a tough winter for the 449th. The other three squadrons are in about the same shape as we are, just waiting for those replacements. Like you," *Hoosier* said with a mischievous, knowing grin. For he knew what was in store for the virgin newcomer.

Bird took a deep breath and tried to collect her rambling thoughts. Throughout her two-month young, fleeting, chaotic life, she had slowly pieced together her purpose for being. But those inescapable, inevitable deeds had always been sometime, somewhere in the distant future. That future was here. Now. The sudden comprehension caused her to start sweating, and a surge of anxiety coursed through her like she had just been hooked up to a portable power supply. One thing she knew for certain, however, was that she was more than a little confused, and everything seemed to be moving too fast.

719th Squadron parking area. Photo possibly taken February 9, 1944. Four replacements during the first week of February had brought the muster up to 15, as visible in the 719th's parking area. Los Lobos was lost February 10th. Crushed stone hardstands and taxiways in white. Crew tents off to right of photo. Some of the olive orchards at top. Runway and 718th Squadron parking area to left of photo. All planes at this time were olive drab. Our Baby, The Buzzer, Paper Doll, Guardian Angel, Lonesome, and Patches identified. [Courtesy 449th Bomb Group Association Collection]

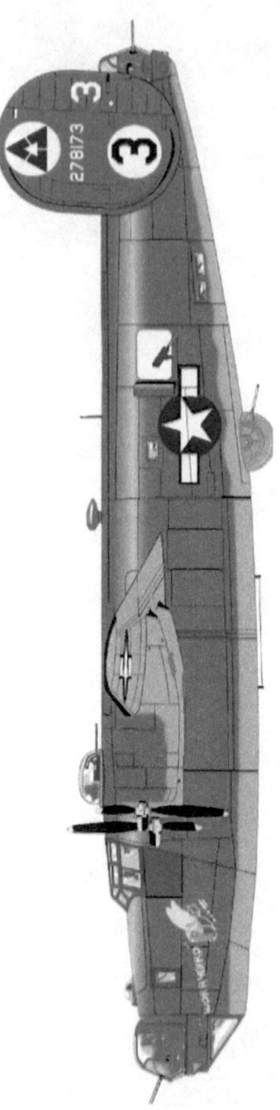

Worrybird's paint scheme in April of 1944. The dark blue triangle in the white circle denotes the 47th Wing of the 15th Air Force. The large three in the white circle denotes the 449th Bomb Group. The small number three on the rudder is Worrybird's personal combat number. The first digit of the serial number was omitted in the tail number. Olive-drab fuselage with light grey underneath fuselage, bottom of wings, and the engine cowlings.
[Image courtesy of Jason Stanley]

10

Roughing It

719th Squadron Officers Tent Area, April 3, 1944 19:00 hrs.

"Boy, these olive trees are fragrant," Harry said, sniffing the air as he jumped down from the back of an Army truck along with Pop, Stan, and Bob in the waning evening twilight.

Their surroundings could have been described as almost surreal. Neat, olive-green, pyramidal canvas tents intermixed in the middle of a flowering orchard. Indeed, the entire countryside was ablaze with blooming olive trees. But in the midst of this horticultural masterpiece, the carved-out blight of war had imprinted its ugly scar, known as Grottaglie USAAF Airfield.

At the moment, Stan's olfactory senses were barely registering, for he was consternated due to what he had learned shortly after landing. "I just can't believe there's a good chance we'll lose *Bird*," he mumbled as he slid his footlocker out of the truck and unceremoniously dumped it on the ground.

"Now, we don't know that for sure. Colonel Gent seemed like a pretty good egg for a commanding officer," Pop replied, trying to assuage not only Stan's concerns but his own. "I told him in no uncertain terms that we were willing to fight for her. As a matter of fact, I think he was taken slightly aback by my passion for keeping her. But then again, he's a flyer first, commander second, and I think he gets it about being attached to one's plane. Or at least I sure hope so."

While not completely mollified, Stan appreciated Pop's efforts and nodded as he dragged his footlocker toward the third Army tent down the row which the PFC truck driver said belonged to Lieutenants Lahr and Zimmerman, Stan's and Bob's temporary destination for the evening. Pop and Harry would be bunking tonight in the adjacent tent belonging to a Lieutenant Schurman.

Upon entering Zimmerman and Lahr's tent, it was obvious that the best way to describe the interior was "makeshift cozy." Four wooden, obviously handmade, bunks were in each corner along with the appropriate occupant's footlocker. Covering the walls were uniforms and accoutrements hung on various improvised hooks. A somewhat rickety looking wooden table with matching chairs was covered with writing materials and books.

But what really caught Stan's mechanically inclined eye was the object that was currently emitting an incredible number of BTUs sitting square in the middle of the rough-sawn, wood-plank flooring.

"Sheldon Zimmerman," said the tall, lanky, twenty-two-year-old 2nd Lieutenant as he gave Stan and Bob a firm handshake. "And the lazy one lying on the bunk is Paul Lahr," he continued with a catching, mischievous grin. With that, a young man of average height with blond hair and blue eyes rolled out of his bunk.

"I only put up with him since he is, after all, our plane's pilot," Paul said, also with a smirking grin, glancing at Sheldon. "But then again, I'm in the right seat making sure he doesn't make any stupid mistakes. Welcome to the 719th guys," as he in turn gave Bob and Stan a firm handshake.

"Bill Stanley, bombardier, though the crew calls me Stan, and this here is our navigator, Bob Simmons." I'm going to like these two, Stan thought as he pointed to the object in front of them. "Care to explain what that is?" he asked.

"You like our stove?" Paul replied. "You'll learn soon enough that you have to have some ingenuity, at least mediocre mechanical skills, and most important of all, good scrounging skills to be comfortable around here. I was a carpenter before joining up so I built most of what you see with what limited supplies I could find."

"Most of the wood you see, including the floor, came from German bomb crates. The metal parts of the chairs came from our bomb fin cages. And believe it or not, some guy's tents have cement tile floors taken from the dirigible hangars. Not all the damage you see done to those hangars was from our bombs. American ingenuity at its best. But I have to give Sheldon here full credit for the stove," Paul said, pointing toward his crewmate.[1]

"I can't take all the credit, it was kinda a group survival effort. It was absolutely freezing here last December, and we had to come up with something quick before we all froze to death," Sheldon explained.

"So for a fuel tank we used the anti-icer fluid tanks they were ripping out of the planes. They had quickly learned that those things burn when hit. For the stove itself, we used a five-gallon oil can with some .50-cal ammo box inserts. Those German and Italian plane carcasses had plenty of copper pipe and petcock valves, and ta-da, heat!" Sheldon said proudly.

"So, I'm afraid to ask what you use for fuel. Engine oil?" Bob reluctantly asked.

"Heavens, no. It thickens up like molasses. We use nothing but the best U.S. refined 100 octane aviation gas. But don't worry, only two tents have

---

1. Currier, Donald. *50 Mission Crush*, pp. 53–58. New York, NY: Pocket Books, 1993.

burned down. So far," said Sheldon, pausing for effect and again with the mischievous grin.

"'Fraid you're going to have to sleep on the floor tonight. We'll scrounge up a few G.I. blankets for ya," Paul interjected with the bad news. "That'll soften that wood floor right up. Ha!"

"What about the two here?" Stan asked as he pointed to the two empty adjacent bunks while scowling as he looked at the uninviting floor.

"Oh, those belong to McDonald and Murray. Those lucky dogs are on R&R till tomorrow morning, so they aren't scheduled for tomorrow's mission like we are, though Paul and I will be split between two planes," replied Sheldon as he searched for a couple of blankets.

"Is it a common practice to split the crews like that?" a now confused and concerned Stan asked with a furrowed brow.

"Common? Well, someone is always moving between planes. You know, somebody is always sick, injured, on R&R, special duty, something like that, who needs to be replaced. The Group usually puts up seven or eight planes from each squadron, so the other half, men and planes alike, have some down time. That also gives HQ a pool of replacement men for the day's mission," Sheldon explained.[2]

"Must say I don't like the sound of that. We've come together as a pretty tight-knit crew and have already been through things just getting here that made us even closer. On top of that, we were told we'll probably lose our plane," Bob said pensively.

"Well, I wouldn't worry 'bout it too much. You'll stay together as a crew for most of the missions," Paul said, trying to alleviate some of the newcomers' understandable apprehensions. "Losing your plane though, now that's a real possibility." After a moment's hesitation, and with a grin,

---

2. 449th Bomb Group Association. *Book III: Grottaglie And Home,* p.118. 1989.

Paul glanced at Sheldon and said, "Hopefully it won't be as dramatic as us losing our plane right off. Isn't that right?"

Rolling his eyes, Sheldon said, "You had to bring that up, huh?"

"Do tell, sounds like there's a story there," Bob said as he and Stan took a load off and sat down on their foot lockers.

Sheldon realized there was no getting out of this one, and besides, he thought it could be a valuable learning opportunity for the virgin navigator.

"I suppose after leaving Morrison Field your first stop was Borinquen Airfield in Puerto Rico?" asked Sheldon, and with an affirming nod from Bob continued with the story.

"Well, we had beautiful weather after leaving Florida, but as we approached the island it became more and more overcast. McDonald, my navigator, did the best he could noting pilotage points when he could see them," Sheldon said, as Bob nodded his head with navigational understanding.

"Of course, when we get to what we think is over the airfield, we couldn't raise the tower." With a serious look on his face and pointing at both Bob and Stan, Sheldon continued, "And that's when you learn that when something goes wrong, it's usually the first in a series of things compounding the last. And that's when it snowballs into something you can't control, and things go to hell in a handbasket real quick."

"So, we circle a few times, and knowing our fuel is getting low, I took advantage of a break in the clouds that suddenly appeared and headed on down to see where we were."

"But, instead of Borinquen or Isabela appearing in front of us, it was a damn mountain full of trees, and its peak was above us. I pulled that yoke into my lap and Paul pushed the throttles to their stops."

"Of course, we were too low so we took out a good harvest of trees and we bounced off that mountaintop like we were on a pogo stick bringing us back above the clouds."

Bob and Stan turned to look at each other with mouths agog but remained silent.

"After regaining our composure, but not having time to clean our pants, we took stock of the situation and realized we were in deep shit, to put it mildly. Our number three engine cowling was smashed and full of tree branches, and it started to overheat, so I feathered it. Then the other engines soon started overheating with their cowl flaps full of debris."

"I was about to put it up for a vote if the crew wanted me to gain some altitude for us to jump, or try again, when the clouds miraculously broke, and McDonald gave me a bearing for the airfield where I was able to land."

"Good thing Murray wasn't in his bombardier compartment 'cause he wouldn't have survived. We lost our bomb bay doors, the fuselage was full of tree branches, and the front edges of the wings were ripped off. Don't know how that plane still flew," Sheldon said, shaking his head.

"So that's how we lost our plane, *Hassen the Assassin*," Sheldon finished as he wiped his sweaty palms on his pants.

The reflective silence was broken by Pop and Harry coming into the tent, and after brief introductions they just stood in place with big grins on their faces.

"Well, don't just stand there looking like a pair of Cheshire cats; you know something, so spill it," Stan demanded.

"I just talked to our squadron commander, Captain Swan, and he said we're keeping *Bird*," announced Pop, keeping the grin on his face.

After group congratulations, Bob told Pop that Sheldon had been giving him some navigational pointers from his short but consequential flying experience.

"Do you have any piloting advice that they didn't teach us in flight school?" Pop asked earnestly as he and Harry grabbed a seat on the two rickety, unoccupied chairs.

Sheldon stood for a moment contemplating if he should bare his soul to these four complete strangers about an incident in which he himself still wasn't sure he had done the right thing. "But, then again, if this green pilot learned something that might save him and his crew on some future mission, what's a bit of embarrassment now?" he concluded to himself.

Nodding his head, Sheldon began. "Been almost a month now. Not sure why, but we were to fly Lieutenant Polink's ship, number three, *Los Lobos* that day in the second wave, loaded with frag bombs. Mission was up to Genzano to bomb German troop concentrations," he said with a hint of pity in his voice.

It was one thing to obliterate infrastructure such as marshaling yards, bridges, refineries and such, but it was a whole different matter to be dropping frags to rip apart a mass of humanity, or "soft targets," even if it was the enemy. Of course, people were killed when bombs were dropped on "hard targets" too, but somehow it was just different, collateral, which made it in some way easier to justify to oneself.

Looking directly at Pop, he continued, "When your plane is completely loaded with fuel, bombs, ammo, and men, all 65,000 pounds, it will take every horse those engines have and every bit of headwind to get you airborne. The most dangerous point of your entire flight is not over the target, it's in those few moments when you're trying to gain airspeed and your flaps are still down. There's absolutely no room for error," he declared, pausing for effect.

"Well, we hadn't even gained enough airspeed to pull in the flaps or raise our landing gear when *Los Lobos* decided he didn't need the number three engine. It just quit, dead, with no warning. Never seen anything like it," Sheldon said shaking his head.

"So here we were with an airspeed barely above fully laden takeoff speed, losing what little altitude we had, no hydraulics because of course it had to be the number three engine, and not knowing if we'll lose another one," Sheldon stated.

Staring hard into Pop's eyes, Sheldon abruptly blurted, "You now have about ten seconds to decide. Quick! What are you going to do?"

Taken aback by the sudden question thrown at him, Pop hesitated before attempting to answer.

"Too late! You just killed yourself and the nine men that put their lives into your hands," Sheldon spat with emotion.

A sudden, uneasy quietness engulfed the tent like a smothering, wet blanket that no one was able or willing to shrug off.

Slowly, Sheldon realized he had been a little hard on Norman, though it wasn't as hard as he'd been on himself for the last three weeks. "Oh, Norman, sorry about that. That was unfair on my part."

"Sheldon, there's no need to apologize," Pop said, attempting to soothe the palpable uneasiness. "That's a tough spot to be in. But to answer your question, I suppose depending on altitude and terrain, I'd attempt a go-around landing."

Breathing an audible sigh of relief that the atmosphere had tempered, Sheldon continued his tutoring. "Right you are, but first things first. You're right about determining if the terrain would allow an emergency landing, which in this case it didn't. So, almost simultaneously, Paul has to contact the tower to declare an emergency and to clear the field of planes taking off. Fortunately, I knew we were among the last to take off from the group.

"Second, you have to get the right waist gunner, who's also the assistant engineer, to turn on the emergency hydraulic pump. We're going to need more flaps and, of course, brakes.

"And most importantly, but unfortunately the most difficult to learn, is determining if your combined airspeed and decreasing altitude will allow you a complete come around. There's no chart or quick slide rule computation that will give you the answer. You have to quickly judge for yourself and trust your gut, 'cause it's nothing I or anyone else can teach you," Sheldon said in a serious but soft tone.

"In my case, in those few seconds, my decision was we didn't have what it would take to come completely around," Sheldon said, now looking into Paul's eyes, who nodded, as if giving him confirmation.

Pop slowly realized what he had meant by that remark, and with a tilt to his head, he asked, somewhat in disbelief, "So, are you telling me you came straight on in. A downwind landing?"

"Yes, I am. With a full load, including two hundred frag bombs in the belly to boot." Sheldon let that sit for a bit to let the implications sink in. "But the airstrip was clear, Pellegrino had gotten our hydraulics back, and I am absolutely certain that there was no way we could have circled around."

"So we came in hot and heavy, with a ten knot tailwind and hit that runway hard. Thought that nose wheel was going to come up through the floor. I can see my flight instructor now just shaking his head and cussing me out," Sheldon said with a surprising grin. He had never before smiled when recalling the incident over and over in his mind.

"We ate up those 3,500 feet of runway real fast, let me tell you. Paul and I had those tires just a smokin' as we hit the earthen dike after there was nothing left of the runway. Crushed the front turret and bombardier station all to hell as we went up the dike face. Stopped us, though. Real quick. But a few of the frag bombs kept goin'. Broke out of the bomb racks and slammed against the bomb bay bulkhead. Sure am glad I had the gunners in the tail of the plane to help keep the nose up. Obviously, the bombs didn't go off," Sheldon added.

"Jesus H. Christ," was murmured by someone.

"Well, though I'm Jewish, I do get the sentiment. You know," Sheldon said as he pulled two olive green blankets out of the wooden bomb crate closet, "I often wonder just how many lives this cat has," as he gave the G.I. blankets to Stan and Bob in a not-so-subtle hint that they all were going to hit the sack. There was another mission in tomorrow's quickly approaching early morning hours.

[449th Bomb Group Association Collection]

MANY, IF NOT ALL, AIRCREW pondered the eternal, unanswerable question of their own mortality as Sheldon Zimmerman had—as too, would the newly arrived crew of the *Worrybird*.

So too had 1st Lieutenant Jacob Kury, piloting the doomed ship *Peerless Clipper*. Ever since his arrival at Grottaglie the previous December, lady luck had been at his right side. She first made her presence known on January 30, when the 449th's commanding officer, Colonel Darr Alkire, told him that he was going to personally fly Jacob's plane, the *Lurchin Urchin,* and that no pleading would change his mind. He wouldn't even allow him to fly as co-pilot. The *Urchin* was one of two planes to be shot down the next day by Flak over Aviano, Italy. Colonel Alkire, along with six others would spend the rest of the war as POWs. Three would not.

This included tail gunner Sergeant Tony Lopez, whose parachute prematurely opened within the confines of the diving, crippled plane. He resisted any assistance in freeing himself, telling the others to jump and save themselves. Tony rode the plane down, frantically trying to pull free his entangled chute, until it crashed into a northern Italy mountainside, along with 2nd Lieutenant James Galliher, who was trapped in the damaged front gun turret, and Sergeant Samuel Scott, who was shot trying to escape after parachuting to the ground.

But Tony's story doesn't or shouldn't end there. Tony had been born in Mexico, an immigrant, along with the rest of his family living in Silvis, Illinois. Not only did Tony lie about his age in order to enlist, at seventeen, he lied about his true identity in order to defy his parents' enlistment objections. He had been born Antonio Pompa. Why does someone like Antonio enlist and ultimately die to defend a country that had so marginalized him?[3]

Lady luck had likewise been on Jacob Kury's left side one month later during a March 2nd mission over Anzio, Italy. Immediately after dropping over 130 fragmentation bombs on massing German troops, who were preparing for a vast counteroffensive on the stalled Allied forces trapped on the beachhead, Jacob's replacement plane, *Urchin Lurchin #2,* was hit by intense, accurate Flak.

The first shell took off the end of the right wing and disabled the number four engine. Almost simultaneously, the devastating effects of another shell, actually exploding within the open bomb bay, rocked the crew. Fragments ripped open the overhead fuselage fuel tanks, filling the bomb bay and flight deck with a *"fog of choking gas and fumes."* Miraculously, it was not ignited. Finally, with the severing of aileron and rudder control cables, Jacob gave the bailout order.[4]

Eight crewmen, including Jacob Kury, would safely land within Allied lines and return to Grottaglie. Two, unfortunately, landed behind the German lines, would be captured, and spend the rest of the war as POWs.

Upon his return to base, Jacob was greeted by cheers and slaps on the back. To complete the day, he learned that he had become a father. His wife Lucy had given birth to their first child, Antonia. Jacob was flying high that day, though that evening he commented that *"he had used up a lot of his luck on that mission."* In actuality, he had used it all up.[5]

---

3. http://migration.lib.uiowa.edu/exhibits/show/war/hero-street-u-s-a-

4. *Lebanon Daily News.* March 3, 1944, pp. 1, 11.

5. 449th Bomb Group Association. *Book III: Grottaglie And Home.* 1989, p. 61.

One month to the day later, on April 2nd, Jacob was piloting the *Peerless Clipper*, which disintegrated upon impacting with the remains of *Superstitious-Al-O-Ysius* and *Miss Behavin*. Luck is a lousy battle plan. Eventually, luck always runs out.

11

SOPHISTICATED LADY AND THE HEAVENLY BODY

GROTTAGLIE, ITALY, US ARMY AIR FORCE FIELD, APRIL 4, 1944, 02:00 HRS.

"BOY, YOU GUYS SURE don't give a girl a chance to catch a little shuteye, do you?" *Bird* commented to no one in particular, amid a cacophony of pandemonium emanating from idling trucks, Jeeps, coughing B-24 engines, and the constant yelling, swearing, and jeers from groundcrews and ordnance men.

Then she noticed some men grappling with five-foot-long, torpedo-shaped objects under *Hoosier*'s open bomb bay doors. Except for three thin, yellow bands circling them, they were painted the ubiquitous olive drab. "Hey *Hoosier*, are you awake?"

"Are you serious, *Bird*? Like I could sleep through this," replied an astonished *Hoosier*, marveling at the newcomer's naivete. "Though I must say, before those ordnance guys rudely woke me, I was having the strangest dream. John was flying me to his Gary, Indiana, U.S Steel plant. Dolph

Ornstein, the bombardier, was flying us on a bomb run over the smoke-stacks that were needle thin at best, at least as seen from a few thousand feet. And get this: he was ordered to drop those bombs right down the stacks. Like that was possible. Of course he kept missing, so he'd tell John to take us back around again and again for other pointless tries. So he's blowing the hell out of the plant and some were dropping into Lake Michigan, exploding into giant two-thousand-foot-tall geysers that were soaking me. I kept yelling at Dolph to stop it, but of course he wasn't listening to me, as usual. Fortunately, I woke up to this clatter," *Hoosier* sighed, indicating the commotion around them.

"You know, thinking about it, Hitler sure didn't do anybody named Adolph any favors. Dolph's real name is Adolph. Could you imagine the ribbing he'd get if he went by that? And him being Jewish too. He mentioned that his parents were Slovakian Jewish immigrants. I wonder if he knows if he bombed his parents' hometown when he bombed Slova-kia?" *Hoosier* mused. "And then there's the dream. I've always wondered if any of my crew have dreams? For their own sake, I sure hope not," he added, remembering how sometimes he'd wake up from a disturbing aerial nightmare with his aluminum skin dripping with condensation and his airframe shaking as if all six of his gunners were simultaneously firing their Brownings.

"Odd, I haven't had any of the dreams that you talk about. I just sleep the night through, unless some groundcrew is poking and prodding me for an early morning flight," *Bird* mentioned.

"Don't worry, they'll come. Though I surely hope they pass you by," *Hoosier* lamented sincerely.

"So, getting back to the whole reason I was wondering if you were awake, I wanted to ask what are those things they're loading into you? Are they the bombs I've been hearing all about? You know, what my nose art is riding?" asked *Bird* as she watched another of the objects being attached to a steel cable which soon disappeared as it was winched into the fathoms of *Hoosier*'s open bomb bay.

"That they are. These are 500-pounders, and it looks like this is the last one being loaded, which will make ten. We could hold more, but we wouldn't have as much combat range. So given that, I'd say we aren't headed to northern Italy. Germany, France, Austria, or Hungary would be my guess," *Hoosier* said as he observed a fuel truck pull up to him.

Bird too noticed the truck arrive between them, mostly blocking her view of *Hoosier*. "Say, it looks like most of the squadron is being loaded for today's mission," she commented after looking around from her unimpeded views.

"It does, doesn't it?" *Hoosier* replied as he too paid attention to the commotion engulfing almost the entire 719th parking area. "Let's see, *Consolidated Mess, Lonesome, Dixie Bell, Dragon Lady,* and *Paper Doll* are being tended to one way or another. I can't see beyond you, *Bird*. Can you read the nose art of the ships with armorers or groundcrews about them?"

"Let's see," *Bird* responded as she glanced out her top and tail turrets. "There's number six, which... I can barely make out its nose art," she said, squinting down her Browning barrels. "*Sky Bandit*! Yeah, that's it," she exclaimed proudly. "Uh, *Sweet Mother* and, oh boy, take a look at that nose art. It's *Two Ton Tessie*. So, with you included, that makes nine of the twelve available."

"Thirteen. There's thirteen available. You forgot yourself there, *Bird*," *Hoosier* said with a knowing grin.

"Me! Available?" she cried out. "I don't think so, bud."

Hoosier had to laugh to himself at *Bird*'s response. Of course she wasn't ready. That was all too obvious. She'd need a few days to get acclimated, fitted out, and basically get her act together. That would be the easy part. It's her crew that would need more time and training. Training to forget everything they'd already learned. What did they call it? School. That's it. It'd take one to two weeks of practice missions with veteran flyers, guys who have been in the middle of it. Those who know that close formation flying is the only answer to survival. That will go against everything the pilots learned in school. But this is the real world. Not some textbook or classroom lecture. Books can't kill. *Hoosier* wasn't laughing now.

"Don't scorch your piston skirts there, *Bird*. You don't have to worry for a few weeks, 'cause we've got you covered until you're ready. You just listen to us and trust the pilots," *Hoosier* calmly reasoned.

"It's probably a little early yet for *Toledo*'s scuttlebutt to get through the ranks, so we might as well sit back and let the groundcrews fawn all over us."

"Who or what is a *Toledo*? And what's with the scuttlebutt?" *Bird* questioned as she watched the fuel crew finish topping *Hoosier*'s tanks and move over to *Consolidated Mess*.

"Oh, you haven't met that bumptious, bombastic, know-it-all on four wheels yet?" *Hoosier* said with a hint of a snicker. "He's a headquarters Jeep who thinks he's the Grottaglie manifestation of 'Wild Bill' Donovan."[1]

Remembering back to the previous afternoon, *Bird* realized that the snooping Jeep which had dropped off Lieutenant Lynch and Sergeant VanArkel must have been the notorious *Toledo*. "I do believe I met him, though we weren't introduced. I must say I wasn't impressed with his scrutinizing stares and his departing, gravel-flinging rooster tail."

"Sounds like him. Well, he does serve a purpose. And I must grudgingly admit, he does it commendably well. I just wish he wasn't so cocky about it," *Hoosier* said as the armorers attached the tail fins to his ten-bomb cargo.

"So, believe it or not, we planes know about the day's mission before any of the crew does. And we get to hear what the squadron, and some-times the group commander, really think about the mission. You know, the odds and all, how bad it could be, or what they really think of the lead plane commander," *Hoosier* said with a slight touch of bravado.

---

1. "Wild Bill" Donovan was an American intelligence officer, best known for serving as the head of the Office of Strategic Services (OSS), the precursor to the Central Intelligence Agency (CIA), during World War II.

"Now, wait a minute. Fool me once, shame on you; fool me twice, shame on me. I haven't been in the Army Air Corps even a full two months yet, but I have learned how tight-lipped they are about such things. Now explain to me how we get to know before, say, Pop, my pilot," *Bird* skeptically asked.

"Simple. The utter arrogance of people. They presume that since they're the only things alive that communicate with language, spoken or written, that they're the only things on this war-torn planet that has conscious thought," *Hoosier* scornfully spat. "Oh, they might think some animals can understand a little, like some of the squadrons' dog mascots, but a so called 'inanimate' object like a B-24 Liberator? Or a Jeep? Ha! They'd lock that person up so they couldn't hurt themselves."

"So, it should come to no surprise that *Toledo* should overhear and take notes on everything the driver, and most importantly the passengers, gossip about. That includes everyone from squadron commanders, the S-2—oh, that's the intelligence officer by the way," *Hoosier* paused to explain to the newcomer, "to Colonel Gent, the head man."

"Right about now, *Toledo* will begin picking up the various commanders and headquarters staff to prepare for this morning's mission briefing. That's when the sleuthing begins," *Hoosier* said as he observed the armorer wire each of the bombs' fuse propellers to the bomb racks. "Gosh, it makes me nervous to watch them do that," he shuddered.

"Anyhow, I don't think an informer's boots could hit the ground getting out of *Toledo* at headquarters before the word would be spread. The first Jeep or six-by-six that *Toledo* would come across, the secret info would be regurgitated as fast as he could spew it. Man, you'll be amazed at how fast that boy can talk. Spit at you, too, as he talks. Your front nose gear will be covered with antifreeze spittle by the time he's done trying to impress you with what he knows." *Hoosier* sighed with relief as the fuse safety pins were slid through each bomb's nose fuse. Just one more safety precaution to make him feel better.

The unmistakable whine of a starter motor and the intermittent, coughing ignition of a nearby Pratt and Whitney engine caught *Bird*'s attention. Glancing behind her, she observed *Paper Doll*'s number three engine coming to life with its propeller settling down to a melodious idle. Other engines soon caught and were roaring to life, quickly appearing content with their 1,000-rpm idle.

Soon after, ghostly apparitions began appearing, seemingly floating out from under the blossoming olive trees. Eerily, but delicately illuminated by the almost full, setting moon, *Bird* began to make out the pale and sleep-deprived faces of men as they shuffled past the waiting planes. Following the cone-shaped path of feeble light emanating from their hand-held flashlights, the men passed through the squadron's planes wordlessly. "Say, hey *Tessie,*" shouted *Bird*, hoping *Two Ton Tessie* wouldn't mind the abbreviated nickname. "Where are they going?" *Bird* asked as she watched the men disappear in the direction of the dirigible hangers, their spectral bodies disappearing into the darkness.

"Oh, hey there *Bird*," *Tessie* yelled back, thankful for the distraction from witnessing her bomb-loading. Everyone got tense while those were being put aboard. "You asking where the guys are going? Why, to the mission briefing at headquarters. It's the stone building to the left of the hangars. Usually lasts half an hour or so," she finished as she watched other armorers loading 4,500 rounds of ammo for her various guns. These weapons and their .50 caliber harbingers of destruction gave *Tessie* a fleeting feeling of invincibility while here on the ground. But she knew that once she got near the bomb run, the feeling would evaporate. But for now, she'd relish in her hypnotic fantasy.

Noticing the dim light emanating from the distant first floor windows of the headquarters building, *Bird* pondered what the crews were learning at the moment. Would there be an audible gasp when the destination is revealed? Or would there be smirking glances to one another as one of those short, poorly defended "milk runs" that every crew hopes for was unveiled?

Suddenly recognizing the palpable stillness around her, *Bird* glanced over at *Hoosier* and noticed his engines had fallen silent. "Must be finished checking him out. Hey *Hoosier*! Where's this famous *Toledo* and this scuttlebutt you were talking about?" *Bird* scoffed.

"I was wondering that myself. The word has usually spread to us by now," said a perplexed *Hoosier*. "He must have gotten caught up with something. You know, just like us, he's dependent upon the men. In his case, groundcrews and headquarters staff."

On cue, both *Hoosier* and *Bird* heard the dissonant din of a whiney transaxle and over-revved Willys Go Devil engine approaching, with all sixty horsepower wishing the distracted driver would shift into a higher gear. *Toledo* was making his appearance.

Skidding to a stop adjacent to *Hoosier*'s bomb bay, the driver and a now relieved passenger, Corporal Clyde Roye, retrieved a massive, K-17 aerial camera from the back seat and soon disappeared into the depths of *Hoosier's* midsection. The four rear gunners will moan in protest as they make their way to their combat stations upon seeing the 55-pound camera filling the void of the rear floor escape hatch. Apparently, bomb strike photos were more important than an unimpeded means of escape from a plane that is possibly spiraling to its death.

"Sorry 'bout the late scoop, guys, but I got called into squadron wake-up duty. Imagine that. Me, a headquarters Jeep performing such a menial task," *Toledo* said with disdain, as the first droplets of engine coolant spittle dripped down *Hoosier*'s landing strut.

Glancing in *Bird*'s direction, *Toledo* shouted a staccato greeting, "Hey, you're the *Los Lobos* replacement, aren't you? Heard about you, *Worrybird*. You're going to be combat #3. Sure hope you last longer than he did. He only made it to nine missions." Fortunately for *Bird* she was outside the ballistic range of coolant spittle.

"You must be *Toledo*. *Hoosier* has been filling me in about you. And by the way, call me *Bird* since I'm planning on being here awhile," *Bird* replied with a touch of defiance in her voice. "So, what's the latest scuttlebutt?"

"Oh, wait till you hear. We're bombing a whole new country. Rumania! And get this, the 449th will be the lead group, too. Sure will be a feather in our cap," *Toledo* boasted with a swagger due to the negative camber in her rear wheels.

"Right easy for you to say while you're sitting safely on the ground five hundred miles away from where the action is," *Hoosier* thought to himself. "So what's so important about hitting Rumania, and what's the target going to be?"

"Bucharest marshaling yards, including railroad stations and repair shops. But not just any marshaling yards," *Toledo* related with an ever-increasing upbeat tempo. "These are key to supplying the German Army from Rumania to southern Russia with oil and supplies. Oil was mentioned a whole bunch of times. They say we are really going to start targeting oil refineries and reserves," *Toledo* said, pausing to catch his breath.

"But it's what's waiting for you guys that does have me scared," his now raspy voice blurted. "They said there are sixty-five heavy Flak guns surrounding the yard. And if that's not bad enough, 175 to 200 single-engine fighters and thirty twin-engine ones will be waiting for you guys." With that comment, *Toledo* could have sworn *Hoosier*'s flaps swiftly retracted.

Hoosier's thoughts reflected back to another mission that came with dire German fighter and Flak warnings. Two Regensburg, Germany aircraft factories back in late February were the target. Responsible for over one third of Germany's Me-109 aircraft production, they were heavily defended by fifty-six heavy Flak guns and a hundred single- and twin-engine German fighters. He had been lucky enough not to have been on that mission. Five days earlier, on a mission to northern Italy, he had sustained painful Flak damage; both waist guns and the front turret malfunctioned, and the bomb bay doors wouldn't open properly. The groundcrew, fortunately, hadn't finished his repairs in time to be on the Regensburg run. Six Group planes, including *Guardian Angel* of the 719th and *Pistol Packin Mama* of the 716th did not return, all shot down by the aggressive enemy fighters.

What really chapped *Hoosier*'s hide, though, was that because of solid undercast, none of the 719th's thirty-six tons of bombs hit their target—10/10 weather they called it. The worst possible. "Why wasn't a weather recall code broadcasted beforehand? And if *Toledo*'s sleuthing was correct, over 360 B-24s from the two Wings involved did nothing but rip up a whole bunch of farmland and the northwest part of Regensburg. Yes sir, 3,600 quarter-ton bombs could harrow a whole lot of farmland. You knew damn well that they would send us back there to finish—heck no, not finish but to commence and complete—the destruction of those aircraft factories. And they did, three days later, but I don't want to think about that right now," *Hoosier* thought with a shudder, reflecting on the destructive power both they and the Germans had expended on that day.

"But does the Army Air Corps ever learn from its mistakes? Or are we just Flak and Messerschmitt cannon fodder? What good is sending up our planes and men to a target without weather data? Head on up enough times and maybe we'll get lucky with the weather? Sure, that's a plan," *Hoosier* thought mockingly. "And whose bright idea was it to devise a mission deep into enemy territory with absolutely no fighter escort? I'm amazed we only lost six planes. Only. Sheee-it." *Hoosier*'s front turret oscillated back and forth as the armorer checked its tracking movement. "Six out of our twenty-four that made it to the target. Twenty-five percent gone in one mission. Something has gotta change or none of us will survive this," he pondered, wondering why the Air Corps hadn't come to the same obvious conclusion.

"*Hoosier*. Hey, *HOOSIER!*" *Bird* finally shouted, even though no nearby engines were being run up. "Boy, I thought you had shut down on *Toledo* and me," *Bird* quipped after sensing *Hoosier* was back with them from wherever his thoughts had taken him.

"Oh hey, sorry, guys," a now chagrined *Hoosier* replied. "Not sure what got after me. *Toledo*'s briefing reports usually don't affect me. Besides, they usually end up being a bunch of slag anyhow," he retorted, remembering one of John McCormick's favorite, less vulgar terms for excrement, picked up working on the floors of U.S. Steel. Unlike John, however, *Hoosier* didn't mind repeating curse words picked up from the rest of his crew and the groundcrew. Sometimes they were just so efficient, so delectably perfect in relaying a thought or feeling.

"Hey there, buddy," *Toledo* said with actual concern in his voice. He had seen that forlorn look on Liberators before, and it usually wasn't a good sign. It's as if they had given up the fight before their landing gears had even gotten off the ground. Like they didn't have a chance or couldn't fight back; were impotent. Well, that was just bullshit, to quote *Hoosier* himself.

"*Hoosier*, why don't you tell *Bird* here about *Sophisticated Lady* and what she did to the Luftwaffe all by herself?" *Toledo* asked, trying some of that psychology that he overheard Doc Peterson, the group's flight surgeon, talking about.

"Jeez, *Toledo*, why don't you just spray salt water into my exposed metal parts," *Hoosier* exclaimed as he unsuccessfully tried not to remember the second Regensburg mission.

"So, who's this *Sophisticated Lady* you're talking about? I don't see her around. Is she with one of the other squadrons?" *Bird* asked, rattling off the questions almost as fast as *Toledo*.

Realizing there was no way out of it, *Hoosier* began the battle litany of the *Sophisticated Lady* and *The Heavenly Body*.

[449th Bomb Group Association Collection]

"*SOPHISTICATED LADY* WAS WITH the 716th Squadron located at the other end of our runway along with the 717th. She's no longer with us," *Hoosier* simply stated. No other explanation was needed.

And so, he began. "Our first mission into Germany was to visit the Messerschmitt manufacturing plants in Regensburg. February 22nd, it was. Of course, this mission, like most others, was a SNAFU," *Hoosier* continued. Glancing at *Bird*, he asked, "You're pretty new to the Air Corps. Do you know what that is?" With a swiveling of her turret, *Bird* acknowledged in the negative. "It's a polite way of saying what most missions truly turn out to be: Situation-Normal-All-Fucked-Up," *Hoosier* said, repeating what he had heard not only from ground crews, but from officers as well, all too often.

"Due to poor planning with no weather data, and believe this if you will, absolutely no escorts, we lost six of us that made it to the target. Fifteen had turned back early. Can you believe that?" *Hoosier* said with disgust. "Superchargers out, electrical shorts, gun turrets inoperative, oxygen leaks, oil leaks. You name it, it broke. But the worst part was when they got there they couldn't see a darn thing. The lead bombardier dropped his bombs based on a navigational checkpoint seen an hour and a half earlier. So there went everyone else's bombs, probably landing in some farmer's field or the Danube."

"Danube. What's a Danube? Is that something I should be on the lookout for?" *Bird* asked, feeling like she had just emerged from her primordial slumber back at the Texas North American plant. So many questions. So much unknown, so much to learn from these veterans, she thought to herself.

"You don't need to 'cause your navigator will be looking for it. He'll use that winding, gunmetal ribbon to guide you to your target. Be it in Germany, Austria, Slovakia, Hungary, and now Rumania. It's a river, and for some reason they call it the Blue Danube. Well, maybe if you're standing on its banks, but at 24,000 feet it's anything but. Every time I fly over it I wonder just how much Liberator debris eventually makes its way to the delta and sinks in the depths of the Black Sea. The Blue Danube. Heck, they oughta call it the river of death," a now morose *Hoosier* said.

"All right, I see the way you guys are looking at me," he continued, forcing a smile, trying to mollify *Toledo*, *Bird*, and the other eight 719th Squadron planes who were now being prepped for today's mission and happened to be intently eavesdropping. For they couldn't hear enough of *Sophisticated Lady* and *The Heavenly Body's* story, even though five of them had lived through it. It just made them so proud to be a Liberator.

"So of course, with such miserable bombing results, we went again, three days later. At least this time they had flown a weather reconnaissance flight beforehand, which gave us the all-clear. So, thirty-five of us took off with eight soon returning to the field with the same medley of defects," *Hoosier* said with loathing as he glanced at the maintenance crews working on *Lonesome's* number three engine. But he knew in his heart, if he had one left, that the numerous mechanical failures weren't their fault. Talk about working in horrendous conditions! He had seen them change out an engine in snow, and another time in a torrential downpour, and always in deep mud. No hangar, no covering to protect them from the elements. And then there were the over one million parts that made the planes up. Jeesh, how they kept it straight he'd never know. Always scrounging for some miscellaneous part not to be found in the supply depot. Making do with what was at hand. And it's not like they were treated really well when on a mission, *Hoosier* thought, as he felt the hundreds of Flak, bullet, and cannon hole patches in his skin.

"And then the SNAFU happened, big time," he continued. "We hadn't even made it sixty miles north of here, over Bitonto if I remember correctly, at 8,200 feet, when another Group came out of the scattered clouds at our three o'clock. It wouldn't have been a problem if they hadn't been at 8,200 feet also. You should have seen our lead plane, *Veni Vidi Vici*, turn on his left wingtip starting us in an emergency 360 degree turn to port to avoid a definite group comingling and collision," *Hoosier* remembered in astonishment.

"Well, we were scattered all over central Italy, and nine of us attached themselves to the Group that had about taken us all out and turned on a different heading to bomb Graz, Austria. So that left eighteen of us, when soon another three fell out with problems and made their way back to base. So now there were only fifteen of us, but at least we weren't alone. Forty P-38s had caught up with us over the Adriatic and were at our sides. Boy, that gives you a warm, fuzzy, hell-bent-for-leather feeling," *Hoosier* said with those same feelings starting to course through his hydraulic lines.

"Well, that feeling was short lived 'cause those fork-tailed beauties left us as soon as we hit the Austrian Alps about an hour before our bomb run. Talk about feeling alone, high above those mountains with absolutely no clouds whatsoever. No place to hide. But boy, that was a beautiful sight though," *Hoosier* said with a slight contemplative grin of remembrance spreading below the navigator's window.

"After crossing the Alps and getting into Germany, we started seeing other Groups of planes ahead of us, and it wasn't long before we saw billowing smoke columns rising to about 5,000 feet on the horizon. We didn't need the navigator to tell us the direction of those Regensburg Messerschmitt plants."

"After arriving at the IP—that's the initial point where we tighten up our formation after the last navigation fix to start our bomb run," *Hoosier* explained for *Bird*'s benefit, "that's when the Flak hit. Heavy, intense, and accurate."[2]

"*Sophisticated* got hit and lost her number two engine. The bombardier kept her on the bomb run and dropped her ten 500-pounders right on the target. We all hit it. That place was nothing but one big massive ball of flame. Those licking flames reached 2,000 feet into that black, boiling smoke, too. I'm not sure what hell looks like, but that wasn't too far off, I bet. Made us feel good 'cause we knew we wouldn't have to go back there any time soon, let me tell ya."

"But there wasn't any time to celebrate 'cause fifty Me-109s, 110's, Ju-88s and Focke-Wulf 190s came at us hard. I saw one of us explode in midair but I couldn't catch the name, there was nothing left but falling fragments. *Shack Wolf* caught fire from the Germans' 20mm cannon fire and went spinning out of control and disappeared. But then the fighters were gone. Just like that. Just as if they had been called back to base. Well, they hadn't, 'cause they just saw easy prey, a Tail-end Charlie. *Sophisticated Lady* was struggling to keep up with us on three engines and was lagging behind. The remaining twenty-one German fighters all went after her and left the rest of us alone."

"Now all that I'm about to tell you I didn't witness. *The Heavenly Body* saw that *Sophisticated Lady* was about to be eaten for lunch and needed assistance. So she dropped back to help. Now except for turning tail and running in the face of the enemy, to leave formation to help a straggling brother or sister will get you into some kind of hot water," *Hoosier* stated in a firm, no-nonsense tone.

---

2. Flak was described in after-action reports by its caliber: heavy, moderate, or light; intensity: slight, moderate, or intense; and accuracy: accurate or inaccurate.

"Wait. What?" exclaimed a disbelieving *Bird*. "Do you mean to tell me that I can't go back and help one of you guys if I see you're in trouble? Just leave you behind to the wolves?"

"That's right. Remember there's a reason we keep such a tight formation when flying over enemy territory. We all rely upon each other for mass defensive protection. We start heading off willy-nilly, that Group protection breaks down. The one is not more important than the whole," *Hoosier* patiently explained.

"Thing is, *Heavenly Body* and *Sophisticated* had been together since the 449th's training days in Bruning, Nebraska. They were close and inseparable, and there was no way one was going to leave the other behind for a certain fate of death. The last the Group or myself saw of those two was *Heavenly* tucked up beside *Sophisticated* with a swarm of German fighters prancing around them out of gun range waiting for the kill."

"But as it turned out, it was the Germans who were in trouble. For even though they were experienced fighter pilots, having shot many of our bombers out of the sky, they hadn't encountered anything like the gunners on those two Liberators," *Hoosier* said with pride.

"For an hour and a half over the crystal blue skies of Germany, Austria, and Yugoslavia, this mélange of combatants battled for their very existence. The German fighters darting and striking like swarming hornets, relentlessly chasing a retreating victim. But this victim wasn't defenseless. Not with *Heavenly*'s ten Brownings chattering away along with *Sophisticated*'s own."

"The Germans had their own firepower, however, and were using it relentlessly. Between the 20mm cannon, 8mm machine guns, and wing-mounted rockets, *Sophisticated* was taking a terrible beating. To help protect her, *Heavenly* was forever flittering around her to stay between her and the rushing onslaught. But it wasn't enough protection. The Germans had become maniacally obsessed with knocking her out of the sky no matter what the cost. But what a cost. *Sophisticated*'s gunners had become possessed with an adrenalin-aided passion for survival. The flight path of this acrobatic, aerial campaign could be traced by a 250-mile-long trail of German fighter debris."

"But it had to end in the eventual obvious conclusion. Now with *Sophisticated*'s number one engine knocked out by cannon fire, her tail section perforated by 8mm bullets taking out her elevators, and finally her number four engine giving up the ghost from a severed oil line, the pilot, Lt. Gil Bradley, finally gave the bailout order over northern Yugoslavia. This wasn't before everything not bolted down was seen being thrown out the waist windows and open bomb bay. Machine guns, Flak jackets, books, the Sperry bombsight, cameras, personal effects, you name it. But it was impossible for them to stay in the air for long on one engine."

"*Heavenly* circled nine parachutes before they delicately reached the earth while *Sophisticated Lady*, in a steep dive, crashed outside the small Yugoslavian village of Todorova. It was obvious from there only being nine chutes that someone had gone down with the ship," *Hoosier* concluded, with the early morning silence blanketing everyone's somber thoughts for the moment.

"When *Heavenly* finally arrived at base, nine hours after takeoff and flying on fumes, the last of the Group to land, the crew was interrogated by the S-2, and their account was scoffed at and dismissed as a firefight-induced fabrication. *Heavenly*'s account of the running battle of *Sophisticated Lady* wasn't filed and reported. All the S-2 had to do was ask *The Heavenly Body* for her account and it would have corroborated the crew's. Silly human," *Hoosier* scoffed. "While they stated that they had shot down three German fighters, which was certainly possible and commonly done, it's what they insisted the crew of the *Sophisticated Lady* had done that was beyond belief for the intelligence officer. For they maintained, and their individual accounts corroborated one another's recall, that *Sophisticated* had downed fifteen German fighters. Fifteen!" *Hoosier* added with emphasis, his hydraulic fluid now flowing with an energized feeling of, well, a devil-be-damned attitude. One that he hadn't felt in a long time. With that slow realization coursing through his lines, *Hoosier* glanced at

Toledo through his open bomb bay, meeting the side glance of the Jeep's headlights, now dimming in the astronomical twilight of the predawn. A wordless "thank you" passed between them, unseen or heard by the others.

THE BATTLE ACCOUNT of the *Sophisticated Lady* would not have to wait long to be vindicated. The very next day, April 5th, a truck dropped off the returning nine members of her crew at Grottaglie. They had survived a thirty-nine-day cat and mouse adventure through German-occupied Yugoslavia, surviving with the help of pro-Allied Yugoslav partisans, led by Josip Tito.[3]

Their battle report to the now chagrined S-2 affirmed everything the crew of *The Heavenly Body* had previously reported. To his credit he admitted his mistake and passed up the now confirmed fifteen "kills" of the *Sophisticated Lady* to headquarters. This story was too good to just keep hidden in a headquarters file cabinet.

Soon the military newspaper "Stars and Stripes" had picked up the debriefing report, interviewed a few of the crew, and published the story, complete with pictures. Unfortunately, the pictures did not include *Sophisticated Lady*, whose remains were still scattered over a farm in northern Yugoslavia, but showed pilot Lt. Gilbert Bradley's original plane, which he normally flew, the *Pistol Packin Mama*. The *Mama*, flown by Lt. Robert Bird three days earlier due to Bradley and his crew standing that mission down, had been shot down on that first Regensburg raid. Lt. Bradley had

---

3. Josip Tito was the communist leader of the Yugoslav Partisans, often regarded as one of the most effective resistance movements in German-occupied Europe. He also served as President of the Socialist Federal Republic of Yugoslavia from 1953 to 1980.

then flown Lt. Bird's orphaned plane, *Sophisticated Lady,* on her infamous February 25th mission over Regensburg. It was a confusing case of mistaken identity that the "Stars and Stripes" either didn't pick up or ignored. All to the detriment of the true history of the *Sophisticated Lady.* This led to word-played front-page headline stories in U.S. newspapers, such as: *"Pistol Packin' Mama Shot Those Nazis Down With Metuchen Man Pouring Lead."*[4]

What the Germans never understood, nor gave credit to, was the inborn tenacity, the individualistic grit, of the common young American men they faced on the battlefields of the ground, sea, or air. This included the six gunners of the *Sophisticated Lady*: a truck driver hauling fruit from Benton Harbor, Michigan; a farmer keeping his widowed mother's farm solvent outside of Delavan, Minnesota; a sawmill employee working alongside his father in Ada, Ohio; an auditor at a Valparaiso, Indiana ordnance plant, who within two years would be dispensing some of that very same ordnance out of his Browning in a futile attempt to save his life; a Jewish thread mill worker from Fall River, Massachusetts, who wasn't about to be shot down in German-held territory; or a line worker at an explosive factory in Metuchen, New Jersey. These men hadn't been given a thing in life; they worked for it all. And they weren't about to have anyone take away their most precious possession: life itself. Not without a fight.

These six men worked as a team, tethered together with the ship's interphone. This they used as a tactical advantage by constantly informing all gunners of an attacking aircraft's distance, azimuth, and angle of attack. This gave the appropriate gunner or sometimes multiple gunners a split-second edge. And at twenty-six rounds per second for the turret-mounted guns, this was enough to give them a lifesaving advantage.

"ME 109 coming in at 12 o'clock level... Nice shooting Herb."

---

4. *The Daily Home News.* New Brunswick, NJ. May 27, 1944, p. 1.

"Formation of Ju-88s preparing for an attack at 6 o'clock high... here they come!"

"Me-110 preparing to come in at 3 o'clock.... Well, come on in, you sons of bitches! What are you waiting for?"

"Nice shooting Paul... we know he'll never come back."

"Do you see him, Prescher? The smoke is coming out of his wings... he must be frozen on the trigger... oh, oh – there he goes, heading straight down."

"Say, Mills, do you see those 88s out there about 5:30 high? Are they afraid to come in.... Here they come, they were lobbing rockets at us!"[5]

On and on it went for a constant hour and a half. When the right waist gunner, Sergeant Roland Prescher, was hit in both legs by cannon-shell fragments, the tail gunner, Sergeant Irving Mills, relieved him. The tail guns' hydraulic system had been blown out by cannon fire. A .50 cal bullet had gone through his flight suit and lodged in the turret's door behind him.

When Sergeant Paul Biggart at the left waist gun position was killed after downing four fighters, Lt. Ken Ebersole, the bombardier, stepped over his almost decapitated body and replaced him, almost losing his footing as he skated across hundreds of four-inch shell casings littering the floor. Once the bomb run was over he was a free man, and as a backup gunner as well as backup navigator, he had a job to do.

The nose turret guns were put out of commission when a 20mm cannon shell severed their electrical system, passing between gunner Sergeant Herbert Clements' legs and exploding beneath his fortunately armor-plated metal seat.

Tech Sergeant Joseph Montagna, the flight engineer manning the top turret, kept on firing even after 20mm cannon shells raked and disintegrated his overhead plexiglass dome, showering him in glass. He had been bending over to check his ammunition supply when the shots came in.

---

5. Ibid

Afterward, even with a 150mph tornadic gale buffeting him, his head exposed to both natural and man-made elements of danger, he shot down two twin-engine Ju-88s and a twin-engine Me-110 before running out of that scarce ammunition.

The last turret-mounted Brownings defending *Sophisticated* were the ball turret guns manned by Sergeant Frank Grubaugh. With his interphone shot out and the turret door jammed shut by cannon fire, he thought he was the last man on the ship. He now knew how the solitary Captain Hendrick Van Der Decken felt piloting the doomed *Flying Dutchman*. Before his guns fell silent due to running out of ammunition and sending the last three fighters scurrying back to Germany with their tails tucked between their legs, Frank had personally shot down six of their less fortunate German comrades.

With *Sophisticated* rapidly losing altitude, Lt. Bradley gave the bailout order, which was passed down the ship with hand signals. The entire electrical system was shot out, rendering the interphone system inoperative and now useless. It had served its purpose with aplomb. Helping their fellow gunners out of the cramped, entombing turrets, the men quickly jumped out of *Sophisticated*, their life preserving airborne platform, which plowed into the backyard of a rural farmhouse less than four seconds later.

The *Sophisticated Lady* still holds the world's military record of having downed the most enemy aircraft in a single mission. Any country, any war. Judging how current aerial combat is conducted, her record will long stand.

All men of the *Sophisticated Lady* and *The Heavenly Body* received the Distinguished Flying Cross, or DFC, in eventual recognition. Lt. Edward Drinan, pilot of *The Heavenly Body*, also received the Silver Star. So much for being severely reprimanded for leaving the safety of the formation and endangering its cohesive defensive posture.

Sergeant Paul Biggart's body was removed from the crushed, smoldering remains of *Sophisticated Lady* by the family living in the adjacent farmhouse. He was given a Christian burial in the village cemetery, while his mother and father, in rural Indiana, 5,000 miles from their twenty-two-year-old son's eternal resting place, received their forever young, only child's posthumous DFC.

12

Boy, I Feel Low

Grottaglie, Italy, US Army Air Force Field, April 4, 1944, 06:00 hrs.

"Yeow, geez! Watch where you're walking!" Bob exclaimed in pain as he thrust his aching left hand under his right armpit after bolting up from a deep slumber in excruciating surprise. "What time is it anyhow?" he asked as he winced and tried to straighten his aching back. He had slept on hard ground in a sleeping bag before, but this wood floor with only a thin blanket for cushioning had to have been the hardest "mattress" he'd ever slept on.

"Oh, sorry there, Bob. I forgot you guys were on the floor," Sheldon Zimmerman apologized. "It's 0600 and the sun will be up in a bit," he said as he searched for matches to light the kerosene lamp to add some feeble light to the predawn filtering through the tent flaps.

"Drop your cocks and grab your socks, guys! Time to get up," Paul Lahr merrily sang as he stepped through the now silhouetted tent flaps, striding over the lone remaining prone figure who was slowly rising from his fitful slumber. "Sheldon and I have already been to the briefing and are heading over to the squadron mess for some powdered eggs and coffee. That'll put some hair on that chest of yours, Stan."

Rubbing his eyes and trying to twist some feeling into his numb back, Stan just mumbled an incomprehensible morning greeting. "You'll have to forgive Stan's grumpy manners," Bob said, he himself wincing while straightening his back. "For a farm boy, he sure hates to get up early."

"Hey, I'm just trying to catch up on twenty years of missed early morning shuteye," Stan said, preemptively stifling a burgeoning yawn. "So, what's the plan today, Sheldon?"

"Well, while you guys are trying to find a tent of your own, with beds I might add," Sheldon responded with a smirk as he watched the *Bird*'s two officers still trying to work the kinks out of their stiff bodies, "Paul and I are going to be laying waste to Bucharest's marshaling yards. Paul is going to be in the right seat of the *Consolidated Mess* with Tony Polink as pilot. He's a good egg, one of the original pilots still left. To prove it, he made Captain," he said, glancing at Paul, giving him a shot of mission confidence. "He'll also be leading the lower left 'C' box of six of our squadron's planes. The other three will be in the lower right 'B' box mixed in with three others from the 718th. I'll be right behind him in the right seat of *Paper Doll*, another one of the original planes, piloted by another original, Rich Garrison. We're both in good hands," Sheldon finished with conviction.

Left unsaid was the part of the briefing that mentioned over two hundred enemy fighters and sixty-five heavy Flak guns awaiting them. Why alarm the new guys? The thought of what they were up against would probably liquefy whatever was in their bowels, Sheldon thought. Besides, the briefing officer did say they had no idea of the capabilities and experience of the Rumanian Air Force, he thought, trying to alleviate the dire concern creeping into his own consciousness.

"Hey, a valuable hint on picking your tent location," Paul interjected. "Get one furthest back, it'll be less in the downwind direction of the latrines. Let me tell you, when they burn them, pee-ew, the Kansas City stockyards have nothing on them, right Harry?" he said, glancing at Harry who had entered the tent with a look of wrinkle-nosed disgust as he recalled visiting those odiferous temporary refuges of thousands of bovines.

"We've got to get going, guys, if Paul and I are going to get something to eat and a bit more coffee in us. We're supposed to be on station in our planes at 0700, and taxiing out at 0810," Sheldon said as he checked the time on his government issued A-11 wristwatch and then proceeded to reach for his flight suit hanging in the crude, homemade closet.

Hands were shaken, and the last words they heard from either Sheldon or Paul was one of them saying, "We'll catch you later" over their shoulder as they disappeared amid the tents and olive trees as the cusp of the morning sun broke over the eastern horizon.

Two hours later, Stan stared down with a leery eye at the powdered egg remains and black coffee in front of him in the crude officers' mess. The coffee looked and poured like the crankcase oil pouring out of his Model T Ford after far too long between oil changes. He swore it also had the faint odor of Standard Oil Red Crown gasoline, too. What he'd give for some of the fresh cream that would rise to the surface of the six-gallon Pittsburg Pottery crock that cooled in the corner of the farmhouse kitchen. Such thoughts had become more frequent, permeating his mind at the slightest hint of something that triggered the mystic memory chords of home.

"Wonder why we haven't heard the Group take off yet? It's pushing 0900," wondered Pop out loud, breaking Stan's brief reverie.

"Could be anything," replied Bob, chewing his gristly-assed, though much appreciated, bacon. "Most probably weather over the route or target, waiting for it to clear." As navigator, Bob had taken classes in meteorology too, a testament to their dependence on, and the importance of, weather. "Of course, we could also be waiting on something from one of the other three Groups; who knows?"

Pushing his chair away from the table and his half-eaten breakfast, Pop announced, "It's a beautiful morning, let's go find us a tent." A hearty cheer erupted from the group and they all pushed their chairs across the stone floor of the bomb-scarred building serving as the officers' mess and soon departed out the door into brilliant sunshine in search of what would become their home.

WITH ALL THE ACTIVITY that had erupted around *Bird* during the previous few hours, she hadn't noticed the pilot standing next to *Hoosier Honey* engaged in a deep conversation with another young officer. With his back against *Hoosier* and facing *Bird*, she realized his eyes would drift over and stare intently, if not actually bore into her. That's when the sudden recognition hit her. "Why, that's Lieutenant Lynch, who taxied me to this spot yesterday, who poured out his personal thoughts—no, demons—to me. I barely recognized him in all of that high-altitude flying gear."

As they finished their conversation, they slowly walked around *Hoosier* after being joined by another man who was just wearing coveralls and a flight cap. They methodically traipsed from one engine to another, pausing to point at something, wave their arms, or put their arms akimbo as they listened to the flight cap man. Soon all three knelt at the front landing gear to examine it and the tire closely. "I expect one of them is going to kick her tire, make an offer, and shake the other guy's hand in a sec, like he's buying a used car," *Bird* chuckled to herself.

"What was that, *Bird*?" *Hoosier* asked. "Were you talking to me?"

"Oh, nothing. But who are the guys with Lieutenant Lynch that are giving you the once over?"

Glancing under his nose, *Hoosier* assessed, "Well, the other officer is Lieutenant John, John McCormick, my pilot. The tall, thin one is my new crew chief. I haven't been introduced but he sure has been all over, poking and prodding me with tools and telling the mechanics one thing or another. You'll get your personal crew chief, too. Be nice to him and he'll help you get through this," *Hoosier* replied as he watched them look at his elevators and rudders. Sure hope they like those aluminum patches in my tail. I think they make me look suave myself, *Hoosier* thought without a hint of modesty.

Bird then noticed the flight engineer she had met, oh what was his name? Something strange, he'd said his parents were Dutch. Art. Art Van Arkel, that's it. He was up out of the escape hatch and onto the wings, checking the fuel caps and safety-wiring them shut. He was then back down the hatch and she caught a glimpse of him discreetly checking the bomb racks. Jumping out of the bomb bay, he then ran his outstretched finger along the bottom of each engine, closely examining the finger after each wipe. Checking for dripping engine oil? she pondered. Boy, that is one busy man. Seems kinda unfair since most of *Hoosier*'s crew are just lollygagging about, lying in the shade of his wings. Almost like they're impatiently waiting for something. Hmm. Now that I look around, it looks like the crews of all nine of the mission-bound planes are doing the same thing, *Bird* noticed.

"Hey *Hoosier*, what are all the guys waiting for?" *Bird* asked. "All they're doing is standing around smoking their Lucky Strikes,"

"Typical Army. Hurry up and wait is their motto, don't you know?" said *Hoosier* as he heard Lt. Wilfred Stagman, his navigator, inform the rest of the crew about what to expect on this flight. He heard nervous laughter and caught the fidgeting hand and feet gestures typical of men who had more on their minds than they were letting on.

One Lucky Strike later, a six-by-six truck pulled up and began disgorging its cargo to the anxiously waiting men. Handed out were what they would need in case everything didn't go as planned. Parachute packs, "Mae West" life preservers, Flak vests, and steel helmets, better known as "brain buckets" to crunch one's head into if the Flak got really bad. Of course, no one in the crew knew exactly how to use a parachute. Sure, they were told how to, but it's not like they had practiced. The Army Air Corps had stopped actual parachute drop training due to too many accidents. Besides, no one had complained about their parachute not opening.

As *Bird* was looking at *Hoosier*, behind him toward the control tower she saw something arc across the sky. And she didn't know what to think. "*HOOSIER*! Holy smokes, look at the green fireworks behind you."

"Fireworks nothing, girl, that green flare means the mission is on," *Hoosier* said with sudden dispatch after glancing out his top turret. "Climb aboard, boys, button down the hatches, and fire 'em up. I'm not sure when we'll get back, since none of us have been to this Rumania before," *Hoosier* declared as his number three engine's starter began its familiar whine and its prop started to slowly turn over. With a cough and the usual jet of black smoke exuding from its exhaust port, it soon caught and settled down to its rhythmic idle. His other three engines quickly joined in on a speedy start and smooth idle, due to the previous early morning start-up and test run. "Catch you when we get back, *Bird*," *Hoosier* yelled over the growing din of thirty-six Pratt and Whitney engines in clamorous mechanical chorus.

"See you, *Hoosier*. Have a good flight!" *Bird* yelled, though she doubted *Hoosier* heard her, and besides he was probably too busy jockeying for his proper squadron position on the taxiway. "Have a good flight? Sheesh! What an absolutely ridiculous thing to say to someone about to head into possible oblivion," *Bird* said to herself disgustedly. Of course, what do you say in a situation like that, she pondered, not coming up with anything better.

Soon, at 09:51 to be precise, upon checking her onboard chronometer, a full power takeoff could be heard emanating from the south end of the runway. As it clawed desperately for speed, *Bird* noticed the front nose wheel of a fully laden Liberator lift off the ground about two thirds of the way down on what was a very short runway. Once airborne, she wondered how anything shaped so cumbersome, so ponderous, carrying so much weight, was capable of flight.

As the plane drew level with her, barely twenty feet off the ground, *Bird* made out the nose art of *Honey On The Moon*, ship number twenty-five, piloted by Captain Rex Tompkins, the Group Operations Officer. A flittering auditory memory fragment briefly brought her back to the North American assembly line, listening to the tinny overhead speakers. The hideous audio fidelity of the paper-coned box speakers could not hide the rich, gravelly voice of "Fats" Waller and his band playing "*There's Honey on the Moon Tonight*," one of her favorites. But the person briefly visible in the co-pilot's seat caught *Bird*'s discerning eye, giving her a start and instantly bringing her back to the present.

"Well, I'll be," *Bird* said after recognizing Colonel Thomas Gent as he glanced out the starboard side co-pilot's window, momentarily catching *Bird*'s intent gaze. "He's certainly no armchair commander, that's for sure," she said as another bomb and fuel-laden B-24, *Harper's Ferry*, gained speed as it traversed the runway thirty seconds after the *Honey* had barely become airborne.

No Army Air Corps Group Commander worth his salt led from his desk chair. Colonel Gent's predecessor, Colonel Darr Alkire, had found that out when he went down piloting the *Lurchin Urchin* two months earlier. As commander, Colonel Gent slowly circled the field, like a patient mother duck waiting for her thirty-one straggling ducklings to follow her lead.

It took thirty-one minutes to get all thirty-two planes airborne, as the last plane, *Star Dust*, flown by Lt. "Spider" Webb had last minute problems, delaying the completion of the Group's flight formation by nine minutes. Colonel Gent was not a happy man; they had a rendezvous to make with almost one hundred and thirty B-24s from the other four Groups currently making up the 47th Wing of the 15th Air Force.

Bird had waited patiently for the eight planes of the 718th Squadron to finish their takeoff, for her apprehensively awaiting 719th Squadron would be next. Funny, she thought. I haven't been here twenty-four hours, and yet I already have a feeling of belonging. Comradeship. Fellowship. It was a nice, warm, reassuring sensation. Finally, the last ship of the 718th, *Gidi Gidi Boom Boom* lifted off from the confines of the airstrip. And then a moment later she saw *Sweet Mother,* the first of her patchwork family, lift her nose wheel off and slowly clamber into the sky. She was quickly followed at thirty second intervals by *Sky Bandit, Two Ton Tessie, Consolidated Mess, Dixie Belle, Lonesome, Paper Doll, Dragon Lady,* and bringing up the rear of the squadron, *Hoosier Honey.* Upon drawing even with their squadron parking area, they all looked longingly at the four solitary Liberators remaining behind.

Now there was nothing to do but wait.

"STAN, POP, YOU GUYS are the tallest, get under there and raise the tent pole," commanded Harry as he and Bob attempted to steady two opposing tent wall corners. However, raising over three-hundred square feet of heavy canvas with a spindly twelve-foot wooden pole proved problematic, and soon tent, pole, and two bemused Army officers were all entangled on the muddy, olive blossom–covered ground.

Hysterical laughing erupted from Bob and Harry as they watched the ghostly canvas-covered apparitions of Pop and Stan trying to extricate themselves from their fabric entombment. Laughter can be contagious even in the direst of times, and soon all four were in uncontrollable fits.

While necessity is the mother of invention, it is also the driver of hard work and rewarding accomplishment. Soon the farm boy, business manager, baker, and civil servant turned air warriors had erected their own tent domain after tightening up the last of twenty-eight hemp guy lines.

Admiring their work, Pop suggested that they get their scant belongings from Sheldon and Paul's tent and bring them over. As they went inside the other officers' tent to collect their gear, they realized just how much work they still had to do to make their shell of an abode comfortable, let alone habitable. As they stood admiring the wooden floor, stove, tables, shelves, bunks with mattresses (thin though they were), and even closets, a slight depression fell over them. "Let's go to the mess and get some lunch after dropping our gear off," Pop suggested, trying to get their minds off the seemingly endless task before a general malaise set in.

"Mind if we sit with you guys?" asked Harry after grabbing his tray of difficult to identify, questionably edible foodstuff.

"Nope," answered a tall, well-built young man with sparkling blue eyes peering out from underneath his officer's fifty-mission crush hat. "Andy Widness," he said, extending his hand and giving Harry a firm shake. "Sitting next to me, shoving half a loaf of white bread in his mouth, is Lorin Robinson," he grinned, as Harry extended his hand and the rest of the *Worrybird*'s crew sat down with similar introductions.

"Kind of thin in here, isn't it?" asked Stan as he scrutinized at eye level a glob of gelatinous goo stuck to his fork.

"Yes, it is," Andy answered with a nonchalant shrug as he observed Stan. "With the squadron being down three planes and with nine in the air, there's not much of us left here on base. Over at the corner table is Pat Gentry and Don Lapham. They fly *Patches*, number fifteen, while Lorin and I fly *Our Baby*. And last but not least, Norm Rogers and Bobbie Bennett over there," Andy informed, pointing a spoonful of questionable tapioca pudding at two officers who waved back in greeting, "fly *The Buzzer*."

On cue, the low-pitched thrum of four Pratt and Whitneys being throttled back upon landing pierced the air. "Must be the first of the early returns," Lorin said knowingly.

"Just how many planes usually return early?" asked Pop with concern etched on his face.

"Oh, usually three or four is the norm now," Lorin answered. "Used to be a whole lot worse, believe it or not. On a mission in late February, we had fifteen return early. That was nearly half the planes that had gone up," he said with an exasperated nod of the head. "Boy, I didn't know there were so many ways to get reamed out," he added. "Colonel Gent called all the pilots and squadron crew chiefs together and tore us all new ones, if you know what I mean." All at the table nodded with grim understanding.

"It did the trick, though," Andy said as he pushed his plate away. "The pre-flight mechanical check is done by the book by everyone now, and then some. Simple things, like checking the oxygen system, interphones, flight suit heaters, electrical system, any of which go out, you can't continue. You know, weakest link in the chain." Andy let that thought hang in the air as each flyer contemplated how that maxim applied to their individual station in the plane. A rather simple, seemingly unimportant occurrence such as a malfunctioning flight suit heater could run the risk of turning a plane back. Would an aircraft commander have such antipathy toward one of his own crew that he would let, say, a waist gunner, while protecting the plane, suffer the effects of −40 degree temperatures, let alone in an open window while traveling at 165mph?

By the time they finished their meal, topped off with cups of black coffee, they had heard two more bombers return, with the last two taxiing to a stop nearby, indicating they were planes of the 719th.

"HEY *BUZZER, PATCHES, BABY,* they're back already!" shouted an exuberant *Bird* to the other stay-behind planes as *Two Ton Tessie,* followed shortly by *Lonesome,* pulled up to the caliche hardstands on the edge of the squadron's parking area, three hours after departing.

"Naw, they're just early returns, Shug. They must have some sort of mechanical problems," *Buzzer* drawled in that syrupy vernacular commonly found in Georgia. She and her crew had trained at Chatham Field outside of Savannah, after all. "We'll hear all about it 'cause there goes *Toledo* with the crew chiefs heading out to the planes to talk things over with the pilots, Lieutenants Fergus and Geisel, along with their flight engineers."

In this case, the rumor mill ground to a halt due to *Toledo* remaining planted under *Tessie*'s port wing. If the scuttlebutt baton was passed to the six-by-six truck that picked up the crews, the news didn't reach the other planes, since the truck made a beeline to headquarters for crew debriefing.

Toledo didn't leave the shade of *Tessie*'s wing for another two hours, until his driver received a message on his portable handie talkie radio sending him to the adjacent 718th's parking area. The reason for his departure became evident a few minutes later when, again, the steady approaching drone of harmonized Pratt and Whitneys cut through the still air.

"Hey guys, get a load of the nose art on *Wood's Chopper* taxiing to the 718th!" *Bird* exclaimed, forgetting that this was nothing new to them. Not with the 718th's sixteen or so planes sharing the north end of the runway with them. While the plane was named *Wood's Chopper* after its pilot, Lt. John Wood, and its nose was graced with the monogram, it was the caricature below that caught *Bird*'s now wide eyes. It was far from being "the girl from home," or someone's fantasy pin-up girl. For it depicted a muscular arm holding a blood-dripping executioner's axe in mid-downward stroke. Its intended victim was Japan's Minister of War, Hideki Tojo, with his head cradled in a wooden chopping block. The previous victim's severed head was flying through the air trailing a stream of blood.

"Wow. So does anybody have any idea who the unfortunate souls are getting their heads chopped off?" *Bird* quizzed to anyone listening.

"Unfortunate souls? I don't think so," *Patches* replied indignantly, as her crew chief and mechanics stood under her wing gesturing overhead at her number one engine. "From what I hear, the guy on the block is named Tojo and he's head of Japan's Army. They're another country that we're fighting on the other side of the world. As if the Germans weren't enough," she scoffed.

"And of course, the flying head is Adolph Hitler's. He's head of all this German Nazi stuff that's going down. So, if you want to get mad at somebody when you see one of us go down, or an Me-109 is tearing you apart with its cannon fire, get even with him," *Patches* said as an armorer checked out the radius of motion of her front turret by rotating it and her twin Brownings toward *Wood's Chopper.*

"Oh, I was told about him back in Texas," *Bird* replied as she gazed intently at the torso-less head spewing blood. "Strange that the world could be torn apart by a man with such a funny looking mustache."

(For the delicate reader who might be repulsed by the violent illustration just described, rest assured that by the end of April, *Wood's Chopper's* nose art was no more. Its offending aluminum canvas was wiped clean. A 47th Wing Headquarters inspection team took one look at the nose art and ordered the heads and chopping block painted over, leaving only the arm clutching an executioner's axe. The official reason: *"So as not to offend the enemy."*[1] As if dropping high explosives on their motherland, and trying to blast their planes out of the sky wouldn't, at a minimum, irritate them? Sometimes you just have to shake your head at the thought processes of armchair pilots and headquarters staff.)

The 719th gang knew something was adrift when another headquarters Jeep loaded down with officers tore down the taxiway and proceeded to a skidding, dust-filled stop with its driver's side mirror scraping *Toledo's* own. Soon, the entire ten-man crew was in intense conversation with the newly arrived officers. Obvious frustration, bordering on anger, was apparent by their arm and hand gestures.

Shortly, the same six-by-six pulled up to the *Chopper* within jawing distance of *Toledo,* with the crew throwing their flight equipment into the truck for a trip back to the supply depot. Later, after dropping off *Chopper's* crew the truck returned, lumbered up to *Patches'* port wing and ground to a halt. Quickly the tailgate was dropped, and the crew chief and

---

1. Currier, Donald R. *50 Mission Crush,* pp. 132–133. New York, NY: Pocket Books, 1993.

mechanics disgorged its contents: metal scaffolding. It looked like *Patches* wasn't going anywhere soon as a work platform was slowly erected under her number one engine.

"Hey there *Jimmy*, what's 'cookin'? We saw you gabbing with *Toledo*, so what's the latest?" *Patches* inquired of the GMC-built truck.

"Hey there, *Patches*," *Jimmy* replied in his midwestern twang, something he had picked up at the St. Louis Chevrolet plant where he had been built. "First things first, you aren't going anywhere tomorrow 'cause you're getting a new engine, if you hadn't already noticed," *Jimmy* chuckled.

"Yeah, yeah. Forget about me, what's with the commotion over at the *Chopper*?"

"Oh, right. Well, seems he was using a crazy amount of fuel. Like over 330 gallons an hour. And there was no way he could make it home if they continued. Would have made it to the Adriatic on the way back just to disappear in its waters, never to be found. That's what the pilot, Lt. Samuelson said, just like that," *Jimmy* repeated

"But you know, it's the crazy stuff the crew was telling the debriefing officers that has me worried. Of course, anytime the crew is debriefed at the plane instead of waiting till they get to headquarters, you know something is up," said *Jimmy* as he was moved to make room for the expanding scaffold.

"Of course, it started out as a complete SNAFU with none of the other four groups at the San Prancrazio rendezvous point. That didn't stop Colonel Gent, though. He headed on over the Adriatic with our 32 planes when the other Groups finally caught up with us along with 119 P-38s and 49 P-47 Checkertail escorts."

"So, everyone was feeling pretty good with us in the lead, except the weather kept getting worse. Now, get this," *Jimmy* paused for effect. "Not even a hundred miles into a now totally cloud-covered Yugoslavia, we realized we were alone. Totally. Nothing but us in the blue sky with that impenetrable undercast below. All the other Groups were gone, but most frightening, all of the escorts were gone, too." With that, it seemed like all work, sound, even the breeze, had stopped.

It was what was awaiting the Group's remaining solitary twenty-eight planes that now had the entire Grottaglie airfield in a state of perplexed anxiety. Those sixty-five Flak guns and over two hundred German and Rumanian fighters would have their sights set solely on the few planes of the 449th.

"You should have heard Lt. Samuelson describe his leaving the group. Almost mournful. They had made it to northern Bulgaria, about 170 miles from the IP, when he radioed his box leader, Lt. Morton in *Shack Happy,* that they reluctantly had to turn back. Fortunately for them, they caught up with a dozen or so P-38s over Yugoslavia who escorted them home," *Jimmy* concluded trailing off with concern.

Looking at her chronometer, *Buzzer* calculated that with *Wood's Chopper's* flight time back, and the Group's distance to the bombing IP when he had left, whatever was going to happen already had, and the remnants were currently straggling home.

Now they just had to wait. But not for long.

Less than an hour later, the mournful drone of a single B-24 split the air as it came in from the south for a landing. As it decelerated to the northern end of the runway, it turned off onto the taxiway and headed straight for the 719th parking area, where it took the first of many empty spaces nearest the taxiway.

"Hey guys, it's *Dragon Lady!*" *Bird* exclaimed exuberantly, though her delight was tempered by the plane's evident demeanor and outright look of hostility directed toward *Lonesome* and *Two Ton Tessie,* who were doing their best to ignore the surliness.

After a few other of the Group's planes had landed, *Sweet Mother's* landing gear touched down and soon joined *Dragon Lady* at the other end of the parking area, as if purposely distancing themselves from the four stay-behinds and two early returns.

Perplexed, *Bird* thought maybe they were keeping space open for the five remaining planes to return, which would fill most of the eight open squadron parking spots.

Within the next twenty minutes, plane after plane of the other three squadrons touched down, some not waiting for the previous plane to complete its landing, as if they just couldn't wait to get away from the hell they had escaped.

And then silence. A... long... silence.

Eight of the 719th's parking spots would remain empty.

A suffocating pall soon enveloped the 449th Group, but nowhere as palpable as what had enveloped the 719th Squadron, like a death shroud.

"*Mother, Lady*, are either of you going to tell us what happened to the rest of the gang?" *Tess* desperately pleaded. "We know something terrible happened and that you guys hold *Lonesome* and me responsible based on your looks toward us. But come on guys, you know there was nothing we could do," she said desperately. "I lost both our electrical converters, the main and backup, so I had no 24-volt power. And *Lonesome* over there lost his number three turbo. You know he'd start to struggle to keep up or be left behind for those German vultures. So tell us, what happened?" *Tess* asked again in soft, hushed tones.[2]

Slowly, haltingly, in such a whisper as to make it difficult to hear over the radio, *Dragon Lady* reluctantly began her litany.

"We knew it was going to be rough when we realized we were all alone up there once we crossed the Yugo mountains. I swear none of us heard the MCRB recall code. But boy, the other four Groups and the escorts sure thought they did," *Lady* said with scornful venom creeping into her voice.

---

2. AFHRA folder GP-449-SU-OP-S, 4 April 1944, Narrative Report No. 40. From: Headquarters 449th Bombardment Group (H); April 5, 1944.

"Once we got to the IP and began the bomb run," *Lady* paused, her engines sucking in gulps of air, "guys, I hope we never see Flak like that again. You thought Steyr, Austria was bad; it didn't even come close."

"We'd seen fighters off in the distance ready to pounce, but they weren't going to get anywhere near their own Flak," she continued. "Heavy, intense, and accurate it was. They sure had our flight pegged. As soon as we dropped our bombs, a bright flash off my starboard side caught my eye. All I saw was fiery debris behind *Mother* falling from the sky with a hole in the 'B' box where *Sky Bandit* had been. Gone, just like that. He'd only been with us, what, two months?" No one dared answer.

"Well, when we rallied to the right, that's when all hell broke loose. Colonel Gent in the lead box turned way too sharp. Our box on the left outer edge just couldn't keep up. It was like we were playing a game of Crack the Whip," *Lady* said, envisioning herself on the outer edge of the children's outdoor game. "When the Germans see a weakness, either in machine or man, they exploit it. Those fighters came on in 'cause they saw easy prey. About a hundred of them against our now twenty-seven. Me-109s, 110s, Focke-Wulfs, painted in all sorts of colors. Black, gray, silver, yellow, orange or blue props or cowls. Buzzing around us like someone had kicked a hornet's nest. A regular aerial circus it was, except without the clowns," *Lady* said with a humorless smirk.[3]

"Within just a few minutes those fighters came in head-on and I watched *Paper Doll* just get hammered with cannon fire. Her right wing was all shot up, caught fire, and she rolled onto her back and just augured into Bucharest. Either Lieutenants Garrison and Zimmerman were dead or they just couldn't keep her from flipping over."

---

3. In his April 4, 1944 Mission Report, Group Intelligence Officer, Major Arthur Harvey said of the ensuing firefight: "*Whole show might best be described as an aerial circus.*"

"Another bright flash at my five o'clock caught my eye and I watched *Reluctant Liz* from the 717th explode at her center wing. Must have been her fuel tanks. Just a moment later, her wingman, *Miasis Dragon* went into a flat spin out of control with its number two engine in flames from explosive cannon fire."

"Turning my attention back to my front, I saw that *Dixie Belle* was all over the sky right in front of me like a falling leaf with her number three on fire. At least nine of her crew were able to parachute out."[4]

Lady paused to take a breath before she continued. "All that was left of our 'C' box at that moment was myself, *Consolidated Mess,* and *Hoosier.* That didn't last long, though." At the mention of *Hoosier*'s name, *Bird* felt a cold chill like the frigid thin air found at 24,000 feet course through her. She wasn't sure she wanted to hear what happened next. But she knew that learning the truth, no matter how ugly and painful, was inevitable and necessary.

"The three of us tightened up tight. I mean my left wingtip was almost in *Consolidated*'s waist window we were so tight. *Consolidated*'s crew shot down two Focke-Wulfs, including the one that mortally wounded him. That's when he got hit some more from only twenty-five yards out and I saw fire break out in the nose, which quickly engulfed the flight deck. I could see the flames licking at Lt. Lahr's face. Soon a couple of crewmen jumped out the bomb bay, the bombardier jumped out the nose wheel doors, and a few out the waist windows. It was like rats leaving a sinking ship. I saw about half a dozen chutes blossom open on the wind as I watched *Consolidated* spiral into the Danube riverbank."

"Danube!" exclaimed *Bird* to herself. The mention of that river was a clarion call. "That's the river of death, according to *Hoosier,*" she whispered with foreboding.

---

4. 449th Bomb Group Association. *Book III: Grottaglie And Home,* pp. 209–211. 1989.

"Those enemy aircraft kept up the fight for seventy-five minutes, covering over a hundred and fifty miles. I know the S-2 at briefing said they weren't sure how good the Rumanian fighters would be. Sheesh. I can tell him they were good. Damn good. Experienced. Aggressive. Unrelenting. And I can even say brave. Yeah, that's right," *Lady* responded after hearing some guffaws over the radio. "When they are so close that you can see their eyes over their oxygen mask and they're still steadily firing into you while their plane is getting absolutely ripped apart by our Brownings, yeah, I'd call that brave. Misplaced bravery, but bravery nonetheless." No one dared to counter her argument.

"Well, it was only a matter of time before *Hoosier* and myself, all alone of what remained of our box would be the next to be sacrificed. I called over to *Hoosier* and pleaded that we join Colonel Gent's upper 'A' box, which I was able to do," *Lady* said, though a bit reluctantly, as it appeared she had purposely deserted *Hoosier* to the surrounding German wolfpack.

Bird's antenna certainly picked up on what *Lady* implied and was ready to pounce with the ire of a bucking bronco. But *Lady* beat her to it.

"Now, before any of you bitch about me abandoning *Hoosier*, that's not what I did. From my perch above and slightly in front of him, I was able to shoot down nine of those bastards. That's more than anyone else in the Group. I watched *Slick Chick*, who was right behind us in the 'F' box of the 716th, shoot down seven."[5]

"*Hoosier* was starting his climb to join us when two Me-109s started a head on frontal attack. His gunners took one of them out, but the other kept pouring cannon fire and just raked his front. In no time his front end was ablaze along with his number two and three engines." *Lady* paused to gain her composure, then continued.

---

5. AFHRA folder GP-449-SU-OP-S, 4 April 1944, Enemy Aircraft Encounter Forms, pp. 1145–1224.

"Something then caused him to shoot skyward. I had to crane my top turret to watch him, then he winged over and I saw his bomb bay doors open. Five of his crew fell out the doors before I watched him break in half at the waist windows and proceed to fall to his death, landing with two big splashes in the Danube. I swear those splashes reached a couple thousand feet into the sky," *Lady* finished with wonderment.

With the mentioning of tall splashes, *Bird* remembered *Hoosier*'s prophetic dream of the two-thousand-foot Lake Michigan geysers from his dropped bombs. "Was that just this morning he told me about those?" *Bird* queried herself in puzzlement.

"*Hoosier* was the last to be shot down, though those fighters dogged us into southern Bulgaria before their bingo fuel status recalled them. But boy, did they pay the price. Our Group shot down forty of them with another thirteen probable. Yes, sir, I think you can say we broke the back of the Rumanian Air Force," *Lady* finished, with no conviction in her voice as she and the other forlorn Liberators stared at the eight empty parking pads.

EATING GRUB AT THE officers' mess that evening was a subdued, melancholy affair, with the only words spoken being simple monotone requests such as "pass the salt." Upon returning to their unfinished, therefore unlivable tent, *Worrybird*'s officers had a difficult decision to make.

Staring into their tent at the uninviting wet, dirt floor, Stan spoke first. "It doesn't make any sense to sleep in that when there's a perfectly fine, well-equipped tent waiting for us over yonder," he said pointing in the direction of Zimmerman and Lahr's tent.

Looking up, Pop murmured, "You're right, Stan, but it'll feel all wrong." He finally shrugged and shook his head. "Let's head over there and at least take a look," he said as they quietly vacated their tent and wordlessly walked to one that until so recently was full of gaiety.

Upon entering and standing on the wooden floor which stood well off the moist dirt below, and staring at the mattressed bunks, they all knew they would spend the night in the missing aircrew's tent. No one would remember who was the first to lay their thin blanket on the hard, wood floor, but soon three others joined the first. While *Bird*'s officers would sleep in the missing men's tent, there was no way they could bring themselves to actually occupy their bunks. That would make it final. Giving up hope. Putting a nail in Lahr's and Zimmerman's coffins. Trespassing. No, they'd rather suffer a bad back and restless sleep than do that.

That night the four officers' thoughts were their own. Not a single word would break the air. But most of the thoughts were the same, as they wrote in their diaries that night: *"Boy, I feel low." "These nine men depend on me, am I capable of the job?" "Can't see how a man can get through fifty missions."* In the end, they all came to the same inescapable conclusion. They and their planes were expendable.

Top L-R: Paper Doll; Reluctant Liz; Miasis Dragon; Dixie Belle; Consolidated Mess; Born to Lose (Hoosier); Sky Bandit co-pilot Edward O'Rourke; pilot William Thieme. [449th Bomb Group Association Collection]

The eight remaining Liberators of the 719th sat with their turret guns pointed morosely down. *Sweet Mother* and *Dragon Lady* stood sulking over their bullet and Flak-pierced aluminum skin. It was a sad looking lot of once majestic B-24s. No one paid much attention to the Liberator taxiing up to one of the many vacant parking spots. A quick, furtive glance in the newcomer's direction extinguished the futile hope that he was one of the five missing, miraculously returning. For none of them recognized this plane before, not with *Skipper* proudly drawn on his nose.

The newcomer glanced at the eight planes that he would soon call family. He wasn't impressed. He had never seen such a motley collection of dour looking Liberators.

The sullen atmosphere of the whole Group was contagious, and soon the newcomer was starting to feel rather low himself. With another quick glance at the planes, he stopped to stare at one of them. Something was familiar with the way she sat. "*Worrybird*," the newcomer whispered to himself. "Well, that doesn't mean anything to me," he pondered, as his eyes made their way to the tail assembly. There, noticing and finally recognizing *Worrybird*'s serial number, the newcomer's nose broke out in a wide grin that almost crumpled his aluminum skin.

"Well, I've never seen a group of Liberators as low as quail shit in a wagon rut before. That is until now," was soon heard by all, spoken in a loud, Texan, southern drawl.

"*Texican?*"

YES, THE 449th PAID a heavy price that 4th of April over Rumania. It would be the largest single day loss of the Group during the entire war. Twenty-nine aircrew were killed, including Sheldon Zimmerman, Art Van Arkel, and Adolph (Dolph) Ornstein; twenty-one became prisoners of war, including Charles Lynch and Paul Lahr; seven B-24s were lost, with an additional seventeen damaged, three severely. Twenty-five percent of those engaged had been exterminated.... again.

The psychological toll on the involved and on the non-involved combatants cannot be expressed thoroughly enough, certainly not by someone who never had the honor of serving in any of the various branches of the U.S. Armed Forces. The words of one of the 449th combatants of April 4, 1944 speak for themselves as to the mental anguish suffered that day.

Lieutenant Paul Lahr survived the crash of the *Consolidated Mess* and was captured by Rumanian forces. Paul spent a few weeks in a Cervenia, Rumania hospital recovering from facial burns received when his flight deck erupted in an inferno. The following is a partial transcript of a letter he sent to the Army Air Force following the war concerning three of his fellow crewmen who did not survive: Clinton Wilson of Hartsville, New York, Angelo Bursio of Petaluma, California, and John Sickley of LaSalle, Illinois:

...After we had examined the plane wreckage, I requested to see the graves of our men. So, under guard, I was taken to the town cemetery...The cemetery is small but landscaped beautifully. The Romanian peasants gave our three soldiers a religious burial and put their resting place side by side in line with Romanian soldiers who were killed in combat. Each grave had a cross with a box attachment where the peasants put flowers and burn candles. At the time I saw the graves, each one had some flowers on them.

.... When I was taken inside the small cemetery I was asked if I cared to be alone before the three graves, and for some reason I can't quite explain I did. So I replied that I would appreciate a few minutes. Everyone, civilians and soldiers, all left the cemetery and I was alone at the graves. For the first time in my life I felt helpless. I couldn't do or say anything. Then I prayed, prayed with sincerity only such an experience could withdraw from a man. After praying I seemed to be unconscious of anyone and everything except the three lads whom I couldn't see, and myself. But I spoke to each of them; seems odd now, but I did. The phrases were useless, but I meant them for I felt I was speaking for the rest of the crew, our friends, our country, and yes, their parents. I said things like "Sorry, great job, thanks, will always remember...

and a few others I can't recall now. After what seemed like hours I felt a hand on my shoulder and a soldier motioned we were to leave. Even then I said "So long, fellas." Gosh, a turkish bath could never make me sweat the way I had those last few minutes...[6]

No wonder Stan had written about Sheldon Zimmerman and Paul Lahr, *"They seemed like such swell fellas."*[7]

---

6. Lt. Lahr's complete letter may be found in the 42-52159 MACR. See https://www.fold3.com/

7. Stanley, William G. Personal WWII Diary: April 4, 1944 entry. Author's collection.

13

Stanley, What The Hell Are You Doing Here?

Back Alley Of Grottaglie, Italy
April 25, 1944   14:00 hrs.

"GUYS, THERE IS NO WAY we're going to find a store in this maze. I'm not sure I even know how to get back to base," Bob said as he stopped to lift his right foot and, with a disgusted look on his face, attempted to scrape off the clinging, odiferous street filth on a nearby cobblestone curb.

"Some navigator you are," Harry teased as he deftly sidestepped Bob's fragrant street nemesis, only to find himself toe-to-toe with a broken wooden crate of unidentifiable, liquified vegetable matter.

"Welcome to Grottaglie!" Pop exclaimed as a wave of fetor-induced nausea wafted over him. Three-story, plastered stone buildings towered over each side of the narrow, refuse-strewn alleyways and streets. The stagnant, fetid air remained at street level, much to the discomfort of the four Yanks.

After walking ahead to the corner of the next six-foot-wide alley, Stan was suddenly approached, practically accosted by, a small runt of a lad, maybe all of seven years old. He had blond hair, a dirt-smudged face, and was barefoot, missing front teeth and dressed in not much more than rags.

"Gotta cigarette, Joe? Chewing gum, Joe?" the young lad asked, apparently depleting his entire English repertoire. However, in this street urchin, Stan saw opportunity.

Mimicking a sweeping motion that would have made Marcel Marceau proud, Stan asked the kid, while pulling a wad of Allied Military Lira notes out of his pocket, "Broom?"

"*Si, una scopa!*" exclaimed the grinning, wide-eyed child when he realized that easy money could be made off these Yanks. "Broom? Come on, Joe." And with that, they were off.[1]

"Stan, where the hell is this kid taking us?" Pop asked as they hurried after the running runt, who kept looking back over his shoulder, encouraging them on with windmilling arm motions.

"Have faith in our little Italian guide, Pop," Stan yelled over his shoulder, though he himself was beginning to wonder after turning yet another corner in the tortuous street labyrinth and watching the boy enter the first floor of what appeared to be a residence. "Did he just bring us to his home?" Stan wondered as he and the rest of the gang entered the open wooden doorway.

"Broom, Joe!" exclaimed their grinning guide as he pointed to a tall wooden barrel with corn broom heads barely peeking over the rim.

After his eyes adjusted to the darkened house interior, Stan realized this was no house, it was a store! A store that would have done Cannon's Dry Goods proud, back home in Cunningham, Kansas. Not only did they find the much-needed broom, but lamp wicks to illuminate their late evening

---

1. Stanley, William G. Personal WWII Diary: April 25, 1944 entry. Author's collection.

diary entries, ceramic water jugs, cups, and a large clay pottery bowl. And all of this purchased for two packs of Lucky Strikes, costing the Americans ten whole cents. However, on the Italian black market, the street urchin and store owner would get many times that amount.

"You know what, guys?" Stan said as he observed their grinning street guide leaning in a corner smoking the remnants of a cigarette butt. "Except for the cigarette, that kid reminds me of my youngest brother, Norman. Of course, if Norman was smoking a cigarette, he'd be bent over retching his guts out." Stan chuckled as he remembered himself having the same reaction after his first and last cheekful of chewing tobacco, while hiding in their family's barn.

"Hey, Stan. You've got a way with 'Norman' over there," Harry quipped as he nodded toward their smoking guide, who at the moment was flicking the remains of the butt out an open window. "Ask him where there's a grocery store. We need to get some real eggs. I've about had it with that powdered stuff."

Grinning in anticipation of the challenge, Stan pointed at the now alerted lad, walked over to their newly acquired pottery bowl, and proceeded to mimic cracking an egg. "Eggs," Stan said as he again pulled a few Lira notes out of his pocket.

"*Uova*, eggs for Joe?" questioned the surrogate Norman. "Come with me, Joe," the tyke instructed after the crew had all nodded in the affirmative.

Upon exiting the store, the ersatz Norman rattled off a litany of Italian down an empty alleyway. Within a few moments, four other young Italian ragamuffins appeared and offered to carry the recently purchased goods.

"Come, Joe. Eggs." And with that, they were off again, not only with a guide, but now with several rambunctious porters in tow who jostled over the privilege and the possibility of finagling a Lira or two by carrying the recently purchased items.

By the time Norman guided them into a small food market, their troupe of dirty, barefoot, young street urchins had grown to an army of twenty. And what a mélange of "recruits." While most of the kids were wearing ragged, loose-fitting cotton pants and shirts, once having been a shade of white, more than a few were wearing various pieces of military uniforms from every conceivable army: German, Italian, British, and American. This pint-sized army was apparently comprised of allies of street survival.

After the purchase of dozens of eggs, a box of oranges, and other sundry foodstuffs, Pop thought it would be a good idea to tip their well deserving "army" before they started back to base. Bad idea.

Pulling a wad of one-Lira notes out of his pocket, Pop began distributing the much-anticipated earnings to the eagerly awaiting lads. However, even before he had finished unrolling the wad, the verbal street telegraph had alerted all youngsters in a five-block radius that easy money was to be had at the market. Even with a depreciated, inflation-ravaged value of one U.S. cent per Lira, the kids wildly accepted their payment as if they were gold Spanish doubloons. With grinning faces, wide, appreciative eyes, and shouts of *grazie* the army of urchins brandished their pay. By the time Pop had depleted his Lira stash, their ranks had grown to a raucous fifty.

"Wow. What are we going to do with this bunch now?" asked a bewildered but amused Bob as he and the rest of the crew observed their small ragtag army of boisterous, recruits milling about, spilling down the crowded alleyway.

With a spreading grin and a twinkle in his hazel eyes, Stan announced to his tentmates that he had another plan.

"What else do you do with raw recruits?" he asked his fellow officers. "You drill and march them in cadence and instruct them. Now watch this," he said as he meandered his way to the front of the mob after grabbing a crate of oranges from one of the porter kids.

"Attention!" Stan barked at the top of his lungs as he stretched his six-foot frame standing atop the wooden crate.

"I said, attention!" Stan barked loudly again which quieted the boisterous bunch to a low questioning murmur.

Then, stepping off the orange crate, Stan started an exaggerated march-in-place motion while barking "left, right, left, right, left, right ..." while nodding to Pop, Bob, and Harry to do the same.

As they spread themselves along the side of the mob, they too started to march in place to Stan's repetitive orders, instructing the raw recruits how performing in time with the simple cadence was properly done. The ragtag army of ragamuffins were soon stepping in time while cheerfully shouting "left, right, left, right ..." which almost doubled their English vocabulary.

It was now time for Stan to take it up a notch.

Handing the crate of oranges to the largest "soldier," Stan began the English lesson instructions in earnest. And it wasn't with a simple U.S. Army march cadence. He began singing in a fine tenor voice, in time with his marching:

You are my sunshine, my only sunshine
You make me happy when skies are gray
You'll never know, dear, how much I love you
Please don't take my sunshine away.

Stan sang, motioning to the others to join in.

The other night, dear, as I lay sleeping
I dreamed I held you in my arms
When I awoke, dear, I was mistaken
So I hung my head and I cried.

"All right, the chorus again," Stan shouted, keeping time by mimicking an exaggerated baton-wielding director.

You are my sunshine, my only sunshine
You make me happy when skies are gray
You'll never know, dear, how much I love you

Please don't take my sunshine away.

Slowly but surely, the army of youths caught on to the lyrics, though heavily tilted with an Italian accent. They soon were marching and singing themselves through the deep, meandering alleyways of Grottaglie, bringing much needed laughter to both the American servicemen, themselves, and to the beaten down, war weary populous of the town. As with most wars, of any era, in any country, on every continent, the innocent civilian population suffered from the loss of their youthful men, their husbands, sons, brothers, and fathers, leaving behind the elderly, the infirm, young mothers, and children to fend for themselves, to survive. Laughter was a rare commodity in war.

Once they got out of town, Stan thought it was time to change it up. These kids might be hungry, poor, and dirty, but they sure picked up *You Are My Sunshine* quick enough, he figured. Time for something a bit more challenging. Besides, they had more than a mile to get to base.

And with that thought, Stan broke in with a different tune, once again catching the recruits off guard. But within a few verses, they too were singing along, though Bing Crosby and the Andrews Sisters didn't have a thing to worry about. By the time the ragtag army entered the 719th's cluster of tents, and finished the last refrain of *Pistol Packin Mama*, they knew one thing for sure; they wouldn't want to tangle with a woman from Texas. They all toted guns!

"Slept late today and went to town in the afternoon. What a time! ... Really cute kids but so dirty. They carried all the stuff we bought and sang 'Pistol Packing Mama' and 'You are my sunshine.' Really had the time of our lives. One little kid was really cute, a little runt with two front teeth out,

and smoked cigarette butts, but he still reminded me of Norman. What a time. Scheduled to fly tomorrow. [2]

With that day's final diary line written, Stan laid his U.S. Army Service Writing Tablet and pencil on the small table, and with a cupped hand blew out the lamp, sending the tent into darkness, save for the remnants of evening twilight extinguishing itself under the horizon. The next morning's mission wakeup call would come early enough.

Settling himself under his covers, jealously listening to the soft snores of one of his tentmates, Stan's mind began to race, and he knew sleep was going to be elusive and a long time in coming.

"What a month," he thought to himself. "Today had to have been one of the most enjoyable in my life, and yet it was only ten days ago that I experienced one of the most terrifying in that same short life," Stan reflected, as his mind began to involuntarily recount the events of April 15th, his first mission....

...THE WHINE OF THE JEEP engine and the crunching of the caliche gravel under its knobby bar grip tires alerted Stan that they were about to get their 04:30 wakeup call. Not that he needed it. He wasn't sure if he had ever fallen asleep, not with his wandering, nonstop mind alerting him to every conceivable thing that could possibly go wrong this day. His first mission. Something he had been dreading and wishing for at the same time. The incongruousness of his life was beginning to dawn on him. "My God. What's it going to be like to complete fifty missions?" With effort, Stan decided to try and not think about it. One day at a time.

---

2. Ibid.

"Wake up, sirs! It's 04:30," was soon heard filtering through the tent flaps from the unfortunate corporal whose thankless task it was to alert the squadron's seven to nine crews of the pending day's mission.

After dressing, a cold-water shave, and whore bath out of their Flak helmets, followed by an unappetizing breakfast of powdered eggs, fried Spam, and black coffee, it was time to make their way to the headquarters building for the mission briefing and to face the music. A musical performance he'd rather not be a part of.

With flashlights in hand, walking through their parked planes, which were having their final mission prep performed, each man's thoughts were his own. While Pop was concerned about his first mission performance as commander of not only the *Worrybird* but of the nine men entrusted to him, Stan was praying that he wouldn't freeze on the bomb run and screw it up, thereby disappointing the rest of the crew.

After entering the headquarters building, Stan peered at the other 151 men seated in the briefing room, consisting of the officers of the 38 planes involved in the day's mission. "What the hell?" he thought, as he swore he saw some men dozing off, trying to catch a few winks. He then observed more than a few men fidgeting with nervousness or jackhammering one of their legs on the stone floor. He glanced askew at his own right leg performing the same solo dance and placed his hand on his knee to stop the motion, lest someone think he was nervous. "Ugh, I think that Spam may come back up," he thought as he tried to remain outwardly calm. What he saw next almost caused him to immediately upchuck his entire breakfast on the floor.

As Captain Burr Tarrant uncovered the large wall map of southern Europe, all eyes anxiously traced the red yarn stretching northeast from Grottaglie across the Adriatic Sea, Yugoslavia, most of Rumania, and stopping 525 miles distant, at a pushpin innocuously marking the terminus of the day's mission: Bucharest.

It had only been eleven days since the successful April 4th bombing of the same marshaling yards, resulting in the destruction of 1,460 railroad cars, numerous locomotives, repair shops, switch yards, and miles of track. But oh, at what a cost! It still hurt to remember the seven planes lost with the 71 souls aboard. Now they were headed back to finish the job and to obliterate any repairs the efficient, industrious Germans and Rumanians had completed.[3]

"Left waist to pilot," was heard over the interphone two hours after *Bird*'s 08:40 takeoff as the Yugoslavian coast was appearing 13,000 feet below through increasing cloud cover.

"Go ahead, Joe," replied Pop, surprised to hear from one of the crew so soon in the flight, hoping he wouldn't be reporting something amiss or a malfunction.

"I just observed Lieutenant Fergus's plane, number ten, open its bomb bay doors and drop four bombs, sir," informed Joe Fox.

Pop immediately glanced out his small sliding window to the plane at the back of the box of six Liberators off his port wing, catching number ten's bomb doors finishing their rolling down closing motion.

"He's shedding some weight. Must be having some sort of engine problem and is struggling to keep up," Pop said to Harry, situated in the right, co-pilot seat, and Stan, who was standing behind them on the flight deck. "Bet he wishes he was back in *Two Ton Tessie* instead of trying out *Dragon Lady #2's* replacement." *Dragon Lady #2*, one of the two survivors of the squadron's disastrous April 4th Bucharest mission, had been shot down over Wiener-Neustadt, Austria three days earlier. Her replacement was so new that the crew hadn't decided upon its name, therefore the nose was unadorned with a namesake depiction.

"Two thousand pounds less to keep in the air can't but help them stay aloft," Stan anxiously remarked, hoping his first bomb release wouldn't be

---

3. AFHRA folder GP-449-SU-OP-S, 15 April 1944. Mission #45. Capt. Burr Tarrant Mission Statement.

as useless, wasteful or downright impotent as dropping them harmlessly into an innocent sea.

A few minutes later, Joe again was heard calling Pop over the interphone, "Left waist to pilot. Number ten is falling away from the formation. It looks like he's heading back, but I haven't seen any of our P-38s yet," he said with obvious concern in his voice, discerned even through the tinny, staticky headphones.

"Thanks, Joe. Fergus will probably pass our escorts in a few minutes. They're supposed to rendezvous with us at 10:50. He'll be OK by himself on the way back," Pop replied, trying to alleviate some of Joe's and the rest of the crew's first-mission jitters that were permeating through the interphone. Lieutenant Fergus would be the last of six early returns, leaving thirty-two B-24s to complete the mission.

Forty minutes later, Stan found himself crawling up into his bombardier position at the extreme front of *Bird*'s nose, underneath the front gun turret. Knowing he was staring through two-inch-thick armored plexiglass didn't relieve him of his fear-induced sweat and the feeling he was hanging out in full view of the German Flak batteries and fighter planes with a target beacon on his chest. He also knew from the scuttlebutt that the bombardier position was one of the most dangerous, after the waist gunners, of the ten positions in not only the B-24 but the B-17 heavy bomber as well.[4]

The view that greeted Stan out of his armored greenhouse was not only breathtakingly beautiful but, surprisingly, disappointing. Beautiful in that he was being embraced by the surrounding dark blue skies at 22,000 feet, highlighted with the noon sun occasionally glittering off the 112 B-24s of the 304th Bomb Wing ten minutes ahead of them. Stan felt relief in the fact that a few thousand feet below them was an impenetrable 10/10

---

4. https://95thbg.com/cms/2021/11/20/95thnbspbomb-group-casualties-analysis

cloud cover that would prevent the 90 German Flak guns from visually locating and tracking them. This, however, was also disappointing since that same cloud cover would prevent him from identifying the target, or even Bucharest itself, through his Sperry bombsight.

Fortunately for the 450 B-24s over Bucharest, this mission would be historic, in that it would be their first bombing mission without using bombsights to adjust the planes' position on the bomb run, and to calculate when precisely to release the bombs. Today, *Honey On The Moon*, leading the 32 planes of the 449th, carried the first ground attack radar navigation system, known as Pathfinder, or "Mickey," in its belly turret. Theoretically, at least, they didn't have to worry about cloud or smokescreens inhibiting their view of the target. All Stan had to do was synchronize for rate, adjusting for the flight time distance from the lead plane to the *Bird*, and toggle the bombs away when he saw the leader's bombs drop.

Flipping down the red, hinged aluminum bomb release cover away from the toggle switch with a trembling hand, Stan waited impatiently for the appearance of falling 500-pound bombs from *Honey*. "*God, I'm as jumpy as a jackrabbit*," he whispered to himself, as sweat pooled inside his Flak suit, though the air inside the *Bird* was a cool −30 degrees Fahrenheit. [5] And then he saw them: ten dark green, finned bombs silently and blindly falling from *Honey*, stark against the dark blue sky, immediately followed by 269 others. "Bombs away, closing bomb doors," Stan announced a few seconds later over the interphone, letting Pop know that their ten had been added to the others as they disappeared through the cloud cover, and that it was prudent to follow the planes rallying to the right and to "get the hell out of Dodge," as they said in Kansas.

And then it hit. Whistling up through the cloud cover on a reverse-course trajectory of the just-released bombs, came the 88, 105, and

---

5. Stanley, William G. Personal WWII Diary: April 15, 1944 entry. Author's collection.

even a few 128mm exploding Flak shells. While the Germans had been late in developing and using tactical radar, they had quickly caught up to the Allies and were now using their Würzburg-Riese Flak control radar to "cut through the clouds." The Allied air forces couldn't hide anymore.

"God almighty, save me from this," was but the first of many prayers Stan and the rest of the virgin crew recited between themselves and their God. Burrowed down in his Flak suit and trying to expose as little of his face as possible under his helmet, Stan watched the exploding Flak clouds blossoming around them and paradoxically thought they reminded him of his mom's hollyhock flowers. He wouldn't know until after they landed that veteran fliers would call the Flak they encountered slight and inaccurate in their post-mission debriefings.

And then it was over. Like someone had turned off a switch. Just the steady, reassuring drone of the Pratt and Whitneys filling the air. No more Flak, just a few German fighters seen keeping their distance from the 25 escorting P-38s now surrounding the formation, with cobalt blue skies and a southwesterly heading of 242° back to Grottaglie. Prayers had been answered and life was good. "I have survived," thought Stan as he whispered a thank you.

"Left waist to bombardier," was soon heard over the interphone, rudely interrupting everyone's silent post–bomb run reverie. Joe Fox was having a busy day.

"Go ahead, Joe," replied Stan as he tried to stretch some feeling back into his previously scrunched body.

"Hate to tell you this, but we have three live bombs still in the bomb racks. Two in the left back rack and one in the right front," Joe replied. As the plane's assistant armorer, Joe maintained the guns and the bomb racks, and helped Stan arm the bombs before the run. Needless to say, it wasn't a good thing to have live 500-pound bombs hanging precariously in the racks with the bomb doors closed.

"Well damn," Stan responded, breaking radio discipline protocols. Glancing up at his overhead panel, there indeed were lit bomb indicator lights, something he had failed to notice during the tension of the moment. "I'll attempt to salvo them again. Opening bomb doors," he announced as he turned the bomb door main control valve, causing the four doors to roll open.

"Salvoing bombs," Stan said as he again flipped down the safety cover and toggled the bomb release switch. "Bombs drop, Joe?" he asked hopefully, although he knew they hadn't since his panel was still lit up like a Christmas tree.

"That's a negative, sir," Joe replied. "They're still held by the shackles. I recommend reducing altitude to warm the release mechanisms. They're known to freeze up, preventing bombs from releasing. At least that's what I was told," he added.

"Pilot to bombardier," Pop announced, breaking into the conversation. "Once we get out of Yugoslavia, I'll bring us down to 10,000 feet over the Adriatic to warm the bomb bay up and also to get us off oxygen. You know, Stan," Pop said with a trace of concern in his voice, "there's no way we can land with those bombs barely hanging in there," letting Stan know that one way or another those eggs had to drop, and it was up to him as bombardier and chief armorer to get it done.

"Golly Ned, Pop! Why not put a little pressure on me?" Stan thought to himself, though in truth, he was mostly scared at the thought of personal failure if he didn't have the ability to get the job done. "I'll get them to drop, Pop. Let me know when we've reached 10,000 feet," he responded with more optimism in his voice than he felt.

Two and a half hours later, Stan stood at the front of the bomb bay staring at the noses of the three culprits that had ruined what should have been a joyous, exhilarating, successful return trip. Further toggling had failed to salvo the stubborn bombs, even after warming up to the seemingly tropical 25° air found at 10,000 feet. He then noticed that Joe had reinserted the safety pins into the bombs' fuse-arming pinwheels. "Safety first," Stan sarcastically joked, though no one could hear him even if they had tried over the hurricane-like gale roaring through the open bomb doors and droning engines less than ten feet away.

Stepping onto the nine-inch-wide catwalk, Stan positioned himself opposite the single bomb hanging at waist level immediately to his left and gave it a hearty push. Nothing. Not even a budge. "This thing is acting like it's welded to the plane," he fumed. Time for more drastic measures. With both hands, grabbing hold of a structural cross member above his head, Stan leaned back, raised his bent right leg and gave it an angry, lost-his-temper kick. And that's all it took. As it slid down the bomb rack rails, Stan kept pressure on it with his foot by following through with a kick that would have made his high school football coach proud. Giving Joe, who had been watching from the opposite side, a thumbs up, the initial success was passed through to Pop over Joe's interphone.

Eyeing the gaping 19-foot span of the bomb bay toward the remaining two bombs, Stan decided that it would be best if he didn't look down before crossing. It's not that he was afraid of heights, for he had climbed the family's windmill many a time. It's just that falling 30 feet to the hard-packed Kansas soil was one thing, maybe breaking a few bones at worst. Falling 10,000 feet to the just-as-hard waters of the Adriatic was another. There was no room to wear a parachute between the bomb racks, and there was no such thing as a safety line on a B-24.

Putting one foot in front of the other, Stan found himself reluctantly having to look down to make sure his five-inch-wide, A-6 insulated flying boots were centered on the ridiculously narrow steel catwalk. He felt like a clumsy circus acrobat walking a tightrope, with one difference: they had a safety net beneath them. To make matters worse, the afternoon sun was starting to broil the atmosphere, causing rising thermals to occasionally rock the ship, though Pop was doing his damnedest to keep her steady.

Finally reaching the other end of the bomb bay, Stan repeated his previous, successful release method on the bottom bomb, and it too slid out of its shackles and disappeared beneath the plane. "Well, that was easy," Stan said in surprise. That left just one more. Glancing at it, Stan instantly knew he had a problem. "This one's going to be a bitch," he said matter-of-factly.

Staring at the bomb was easy since it was at eye level. There was no way he could do what he had done previously and kick that high. He'd have to have the dexterity of a can-can girl to be able to get at it with his feet. Before he had even completed questioning himself as to how he was going to accomplish this seemingly impossible task, he knew the answer, and he didn't like it. But he had no choice. He had tried to pry the bomb out from its clinging shackle with a screwdriver, to no avail. He was out of options.

Taking a deep breath, Stan grabbed the overhead cross member with both hands, and as if he was on playground monkey bars, pulled his torso up, bent his knees until his back was parallel to the open bomb floor, and kicked up and out at the offending 500-pound cylinder of TriNitro-Toluene. And nothing. Again with the aerial kick and, as before... nothing.

Bent over, leaning against the bomb racks, buffeted by the bone-chilling wind, panting hard due to the low oxygen levels, his insulated flight suit drenched with cold sweat from exertion, Stan finally lost his temper. Not a hit-your-thumb-with-the-hammer-type of lost temper, but a real vein-popping, clenched teeth, terror-eyed temper. The accumulation of excessive adrenaline and cortisol stress hormones in his bloodstream, having witnessed friends die, being 6,000 miles from home, not having received a single letter in over 45 days, and putting his 20-year-young life on hold, finally all came to a heavy boil.

Straightening up, grabbing hold of the overhead handhold, Stan swung up again and, focusing all of his built-up stress, anxieties, and rage into his coiled legs, kicked the bomb one last time out of its clenching shackles, sending it into a long freefall into the depths of the waiting Adriatic.

Staring down at the blue sea far below him, trying to get his heart rate and breathing back under control, Stan screamed into the unrelenting, unresponsive gale: "*Stanley! What the hell are you doing here?*" A question he was unable to answer at that moment, and the roaring silence of the wind offered no clues.[6]

Now, ten days later, lying in bed, Stan still hadn't totally answered that gnawing, unending question. It had now been almost two full months since he had heard anything from home, or anybody for that matter. That would certainly have helped to quell his anxieties and fears before and during the missions. "I've got to get some sleep; briefing is at 04:30," Stan told himself as he started to slip into the ether that lies between consciousness and dreams. Finally, his last image of the night before succumbing was of home, as he admired his mother's flower garden full of blossoming hollyhock flowers.

---

6. Stanley, William G. WWII oral remembrances with family.

14

SEEING THE ELEPHANT

719TH SQUADRON AIRCRAFT PARKING AREA, APRIL 26, 1944, 03:17 HRS.

WHILE STAN WAS ATTEMPTING to finish off the day through sleep, *Bird* and *Skipper*'s day would never end and would roll right on through the night as they got ready for the next morning's mission.

"Frag bombs, damn, I hate those things," *Skipper* said as he watched with discerning eyes as armorers unloaded clusters of the obese 20-pound hand grenades off the deuce-and-a-half truck that had pulled up to his open bomb bay doors.

"Relax, *Texican*, er, I mean, *Skipper*," *Bird* said, quickly correcting herself. "Sorry 'bout that," she said sheepishly. "I'll get used to your new name one of these days. Must be hitting an airfield tomorrow based on those clusters of frags," she added, hoping that by quickly changing the subject, *Skipper* wouldn't have noticed the slip.

Skipper appeared to have missed the slight because his mind was elsewhere in both place and time. Two weeks earlier, he had been on his first mission, April 12th, loaded with clusters of larger 100-pound fragmentation bombs to be dropped on the Wiener-Neustadt aircraft assembly plant, Messerschmitt's largest Me-109 factory. Even after being bombed four times prior, it was still producing fifteen of those terror-inflicting fighters per day to help fill the depleted ranks of the German Luftwaffe.[1]

"Sorry there, *Libby*, er, I mean, *Bird*," *Skipper* said with a smirk, hidden only by the high beam headlights of the offloading deuce-and-a-half, blinding *Bird*'s vision as it pulled up to her doors. "I was having a flashback to my first mission after noticing those bomb clusters. You know, that was a cruel trick having a couple of your magnetos go out at the last minute so I had to replace you," *Skipper* said in jest. Or so he thought.

"Now, you hold on there, *Skipper*," replied *Bird* indignantly, spitting out a few drops of engine oil from her number four cowling. "You just ask Sergeant Lambertz, my crew chief, if you think I was shirking. You know I'd take a Flak burst for you or anyone else in the squadron," *Bird* passionately responded, now with her feelings deeply hurt.

"Whoa, girl. Don't get all pouty on me," *Skipper* replied, realizing he had gone too far this time teasing her, and he had to make amends quick. He had watched squadron plane tempers flaring this month in the parking area and on the tarmac. Twenty-four planes out of sixty-four in the 449th Group had been lost so far in April, eight of them from the 719th Squadron's sixteen. Fortunately, once in the air, perceived grievances were left behind back on the ground, and it was all business as they pulled together to survive the mission. After all, their crews needed every bit of help they could get.

"Hey *Bird*," *Skipper* called out, with no response except for the sudden hum of *Bird*'s electrical system as groundcrew hooked her up to the ground power unit. "*Libby*," he continued in a softer, affectionate tone,

---

1. https://15thaf.org/55th_BW/460th_BG/Stories/PDFs/Wiener%20Neusta
dter%20Flugzeugwerke.pdf

"I can be a loud-mouthed Texan, a braggart and a jerk sometimes. Don't I know it. But I didn't mean what I said to you. You mean too much to me, and, well," *Skipper* struggled, trying finally to put into words what he had felt for a long time coming, "I care for you, gosh darn it!" he reluctantly yelled through the pre-flight maelstrom.

Even over *Buzzer*'s engines coughing into life for its pre-mission warmup, *Bird* heard those words for which she had been hoping and waiting. She thought there had been more than combat zone camaraderie between them. With the jesting, the occasional wink and nod, the pangs that ran through her when either of them was left behind on a mission, watching the other take off fully loaded, possibly never to return. "Braggart, huh?" *Bird* coyly remarked as the armorers filled her bay with bomb clusters.

"Hey, it's not easy for the best Liberator in the group to admit he has shortcomings," *Skipper* playfully responded with relief, heavy on the Texan drawl. *Bird*'s front and tail gun turrets rolled in response as the gun armorers tested their rotational movements.

"Though seriously, *Bird*," *Skipper* said in a heavy tone as a fuel truck pulled up to his starboard wing to top off his tanks, "it was the sudden nature of being thrown into battle with absolutely no warning whatsoever that put a burr under my saddle.

"Sure, I had been flying almost since the day I got here. But that was practice formation flying in friendly skies with Lt. Liddycoat and his familiar hands at my controls. Boy, I'm still not used to that, not with our wings almost touching," *Skipper* said, though with fond memories of flying with *Bird* on one side and Lt. Warren Rustad in *Nancy Jane* on the other.

But there were no fond memories of his first mission. Within an hour and a half, *Skipper* had come under moderate but accurate Flak for the first time after penetrating only 30 miles into Yugoslavia. Cringing at every blossoming explosion, he just waited for the painful, jagged tears to appear in his wings or fuselage. While most planes, including *Skipper*, survived unharmed, *Veni-Vidi-Vici,* located in the back "C" element of the formation had his left-wing gas cell and lines ripped open. Fortunately for the crew and *Veni,* the wing tanks didn't explode and they were able to turn back to base. That wouldn't be the last time the group would be incomprehensibly led over known Flak positions, either enroute or on the return.

Two hours later, *Skipper* approached the Initial Point with virgin trepidation, even with P-38 Lightnings and P-47 Thunderbolts escorting them. At least for the moment.

"I had the strangest mixed emotions over the target," *Skipper* continued. "I was proud that I was flying right wingman to Colonel Swan, leading in *Giddi Giddi Boom Boom* at the front of the group. And I was scared to death, I don't mind telling you, because, again, I was at the very front. I swear I thought the Flak and enemy fighters were all aiming and coming just for me," he recalled with a shudder. "It was good to see *Two Ton Tessie, Lonesome,* and *Dragon Lady* behind me in our box, though; made me feel not so alone, like we were in this together."

"But then the strangest thing happened that I just haven't quite figured out," *Skipper* pondered. "I caught *Giddi Giddi*'s bomb doors opening as we approached the IP when all of a sudden I thought I saw her disintegrate into thousands of pieces right before my very eyes. I swear I did," a perplexed *Skipper* swore. "But a few seconds later, there she was! Then I realized some of the crew had thrown thousands of bright, shiny, what appeared to be strips of metal out the bomb doors and waist windows. Just strange, I tell ya. I've seen it on other missions since, too," *Skipper* said, remembering almost ingesting some in his air intake over Sofia, Bulgaria as he was flying in the lower "C" element.

"Window—that's what they call it," *Bird* replied, relishing in the moment at being able to tell *Skipper* something new for once.

"Window? What's that you say?" *Skipper* replied, not being sure if he heard correctly as they were starting up his number three engine.

"Yep, you heard right. Window. Invented and named by the Brits. It's thousands of strips of aluminum that the lead ships in the "A" element throw out after reaching the IP. They drift down in a cloud and somehow are supposed to confuse the German's Flak directional control radar. At least that's what *Toledo* told me," *Bird* finished proudly, feeling like a student who had just perfectly recited a difficult mathematical theorem to her professor.

"*Toledo*! That clinking, clanking, clattering collection of caliginous junk?" *Skipper* yelled indignantly. He had been waiting for the perfect moment to use his favorite line from the *Wizard of Oz*, which he caught pieces of on a makeshift USO outdoor movie screen just a few nights before. Now had been that moment.

"He doesn't know what he's talking about because that Window crap didn't help *Dragon Lady,* now did it?" *Skipper* spat. "For right after we rallied to the left, all hell broke loose with heavy, intense, and, by God, accurate Flak. One of those exploded right underneath *Lady*'s number four engine and another right under her port wing. Remember, she was only a hundred feet behind me so I felt the concussion waves hit my tail. She feathered her number four and started spewing oil all over her port wing. God, she was a mess. It was only a matter of time for her to start losing altitude and speed. And that's when she was jumped," *Skipper* yelled as his number three was revved to 2,400 rpm.

"Let me tell you, something needs to change with our so-called fighter escort coverage," *Skipper* continued, feeling his oil temperature rising. "While the P-38s were leaving us because they'd reached their fuel limits, the darn P-47's that had just arrived were drawn off by a group of German fighters. Man, they took that bait hook, line, and sinker. Just left us all alone to the fifty remaining fighters."

"Those fighters saw *Lady* losing altitude and they took after her like a pack of coon dogs chasing a tired coon up a tree. I heard that *Lady* got five of those bastards before she went down though. I wish she had gotten more 'cause a wave of twelve came out of the sun flying through the formation with guns and cannons blazing a few minutes later."

"Now, I don't know if it was because *Shasta Shack* was the only silver ship in the formation, and that sparkly gem was too much for those fighters to ignore, or what.[2] But her number two engine caught a bunch of cannon fire and exploded in flames, sending her into a spin from which she never recovered. That bright, shiny aluminum is fancy all right, but I'd hate to be the only one in the crowd with no clothes on. Say," *Skipper* paused, cocking his front turret, "Remember when we were dreading the paint booth 'cause they were going to cover our beautiful gleaming aluminum skin? We were such virgins. Anyhow, *Nancy Jane* and I flew in with her just a short week ago, too. If I remember correctly, didn't she replace your friend *Hoosier*?" *Skipper* paused in reflection.

Unknown to *Skipper*, one more Liberator, *Blind Date*, was also shot down during that aggressive pass-through attack. Being at the Tail-end Charlie position, and a member of a different squadron, *Skipper* never saw or heard it happen.

With the sudden mention of *Hoosier*, *Bird* felt a momentary pulse of melancholy course through her. Either that or it was the high-pressure hydraulic fluid now flowing through her lines as the ground crew turned on her auxiliary pressure pump.

"Yeah, *Shasta Shack* replaced *Hoosier* just last week, believe it or not. And unlike in craps, it sure doesn't pay to have number eleven as a combat number around here," *Bird* said, referring to a winning "natural" roll of eleven in the popular craps game being played on the base. In turn, *Hoosier* had replaced the previous number eleven, *Battlin Betty Ann*, lost in the Atlas Mountains in December.

---

2. Shepherd, D. William. *Of Men and Wings*, p.101. Panama City, FL: Norfield Publishing, 1996.

"You know, *Skipper*? I was thinking after my first mission, about how little control we, or even our crews, have over our ultimate destiny," *Bird* began, still with a hint of despondency in her voice. "But let me tell you, it sure helps having a pilot like Pop. I do believe he betters our odds up there. You should have seen what he did during yesterday's mission to the Ploesti marshaling yards. Made me feel lucky to have a man like that holding my yoke," she attested.

"Good thing you weren't on that mission. Lordy. I hope we don't have to go back there again. Did you know Ploesti is the fourth most defended area in German-held territory, after Berlin, Munich, and Vienna, Austria? During the briefing *Toledo* said there were audible gasps when the crews were told there were 157 heavy Flak guns waiting for them. But fortunately, most of them were surrounding the adjacent refineries," *Bird* said, ignoring *Skipper's* scowl upon the mention of *Toledo* again.

"So up to the bomb run things weren't bad, not with our escorts holding back most of the enemy fighters. Then the Flak hit. Heavy, intense, and accurate, even though we dropped boxes and boxes of Window from lead element planes. Funny thing, for the first time I could actually see the guns firing at us. I was watching the bombs drop to check their accuracy when I saw patterns of red flame flashes on the ground. Looked like an angry swarm of sparkling fireflies," she said.

"I didn't realize that something so terrifying could be so deadly silent. At 24,000 feet it takes about thirty seconds for those shells to reach us. Time was ticking down and all you could do was wait and try not to count. But of course you do, and within a few seconds of counting down to zero that Flak started exploding all around us and knocking us around a bit. But amazingly, we weren't hit, along with most of the others in the Group.

"Then things went to hell in a handbasket really quick," *Bird* continued.

"As the lead 'A' element of the Group rallied to the left over the countryside after the bomb run, the lead pilot of our 'B' element led us over the refineries themselves that were rimmed with Flak batteries, plus some that were mounted on railcars. No Window had been thrown out since we weren't supposed to be flying over the refineries. Boy, did they open up on us. A ten-inch piece tore through me aft of my starboard bomb door and went in between Sergeants Allen and Yeates who were standing back-to-back at their waist guns. Don't quite know how to explain why they weren't mauled by that piece of hot iron," *Bird* said, as the ground crew checked the movement of her right and left flaps.

"Needless to say, Pop was pissed, and that's putting it mildly. You should have heard some of the words he used to describe that pilot. Amazing thing, too, is the fact that he was a major!" *Bird* exclaimed incredulously.

"Hey, *Bird*. Just because someone has silver or gold bars, oak leaf clusters, an eagle or even stars on their uniform, doesn't mean they can't have shit for brains," *Skipper* eloquently stated the obvious.

"Well, Pop suffers no fools, especially when they jeopardize the safety of his crew and myself," *Bird* replied, trying not to giggle at *Skipper*'s innate ability to use foul language as if it was proper Queen's English.

"As soon as he safely could, Pop put me on my left wingtip and hooked up with a box of the 'A' element and left the jerk pilot behind before he got us into more trouble. Now that was using his head, and with that kind of thinking I may have a better chance of surviving all of this," *Bird* said, still with a bit of bewilderment in her voice. "Do you know that once we were over Yugoslavia that Major pulled up and flew off my wing? I think he came to the same realization that I did, that maybe Pop knew what he was doing," *Bird* proudly said.

"But even with a pilot like Pop at my controls, I think it pales in comparison to our, well, fate, or luck of the draw, whatever you want to call it," *Bird* said resignedly as she now watched the armorers load the .50caliber belts into her turrets. Maybe those will prevent an untimely fate, she thought to herself.

"And sometimes events happen to you, and at that particular moment, you think things couldn't possibly get any worse, or 'why me?' Like the hailstorm over Pensacola that I told you about. That could have ended it right then and there for me and the crew. Nothing but bad news. Then again, because I had to wait ten days for parts, I arrived here ten days late. If that hail hadn't ripped me to shreds, I'd have been here early enough to have been part of the April 4th mission. Could Pop or I control that hailstorm? No. Would I have been one of the two survivors of that mission?" *Bird* asked, not expecting an answer because there was none to be had.

"Or those Flak shells that took out *Dragon Lady*. A fraction of a second quicker on the 88 Flak gun lanyard, or a shift in air currents aloft, could have caused those shells to explode under you, *Skipper*. Beyond our control, as I said," *Bird* judged forlornly as she considered life without *Skipper* due to a whim of chance.

"My first mission was only three days after I arrived, April 7th. There were too many losses from that April 4th mission for me to just sit around. Ready or not, they put me in the air. Pop was too green to pilot a combat mission so I went up with Lieutenant Gentry and his crew. They left *Patches* on the ground for some much-needed rest and repairs. I sure wasn't comfortable with a stranger's hands on my yoke. Certainly not on my first mission. I remember saying to myself over and over, 'I want Pop.... I want Pop'. It sure wasn't like what the recruiting poster said when we signed up for this," *Bird* said, repeating an often-heard remark by some of the crewmen, especially during the heat of a mission.

"The lead ships started throwing out Window at the beginning of the IP all the way through the bombing of Mestre up in northern Italy. This time I think it mostly worked. While the Flak was heavy and intense, it wasn't very accurate. Except for *Pugnacious Peggy* of the 716th Squadron off my starboard in the middle box. She absolutely got shredded. Her elevators and right wing were full of holes, her number one and two props were feathered, and gas was pouring out from some of those holes in her right wing. They started throwing everything out but the kitchen sink, but she kept losing altitude till she ditched in the Adriatic. Hardly anyone survives ditching in the sea, plane or crew. So, what makes me so different that that

Flak didn't shred me? Nothing, that's what. And all I kept thinking was 'sure am glad I'm not that poor bastard'," *Bird* murmured, ashamed of her selfish attitude.

"Not that I had much time to think about *Peggy's* problems 'cause I had problems of my own," *Bird* continued after a short embarrassing interlude. "Even in the middle of that Flak, those German fighters came on in. About 30 of them, 109's and 190's. Five minutes after we dropped our 500-pounders, while we were still rallying, an FW-190 came at me from five o'clock high. It started firing its four cannon at me from 800 yards, all the way up till it was only 100 yards away. I swear, from my tail turret I could see that pilot's young face grimacing as .50 cal slugs found their way into his now blood-smeared canopy. He went down underneath me, smoking, until he blew up into small pieces at about 10,000 feet. I just had to watch him go down; I was mesmerized and couldn't take my eyes off him," *Bird* said in a foggy voice as she remembered the descending, smoking craft and falling, flaming debris. "Do you know, in those 700 yards he fired over 400 cannon shells at me and not a one hit me? Amazing. Was the pilot that inexperienced or was he too scared watching Sergeant Route's twin Brownings sparkle at him?"[3]

"And that's another thing. As much as I like and appreciate Sergeant Fox in my tail turret, I sure was glad I had Sergeant Route in it that day, let me tell ya. That man was experienced. He's had over twenty missions in the air, real combat training using those guns, and he knows how to survive," *Bird* finished, with strong emphasis on her last word of the early morning: Survive.

Skipper had always considered himself more of a talker than a listener. But in this case he knew *Bird* was hurting, questioning herself, and he thought it best to just listen for once. Not that he disagreed with anything

---

3. AFHRA folder GP-449-SU-OP-S, 7 April 1944. Mission 42. Ship #3 Combat Claim Form.

she said, because he didn't. He had those same "out of control" feelings himself. If not during his first mission, certainly on the following day's. That one really spooked him and caused him to question how he was going to survive this madness. For that's what it was.

The four-hour April 13th flight to the IP went without a hitch with Lt. George Fergus, Jr. at *Skipper*'s controls this time. Loaded with 115 fragmentation bombs, their target was the Vesces airdrome nine miles outside of Budapest, Hungary. This was the final assembly and testing site for two-thirds of the twin-engined Messerschmitt 210 and 410 heavy fighters and Schnellbomber.

Skipper felt good about this mission. Thirty-six P-38s and thirty-three P-47s were sticking tight with them this time. In the twelve-ship "A" element in front of his "B" element he could see many familiar faces, or at least tail turrets and assemblies. *Consolidated Mess #2*, being flown by Lt. Davis and navigated by *Bird*'s rookie navigator, Bob Simmons, was at his two o'clock. Good ol' *Buzzer*, piloted by Lt. Easters and co-piloted by *Bird*'s pilot, "Pop" Blomgren, was in front of him. But best of all, *Nancy Jane*, piloted by Lt. Rustad, was immediately off his left wing, not fifty feet away.

Skipper's original pilot, Lieutenant Liddycoat, *Nancy Jane*'s pilot, Lieutenant Rustad, and *Bird*'s pilot "Pop" Blomgren and their crews, had all come from three months of training together at Tonapah, Nevada. The fact that they all ended up in the same bomb squadron was one of those twists of fate. The "Three Tonapah Amigos" they were called.

"Not bad, survived another one," *Skipper* said to himself, what with little, inaccurate Flak, German fighters held off by the escorts, and Lt. Hinds, the bombardier, announcing "bombs away" over the interphone. He was feeling good as he sensed his bomb doors beginning their closing motion, when a blinding flash of light followed by a concussive blast and inferno of heat struck all along his port side. Immediately *Skipper* felt rudder and aileron controls actuating as Lt. Fergus fought for flight control. *Skipper* was physically pushed aside. At the same moment he felt searing hot pain peppering his side. It was like running through riverbank catclaw on horseback and you were dumb enough not to have worn your leather chaps. He felt a large piece of steel penetrate the armored glass of his ball turret, and from Sergeant Vito Corso's screams, he knew he had been seriously hit. Then *Skipper* looked to his left.

The sight that met him was surreal. There were so many disjointed, incomprehensible fragments that he momentarily couldn't determine what he was seeing and what had just occurred. *Nancy Jane* wasn't there. At least the *Nancy Jane* that he had previously known. In her place he saw an orange-yellow ball of flame engulfing the right wing of a B-24 carcass as it began to flip over, exposing the top of its fuselage and overhead cockpit windows. *Skipper* caught a fleeting last glimpse of Lt. Rustad and co-pilot Lt. Keeler at the controls.

In what seemed to be slow motion, its left wing broke off and began a slow, fluttering descent to the ground with its number one and two engines still running at over 2,000 rpm as if it still had an airframe attached to it.[4] Slowly, the remnants of the right wing broke in half and folded itself up and over the fuselage like a hand trying to cover one's eyes to prevent observing the inevitable truth. In the middle of all this, *Skipper* caught a few blurs of what appeared to be fragmentation bombs slipping through the airspace just recently occupied by *Nancy Jane*. And then she was gone, dropping out of sight as she plunged earthward.

What *Skipper* couldn't see Pop could see from *Buzzer*'s vantage point. And what he saw would be forever seared into his memories, like a perpetual horrifying snapshot of time and place. Along with the burning mass of what had been *Nancy Jane*, five silk parachute canopies caught the wind and momentarily blossomed alongside, long enough to catch fire.[5] All

---

4. Stanley, William G. Personal WWII Diary: April 13, 1944 entry. Author's collection.

5. Blomgren, Norman E. The War Diary of Capt. Norman E. Blomgren: April 13, 1944 entry. Author's collection.

plummeted to earth as one. There were no survivors of the ten-man crew. Co-pilot Ken Keeler, bombardier John Bowen, tail gunner Ralph Legrow, and waist gunner Frank Spano would spend eternity together in a common grave in section 12 of Arlington National Cemetery.

Skipper thought long and hard about what *Bird* had said about uncontrollable events, destiny, and fate. It very well could have been him underneath that B-24 from the 376th Group, dropping its bombs from too high an altitude and being mispositioned too far ahead, above the totally unaware 449th. Skipper's left wing had been only fifty feet away from the falling rain of armed fragmentation bombs.

"So many ways to die, and they just keep coming. Who would have thought that one way was to be bombed by a fellow Liberator?" *Skipper* thought silently to himself, not wanting to disturb *Bird*. "Flak, enemy fighters, mid-air collisions, takeoffs, landings, weather, mountains, and running out of gas." *Skipper* finished counting the almost endless possibilities, though he found himself chuckling with the memory of the last method.

It seemed so long ago, a different lifetime, but it was only a little over a month ago that he and his crew had almost disappeared into oblivion, without a trace. During their long flight over the Atlantic, it was obvious to Lt. Liddycoat that they were going to run out of precious gas before they reached the shores of Africa at Dakar. They had thrown everything overboard that wasn't bolted down, to no use, when he gave the order to prepare for ditching when they were still 50 miles from shore. Nobody survives ditching.[6] That's when *Skipper*'s flight engineer, Tech Sergeant Ken Thompson, adjusted a few more fuel cell distribution valves that

---

6. Birdsall, Steve. *Log of the Liberators*, p. 59. Garden City, NY: Doubleday & Co., 1973. During ocean "ditchability tests," it was determined that a B-24 crewmember had one-tenth the survival chance of a B-17 crewmember under similar conditions due to the fuselage breaking in half behind the flightdeck.

miraculously gave them barely enough fuel to land at Dakar, with two engines sputtering to a stop as they completed their landing rollout.[7]

As the ground crew finished up *Skipper*'s preflight checks and engine warm-up, and while he waited for dawn and the pending day's mission to a place unknown, he couldn't help but think of how far he and *Bird* had come since their early days as newborn innocents in Dallas. It was only three months ago that they were quizzing one another with such benign questions as what was their purpose, what would the bomb racks carry, how could their Brownings inflict damage from high in the sky, exactly how were they going to fly?

They were now trying to answer lofty questions such as ones pertaining to their ultimate fate. To *Skipper* the answer was simple, and one he had learned way back at the North American Aviation assembly plant. He was not in control. And for the most part neither was his crew, something *Bird* was just coming 'round to realize. Their fate truly was just a roll of the proverbial dice. There was nothing they could do about it so they needed to just take it one mission at a time, use their heads, and then, and only then, they might just get through the war alive. There were just too many ways to die, with more being devised every mission. To *Skipper* it was like fighting against a tide with no ebb. And the best way to survive that was not to fight it at all and just go with the flow.

---

7. 449th Bomb Group Association. *Book II: Tucson to Grottaglie*, p. 33. 1985.

15

POKER, SCRAMBLED EGGS, AND SEAGRAM'S

WORRYBIRD'S OFFICERS TENT,
719TH SQUADRON AREA MAY 1, 1944, 16:30 HRS.

"ALL RIGHT, HOW ABOUT a little simple five card stud with, let's say, deuces and jacks wild?" Harry said as he deftly dealt cards out to Bob, Stan, and Pop, who watched impatiently as their cards flew through the air fogged by heavy blue-gray cigarette smoke.

"Let's make this the last hand; the rest of the crew will be here shortly," Pop said. "Besides, I don't want them to see how poor of a card player you are, Bob," he remarked with a grin, comparing his own pile of bills to the pocket change in front of Bob.

"It sure looks like I'm paying the rent this month, doesn't it?" Bob said sardonically, trying to hide his disgust as he flipped the last card into his hand, realizing yet again he had nothing.

"Well, Bob, if you worked on your poker face a bit, you might have a larger pile in front of you," Stan said, as he too had a small pile of greenbacks in front of him. At last count he thought he was up just shy of $15. Not a bad evening.

"Do you think you got enough eggs at the market today?" Harry asked Pop as he assessed the hand he had dealt himself. "You know how much those boys can put away."

"I sure hope so. Got two dozen and I was lucky to get them. Shelves were kinda sparse and they cost me four packs at that. I wouldn't have gotten those if it hadn't been for Salvatore and his mother. They knew where to find them," Pop said as he raised Stan's bet by a dollar. Salvatore was a Grottaglie youngster hired as a "houseboy" to help keep things clean, run shopping errands, and get their sweaty clothes to his mother to be washed and ironed. Even amidst war's carnage they had to keep up appearances.

"Well crap, I fold," Bob sighed.

"You wouldn't know that four bachelors live here the way he keeps this tent clean. That's $2.50 to you, Harry," said Pop.

Shaking his head, Harry threw in his cards, got up, and refilled his cup with their precious Seagram's V.O. "Yeah, and his mother sure knows how to get our uniforms clean. And folded too," he said as he attempted to drown his gambling sorrows.

"That's a dollar to you, Stan, to stay in," Pop reported coolly with a blank expression on his face. "Say, let's give him another pack of cigs and maybe some more soap for his mother. I'm feeling generous."

"Oh, that's easy for you to say with that stash of green in front of you," Bob said as he stood up and palmed the few coins off the table that he could claim as his. "But I'm good with that," as the others also nodded approval.

Stan looked down at his hand that, except for a miserable black three of clubs, would have been a flush of red hearts. He then looked at Pop's carved-in-stone face and his pile of green and, deciding that discretion was the better part of valor, threw his cards down.

Rubbing his hands together, Pop joyfully exclaimed, "Come to Pop-pa!" and proceeded to add to his winnings. "Anytime you guys want to hand over your pay, just deal a hand."

"Pay, what's that?" Stan exclaimed as he filled his cup. "Someone sna-fued my pay voucher and they don't know when they'll figure it out. Good thing I took some of your pay, Bob. You too, Harry," he said as he pointed toward the two poorer officers with his cup before bringing it to his lips and, with his head tilted back, gulping the entire contents down.

"Whoa there, boy!" Pop said, trying not to laugh at the contorted, shocked look on Stan's face as the blended whiskey set fire to his throat. "It's not like we can head back to Trinidad and pick up another case of that stuff." The boys had picked up a two cases of the honey-brown refreshment along with other required combat zone necessities during a brief stop on their trans-Atlantic trip.

"Hello in the tent!" was heard bellowed from outside before the re-mainder of *Bird*'s crew came through the tent flap carrying their cups and mess kits, all in a buoyant mood. The entire crew always looked forward to the egg fries with their lieutenants.

"Damn, the boys sure needed this," Pop thought to himself as he began picking up cards. "Heck, I needed this if I'm honest with myself. We were beginning to get a little testy with one another. Thank goodness those were red flares they shot from the control tower this morning. That would have been four missions in as many days."

"Let me finish picking up my winnings here to make some room," said Pop as he folded the bills and inserted them into his money clip.

"Stan, why don't you light the stove and get those eggs cooking while Blankenship and I go outside and have a smoke? And the rest of you guys, fill up those tin cups of yours while the Seagram's lasts," Pop said as he gestured Bill toward the tent flap.

As he exited the tent, Bill fidgeted as he fumbled for the Lucky Strike pack in his pocket. He knew what Pop wanted to jaw about.

After lighting his cigarette, Pop looked at Sergeant Blankenship with an appraising eye. He was a good man. A great engineer. That's why it had been tough bawling him out yesterday after the mission. But it very well could have been their lives. All because of a stupid rookie mistake. Some planes don't make it back because of stupid mistakes.

Finally, Bill's nerves had had enough. "Listen, Lieutenant. You bawled me out good yesterday," he began, "and I deserved it. Boy, didn't I? Letting an engine run out of gas like that. And on landing approach, too. Dumb is what it was. And to be honest, I wasn't paying good enough attention to the gauges." Bill looked Pop square in the eyes as he took a drag. He wasn't sure there was anything Pop could say that could make him feel any lower than he already did.

"Yep. That's what I thought. A good man," Pop told himself.

"Sergeant, it's water under the bridge. I know you realize that could have been a mission critical mistake. Had that happened on the recalled Ploesti mission last week, with us returning with a full load of bombs and gas, all 65,000 pounds, well, I would not have been able to recover from the loss of power in time and we wouldn't be here talking about it." Pop let that set in for a few long seconds.

"I know it won't happen again because I know you're a good engineer. And I'm not the only one who knows that," Pop paused for effect. "Congratulations Staff Sergeant Blankenship, you've been promoted," he said with a grin as he thrust his hand into Bill's, shaking it firmly. Now he knew the adrenaline rush Ebenezer Scrooge felt when he told Bob Cratchit that he was going to get a raise and not be fired.

"As I said, water under the bridge. I came out here to tell you of your promotion, not to bust your chops again," Pop said as Bill stood glassy-eyed, comprehension slow to sink in.

"Come on in. Let me buy you a drink," Pop said as he guided Bill back into the smoke-filled, party-infused atmosphere of the tent.

"There you guys are. Pop, listen to what Yeates just told me," Stan said as he finally got the 100-octane stove flame under control, even with a sticky petcock valve.

"Well, sir, you did say something about the Seagram's not lasting," Cecil said as he looked into his half-filled mess cup. "Well you don't have to worry about that."

"I don't, do I?"

"No, sir. I was talking with someone in supply. It appears there's an occasional booze run made to Cairo in an old 'D' model B-24. The *Doodlebug*."

Shaking his head and then chortling to himself, Pop said, "Well, doesn't that beat all? Leave it to some bomber pilot to think nothing of flying 1,000 miles, one way mind you, just for some booze. Where do we place an order?" he asked to a round of lubricated guffaws.

After cracking the two dozen eggs into a large crock bowl, Stan looked up and glanced at each of the other nine members of the *Bird*'s crew. He wouldn't trade a single one of them, he thought to himself as he watched Corporal Windham draw an oversized cigarette out of a crushed, though all-too-recognizable pack.

"Corporal, where did you get a pack of Wings cigarettes?" Stan asked as he picked a bunch of broken eggshells out of the bowl. Cooking wasn't one of his strong suits.

"Oh, my younger brother Pat sent them to me in a care package. He's in flight school back in Texas and he knew we wouldn't get these out here," Joseph said as he lit the cigarette to add to the semi-opaque smokescreen.

"He knew I preferred the king-size Wings to those stubby Lucky Strikes or Chesterfields. Do you prefer them too, Lieutenant?"

"Can't say I ever smoked one, though I've had over twenty packs in my possession, all empty, of course," Stan commented, grinning at the bewildered looks on most of the men's faces as he scrambled the eggs.

"Do you mean to tell me none of you ever heard of their 'Wings of Destiny' contest?" Eight shook their heads, while Joseph smirked and nodded.

"Boy, and me living in Podunk, Kansas, too. Well, fill up your cups and let me tell you," Stan said as he put a cast iron skillet on the stove with a ladleful of lard he had gotten from the officers' mess. Bacon and its grease were found only in their dreams.

"So, Wings cigarettes sponsored a radio show on NBC every Friday night called 'Wings of Destiny'," Stan said, glancing around for any recognition. None was had, so he continued.

"Pilot Steve Benton and his trusty mechanic, Brooklyn?" he added with a quizzical look.

"Don't forget his girlfriend, Peggy, Lieutenant," Joseph added.

"Right. Can't forget Peggy now, can we?"

"While the show itself was lame at best, it was the drawing held at the end of each broadcast that kept me and my younger brother, Rut, glued to that Philco farm radio."

"What did they give away, cartons of cigarettes for kids?" asked Charley Debord to a chorus of laughter.

"No. A Piper Cub airplane. One a week," Stan said, stirring the chunk of lard, helping it to melt into the pan.

"No kidding?" Charley asked, not laughing now.

"No kidding. A person had to send in ten empty Wings packs and write a short essay as to why you thought you deserved a Piper Cub."

"Rut and I would scour the dusty streets of Cunningham for empty Wings cigarette packs. Once we got enough then we'd sit down and write an essay. Boy, were they corny. You know, something like, 'We're two American farm boys wanting to fly above the golden fields of grain of our great nation in a Piper Cub aircraft.' No wonder we never won. But boy, did we ever want to fly," Stan chuckled as he poured the eggs into the pan, adding a boiling cloud of steam to the already smoky tent.

"Well, you're flying now," Pop said, raising his cup toward Stan.

"How about your brother, Rut?" asked Bob.

"That knucklehead got his wings right after he turned nineteen."

"I got a letter from him last week where if I read his hints correctly—have to get past the censors you know—he's going to be flying the Hump helping out Chiang Kai-shek and the Chinese," Stan said as he stirred the golden mixture, sending tantalizing wafts of fresh egg smell toward the boys with stomachs agrowl.

"Boy, you two should have watched what you wished for," Harry smirked.

"Yep, this isn't quite what we had in mind when we wished to fly," Stan said as he motioned toward the plates with his spoon.

"But then again," he said as he scooped eggs onto the plates of his salivating crewmates. "Here's my brother, at nineteen years of age, going to be flying a four engine B-24, or the C-46 or C-47 transport planes, over the Himalaya Mountains into China. I don't think that would have happened in civilian life. Let's eat, boys."

As they enjoyed the real, farm-raised eggs, washed down with tomato juice, Pop asked, "So, did anyone witness the P-51 crash this afternoon?"

"Yeah, all us gunners were out on our end of the runway watching him buzz the field," Joe Fox said. "Apparently, a few days ago someone shot one down by mistake thinking it was an Me-109. So this guy was to give us gunners fast, low-level buzz jobs to give us an idea of what a Mustang looked like at speed."

"Fast, no kidding," Jim Reed said as he scraped egg remnants into his mouth. Couldn't let any of that go to waste. "He had to have been doing 400mph!"

"Well, 400mph, a cocky fighter jock, a pavement scorching altitude, and an unfamiliar airfield sure were a recipe for disaster," Pop said as he wondered if it was appropriate for him to lick his plate.

"Stan and I were down near headquarters when he came buzzing in at about 50 feet and his right wing caught the side of the dirigible hangar."

"That ship just exploded into a thousand pieces," Stan said, gesticulating his arms and scattering globules of his precious Seagram's into the air like the disintegrating P-51 fuselage.

"The engine ended up another 250 yards down the field from most of the wreckage."

"One of the weirdest things to happen about the whole situation," Stan continued as he picked an errant eggshell out of his mouth, "was while I was standing there staring at the smoldering engine, I looked up and the guy standing on the other side said to me, "Aren't you Bill Stanley, Verne's boy?"

"He was a kid from my hometown of Cunningham, with a population of 481. And I think that includes the dogs!" Stan said as he looked into his cup and wondered where the hell his Seagram's had gone to.

"So, besides Stan and Joseph, does anybody else have brothers in the war?" Pop asked, thinking of his older brother Lewis having enlisted in the Coast Guard two years earlier.

"Yeah Pop, besides my brother, Pat, being in the Air Corps, my brother, Jim, is in the Army's 501st Ordnance Battalion. Not sure where he's stationed now though," Joseph added.

"My older brother Harold just enlisted last month in the Army," Bob wistfully said. With just thirteen months separating them, they grew up close.

"My brother Robert is in the Army while my kid brother, George, had enough of the North Carolina mountains so he joined the Navy, of all things. He's on an LST somewhere in the Pacific. At eighteen I worry about him the most," the newly minted Staff Sergeant Blankenship added with a pensive look on his face.

There were obviously a lot of Blue Star Service flags flying on porches across the States because of his crew's families, with more to be added during the coming year. Pop broke the lingering pregnant pause by asking, "Anyone have a good toast for brothers?" as he filled his cup with Seagram's and passed the bottle.

"Well, not sure if it's a toast, but maybe having studied Shakespeare in English Lit at North Texas Teachers College will actually come in useful after all," Joseph said as he raised his cup, with everyone following.

"I may not remember it exactly right, but this is from Shakespeare's Henry the Fifth. He's trying to rally his men for tomorrow's fight, even though they're way outnumbered and there's a good chance they won't survive." No one dared to comment on the disturbing similarity to their own current situation.

Clearing his throat, Joseph began: "*This story shall the good man teach his son. From this day to the ending of the world. But we in it shall be remembered. We few, we happy few, we band of brothers. For he today that sheds his blood with me, shall be my brother.*"

"To brothers, whoever and wherever they may be," Stan added as they all drained their cups.

Tent party with Seagram's. Stan asks Pop, "Are you really going to drink that?" [Author's Collection]

Harry Bursten and Salvatore outside of the Worrybird's officer's tent. Salvatore's pay "going up in smoke." [Author's Collection]

16

Deja-Vu All Over Again

19,800 Feet Above Ploesti, Rumania, May 5, 1944, 13:58 hrs.

"My gallant crew, good morning. *I hope you're all quite well*," Stan sang softly to himself as he used the drift and turn knobs of his bombsight to compensate for the killer crosswind they were experiencing over the Standard Oil Refinery and marshaling yards of Ploesti, almost 20,000 feet below. [1]

G-g-g-crunch-zing-zing-zing. Another Flak shell exploded in front of *Bird,* sending searing hot metal fragments through her skin like a hot knife through butter. To Stan it sounded like being inside the tin-roofed barn on their farm during a central plains hailstorm. Since there were 157 German Flak guns protecting the Ploesti refineries, with each capable of sending twelve to twenty shells a minute into the overhead formations, there were plenty of "hailstones."

---

1. Sullivan, Arthur. *H.M.S. Pinafore.* Root and Sons Music Co. Chicago, 1879.

"Don't stop singing now, Stan!" *Bird* bellowed. On missions like this, *Bird* found that Stan's crooning helped divert her attention away from the aerial terror surrounding her.

"*I am in reasonable health, and happy to meet you all once more,*" Stan continued as he had trouble keeping his eye pressed against the padded eyepiece due to the Flak-induced turbulence.

"Bombs away, Pop! Let's get the hell outta here!" Stan yelled into the interphone as he finished the HMS Pinafore's lyrics with gusto, "*I am the Captain of the Pinafore!*" "Amazing I can remember my lines. Boy, that really was another lifetime ago, a Saturday night High School theater production," Stan mused to himself as another shell exploded in front of the nose turret.

"Damn!" Cecil Yeates exclaimed, sitting behind his twin Brownings in the turret immediately above Stan.

"Cecil, you alright?" Stan yelled up to the compartment above, after extricating what seemed to be his entire body from underneath his Flak helmet.

"I'm OK, Lieutenant," Cecil replied after briefly examining himself underneath his Flak suit. "Can't say the turret is OK, though. There're holes all over. I can see daylight out both sides, above me and below me."

"Gunners, we lost our escort during the bomb run, so be on the lookout," Pop instructed over the interphone, trying to get his crew focused for the onslaught they all knew was coming. The briefing officer had reported between seventy and eighty-five enemy aircraft would be waiting for them.

It took only two minutes after the bomb drop for sixty Messerschmitts and Focke-Wulfs firing rockets to make their presence known.

"109's, twelve o'clock high coming out of the sun, Cecil," Bill blurted over the interphone from his perch in the top turret.

"I'm tracking them. Red noses with yellow fuselage. Three split off. They're coming for us," Cecil responded impassively as he sighted the middle red-nosed Me-109 and pulled both triggers. *Bird* felt her airframe reverberate with the results.

It took only twelve minutes for the aggressive fighters to knock four of the thirty-eight B-24's out of the sky. This included *Bonnies Boys*, flown by 2nd Lieutenant Bernard "Bonnie" Armstrong, which had joined the ranks of the 719th Squadron one week after *Bird* and *Skipper*, replacing the unfortunate *Dixie Belle* lost on April 4th. It took eight German fighters to take her down, however. With *Bird*'s gunners getting in a couple good hits from the 700 rounds fired, she was able to survive two more passes of the Me-109's attacking three abreast.[2]

Once she saw the menacing Messerschmitts depart, *Bird* took stock of her own situation. She definitely felt "draftier" and thought she'd mentally count the Flak, machine gun, and cannon shell holes in her. She lost track at forty. Engines felt good, no fluid losses that she could feel, and the rudder, elevators, and ailerons seemed to be responding to Pop's inputs as they rallied left over the town of Campina. *Good, I can make it back.* Then she remembered she wasn't alone.

"*Skipper*! Can you hear me? Are you there?" she cried out over the radio. There were two planes, *Big Noise From Kentucky* and *Peepy*, both blocking her line of sight with *Skipper*.

After what seemed like ages, *Skipper*'s Texan drawl finally came in over the radio static, droning engines, and buffeting wind. "Well, where else would I be? Laredo?"

A surge of relief swept through *Bird* as if Harry had added a few extra pounds of boost to her turbochargers. "You could have at least said something, you know," she responded with a false sense of outrage. "Are you OK?"

"Couldn't be better," *Skipper* said with bravado. "Except of course the Flak holes in my number one engine and right wing. And then there're the numerous 8mm machine gun holes in my side too," he added nonchalant-

---

2. AFHRA folder GP-449-SU-OP-S, 5 May 1944. Mission 54. Ship #3 Interrogation Report.

ly. "At least my gunners got the bastard. How are you faring?" he added almost as an afterthought.[3]

"Plenty of holes but amazingly none of them hit anything crucial. And somehow all my crew dodged the stuff too. Though Joseph Fox, my left waist gunner was almost killed by one of his own .50 cal bullets."

"Now how in the blue blazes could that have happened?" *Skipper* asked, puzzled.

"A piece of an exploding 20mm cannon shell hit a cartridge in the ammo feed track right above his head, exploding the cartridge. Really a freak thing to happen, I must say."[4]

"Well, we can relax now, though I don't see the P-38 escort that was supposed to cover us on the way back. Typical," *Skipper* said disgustedly as he sensed the Group tightening up their formation to enhance their defensive posture.

Enjoying the scenery of western Rumania into eastern Yugoslavia an hour later, *Bird* realized two things that suddenly sent shivers down her airframe like Cecil's twin Brownings.

First, she had slowly decreased altitude along with the other thirteen planes of the leading "A" element of the three-element Group, and they were now flying at the ridiculously low altitude of 9,000 feet. It was far too low for being in enemy airspace, especially since they would have to climb back to 12,000 feet to clear upcoming mountains. Nothing but a dangerous way to burn precious gas.

But it was the second fact that was most disturbing, if not downright foreboding.

---

3. AFHRA folder GP-449-SU-OP-S, 5 May 1944. Mission 54. Ship #6 Interrogation Report.

4. AFHRA folder GP-449-SU-OP-S, 5 May 1944. Mission 54. Ship #3 Interrogation Report; Simmons, Robert I. Diary: April 3, 1944 to August 29, 1944. May 5, 1944 entry. Author's collection.

Exactly two hours prior, they had flown over the same exact location, though 7,000 feet higher. Either the lead navigator or the lead Group pilot had been sleeping during the morning briefing. They were lost, or worse, they were incompetent. The planned route took them within five miles of Bor, Yugoslavia, but they had been warned to avoid the town in the briefing. Now here they were again for an encore appearance. Below them were the copper mines and smelting plants supplying Nazi Germany with 50% of its copper needs. With no copper, there are no Flak shells, bullet cartridges, generator and motor windings, wire, and a myriad of other military necessities. Therefore, it was heavily defended with Flak batteries.

"Hey *Skipper*, wake up!" *Bird* blurted out, waking him from his droning engine-induced semi-consciousness.

"Wow, girl, you certainly know how to disturb a guy's dreams now, don't you?" an irritated *Skipper* answered.

"Well, I wish I was dreaming, but aren't those the same smokestacks and factories off our left side that hit us with a bunch of Flak on our way up?"

Peering to his left and up ahead, *Skipper* did indeed recognize the factory complex and the telltale scars on the earth from the large open pit mines. Fortunately, on the way up they had caught the surrounding Flak batteries by surprise and there was only slight damage done to the Group flying at an altitude of 16,000 feet. Not this time, however.

"You're right again, *Bird*. Oh damn!"

"What is it?"

"Take a look down there and hold on, because they aren't going to miss at this altitude," Skipper said grimacing, waiting for the inevitable to occur in about ten seconds. Down below he had just witnessed the flashing of Flak gun muzzles that could easily be seen against the denuded landscape.

"Sweet mother of mercy," was all *Bird* could utter before the heavy, accurate, and intense Flak began bursting among the lead element, especially in the front box which included *Bird* and her crew situated two planes behind the lead.

Hot steel fragments again assailed *Bird*'s thin skin, peppering her with holes, including one through Pop's windshield. She lost count at an additional thirty to add to her previous forty.[5]

With *Big Noise From Kentucky* fifty feet off her left wing at her eleven o'clock, *Bird* couldn't miss the devastation being pummeled upon him. A well-placed Flak burst between his number three and four engines set in motion his final death knell.

"Oh no, *Kentuck*!" screamed *Bird*, as smoke and flame immediately erupted from his engines. With a sudden loss of all power from its right wing, *Kentuck* began sliding directly into *Bird*'s flight path. It's pilot, Lt. Paul Harper, regained momentary control before it began losing altitude and drifted out of *Bird*'s sight.

"Can anybody see what's happening to *Kentuck*?" *Bird* asked over the radio.

"Yeah, *Bird*, this is *Buzzer* back here in 'C' element," came the welcomed and recognizable reply. "He's fallen behind the entire formation and has lost a few hundred feet of altitude. It doesn't look good, though he got the fire out on number four."

"There go two chutes," *Buzzer* added a few minutes later as he continued to monitor *Kentuck*'s death struggle.

Fifteen minutes later *Buzzer* reported seeing eight more chutes before *Kentuck* began a lazy clockwise death spiral, crashing into the forested mountains outside of Beocic, Yugoslavia, just a few moments later. By keeping his plane airborne for those additional seventeen minutes, Lt. Harper was able to get his men 45 miles further out of enemy territory. As navigator and keeper of *Bird*'s mission log, Bob noted the latitude (43°50'N) and longitude (21°13'E) of *Kentuck*'s demise.

Big Noise From Kentucky was lost and ten crewmen were wandering the forests of central Yugoslavia trying to evade capture, all because of

---

5. Ibid.

incompetent leadership from the lead plane. Being slotted off *Bird*'s left wing was beginning to look like a very hazardous position.

By the time *Bird* landed she was pooped. It had been a long day, but even longer for her crew. Rousted from a fitful sleep at 04:30, briefed at 05:30, on station in *Bird* at 08:50, takeoff at 10:38, dodging Flak at Bor at 13:05, flying over the target at 13:58, watching helplessly as four of their ships were relentlessly shot down, enduring Flak again at Bor at 15:07, the irrational loss of *Kentuck*, and finally landing at 17:12, none of the crew was in a good mood, even though they had survived their fifteenth mission. Only thirty-five to go.

Climbing out of *Toledo* and quickly scanning over *Bird*, her crew chief, Sergeant Clarence Lambertz, blurted out with emotion, "Lieutenant! What did you do to my plane?" as he saw Pop almost fall out of the bomb bay as his fatigued legs began to give way. Unassisted rudder pedals on a four-engine bomber are a bitch.

With Bob and Harry assisting Pop over to the interrogation tents set up nearby, the looks on their faces told Sergeant Lambertz not to expect a reply any time soon. Besides, he had work to do. He had to get *Bird* back in flying condition, for they had just posted tomorrow's flight schedule, and she was on it. No one but Headquarters knew it, but they were heading back to Rumania.

"Boy, that sure was a rough one, wasn't it?" *Toledo* said, as his leaking engine coolant mixed with the black engine oil dripping from his oil pan onto the compacted tufa stone hardstand. *Toledo* was beginning to show his age.

Bird held back her response to such a ridiculous statement from someone who had sat safely five hundred miles from the carnage, as she caught a glimpse of *Skipper* taxiing up to the parking space next to her. *Bird* had been the first of the squadron to land, with the last, the new number eleven, *Salty Dog*, not landing for another thirty minutes.[6]

"Hey there, *Skipper*," *Toledo* said, now spewing his coolant indiscriminately into the wind. "I was just telling *Bird* here how that sure was a…"

"Nice landing you had there," *Bird* said, quickly finishing *Toledo's* sentence for him, not wanting to be caught in the middle of a verbal shooting match. One battle was enough for the day.

Skipper, sensing he had missed out on something, slowly turned and silently stared into *Toledo's* grill, while *Bird* awaited the predictable tumultuous exchange.

"*Toledo*," *Skipper* began slowly, not wanting to expend his built-up mission rage on this insignificant blowhard. "You're all hat and no cattle." He then stood silent except for the contracting ticking of his cooling engines.

Bird and *Toledo* exchanged side glances, pondering the metaphor, as they too fell silent watching the disembarking crews walk toward the adjacent interrogation tents.

Bird, *Skipper*, and *Toledo* didn't need a radio to hear some of the comments made under the tents as the crews were interviewed by S-2 staff filling out their after-action interrogation reports:

"Why over Flak area twice?"[7]

"Bitching about coming over same Flak that they hit on route out."[8]

---

6. AFHRA folder GP-449-SU-OP-S, 5 May 1944. Mission 54. Up-Down Flight Log.

7. AFHRA folder GP-449-SU-OP-S, 5 May 1944. Mission 54. Ship #3 Interrogation Report.

8. AFHRA folder GP-449-SU-OP-S, 5 May 1944. Mission 54. Ship #23 Interrogation Report.

"Why return over same Flak area at 9,000 feet when had to go back to 12,000 to clear mountains. Lost #26 because of this!" [9]

But the most emotional outbursts were held for the private thoughts put down on paper later that night:

"*This time I was scared, and I admit it,*" wrote Sergeant Francis Hearty after he observed the carnage from the left waist gunner's window in *Honey On The Moon* off *Bird*'s right wing.[10]

"*... We were on our way home...I saw guns flashing on the ground. Then it hit us...I don't see how we got through. One 24 went down and several had engines out. Really rough. They ought to court-martial that lead navigator...*"[11]

"*... They knocked hell out of us again. We lost another ship and many crippled. All this happened because one man didn't use his head. He isn't qualified to lead the Group.*"[12]

Soon, Pop and the rest of *Bird*'s crew would discover just how physically and mentally demanding the role of flying the lead plane could be.

---

9. AFHRA folder GP-449-SU-OP-S, 5 May 1944. Mission 54. Ship #36 Interrogation Report.

10. Hearty, Francis P. *My 50 Missions: Grottaglie And Home*, p. 462. 449th Bomb Group Association, 1989.

11. Stanley, William G. Personal WWII Diary: May 5, 1944 entry. Author's collection.

12. Blomgren, Norman E. The War Diary of Capt. Norman E. Blomgren: May 5, 1944 entry. Author's collection.

17

Go "Home" Tomorrow

Adriatic Sea, Off Santa Cesarea Terme, Italy , May 23, 1944, 15:00 hrs.

"STAN, WATCH THE BOOM, it's going to be coming around your way. I don't want to see you knocked off the boat since you say you swim about as well as a rock," Pop said as he pushed the tiller to starboard to catch a bit more of the wind.

As Stan ducked the head-knocking boom, he momentarily hung his head over the side just in case his five-course lunch should happen to reappear. With the sea being a little rough, he now knew that he wouldn't make much of a sailor.

"I can't help the fact that the closest body of water to our farm, the Ninnescah River, was more sand than water. Heck, you were lucky to get your ankles wet," Stan said, staring into the foamy blue-green water, wishing he was back on the Ninnescah, sitting on one of its steady, unmovable rocks.

Turning the boat around to head back to Santa Cesarea, Pop had to begin to tack into the wind. Having lived on Lake Pistakee, north of Chicago, he had grown up with a sailboat tiller in his hand. He knew what he was doing.

Pop was having the time of his life. Except for the wind and the slap of the bow cutting through the breaking waves, there was absolutely no noise. And it was this lack of auditory stimulation that made the biggest impression of all on his senses. Not the warm breeze flowing through his hair, nor the salty taste on his tongue from the ocean spray, nor the absolutely stunning beauty of the seaside landscape. No, it was the lack of noise, or more specifically, the absence of particular noises. Even with cupping a hand to a skyward tilted ear, one could not hear the drone of a single aircraft engine. No over-revved truck or Jeep engines. No crew chiefs barking orders, nor the sounds of air compressors, rivet guns, or the hammering of metal as ground crews tried to get the squadron's planes ready for the next day's mission. War? What war?

Four days prior, the *Bird* and its crew flew what should have been a "milk run" mission to La Spezia harbor in northern Italy. While encountering inaccurate Flak and no enemy fighters, they did encounter their worse nemesis, weather, and again, poor flight leadership. High clouds at the IP caused the "B" flight element to fly over the leading "A" element. The "C" element maintained position, including *Bird* in the second box which Pop was leading. It was a miracle that no repeats of the fatal *Nancy Jane* debacle occurred.

But it was the weather during the return trip over the Tyrrhenian Sea that was most akin to a nightmare. Heavy, banking cumulonimbus clouds and rain squalls prevented them from flying in formation at cruising altitude. They were soon forced to fly under the cloud base just above the frothy, stormy sea below.

While skimming above wavetops during rain squalls was taxing enough for the flight crew, there was the precarious matter of the escort planes. The fifty P-38s and thirty P-51s relied upon the bombers to guide and navigate them home, lest they become lost in the enveloping curtains of rain and clouds. The escorts' positioning was below the homebound bombers. One hundred and seventeen planes sharing the same thin ribbon of visible airspace between the low cloud base and sea for three and a half hours compounded the harrowing situation. By the time *Bird* landed, Pop's and Harry's nerves were frayed, and their arms and legs were tensed into painful knots.

To compound the situation, there was no ground transportation waiting to bring them to the debriefing area now located at the far end of the runway in the parachute storage facility. It was a long, painful walk. Sample comments from the Interrogation Reports such as *"No transportation from ship to interrogation!"*[1] and from a *Ghost O' The Omar* crew member, *"Let's put less rank and more brains in lead. Very poor leadership,"* says it all.[2]

Upon returning to his tent after having a quick lunch, Pop was instructed to report to the office of Captain George Clark, the squadron's Flight Surgeon. Here, he and his entire crew were ordered to report to the Santa Cesarea rest camp the next morning for four days of R&R.

Besides their obvious medical duties of treating mission wounds, base camp accidents, administering shots, diminishing the effects of dysentery and the clap, the squadron's doctors were also constantly observing the mental condition of the airborne crews. To this end, they were required to "participate in frequent aerial flights," giving them firsthand knowledge of the mission experiences that psychologically affected the squadron's one hundred and sixty crewmembers. Even though *Bird*'s crew hadn't quite

---

1. AFHRA folder GP-449-SU-OP-S, 19 May 1944. Mission 62. Ships #1,3,6,8 Interrogation Reports.

2. AFHRA folder GP-449-SU-OP-S, 19 May 1944. Mission 62. Ship #66 Interrogation Report.

reached the mission halfway point, Captain Clark had seen something in Pop's crew which demanded a respite.[3]

As their boat slowly cut through the waters off Santa Cesarea Terme, Pop, Stan, and Bob silently viewed the town with wonder. It looked just like a picture from a travel brochure. Stone homes, Moorish-style villas, towers, and hotels seemed to hang in the balance on the karstic, white limestone cliffs overlooking the gem-quality, emerald-turquoise waters of the southern Adriatic Sea.

As Pop sailed the boat through the natural cut into the quarry turned boat dock, they lost all wind propulsion like they were in the tropical doldrums. "Alright crew, get out the oars and put your backs into it," Pop barked with arms akimbo, standing on the bow deck looking every bit the Captain Bligh, except that he was smiling.

After securing their sailboat to the dock, Stan and Bob walked unsteadily to their waiting bicycles as they attempted to regain their land legs. The boys took a dirt side road up into the overlooking hills, enjoying the onshore breeze, limestone outcroppings, and gnarly trees that reminded them of live oaks. If it wasn't for the blue waters of the Adriatic, they could have sworn they were in the Texas Hill Country outside the San Antonio airfields.

Getting back to the hotel, they found Harry playing pool with none other than *Skipper*'s pilot, Lt. Don Liddycoat, and his fellow officers.

"Hey there, Pop, Stan, Bob, some gig you've got going here," Liddycoat said, holding a cue stick in one hand and a stiff drink in the other.

"Don!" Pop exclaimed. "What? Thought you'd leave all the fun behind and come crash this party?" he asked as he eyed the group of boisterous Air Corps officers at the bar giving numerous toasts.

"So, what's going on over there?" he said, watching Lt. Elmer Meade raise a glass in toast.

---

3. 449th Bomb Group Association. *Book II: Tucson to Grottaglie*, p. 44. 1985.

"Meade's crew came in with us. 'Skin' Martin finished his 50th mission over La Spezia. First one to finish in the Group, the lucky bastard," Don said with a slight hint of jealousy.[4]

Hugh Martin, known as "Skin" due to his 5'8", 119-pound frame, had been "C" flight's lead bombardier flying in the *Nancy Jane #2* over La Spezia Harbor. The target was "well plastered," mostly by the "C" element due to his skill."[5]

"There's going to be a larger party after dinner so I'm going to our room to wash up," Don said, watching the Yugoslavian refugees set up the fine tablecloths, silverware, and numerous wine glasses in the adjoining dining room.

"Don't just wash up, have a maid draw a warm bath for you. Though if you're as grimy as I was, a pretty good oil ring will be left behind. Those new cold-water showers back at camp obviously aren't doing the job," Pop said with a smile.

As the Italian waiters brought the after-dinner coffees and desserts, most of the men lit up cigarettes, or in a few cases, cigars. Listening to the orchestral quartet, the clinking of silver spoons and forks against bone china, and observing the men all dressed in their "pinks and greens," Stan mused to himself that this must be some sort of fantasy. The only thing missing to make it complete were women. But all fantasies must end. And after four days, this one did also. "*I go home tomorrow,*" Stan thought to himself as a corner dinner table began to transform itself into a makeshift poker table. "*That's a hell of a thing to say, isn't it? Home.*" Had his outlook on life changed so much that he now considered Grottaglie, Italy his "home"? Pondering that thought for a second, he decided he should just

---

4. AFHRA folder GP-449-SU-OP-S, 19 May 1944. Mission 62. Ship #8 Interrogation Report.

5. Simmons, Robert M. Diary: April 3, 1944 to August 29, 1944. May 19, 1944 entry. Author's collection.

enjoy life as it presented itself. Putting his cigar in his mouth and grabbing his drink, Stan got up to join the game.[6]

"Short-snorter" that Stan made from his poker winnings of 23 May 1944, Santa Cesarea, Italy. Note signatures of H.J. "Skin" Martin, W.G. "Stan" Stanley, N.E. "Pop" Blomgren, Harry Bursten, Don Liddycoat, and others. Short-snorter tradition began pre-WWII and exploded during it. A transatlantic flier had his fellow crewmen sign a bank note. Upon presenting one's short snorter at a bar, those who could not produce theirs had to buy the presenter a drink. A small one, however—a short snort—in case they had to fly the following day. [Author's collection]

---

6. Stanley, William G. Personal WWII Diary: May 23, 1944 entry. Author's collection.

18

THE REAL WAR WILL NEVER GET IN THE BOOKS

20,200 FEET OVER WOLLERSDORF, AUSTRIA, MAY 29, 1944, 10:13 HRS.

DOUBT—AND THE MOST pernicious and debilitating of all, self-doubt—had begun to take hold of *Bird* sometime in mid-May. She was never sure exactly when it had begun, as subversive as it was. Perhaps it was after her landing attempt following a milk-run mission over Brasov, Rumania. That was just one day after losing *Kentuck* and four others from the Group over the Standard Oil Refinery at Ploesti.

As soon as Harry had started lowering her landing gear on the Grottaglie approach, she knew there was going to be trouble. Only she knew that her brakes were locked.

"Pop! Harry!" she screamed to no avail.

"Joseph! Charley! Can't you see my tires aren't moving?"

At their right and left waist gunner positions, Joseph and Charley had reported over the interphone that the bright yellow locking tabs were visible on the landing wheel struts, indicating that the struts were fully down and locked. What they failed to notice was the lack of the usual slight rotational movement of the wheels generated by the 120mph slipstream.

All *Bird* could do was close her eyes and hope Pop could pull the landing off. She once heard a pilot brag, "Any landing that you walk away from was a good landing." What a typically selfish, uncaring human viewpoint. An airplane could end up a crumpled piece of aluminum leaning against an earthen dike, but as long as the crew walked away, everything was apparently fine. "What a crock," she thought.

As soon as her two main landing gear wheels hit the crushed gravel runway at 100mph, everyone on board realized that the wheels were locked, especially Pop and Harry. If anyone was unaware, it was made obvious when *Bird*'s nose came crashing down, almost sending the front nose wheel up through the floor. Aided by Pop's and Harry's use of her rudders, ailerons, and differential engine throttling, she kept pretty straight, skidding down the runway for 200 yards. *Bird* then thought she was a goner when her right tire blew, causing her to veer toward the runway's edge and almost starting a dangerous ground loop, akin to an automobile performing a parking lot "donut." She should have trusted Pop more; he somehow corrected the potential ground loop and she continued to slide straight down the runway for an additional 100 yards when her brakes decided to unceremoniously release.

From that experience, all *Bird* lost were two ruined tires and a bit of her pride. Seven of the squadron's planes, including *Skipper*, had landed before her and witnessed the whole embarrassing affair. They wouldn't let her forget it, not with the occasional ribbing she would have to endure.

"Hey, *Bird*. Dig any ditches in the runway lately?"

"I smell burnt rubber. *Bird* must be taxiing up."

While the ribbing didn't help matters, it was the sudden disappearance of Pop and the crew and her being passed off to others that caused her to truly start questioning her ability.

"Do the guys blame me for the locked brakes or the broken engine cylinder studs that made them miss the next day's mission?" she pondered. "Have they abandoned me for another plane?"

She further reflected, "And I just couldn't get used to Lt. Isaacs. I mean, he wasn't even from our squadron, for Pete's sake! Besides, I just couldn't bring myself to drop my bombs on those men even if they were some of Hitler's boys." *Bird* had feigned poor visibility in not dropping her bombs on a German troop concentration ten miles southeast of Rome. Lt. Isaacs brought them on home.

"Then the next day they pass me off to Lt. Eaton, and while he's at least from our squadron, I sure didn't like the way he used my throttles and mixture controls. Maybe that's why he had to turn back after flying only a quarter of the way to Weiner-Neustadt while using over half my fuel."

"And then it wasn't but two days later that they gave him a brand new plane to fly. A silver job too," she said disdainfully, wondering if he had gone and complained about her. "What? One of us drab olive-greens isn't good enough for you?" she scoffed. Olive-green planes were now in the minority. Everyone wanted the new replacement "silver jobs" now.

"So, what do I do when Pop and the guys suddenly climb into me for a mission one morning after disappearing on me? Do I put on my best performance 'cause they came back for me? Heck no. I go and blow an engine cylinder," she thought disgustedly.

"What the bloody hell was I thinking? I wasn't thinking, that's for sure."

"So, of course with me out and the boys scheduled to fly to Nice, France the next day, they went looking for a plane. And they didn't have to look far, not with Lt. Liddycoat and his crew taking advantage and disappearing for a few days. *Skipper* was now available. I could tell he was pissed when given the news early the next morning as they loaded him up with 500-pounders."

"*Bird*, I'm madder than a sack full of cut snakes," *Skipper* bellowed as the armorers prepped him for the mission just after midnight.

"I'm supposed to be getting a few days rest and care, just like my crew, but no, you have to go get yourself hurt again so I have to pick up the slack. Again," *Skipper* added, glaring at *Bird* with the scaffolding tucked under her cowl-less number one engine.

Skipper couldn't understand it. *Bird* just wasn't the same. She had started out with the same uncertainties and questions of survival as they all had, but she had eventually gotten over the anxieties. "Missions were becoming habitual" for all of them.[1] But over the past few weeks *Bird* had missed five missions because of something mechanically wrong with her, and even turned back on one. *Skipper* hadn't missed a single mission yet.

As Pop and Harry slid into their seats and Bill began pre-engine start-up checks, *Skipper* could sense the confidence emanating from their handholds and from their simple, direct, no-nonsense commands.

"Now I see why *Bird* gloats about her crew," thought *Skipper* as he observed Bob double check his navigational charts while Stan checked out the Sperry bombsight usually used by Lt. John Mills.

"This should be an interesting mission," *Skipper* yelled to himself over the roar of his engines as he lifted off the runway. With a quick, furtive glance down and to his right, he caught a chagrined *Bird* staring forlornly up at him. *Skipper* felt a sudden pang of regret at the way he had talked to her, while at the same time he also felt a building frustration within. "Women!" was all he could come up with.

"Fight your foes on their soil! 'Old Glory's' honor revive! Drop the bombs, don't recoil. Be gallant, brave and survive!" Stan sang as he watched the Var River bridge violently lift up and then fall into the river through his

---

1. Simmons, Robert M. Diary: April 3, 1944 to August 29, 1944. May 25, 1944 entry. Author's collection.

bombsight as if it had been pulled by some form of celestial marionette strings.[2]

"This bombardier must be crazy, singing at a time like this," *Skipper* thought. The Flak gunners had found the 449th's altitude, according to the heavy, accurate, and intense shells now bursting among the planes. The familiar sensation of hot steel shrapnel tore through him with a blinding flash. Then a broiling fireball erupted immediately below him, causing eerie, insidious shadows to dance inside his fuselage.

"Jesus!" Stan exclaimed as he tore his eye away from the bombsight to stare down at what had been the bright, silver-bodied B-24 *High Life* just moments ago. A Flak shell had exploded inside its open bomb bay seconds after the bomb drop, instantly igniting the plane's remaining 1,300 gallons of aviation fuel. Pilot Gerald Warner and his crew never knew what hit them.

While he watched the remains of *High Life* break in half behind the top turret and fall silently into the surf of a beautiful French Riviera beach, the war came intimately closer to Stan and again reminded him of the fragile randomness of life. As he was intently watching and praying for signs of parachutes to emerge from the spiraling wreckage, another Flak shell burst in front of *Skipper's* nose, sending a chunk of steel through the armored plexiglass immediately above the bombsight's eyepiece where Stan's head had been just moments before, striking him harmlessly in the chest of his flak jacket.[3]

Usually, *Skipper* would have been in a jubilant mood as he taxied up to his parking spot, back from a successful mission. But he wasn't. Not even the sight of the returned Lt. Liddycoat waiting impatiently in *Toledo's*

---

2. *Be a Hero, My Boy!* Minkus, Mark and Kane, Henry. New York, NY: Patriotic Music Publishing, 1943.

3. That Flak fragment sits innocuously on the shelf containing my father's WWII mementos.

driver seat gave him reason to celebrate, for the look on the Lieutenant's face would have given the devil cause to retreat.

"Blomgren! What the hell do you mean bringing my plane back full of holes!" Don Liddycoat screamed as he jumped out of *Toledo*'s seat as soon as he saw Pop stiffly descend through the open bomb bay doors.

Before an astonished Pop could respond, Don ripped into him some more as he advanced hell-bent, with long, purposeful strides. "Of course, what should I expect from some tall, lanky Swede who's more at home at the tiller of a boat than at the controls of a 65,000-pound aircraft?" As Don finished his tirade a broad smile emerged on his face as he thrust his hand toward a now beaming and relieved Pop.

As Stan, Harry, and Bob tried to find room for themselves and their gear in the back seat, *Toledo* cast an appraising eye at *Skipper* who was staring at *Bird* who was doing her best to become invisible.

"*Skip*, I don't know what's going on between you and *Bird*, but I gotta tell ya it's just a crying shame to see something come between you two. Why, you two were closer than two hogs rolling in mud," *Toledo* said, as Don started him up after all the boys and their gear were stowed, causing him to squat down on all four wheels.

"Oh *Toledo*, it's too complicated to jaw about right now. Besides, it's up to *Bird* to figure out. Time will tell," *Skipper* said, though that's the one thing they didn't have: time. "We'll see how she handles the next mission."

"Handles? What do you mean how she'll handle the next mission?" *Toledo* yelled over his screaming engine as he was driven away in a white cloud of dust, not able to hear an answer.

Three days later *Bird* thought she was ready. She had been off for three days with Sergeant Lambertz and his ground crew checking her over with the skills of a proctologist. Feeling good with a new number one engine on her left wing and with Pop, Stan, and Harry having put her through the paces the previous afternoon, she was ready to prove to Pop, *Skipper*, and the whole squadron that she was back and ready for whatever could be thrown at her.

"Mind over matter. Yeah, that's all it is," *Bird* thought to herself the next morning as she watched her boys, for that's what she considered them, jump out of *Jimmy*, the GMC six-by-six truck.

"Hey *Bird*, wait till I tell you what *Toledo* told me is waiting for you all," *Jimmy* said breathlessly. It had been a busy night.

Bird didn't really listen. She loved the early morning with the sun just breaking the horizon, calm breezes, and the air cool and crisp with a hint of early morning dew condensing on her metal surfaces. Even with *Jimmy* blathering about 113 Flak guns and 175 enemy fighters waiting for them at the Wollersdorf, Austria airfield complex, she wouldn't be deterred from enjoying a piece of the morning. Not with the old crew on board, with Pop and Harry going over the checklist, and Stan looking over the bombsight singing softly to himself, with *Bird* listening to every word: "... *just hear those motors purring, whirring above over the land we love. So raise your hand up high to the army of the sky* ..."[4]

"Stan, you're no Dinah Shore," Bob yelled jokingly before Harry started cranking engine number three to life.

Bird couldn't hear Stan's entire response over the drone of her engine, but she caught something to do with not having her body either. It was great to hear the boys' jovial pre-mission banter again. She had missed it. "Yessiree, I've got this," *Bird* told herself again, though she knew her nerves were flying on thin air.

Once over the Adriatic, looking out over her right wing, a welcome surge of pride and sense of strength coursed through her as she viewed the eleven ships of the 719th leading the thirty-eight Liberators of the Group. She herself was leading the "A-3" box with *Skipper* tucked in on her left wing.

---

4. *Wings Over America*. Edwards, Leo and Hackerman, Ian. New York, NY: Belwin Inc., 1939.

It didn't take long for a tinge of sadness to interrupt her stream of bravado. The image of her squadron comrades floating gracefully beside her was much different than just a month ago. Had she looked out over her squadron in mid-April, she would have seen them all in the ubiquitous drab olive-green, attempting to be camouflaged from high-flying enemy aircraft against the greenish landscape below. What a fool's folly that had proven to be. Now half of them were in their natural metal finish, bright aluminum. Each one of them was a silent reminder that they had replaced a previous drab olive plane like herself. How long before they all would be bright aluminum, gleaming brilliantly against the dark blue skies at 25,000 feet?

"Shake off those thoughts, *Bird*. They aren't good for you," she told herself. "Remember: mind over matter."

Three hours later, with only twenty minutes remaining before the target, a voice was heard over the Group radio frequency calling for Lt. Colonel Gent, flying lead in *Hot To Go*, situated off *Bird*'s two o'clock. It was a new silver plane received into the 719th two weeks prior. "Pump up three lead, this is ship seven, over." Pump up three was this mission's call sign for the planes of the 449th.

"Gent here, go ahead, Fergus."

"I've lost a supercharger and am having trouble keeping up under full power."

"You need to stay with us for your own safety. If you can't, jettison bombs to lighten the load."

With the mention of ship number seven, a shiver of apprehension vibrated through *Bird*'s frame. She knew instantly who was in trouble: *Tess*. She was one of three remaining original planes of the squadron, and one that had greeted her into the family. *Two Ton Tessie*, flown by Lt. George Fergus, who had recently celebrated his 21st birthday and was just about done with his 50th and final mission. Living in the tent next to Pop and the gang, *Bird* had overheard many a "Fergus story" regaled from the flight deck.

Glancing to her right, *Bird* caught sight of *Tess* falling lower and behind her allotted slot in the "A" element. Within a few minutes, ten armed 500-pound bombs slipped from her bomb racks, diving for a lone factory in northeastern Austria that her bombardier, Lt. Foss Robinson, had spotted through his bombsight. Might as well hit something of possible importance. Thirty-five seconds later, the factory, which could have been producing anything from lethal ordnance to lederhosen, exploded.[5] A great shot, though not surprising. "Precision daylight bombing" was truly achievable given an experienced bombardier with no Flak, smoke screens, or enemy defenses hindering his motions.

Five thousand pounds lighter, *Tess* was able to catch up and fall back into her position, safe among her protective squadron.

"*Tess*. It's me, *Bird*. You doing OK over there?" *Bird* asked with concern. It was a long way back to base with an engine trying to operate at 25,000 feet without a supercharger.

"Hey, *Bird*, I'm doing OK for now, but something isn't quite right with the supercharger in another engine, my number two," *Tess* said, slightly out of breath, as if she had emphysema.

"Pump up three lead, this is ship seven, over," was soon heard again.

"Gent here, good to see you back, Fergus."

"Not for long, Colonel, I just lost another supercharger and am falling back."

"Contact escorts on VHF channel Able Colon, call sign Airslug. Hopefully they can spare a few P-51's to cover you. See you back at base and good luck."

It was short and to the point, but Colonel Gent had a lot on his mind at the moment. He knew the safety of the Group and the success of the mission easily trumped concerns over a single plane and ten men. The

---

5. AFHRA folder GP-449-SU-OP-S, 29 May 1944. Mission 69. Ship #11 Interrogation Report.

well-being of a friend and his crew met the cold, hard, sacrificial demands of war. As lead pilot for the Group, he controlled the movement of all thirty-eight planes, and they were two minutes away from the all-important Initial Point, the IP, over the hamlet of Altenmarkt, fourteen miles from their target. It was time to concentrate on tightening up the Group, turn them on a true 140° heading to target, and turn the plane over to the bombardiers for the bomb run.

Tess didn't get an escort. The twenty P-51s were about to have their hands full with seventy enemy aircraft that were flanking the Group from high above, some of which noticed *Tess* dropping back and eventually turning around. All alone.[6]

It took only three minutes for some of the circling jackals to pounce on the isolated, vulnerable *Tess* trying to hightail it home. Diving to get into the thicker, denser air at lower altitudes to give his supercharger-less engines some much needed oxygen, Lt. Fergus hoped his six gunners could fend off the attacking pack of bandits.

They couldn't.

Bird watched out her tail turret as *Tess* was shredded by cannon fire, causing engines to flame before she went into a flat spin, crashing into the picturesque downtown of the village of Ybbs an der Donau, Austria. But not before ten parachutes were observed billowing in the wind. Lt. Fergus and his crew would spend the remaining year of the war as German POWs. *Tess,* however, was a burning crumpled mass of aluminum on the banks of the Danube.

Bird swore her skin was beginning to sweat, even at −20°F. She tried to fight the insidious, creeping self-doubt again beginning to circulate through her. "Mind over matter. Mind over matter," she began to repeat to herself, to no avail. She was becoming damn tired of coming face to face

---

6. AFHRA folder GP-449-SU-OP-S, 29 May 1944. Mission 69. Narrative Report.

with her own mortality day after day. She needed help. And it came to her from the unlikeliest of places: her nose.

"*Freude schöner Götterfunken, Tochter aus Elysium, Wir betreten feuertrunken, Himmlische, dein Heiligtum! Deine Zauber binden wieder, Was die Mode streng geteilt; Alle Menschen werden Brüder Wo dein sanfter Flügel weilt*," Stan sang as he tried to distinguish the target's aiming point through smoke and flames from the preceding Group's bomb strikes.

Though *Bird* found it bizarre to be listening to the final Germanic movement of Beethoven's 9th Symphony, "*Ode to Joy,*" while bombing the German war machine far below, the martial tone and cadence brought her out of her spiral of panic-induced self-doubt and reminded her of the task at hand.

Having practiced her German with the help of *Buzzer, Patches,* and poor *Tess,* the oldest planes in the squadron, she liked and appreciated the translated last two lines of the poem set to music:

All people become brothers,
Where thy gentle wing abides.

On either side of *Bird*'s wings, it was anything but gentle at the moment. As Stan toggled the bombs, angry black bursts of Flak began exploding all around and within the leading "A" element of the Group.

With *Bird*'s nose stuck out in front of them all, *Skipper* mumbled to himself that he "thought 'Pop' Blomgren and *Bird* were a goner."[7]

After fourteen minutes of surviving the relentless pounding of Flak hell served up by the 113 guns, it was the Luftwaffe's turn to inflict damage.

It wasn't just machine gun and 20 or 30mm cannon fire directed at them, but it seemed like every twin engine Me-110 or Ju-88 held four

---

7. Blomgren, Norman E. The War Diary of Capt. Norman E. Blomgren: May 29, 1944 entry. Author's collection. That night, Pop recalled his wingman's thoughts of the mission—that was Don Liddycoat, *Skipper*'s pilot.

wing-mounted rockets capable of sending a 90-pound, 210mm exploding warhead at them. And they did.

Bird felt powerless to do anything to stop them, as did her gunners. Approaching head on at a combined closure speed of over 460mph, it was a deadly game of chicken, in which the Germans would purposely flinch first. At a distance of 800 to 1,000 yards, *Bird* would observe a small explosion under both wings of the quickly approaching planes, usually three or four abreast, just before they suddenly veered off before coming within the range of *Bird*'s gunners.

Leaving eerie, white contrail streaks, the approaching warheads would mesmerize *Bird* and her crew. For unlike the invisible Flak shells, one could watch these death-on-rails as they approached on their two-second journey, and all you could do was close your eyes and crouch into your Flak helmet.[8]

During the bombing run, *Suzan Jane*, flown by Lt. Frank Henggler in the "C" element behind *Bird*, was hit by a lethal combination of rockets, 20mm cannon fire, and Flak, sending her to her death in the smoking ruins of the Wollersdorf Airfield complex.

Fourteen of the Group's planes were damaged plus two lost. Everyone, man and plane alike, hoped they would never have to visit there again.

Landing three hours later, as Pop brought her to a stop back at her safe parking spot, *Bird* couldn't stop herself from shaking. So much for mind over matter. All she could do was try to extinguish her internal anxiety-ridden crisis and attempt to put on a calm, reassuring facade of strength. But then again, she didn't have a poker face like that of Pop or Stan. She was really wondering if she could do it all over again. As it turned out, she couldn't.

---

8. Stanley, William G. Personal WWII Diary: May 29, 1944 entry. Author's collection.

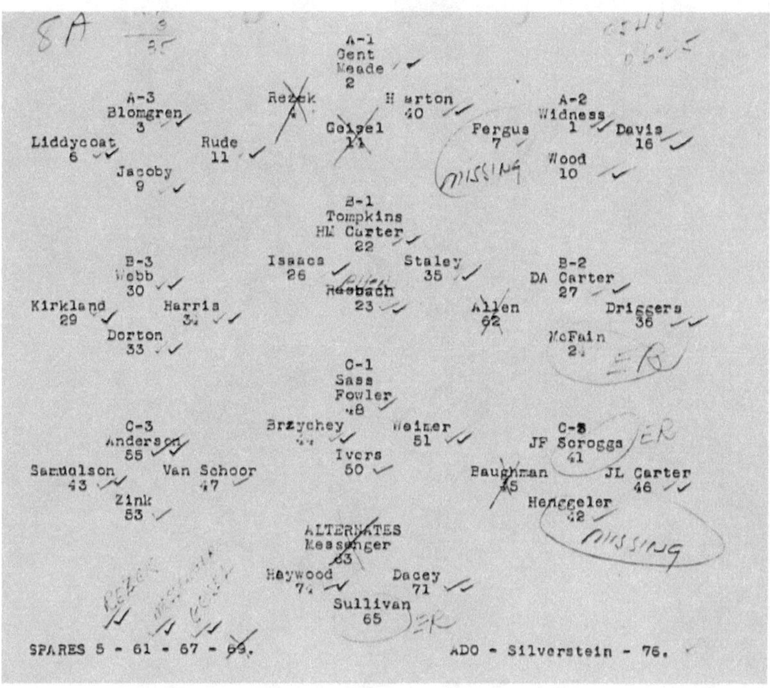

Flight formation map of May 29, 1944 Mission to Weiner-Neustadt, Austria. Markings are those from an Intelligence Officer, or perhaps someone in the flight tower checking off planes as they returned, or circling those that did not, such as #7, Two Ton Tessie or #42, Suzan Jane. ER indicates those that returned early, while those crossed out indicate planes that did not take off and were replaced by a spare. Worrybird, #3, is out front in the A-3 box, with Skipper, #6, flown by Don Liddycoat, off her left wing. [AFHRA folder GP-449-SU-OP-S, 29 May 1944. Mission 69]

19

I CAN'T UNDERSTAND IT!

19,600 FEET OVER SIMERIA, RUMANIA, JUNE 2, 1944, 09:36 HRS.

IT WAS JUST ANOTHER of the early morning pre-mission rituals the following day as *Bird* watched the men saunter through the parked planes on their way to the 04:00 mission briefing. It gave her time to think. At least the shaking had stopped.

It was barely two months ago that *Tess, Consolidated Mess, Dragon Lady, Dixie Belle, Hoosier,* and others, all gone now, had told her that you put yourself on the line for all of them, your family. But that family had disintegrated. There was no cohesion now with the shiny new replacements filling the void. There was no time to get acquainted with the fresh fish, not that she wanted to. Why make friends with someone who may be savagely torn from you, leaving yet another invisible wound in your existence? Another hole in one's fabric of nerves which was already barely holding together?

No, she was in this to survive, and if she could do that while protecting her crew and, on the outside chance, *Skipper*, that was fine with her. She'd get her chance today.

She was already on edge when her wheels left the ground two hours later. She had learned they were heading back to within twelve miles of yesterday's target to hit another aircraft assembly plant in Ebreichsdorf, outside of Vienna. So much for wishing not to return.

It was while she was jockeying into her assigned formation slot leading the high "C" element 3,000 feet over Manduria, Italy twenty minutes later that she noticed who was leading the 449th's thirty-eight planes today. She mumbled to herself in panic, "Mother of God. We're going to be nothing but cannon and Flak fodder!"

The Army Air Corps, in its infinite wisdom, was once again putting their lives into the hands of the lead pilot who had led the disastrous bombing of La Spezia harbor two weeks earlier. But worse, this was also the same pilot who had led the Group's May 5th mission over the same Flak positions on their way to Ploesti and on the return, which caused the totally preventable demise of *Kentuck*. Obviously the Air Corps was slow to learn, or was hard up for lead pilots. All *Bird* knew was that she and her crew were going to have nothing to do with today's mission. Not if she could help it.

"Impish one three lead, this is ship three, over," Pop called over the VHF radio with that day's 449th call sign.

"Lead here, go ahead Blomgren."

"Sir, number one and number four generators are out and we've developed a bad gas leak. Request early return."

"Roger. Proceed back to base. Out."

Skipper, who had heard the open channel conversation, noticed *Bird* losing altitude and turning back. "*Bird!* What are you doing?"

"*Skipper*, come on back with me, please. There's nothing but disaster up ahead with that lead pilot. He's the one that killed *Kentuck* and about made us run into each other over La Spezia! Remember?" *Bird* pleaded.

"No can-do *Bird*, I'm feeling fine," *Skipper* said. "I've got to stay with the Group. I'll see you back home." *Bird* could only hear his last words faintly as the distance increased. *Skipper* himself was wondering if he and *Bird* were beginning to drift apart. "Is it possible that *Bird* was intentionally running away?" he reluctantly pondered.

Seven hours later, *Bird* sat anxiously watching as the planes returned, silently counting them off, one by one. As she hit thirty-five, she finally could breathe once more. Subtracting the two other early returns, all had come back, with twenty bearing Flak scars. Later she would learn that six men came home injured, mostly bombardiers and navigators, including *Skipper*'s.[1]

But it was when she saw the set, furrowed look of all eleven of the squadron's planes from the mission that she knew there had been some other kind of trouble.

The Group's radio wave scuttlebutt quickly circulated among the planes, still hot under their engine cowlings, as they repeated their crews' immediate mission recall at the post-mission interrogations:

"'*B' section crossed over 'C' section spoiling bomb run,*" *Salty Dog* and *Headin Home* remembered.

"*From IP to target, bomb run all screwed up. Bomb results all fucked up,*" the veteran *Patches* said, not mincing any words.

"*Lead navigator poor on bomb run, went through too many Flak areas,*" *Hoppy* and *Bucket of Bolts* concurred.

"*Leaving target excess speed was used. 'Tail end Charley' had to pull 45 inches Hg, 2,500 RPM for 20 minutes to catch up,*" *Cinnsy's Margie* bemoaned.

---

1. AFHRA folder GP-449-SU-OP-S, 30 May 1944. Mission 70. Injury and Damage Report.

Ghost O' the Omar didn't hold back his feelings either, *"Leadership today was 'piss poor,' inexcusable. Even on bomb run which was in a turn, our ship was tipped over. It's a wonder bombs didn't tear thru side of ship."*

And as confirmation, *Shamrock* added, *"Lead piss poor, 30° bank on bomb run. Threw bombs."*

And perhaps the most poignant of all came from none other than *Skipper*: *"Lead fucked up on bomb run."*[2]

The following day's reconnaissance photos told the story of a mission absolutely mishandled and wasted. Of the 346 bombs dropped, 240 of them plowed fields outside the town of Sollonau, eight miles southwest of the intended target. So much for "precision daylight bombing." It would be the worst bombing performance of the 449th during the war.[3]

Perhaps that mission's Deficiencies and Suggestion Report, including the above comments drafted by Major Arthur Harvey, the Group's Intelligence Officer, and forwarded to Colonel Gent and Lt. Colonel George Blasé, the Group's Air Inspector, finally did the trick. That pilot would never fly Group lead again. Or would he?

Bird felt somewhat vindicated, but it didn't make her feel any better. She didn't see much difference between what she had just done and when Pop had left his position in the "B" element led by the same pilot during the April 24th Ploesti mission. Pop had called that lead pilot a jerk and left him before *Bird* and her crew were led into trouble. "Using his head" is what Pop had said about protecting himself and his crew. *Bird* decided that that's what she had also done: used her head.

In the next morning's pre-dawn hours, as the boys were methodically checking out her well-being and their own on-board stations, *Bird* had

---

2. AFHRA folder GP-449-SU-OP-S, 30 May 1944. Mission 70. Ship # 5, 11, 15, 33, 34, 43, 66, 72, 6 Interrogation Reports.

3. AFHRA folder GP-449-SU-OP-S, 30 May 1944. Mission 70. Strike Assessment Report.

a decision to make. Would she be a part of this mission? *Toledo* had just told her some discouraging news. It wasn't the threat they were going to encounter: 234 Flak guns, plus up to 150 enemy aircraft doing their best to prevent them from doing more harm to the Ploesti refineries. No, as incredulous as it sounded, the jerk lead pilot from yesterday was up again as lead. *Bird* had lost about all faith and confidence in the Air Corps.

It wasn't until *Bird* was out over the Adriatic that she finally decided. If she was to turn back, it was prudent to do so before you got into enemy territory.

It would have served *Bird* well to have listened to Pop as he radioed to the lead to again report he had lost two generators and to request an early return. But she had pretty much shut down listening to anyone, just so she wouldn't have to hear the pleading, grumbling and, worst of all, disappointment from her fellow squadron planes, especially from *Skipper* who was off her wing.

If she had listened closely, however, she would have realized it wasn't the "jerk" pilot who had been listed on last night's mission schedule to lead, responding to Pop's request. It was instead Lt. Colonel William Tope from HQ flying as lead in ship #68, *Fickle Finger*. Obviously, a lead pilot and aircraft change had been made at the last moment. Perhaps the previous evening's Deficiencies and Suggestion Report had finally come to the attention of Colonel Gent.

It turned out to be a well led, though costly, mission. While all thirty-seven 449th ships returned, twenty-eight incurred Flak damage. Sixteen B-24s from the other three Groups that joined in the attack were shot or knocked down by enemy aircraft or Flak.

Bird caught a lot of grief concerning her "unexcused absences," even after her ground crew opened her number four engine cowling and its generator unceremoniously dropped to the ground beneath her. The grief she received from her fellow squadron mates continued unabated all through the night and into the morning. Not that she would have gotten any sleep anyway. A damn bothersome German reconnaissance plane had been flying night missions over the field every night for the past week. Of course, the defensive ack-ack batteries around the field opened up on him every time, but so far the prey had been illusive, as was sleep for the planes and men of the Group.[4]

"The boys appear raggedy-assed tired this morning," *Skipper* said to no one in particular as he was being fitted with the usual 500 pounders.

"With Vega at our zenith, I'd say it's about 03:00, pretty darn early," *Bird* replied, remembering some of Bob's celestial navigation mutterings.

"You never cease to amaze me, *Bird,* with your plethora of eclectic minutia," *Skipper* replied with a good-hearted chuckle.

"You know me, *Skipper,* always listening and soaking it all up like a sponge," *Bird* countered, glad for the friendly, though recently elusive, bantering.

"Just remember I'll be up there for you. *Jimmy* said all of us are flying as alternates this mission so we'll be spread out all over, depending upon where we'll be needed to fill gaps in the formation," informed *Skipper.* Based on *Bird*'s expression, she hadn't heard the disturbing news.

"Ooh, I don't like the sound of that, but thanks for the warning. I would have wondered if the gang was being torn apart," *Bird* said, as she and *Skipper* stared at each other in the kind of wordless communication that can only transpire between two who have been intertwined via shared traumatic experiences.

"Engineer to pilot," Bill Blankenship reluctantly called over the interphone five hours later as *Bird* crossed the Rumanian border. They were on their way to the Simeria, Rumania marshaling yards, 120 miles ahead.

"Go ahead, Bill," said Pop.

"Hate to tell you this, but I'm reading 0 Amps on number four generator and number two is fluctuating and slowly dropping. I've toggled the

---

4. Stanley, William G. Personal WWII Diary: June 2, 1944 entry. Author's collection.

generator switches with no change in reading," Bill reported, now awaiting a verbal eruption.

"Jesus H. Chr-," Pop caught himself before completing the sacrilegious exclamation. It wouldn't do for the aircraft commander to appear flummoxed. Turning around to look at Bill in the engineer compartment and fixing him with a quizzical stare, all Bill could do was shrug.

"Watch number two and let me know if it changes, Bill," Pop said resignedly as he turned around and gave Harry a "what the hell do we do now?" look.

"Will do," replied Bill.

"We've got about forty-five minutes to the IP and then a twelve-minute bomb run. Other than a loss of electrical current, all engines are running fine," informed Harry, knowing Pop would want all relevant information concerning mission status and *Bird*'s health before making a return decision.

"What the heck are you doing, *Bird*?" Pop softly questioned to himself, though not so quietly that *Bird* couldn't hear.

"There is no way I am going to turn you around. Not three missions in a row, no siree! So, you just get that out of your head," Pop murmured as Harry glanced over, wondering if Pop was speaking to him. Seeing Pop wordlessly talking to himself, Harry knew that the pilot was just going through his methodical decision-making process; a process that hadn't failed them yet.

"Sure wish I knew what I was doing, Pop, 'cause I don't know what's going on," *Bird* anxiously replied. "Wish I had the gang up here next to me," she said, feeling a further loss of current as her number two generator quit, which caused a flurry of commotion on her flight deck.

"Well, *Worrybird*, or should I say *Libby*? You may not have your 'gang' up next to you but I'm here for you," was suddenly heard in the peripheral. It was a spectral voice out of the distant past, though she couldn't quite place it.

"At your five o'clock."

As Bill rotated the electrically driven top turret situated above his engineer station to assess the impact of the current loss, *Bird* caught sight of the vocal apparition.

It took a moment to retrieve the precariously tethered memory fragment and comprehend who she was seeing. For not only was it a vocal apparition, but a visual one also. It was none other than *Valiant Virgin-ia,* the plane with the buck-naked, perky breasted, blond beauty riding a 500-pound bomb as her nose art. Yes, sir, except for some peeling paint, engine grime covering her wings, random bright aluminum patches adorning her skin, and twenty-eight small yellow bombs painted above her caricature, in contrast to *Bird*'s twenty-five, it was the *Valiant* seen so long ago at Hamilton Airfield, California. She, too, had come of age.

"*Valiant*! Wait. What are you doing here? How long have you been here?"

"Oh, I've been here all along, but you've been too busy playing mother hen to your four other squadron planes scattered up in "A" and "B" element up ahead to have noticed me."

"Yeah, but when did you get into the 449th? I haven't seen you around."

"Well, you sure know how to make a girl feel welcome," *Valiant* scoffed as her pilot, Lt. Floyd Haywood, brought *Valiant* closer to *Bird* after Pop, their flight leader, had ordered the formation to tighten up. They were getting close to the IP.

"To answer your question, I actually got here before you did. As a matter of fact, I saw you arrive as you flew over us way back in April. I'm in the 716th Squadron down at the other end of the runway from you so we never cross paths. We were on that mission together outside Rome a few weeks ago, and then again the other day when you skedaddled back to base. So, you doing OK here?"

Bird struggled to gather her thoughts. Just how much do I tell her? Do I tell her I'm flying on thin air and am tingling all over even without two of my generators? That I question myself about my abilities during every mission? No, I'll keep those thoughts to myself, she finally decided. "I've got two generators out but I'm barreling on ahead. I mean, what else can I do? I'm not about to turn around again, not this close," *Bird* replied with false bravado, mimicking Pop's words and actions.

"Damn right, girl. We Dallas North American Liberators need to stick together," *Valiant* said with forceful conviction.

"You mean you, me, and *Skipper*?"

"Plus a few others, *Miss De Flak, Racy Tomato,* and *Th' Inhoomin Critter* 'bout rounds it out. Most of the rest are those Fords out of Dee-troit, to mimic that twit *Toledo*," *Valiant* said.

"Oh, he pays you a visit too, does he?" *Bird* said as she felt Pop adjust her heading along with the rest of the Group as they reached the IP.

"Sure, he makes it his sworn duty to visit all of us, spreading that claptrap of his. Though I must admit he was right on about this mission," *Valiant* said, noticing her bomb doors opening.

"I missed him this morning so I didn't catch the scoop. What did he have to say about today?" *Bird* asked, as she tried to ignore Stan's singing. Something about into the wild blue yonder. What the devil is a yonder she wondered?

"He said we wouldn't see any enemy aircraft and very little Flak. A real milk run. That's why it didn't surprise me that you didn't turn around. I'm surprised you haven't learned to trust your pilot by now. If you did, you wouldn't have been shaking on the way up. By the way, you notice you aren't shaking now?" *Valiant* said in a somewhat motherly tone.

Bird was about to deny what had been plainly obvious to the most casual observer, something *Valiant* was not. But then she realized that, by golly, she wasn't shaking. Not since she started to talk with *Valiant*, she figured. How about that?

"That's alright. I shake like an autumn leaf in a Texas blue norther right before takeoff. But let me tell you, once my wheels leave the ground, I'm all in. I just focus on my crew and do my darndest to have my bombardier drop those bombs on the target. After all, that's why we're all here, isn't it *Bird*?"

Then *Bird* picked up what Stan was singing, "*Minds of men fashioned a crate of thunder, sent it high into the blue; Hands of men blasted the world asunder.*" *Bird* was suddenly 5,000 pounds lighter as her bomb load fell. Stan finished the last stanza of the official Air Corps song as Pop put her into a right bank rally. "*How they lived God only knew! Souls of men dreaming of skies to conquer, Gave us wings, ever to soar! With scouts before and bombers galore. Hey! Nothing'll stop the Army Air Corps!*"

During the return leg of the mission, *Bird* pondered the words spoken by *Valiant* and those sung by Stan. If she interpreted the not-entirely-flattering lyrics correctly, she indeed was one of those crates of thunder flying high in the sky and blasting the world asunder.

It was the last line of lyrics that stopped *Bird* cold. "*Nothing'll stop the Army Air Corps,*" she repeated over and over. "Certainly, whoever wrote those words wouldn't understand an Air Corps bomber consciously stopping itself from completing the mission. The whole reason of their existence?" she wondered, becoming ill at ease with her actions the past few weeks.

"What was it that *Valiant* had said? After all, that's why we're all here?" *Bird* recalled as she impatiently waited for *Skipper* to land. She had something to tell him. Not an apology exactly. More of an affirmation of faith. Faith in herself. In Pop and her crew. And faith in her mercurial family, no matter how many times the faces would change.

Bird finished the month of June having flown forty missions in total, plus missing an additional nine since her arrival due to last-minute mechanical problems or outright early returns. This would put *Bird* near the top of an uncomplimentary list of Group "Groundhogs," those planes that spent a lot of time on the ground either being repaired or who had the most early returns. *Skipper,* on the other hand, was tied for the top spot on the converse list. A list of "Workhorses," planes that hadn't missed a single mission.[5]

Bird had two more "loss of faith" relapses before finally settling down into her uninterrupted mission groove. The first occurred due to her inability to retract her wheels after takeoff on a June 13th mission to Munich, Germany. After a quick return to the field, Pop and the boys literally ran to a spare ship, *Th' Inhoomin Critter*, and finally caught up to the Group to complete the mission courteously filled with Flak from the 286 heavy ground guns that awaited the Group.[6]

The other instance, two weeks later, found *Bird* unable to release her left brake while taxiing out on a June 26th mission to Vienna. Again, the crew about broke their necks trying to get to a spare ship. In this instance, it was *Harper's Ferry*, an original December 1943 cadre ship that had seen too many missions and had too many hours on its engines. Taking off seventeen minutes after the last plane, Pop had to use excessive power and Stan had to drop four bombs into Lake Balaton in western Hungary not only to catch the formation, but to maintain formation position. That was one tired Liberator.

After Stan dropped their remaining six bombs on the targeted Heinkel aircraft factory, Pop had to feather the number one engine because of a loss of oil pressure.[7] A tired old ship, low on fuel, running on three overtaxed engines and falling behind the formation to become Tail-end Charlie over

---

5. 449th Bomb Group Association. *Book IV: Maximum Effort*, pp. 103–105. Panama City, FL: Norfield Publishing, 2000.

6. AFHRA folder GP-449-SU-OP-S, 13 June 1944. Mission 79. Intelligence Annex to Operations Order.

7. Stanley, William G., Personal WWII Diary: June 26, 1944 entry. Author's collection.

German-held Austria with a reported hundred enemy fighters in the area. Not good.

Fortunately for Pop and the crew, most of the enemy fighters were fiercely engaged with two other Groups that were currently bombing nearby oil refineries outside of Vienna. And to further increase their chance of returning, the crew picked up an escorting angel off their wing, the *Lady In The Dark*, flown by Lt. John Belton of San Francisco.

It's always good to have someone flying off your wing. If not for cover from its additional ten Brownings, then for moral support. And of course, there's the pragmatic benefit of having someone able to report to headquarters where you went down.

[*Courtesy of 449th Bomb Group Association Collection*]

Pop and his crew were cashing in on a chit. For they had paid it forward only two days prior when they themselves had escorted a fellow straggler attempting to make it back from the Group's most dreaded target: Ploesti.

CONFIDENTIAL

Observations confirming claims of others: _______________

Our Group A/C Losses:
(Time) (Altitude) (Place by Name & Coordinates) (Description and No. Chutes &c)

Other A/C Losses:

Crew Injuries: (Name, Rank, ASN, and Extent of Injury) _______________

Extent of Damage to own A/C from FLAK:

Extent of Damage to own A/C from FIGHTERS:

Damage from other reasons:

PRO STory or possible citations

Other comments or suggestions (Include Radio and Armament deficiencies, etc.)

Interrogated by _______________

ARTHUR HANEY,
Major, Air Corps,
Group S-2.

Typical interrogation report of a rough mission. June 6, 1944 mission to Ploesti, Rumania, ship #16, Consolidated Mess #2, Lt. Leland A. Davis pilot. "Turned into flack over target and into Belgrade [38 miles off course]. Third straight day low element of B unit has been in trail of attack unit A and too close so in prop wash and makes poor formation. Most fuck up formation ever been in from start to finish." Lt. Davis will receive the Silver Star and the Distinguished Flying Cross, the DFC, for bringing Consolidated Mess #2 home from the later July 9th bombing of Ploesti. This was accomplished without a right rudder, ailerons, #3 engine, no hydraulics or instruments. [AFHRA folder GP-449-SU-OP-S, 06 June 1944. Mission 75]

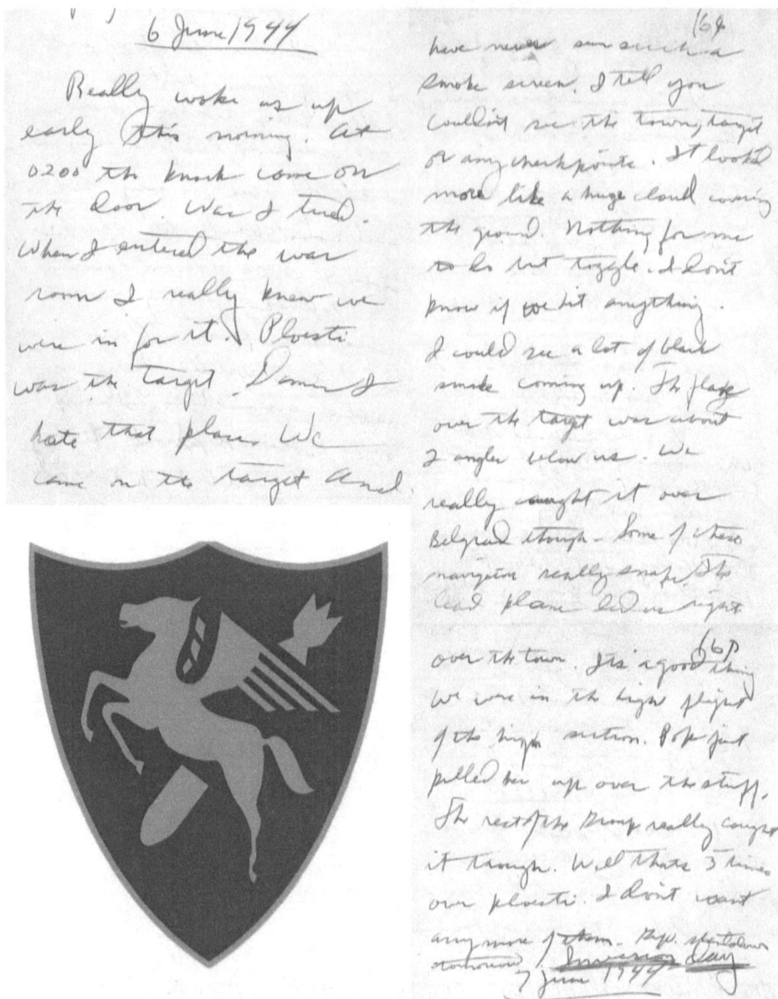

Diary entry of William "Stan" Stanley detailing experience of June 6, 1944 bombing of Ploesti, Rumania. Worrybird was leading the five ship B-2 box as opposed to Lt. Davis in Consolidated Mess #2 leading the adjacent B-3 box as mentioned in the previous interrogation report. [Author's Collection]

Diary transcription:

June 6, 1944

Really woke us up early this morning. At 0200 the knock came on the door. Was I tired. When I entered the war room I really knew we were in for it. Ploesti was the target. Damn I hate that place. We came on target and have never seen such a smoke screen. I tell you couldn't see the town, target or any checkpoint. It looked more like a huge cloud covering the ground. Nothing for me to do but toggle [the bombs]. *I don't know if we hit anything. I could see a lot of black smoke coming up. The flak over the target was about 2 angels* [two thousand feet] *below us. We really caught it over Belgrade though. Some of these navigators really snafu. The lead plane led us right over the town. It's a good thing we were in the high flight of the high section. Pop just pulled her up and over the stuff. The rest of the Group really caught it though. Well that's 3 times over Ploesti. I don't want anymore of them.* [Unknown to Stan, he will bomb Ploesti four more times.] *Grp. standdown tomorrow. Invasion Day.*

Pop was proud of his action of *"pulling up high above the rest of the ships so that my element of five ships were clear of the trouble."*[8] Other ships of the Group were not as fortunate, such as #74, *Valient Virgin-ia*. Lt. Floyd H. Haywood was piloting *Valient* 2,000 feet lower, in the furthest back C-3 box. Flak took out his number four engine causing him to be Tail-end Charlie. After *Valient* dropped her bomb load, two Me-109s and an FW-190 shot away her ailerons, flaps, number one engine, and hydraulic system. Lt. Haywood was still able to get her home to Grottaglie, though

---

8. Blomgren, Norman E. The War Diary of Capt. Norman E. Blomgren: June 6, 1944 entry. Author's collection.

as he stated in his interrogation report: "*Came back on wing—two engines and a prayer.*"[9] Lt. Haywood received the DFC for his actions.

9. AFHRA folder GP-449-SU-OP-S, 6 June 1944. Mission 75. Ship #74 Interrogation Report.

20

DAMN, I HATE THAT PLACE

LT. WILLIAM STANLEY WAR DIARY, JUNE 6, 23, 24, JULY 9, 15, 1944

THE MAXIM "An army marches on its stomach," attributed to both King Frederick the Great and Napoleon Bonaparte, certainly was true of armies before the 20th century. By World War II, however, armed forces had become so mechanized that it wasn't food that was required to move vehicles, supplies, men, and instruments of war. It was oil. Indeed, oil was required to wage, and more importantly to win, a war, and Nazi Germany didn't have enough of it to maintain its farcical "Thousand-year Reich."

What they did have, however, were large lignite coal deposits and world renowned petrochemists who, in the 1920's and 1930's, invented the world's first synthetic liquid fuel process. By 1943 this synthetic petroleum was supplying Germany with 52% of its needs. However, with domestic oil reserves supplying only 11% and Western and USSR imports cut off, where would they obtain the rest? The answer was Rumania with its huge petroleum reserves and Europe's largest refinery complex of thirteen separate refineries surrounding the town of Ploesti. Following the bloodless transformation of an independent Rumania into a German ally in the summer of 1940, Hitler had gained Ploesti without firing a shot.[1]

One of the outcomes of the January 1943 Casablanca Conference between President Franklin Roosevelt and England's Prime Minister Winston Churchill was the establishment of the Combined Bomber Offensive and the agreement that the refinery complex at Ploesti had to be destroyed. Churchill had labeled the Rumanian refineries the "taproot of German might." And the only way to eradicate an invasive, toxic weed is to pull it up by the roots.

Planning for the first large-scale bombing of Ploesti began immediately. What would eventually be known as operation TIDAL WAVE was set for August 1, 1943. Five Groups totaling 177 B-24s of the Air Corps' 9th Air Force, loaded with 500 and 1000-pound bombs, took off from Benghazi, Libya, 1,200 miles from Ploesti. Fifty-four of the planes and their crews were lost to enemy fighters, Flak, and accidents enroute. Fifty-five more were damaged. It would go down in history, a day forever known as "Black Sunday."

While refinery output dropped by 40% immediately following the bombing, within a few weeks output was back and actually exceeding pre-bombing levels. The tenacity and efficiency of the Rumanian and German refinery construction crews, aided by thousands of enslaved laborers, could quickly repair extensive damage caused by a single, uncoordinated bombing mission.

It was obvious that an unrelenting, multi-group bombing campaign would be required to destroy this strategic target. That campaign began

---

1. https://defense.info/re-thinking-strategy/2018/10/oil-and-war/ ; Stout, Jay A. *Fortress Ploesti: The Campaign to Destroy Hitler's Oil*. Havertown, PA: Casemate, 2003.

April 5, 1944 with *Bird*, still the virgin, watching as twenty-seven B-24s of the 449th took off for the first of their eleven missions over Ploesti. *Bird* and her crew would visit Ploesti in seven of those missions. She didn't have any good memories of those seven except possibly her fourth trip on June 24th, targeting the largest refinery of them all.

<u>24,500 feet over the Romano-Americano Refinery, Ploesti, Rumania June 24, 1944, 09:44 hrs.</u>

"BOY, I HATE THIS PLACE," Stan whispered to himself as he was given control of *Bird* as they entered the bomb run.[2] He had never seen such large blossoms of Flak as when they had reached the IP a few minutes earlier. Since Stan's last visit on June 6th, the Germans had added an additional 92 Flak guns so that 234 of them were now doing their best to knock *Bird* out of the sky before Stan dropped her devastating cargo. It was no time to be singing.

Leading the high "B" element, *Bird* knew she had to be at her best. Her fellow brothers and sisters relied upon her, Pop, and Stan to place their bombs on target so the rest could follow suit.

She wasn't sure which sensation she was aware of first. The sight of a bright red explosion of seven and a half pounds of high explosive, the expanding black cloud enveloping her right wing, or the searing hot tear of her number four engine nacelle.

"Pop! Harry! Feather my number four before it rips me apart," *Bird* exclaimed before she suddenly felt its propeller blades turning into the wind, causing its spin-induced vibration to cease. Harry was on his toes. Almost simultaneously, Harry advanced the throttles on her three remain-

---

2. Stanley, William G. Personal WWII Diary: June 24, 1944 entry. Author's collection.

ing engines, causing a disconcerting change in the tone of her engine drone. They had to remain in lead, it was too late for a lead change.

"I can do this," *Bird* told herself with firm confidence. Though *Skipper* wasn't with her today, others were, situated immediately off her wing and behind her in their five-plane box. *Consolidated Mess #2* in its bright silver skin was off her left wing, while ol' *Buzzer*, an original ship, was off her right. It always felt good to have one of the old guards with her. Directly behind her was *Our Baby*, who had arrived in the squadron two weeks before her. And behind her was *Racy Tomato*, who had replaced the unfortunate *Kentuck*. While she belonged to the 718th Squadron, she was also a Dallas North American, having come off the line one month after *Bird*, therefore she too was in her bright skinned "birthday suit."

On so many of her missions, *Bird* wished she could have closed her eyes to the lurking dangers, seen and unseen, she was about to fly into. As if that would have protected her. She should have heeded the old adage, "Be careful what you wish for."

For a split second she was aware of another red flash in front of her right wing, this one between her feathered number four and the straining number three. She certainly felt the iron fragments entering her right wing that somehow missed her rubber fuel cells. She was then suddenly enveloped in total darkness. At first, she thought she had entered an opaque, solid wall of Flak bursts. When it didn't eventually clear, she knew that the prior burst had done more damage than she thought. A piece of iron shrapnel had severed vital wiring from her generators to the cockpit. All twenty-seven of her instrument panel gauges went dead. She and Pop were now flying blind.

"Sweet Mother of Jesus, help me now!" *Bird* prayed. Ever since Pop and Stan had brought onboard their rosaries, personally blessed by Pope Pius XII from their Vatican visit in the newly liberated Rome, she considered herself Catholic. Never mind that Pop and Stan were Protestant; they figured they could use all the spiritual help they could get. *Bird* didn't completely understand religion, but most of her crew did in one form or another, so she figured it sure couldn't hurt to at least go through the motions.

Fortunately for *Bird*, Stan, and the rest of her flight element, the A-5 autopilot on Stan's Sperry bombsight still worked. As long as Pop kept *Bird* at a steady 160mph, based on the engine drone, Stan could make the fine adjustments, for he had the smoke covered Romano-Americano refinery in his crosshairs.

Bird felt 5,000 pounds lighter as her bombs were let loose, falling into the smoking maelstrom below, when she suddenly sensed herself banking right. Flying with your eyes closed was not all that it was cracked up to be. She couldn't comprehend what was happening or be able to prepare herself for the next onslaught. She felt helpless, not that she didn't completely trust Pop and the crew, for she had finally learned to do just that. It's just that she felt utterly useless in not being able to help them, for they soon could have used her acute eyesight. In their turn to the east to skirt the nearby Bucharest Flak batteries, a deadly nemesis came out of the sun.

"109s, three o'clock level! Where the hell did they come from?" Bill blurted over the interphone as he finely adjusted the azimuth of his top turret, pulling the triggers, and thus bringing his twin .50s to bear on the now firing pair of quickly approaching Me-109s. Joseph in the ball turret, a second behind Bill, began adding to *Bird*'s tremendous defensive firepower. To complete the broadside, Sergeant Mark Turkiewicz, filling in for Charley Debord, who would normally be in the right waist gun position, sighted in on one of the bright red ME-109s and pulled the trigger on his single Browning.[3]

While *Bird* couldn't see without her instruments, there was absolutely nothing wrong with her hearing and tactile sense of touch. "What in the hell is happening, guys?" she yelled as her airframe violently shook with

---

3. AFHRA folder GP-449-SU-OP-S, 24 June 1944. Mission 83. Ship #3 Interrogation Report.

the explosive power of four hundred .50-cal cartridges spent in the fleeting matter of four or five seconds. She swore that the tumultuous concussions actually stopped her in mid-flight. Her keen auditory sense gave her the answer, however, as the unmistakable high-pitched whine of two German-built, Daimler Benz V12–engined Me-109s swooped underneath her, exiting her at the eight o'clock where they prudently took up station just out of gun range. Quickly searching her fuselage for additional holes beyond the ones in her right wing, she found none. "These Germans and Rumanians are becoming poorer shots, thank God," she thought, evoking a deity that not too long ago she hadn't even acknowledged. There are no atheists at 24,000 feet above the foxholes. But she had forgotten about the Bulgarians.

"Daylong Four, this is ship #1," was heard on the VHF group frequency.

"Go ahead Holland," replied Colonel Thomas Gent in the lead plane, #60, *Miss 'N Moan*.

"We have two engines out, am losing altitude and cannot keep up with the formation. We'll see you back at base," Lt. William Holland, flying *Our Baby*, replied.

"Good luck. Gent out."

Our Baby and her crew would need it. She was in the same airspace that *Gidi Gidi Boom Boom* had occupied a few hours earlier when she lost an engine enroute and turned back alone. She was last seen with five Bulgarian Me-109s attacking. She never came home.

Bird was well aware of *Our Baby's* plight, for she was part of her box flying immediately behind her tail turret. "*Baby*, hang in there," she pleaded, not being able to see *Baby's* feathered number one and two engines.

"Hey there, *Bird*. I must admit I've felt better," *Baby* replied, almost out of breath. "My number three and four are barely hanging in there with their superchargers out. My boys have thrown everything out that they can, including guns and ammo, so I'm defenseless up here."

Bird really felt useless now. She wanted to help *Baby* but couldn't do it alone. She needed her boys.

"Listen up, guys," was soon heard over the plane's interphone as Pop got everyone's attention. "You all know the score concerning *Baby*. If she's left alone, five will get you ten those bastards out there will get her in a flash," he stated, glancing out his side window at the two red specters paralleling them 1,000 yards out. "I know we're hurt but we can probably make it back. They can't. They won't. As aircraft commander, I can order us to stay behind to escort her in. But that decision isn't just up to me. It's up to all of us. So, I'm putting it up to a vote and it has to be unanimous," Pop finished, glancing over at Harry, who determinedly nodded in the affirmative. One by one, without hesitation, they all voted agreement. Though *Bird* and *Baby* were two wounded kites, the crew of the flanking 109s didn't want to tangle with that many Brownings. They didn't want a part in the bloody sequel of *Sophisticated Lady* and *The Heavenly Body,* and soon departed for safer skies once *Bird* and *Baby* hit the Yugoslavian border.[4]

Our Baby did make it back with the help of its number two engine, which miraculously came back to life. Running out of gas, she landed at Brindisi, Italy, with its runway only 600 feet off the Adriatic.

"*... By his brilliant display of courage and skill and by his unselfish devotion to duty...*" read part of Pop's citation for that day. He will shortly be presented the DFC for his actions. Too bad an inanimate object such as a B-24 wasn't eligible. For surely *Bird* and *Our Baby* deserved one also.[5]

Luck eventually ran out for *Our Baby* over the Budapest, Hungary marshaling yards two weeks later. Trailing smoke from her feathered num-

---

4. Letter of WWII reminisces from Robert Simmons to William Stanley, December 27, 2001. Author's collection.

5. AFHRA folder GP-449-SU 1-3 Citations. Feb 1944 to Aug 15th, 1944. Norman E. Blomgren.

ber four engine, and having prematurely jettisoned her bombs at the IP, she turned for home. This time she had no escort and was shot down by a pack of angry Me-109s. Nine of her crew became POWs. The twenty-year-old bombardier, Lt. Willis Englehart, of Azusa, California, never made it out of the plane as it crashed into downtown Budapest.

Ship #20, "*Mickey*," 24,000 feet over the Concordia Vega Refinery, Ploesti, Rumania July 9, 1944, 10:20 hrs.

STAN'S HANDS WERE PERSPIRING so much that he thought his thermal gloves had filled up with cold sweat. With both hands tightly gripping the control and firing handles of the front turret guns, his eyes darted back, forth, up, and down, searching the crystal blue skies for distant moving specks or a fleeting glint of sunlight where no reflection should have been. He shouldn't be here, he thought. "*I hate this place*," he hissed.[6]

Over the previous two weeks, if Pop and his crew weren't on a mission, they were practice-bombing with an improved offset, synchronous version of the Pathfinder Force (PFF) radar system, otherwise known as "Mickey," found in ship #20. The radar dome that replaced the bottom ball turret, if one squinted enough, had a strange resemblance to Mickey Mouse of Steamboat Willie fame. While ship #20 hadn't been given a nose-art moniker, they improvised and casually named her *Mickey*. A last-minute crew change had replaced Stan as *Mickey*'s lead bombardier, and instead had posted him as the front turret gunner and observer. While he had practiced just last week on the waist guns, ripping to shreds static German and Italian fighter hulks sitting harmlessly on the flanks of Grottaglie, operating a powered turret with dual guns and controls was a bit more complicated. "Cecil Yeates should be here, not me," Stan whispered as he

---

6. Stanley, William G. Personal WWII Diary. July 9, 1944 entry. Author's collection.

momentarily caught the reflective glint of ten Me-109's approaching them at his ten o'clock.

Then he heard familiar accents, incessant jabbering, and absolutely terrible radio protocols, and he knew he was at least safe from enemy fighters.[7] A broad smile, covered by his leather-rubber oxygen mask, broke out across his face. The Red Tails of the 332nd Fighter Group in their P-51 Mustangs had arrived as escorts.[8]

They had protected *Bird* and her crew once before, flying that time in P-47 Thunderbolts on June 16th as they bombed a synthetic oil refinery in Bratislava, Slovakia. Unlike most of their white fighter escort counterparts, the black Tuskegee Institute–trained pilots did it right. They stuck to the lumbering giants like glue, daring the German or Rumanian fighters to attack. They would eventually lose a few bombers under their care, but at a far lower proportion than was usual.[9]

Weaving back and forth, above and below, looking pretty, they intimidated the ten approaching Me-109s, who prudently decided to fly above the 449th to attack the planes of the following 98th Group.[10] Stan relaxed his grip on the turret handles, exhaling a sigh of relief, and pulled his fingers away from the triggers. Then he watched as large red, white, and black Flak bursts began to blossom below him, totaling engulfing the leading "A" element of their Group, flying 2,000 feet below and slightly ahead of them. *Bird,* on this day being flown by Lt. Henry Krawiec, was among them at

---

7. Stanley, William G. WWII oral remembrances with family.

8. https://tuskegeeairmen.org/wp-content/uploads/2020/11/TAI_Resource s_312_Missions.pdf

9. https://www.nationalww2museum.org/sites/default/files/2017-07/tuskeg ee-airmen.pdf

10. AFHRA folder GP-449-SU-OP-S, 9 July 1944. Mission 95. Special Narrative Report No. 95.

the very front. All Stan could do was helplessly watch. He felt like a prize boxer antagonizing his foe by thrusting his chin out, just daring them to land a punch. A potentially lethal punch.

Looking ahead and below through *Mickey*'s windshield, Pop didn't like what he saw. The most obvious object in the clear sky was a 20,000-foot-tall column of black smoke rising from the area of the distant Xenia Oil Refinery. The 5th Wing of the 15th Air Force had found their mark fifteen minutes earlier. As expected, a grey-white opaque smoke-screen covered not only the town of Ploesti, but the surrounding thirteen refineries. That was of no concern, that's what all the training and Mickey was for. Their target for the day was the Concordia-Vega Refinery, which had been visited once before in May. Its production, however, had gone back up to 1,200,000 gallons per day of refined oil and the precious, vital gasoline.

What was of concern was the killing Flak barrage now enveloping the "A" element below them. According to the morning's 03:45 operations briefing, Pop was supposed to lead his "B" element down to near the same altitude at the IP and follow the "A" element into the developing Flak stormfront.

"Bob, time to IP?" Pop queried over the interphone.

"Ten minutes. You should begin your descent to 22,500 feet now."

Pop didn't reply, as he was contemplating an alternative. An alternative that could possibly save lives, including his own. The Germans quickly made up his mind for him. A well-placed Flak burst destroyed the number two engine, cut control cables, and took out the hydraulic system of *Th' Inhoomin Critter* flying off *Bird*'s left wing. Seconds later they jettisoned their ten bombs to stay airborne. In quick succession, the ship behind *Bird*, known simply as *#66*, caught another burst that inflicted similar damage. Pop had seen enough carnage down below them.

"Foothold Three, this is 'B' lead," Pop called over the Group's VHF frequency. "B element is to remain at current altitude of 24,000 feet. Bombardiers, note new bombing altitude," Pop announced.

"Yes, sir. They made me a lead pilot for a reason," Pop thought. "And that was because I can think on my feet, use my head. Sometimes conditions in the air during the engagement cause the operational orders to be discarded, altered at the moment. This was one of those moments," Pop realized, as he reached the IP and changed course to the prescribed 176° angle of attack, handing the ship over to *Mickey's* bombardier, Lt. Harry Crisman. He wasn't about to bring his thirteen ships down into that maelstrom. Orders be damned.

While *Mickey*, leading out front, wouldn't receive a single Flak hole, two in its element received much more, despite trying to fly over the devastating barrage occurring down below. *Shacking Stuff*, flying in the four-ship diamond-shaped box off Pop's left wing had her rudder cables cut, her electrical system shot out, and two of her engines damaged and smoking. Like *Th' Inhoomin Critter*, ship *#66*, and now *Shacking Stuff*, the ship fifty feet behind Pop also wouldn't be able to make it back to Grottaglie. It was *Skipper*.

Pilot Lt. Robert McGlasson had troubles rallying right after dropping *Skipper's* bomb load. Flak had damaged his rudder and elevator cabling, and also disabled his number one engine. It was going to be a long trip home in an unfamiliar aircraft. *Skipper's* usual pilot, Don Liddycoat, had completed his 50th mission the day before, beating Pop and his crew to the crucial lifesaving milestone which meant one thing: home.

By the time the Group had completed its rally to the east of Ploesti, the view out their starboard windows brought them a great sense of accomplishment, and relief, because they knew they weren't going to have to bomb that refinery again. Even through the obscuring smokescreen, they could observe red broiling fires and explosions. And four columns of churning black smoke had already risen to 10,000 feet, ultimately rising to 25,000 feet, visible 150 miles from the devastation.[11]

The Group had 410 miles to fly, however, before reaching the safe airspace of the Adriatic. Slowly the cripples, those that couldn't keep up, grouped together, trailing the main formation. They included *Th' Inhoomin Critter*, *#66*, *Shacking Stuff*, *Harper's Ferry*, *Skipper*, and *Bird*.

Though she was among friends, particularly *Skipper*, *Bird* didn't feel well. Not that any of them did. While she thought she could stay airborne, with the help of Lt. Krawiec at her controls, three of her engines had been hit and were running hot. And then there was her body. She had been ripped to shreds with huge holes, causing not only turbulence inside of her, but outside too, creating drag. Drag that was slowing her down. The seventy holes she received back on May 5th, the first time she had visited this place, were nothing compared to what she had received today. "God, I hate that place," she swore as she began to lose altitude.

"*Bird*, are you OK? Where ya going?" *Skipper* asked with concern as he noticed *Bird* wasn't off his wing anymore.

"Hey *Skip*," *Bird* replied, always soothed by *Skipper*'s Texas twang. "I've lost my oxygen so the crew is taking me down to 10,000 feet. I'll be down below you, don't you worry now," she said as she observed the fast-approaching Yugoslavian mountain peaks. She estimated she'd have a few thousand feet to spare, no problem.

The one who was having problems, though, was *Shacking Stuff*, who was losing even more altitude than *Bird,* and was lost out of sight 155 miles from the coast. Having now lost her number two and three engines, her entire electrical and hydraulic system, and flight control cables, it was doubted that she could make it out of enemy territory. But they should have given *Stuff* and her crew more credit.

---

11. AFHRA folder GP-449-SU-OP-S, 9 July 1944. Mission 95. Ship #5, 22, 45, 53, 55, 56 Interrogation Reports.

For over an hour the crew, having shed *Stuff* of all unnecessary weight, including her defensive Brownings and ammo, prayed that Lt. Cornelius Van Schoor could keep her aloft. Previously a high school graduate book-keeper at the Union Salt Company of Cuyahoga, Ohio, "Gerald" knew that even if they got out of Yugoslavia, there was no way they would ever make it across the Adriatic. He altered course for the island of Vis, fifty miles off the coast. British-held, it was an impenetrable thorn in the side of Germany's Balkan perimeter. But most importantly, it had a runway. A short 3,300-foot one, but a runway nonetheless.

Hitting the airfield at 95mph, with no hydraulics and therefore no brakes, "Gerald" had a plan. He had the waist gunners, Tech Sergeants James Edwards and Ralph McDaniels, hook their parachutes to the waist gun posts. As soon as *Stuff* hit the runway, they simultaneously threw the packs out the waist windows and pulled their ripcords. Reminiscent of fu-ture NASA Space Shuttle landings, *Stuff* was able to stop and successfully end her mission. Lt. Van Schoor would receive the DFC for his actions, but alas, not the ship that had brought him and his crew safely back down to terra firma.[12]

The one who was never seen again for certain, though, was *Th' In-hoomin Critter.* Thirty minutes after the disappearance of *Shacking Stuff,* having thrown overboard everything not bolted down, it was obvious to Lt. Clyde Drigger and his crew that their ship was doomed. Filling up with leaking explosive gas fumes, they safely parachuted out over a stretch of mountainous terrain twenty-five miles long, while *Critter* continued its pilotless journey for an additional ten miles before crashing thirty-five miles outside of Sarajevo. The crew would eventually evade German cap-ture with help from Chetnik guerrilla forces and ultimately return to base.

---

12. AFHRA folder GP-449-SU-OP-S, 9 July 1944. Mission 95. Ship #42 Inter-rogation Report.

Approaching the Yugoslavian coast, the crews of the four remaining ships breathed a sigh of relief after the angst of encountering enemy fighters. A group of four Focke-Wulf 190s had eyed the group twenty minutes prior but decided discretion was the better part of valor and departed.[13] However, three of the group's engineers reported to their pilots that they would not have enough fuel to make it back to Grottaglie, and maybe not even enough to make the 120-mile journey across the Adriatic.

"How y'all doing back there?" *Skipper* asked *Bird* and *Harper's Ferry*, which was trailing a bit behind. "I'm hanging in there, *Skipper*," *Bird* replied in a wheezing voice. Her engines were operating, just barely. "*Harper* just told me his crew threw out their guns and ammo and are going to try and land at Bari on the coast. They know they don't have enough to make it to base."

"Well, neither can I and *#66*. We're going to split off and try and land at Gioia. That'll save us thirty miles. That poor bastard only arrived here last month and hasn't been given a name yet. She keeps getting passed around like a prickly pear cactus, no one claims her," *Skipper* said in an exasperated tone. "I've been calling her *Dallas* since she was made there about two months after us. She liked that, kind of calmed her down. She's as jittery as a jackalope, though. Flown out of Love Field down to Tucson and up to Hamilton Field, just like us. Boy, doesn't that seem ages ago," *Skipper* mused, feeling nostalgic all of a sudden, even through the pain.

"You're a good ship, *Skipper*. I'll see you when you get back," *Bird* softly replied, though silently wondering if she herself could make it back.

"*Dallas*, pull up!" *Skipper* screamed thirty minutes later as they made their approach to Gioia's airstrip. *Dallas* had reported she was about out of gas so was landing first. One mile from the field, *Dallas* used up the last

---

13. AFHRA folder GP-449-SU-OP-S, 9 July 1944. Mission 95. Ship #22 Interrogation Report.

of her fuel and didn't have enough altitude to glide, not that a "flying can of Spam" could.

Twenty-one-year-old Lt. Hubert Westbrook from Nashville, Tennessee, on only his third mission, tried to keep *Dallas*'s nose up as he prepared to crash. Passing over a 90-foot escarpment, she then plowed into the cultivated fields and olive groves with the beckoning airstrip lined up just beyond. While the ship remained in one piece, all it took was one spark to ignite the volatile high-octane gas fumes that filled the empty wing and overhead fuel tanks. All four officers and the flight engineer, situated in front of the wings in the flight deck, burned to death. The rest of the crew jumped safely out of the waist windows.[14]

Passing over the exploding flames, and inhaling *Dallas*'s spirit-infused acrid smoke, *Skipper* had a momentary lapse into despair before he snapped back to the emergency at hand, for his three working engines inevitably began to sputter and miss with their lack of fuel. Lt. McGlasson had his hands full with engines cutting out and intermittent rudder and elevator controls, as he attempted to feather out the landing of a non-powered, barely flying brick.

Witnesses described it as a "controlled crash." McGlasson was able to keep *Skipper* on the runway and come to a stop in time with no injuries to the crew. "What do humans call a successful landing? One in which everyone walks away?" *Skipper* scoffed as he sat at the end of the runway, suddenly feeling very old.[15]

If *Skipper* was to crash anywhere, Gioia dell Colle Airfield was the place. Here were stationed the 38th and 41st Air Depot Groups of the Air Service Command, delegated with the maintenance and major repair and

---

14. AFHRA folder GP-449-SU-OP-S 9, July 1944. Mission 95. Ship #48 Interrogation Report.

15. AFHRA folder GP-449-SU-OP-S 9, July 1944. Mission 95. Time Up, Down Report.

rebuild of the Air Corps' fleet of planes. Even so, *Skipper* wouldn't be flying again for the ten days that he was in their hands.

Bird did make it to Grottaglie, barely. Her fuselage, wings, and bomb bay were shredded with holes, and three of her engines were severely damaged. With Grottaglie not having the superb repair facilities found at Gioia, *Bird* wouldn't fly again for thirty days.

A lot would happen in those thirty mission-filled days. From losing a few more of her cherished olive drab family, to the sudden realization she'd never fly with Pop and his crew again, to the most devastating of all: she would never fly with *Skipper* again.

Worrybird after her 40th mission of June 14, 1944, to bomb an oil refinery in Osijek, Yugoslavia. Beginning to show her age. [Author's Collection]

Grey-white smokescreen over Ploesti Xenia oil refinery, 10 August 1944.
Black smoke column well over 20,000 feet. B-24s regrouping during rally.
[Courtesy of National Archives]

21

THAT OLD GANG OF MINE

*B*IRD WAS BUMMED, RESTLESS, and though she couldn't quite believe it herself, she was actually looking forward to getting back up there, where life was fragile. To revenge her friend, if nothing else. *Sweet Mother* had pulled up next to her at about 13:00 after getting back from a mission to the Budapest marshaling yards and told her the story. Over the target *Our Baby* was hit by Flak and began trailing just behind and below the formation. It was enough. Me-109s spotted the easy prey and shot her out of the sky. And now, just a few hours later, they were all being prepped for tomorrow's mission, which, if rumors were true, was to Ploesti again. *Bird* just sat there with scaffolding under all her engines. Useless to the cause. "*Skipper* would have said something eloquent like, 'I'm about as useless as tits on a boar'," *Bird* thought, smirking as she glanced over at the vacant parking spot where *Skipper* usually sat. *Bird* wasn't worried for her friend, her soulmate. She had heard he was in good hands and would return in a week or so, as good as new, or thereabouts.

<u>24,500 feet over the Romano-Americano Refinery, Ploesti, Rumania, July 15, 1944, 09:44 hrs.</u>

STAN HAD NEVER SEEN FLAK quite like this. Briefly he took his eye away from the bombsight's padded eyepiece and glanced out the bombardier's compartment front window. He could actually watch dancing Flak shadows between his ship, *Nancy Jane #2*, projected onto the fuselage of Pop's ship, *Mickey*, leading the high "C" element of twelve planes. It was like some macabre scene out of a black-and-white horror movie.

At some other time, he would have been singing to calm his nerves, because he had to admit he was scared. But this time the gang was all split up. Pop and Bob were just ahead in *Mickey*, he was in *Nancy Jane*, and Harry off his right wing was in *Salty Dog*.

After dropping his share of the 1,520 tons of bombs that landed on Ploesti's refineries that morning, and banking right then left to avoid some of the 241 Flak guns, Stan looked back and *"[his] heart almost did a flip-flop at what [he] saw."*[1]

A huge column of smoke was rising to their 20,000-foot cruising altitude like a huge cumulonimbus cloud, with the top flattening out into an anvil. Stan expected cloud-to-ship lightning to start at any moment. Obviously, they had hit it good.

What also made Stan's heart flip-flop was watching what at first glance he thought were parachute-less bodies jumping out of a ship in the "A" element in front of him. Looking closer he realized they were ten empty Flak suits, shortly followed by ammo and machine guns. Ship #55, *Dry Run*, had feathered two of its engines due to Flak damage and was attempting to remain with the formation. *Dry Run* made it as far as northern Albania before it gave up the ghost.

---

1. Stanley, William G. Personal WWII diary: July 15, 1944 entry. Author's collection.

Heard over the interplane VHF radio frequency were the final words of some of *Dry Run*'s crew addressed to the rest of the Group before bailing:

"...don't steal all of my clothes..."
"...mail my letters that are on my desk..." "...write home to my folks for me..." "...see you in a month or so..."

And then, the last to leave, twenty-two-year-old pilot Lt. Auty Blanton, from Charlotte, North Carolina, said "Good luck," and jumped.[2]

"Incredible," Stan thought. "Here were these guys so calmly bantering and joking when they were about to jump from a stricken plane at 10,000 feet into mountainous, enemy-held territory. And they have the brass to tell us 'good luck'!

"...I tell you it did something to you. It made you feel proud to belong to the same bunch of fellas that they belonged to. It made you want to fight all the harder. Those guys knew what they were up against and yet they could joke in the face of it all,"[3]

Stan wrote as he finished his diary entry concerning the plight of *Dry Run* and its crew. He glanced over at Pop and Bob, sleeping so soundly with what could almost be mistaken as grins on their lips. For they were done. Finished. No more Flak, enemy fighters, stress of command, 02:30 wake up calls. No more Ploesti. Today had been their 50th mission, that seemingly never-achievable final curtain. And yet they had reached it, and

2. Ibid; Blomgren, Norman E. The War Diary of Capt. Norman E. Blomgren: July 15, 1944 entry. Author's collection.

3. Stanley, William G. Personal WWII Diary: July 15, 1944 entry. Author's collection.

incredibly, they had survived unscathed. Maybe tonight, the first in a long while, they'd sleep peacefully. Especially since they had been assured that they weren't going to be screwed out of their last mission credit.

The previous seven missions to Ploesti had been granted double mission credits because of the extreme danger of the German defenses and the length of time under duress. When the returning crews landed this time, however, they were greeted with the unbelievable news that this mission, along with all future Ploesti missions, had been deemed worthy of only a single credit. That would have put Pop and Bob back at the tantalizingly close 49. They quickly marched into acting Group commander Lt. Colonel George Blasé's office and respectfully berated him for the unjust turn. He assured them both that Colonel Gent would grant them a double since they had trained specifically for that mission, a mission they had actually requested in order to put them "over the top."

The single credit news had raced through the Group's planes like a bomb bay fire:

"I tell you what," announced the eloquent and scantily clad *Classy Chassy*, *"...we invite the General to visit Ploesti on our next mission. Single sortie, huh! No flak vest will be issued..."*

One Night Stand expressed similar sentiments: *"...Ploesti too long and rough a mission for single mission credit. CHICKEN SHIT! General dissatisfaction. We also extend a personal invitation to strategist who cancelled double sortie credit to accompany us next time. No flight deck position and wrapped in flak suits will be allowed..."*

And *Honey Chile* wondered, *"...has he ever been there? Single mission to Ploesti! Awful. Getting tougher all the time."*[4]

---

4. AFHRA folder GP-449-SU-OP-S, 15 July 1944. Mission 98. Ship #48, 49, 50 Interrogation Reports.

Indeed, it had. Since their first visit in April, the number of Flak guns greeting them had doubled. The next and last time Stan visited, there would be 278 guns waiting for him.

23,800 feet above Gulf of Trieste, July 19, 1944, 09:56 hrs.

FOR THREE HOURS it felt good again. To be above where eagles soar, inhaling the thin air at nearly 24,000 feet. To be flying again, even if he was on his way to Munich. Then again, after having spent the last ten days in the good hands of the Air Service Command at Gioia, *Skipper* should really have felt better. For the past thirty minutes or so, he had been having a hard time sucking in air in number two. And it was getting worse. He knew he was in trouble when he felt Lt. John Campbell, his copilot, increase his throttles, yet he didn't feel a surge in speed. If anything, he was starting to drop back, slowly but surely.

"DST lead, this is 6P over," Pilot Lt. William Holland radioed the "B" element lead pilot, Lt. Charles Domos in *Mickey*.

"Go ahead, Holland."

"Am having troubles keeping up, am pulling 43 inches at 2,550 rpm. Requesting bomb jettison."

"Roger bomb drop. OK to drop one, repeat, one," Domos replied, hoping that since they were carrying 1,000-pounders, one would do.

It didn't. With the jettisoning of the four remaining bombs, *Skipper* then felt like he could keep up. But why? Just to be Flak fodder? His bomb bay was now empty. That question was answered when he felt himself banking over into a reciprocal course. He was heading back.

"Damn! My first early return," *Skipper* exclaimed. He was going to have to eat some crow when this came up in conversation with *Bird*. He had been awfully rough on her for the same thing back in May. Not exactly understanding. "Yes sir, I'm going to be eating an entire crow pie," he ruefully admitted as he headed back to base over the Adriatic.

Stan, riding in *Mickey* as lead bombardier for the first time, didn't like hearing that *Skipper* was heading back. That meant two and a half tons less bombs to be dropped on the target. He alone was responsible for the Group's success or failure at hitting the Dornier-Werke aircraft factory in Neuaubing, seven miles west of downtown Munich. The pressure was causing him to sweat even more than on a typical Munich mission. Not that any mission to Munich was typical. With 294 Flak guns rimming the city, only Berlin and Vienna had more.

Stan had only himself to blame. Bombing accuracy was measured as C.E., Circular Error, defined as the radius from target center in which half the bombs fell. Typical Air Corps bombing cadets averaged a C.E. of 400 feet at graduation. In actuality, over the skies of Europe, a mission C.E. of over 1,000 feet was typical. In Stan's bombing practice a few weeks earlier, he'd averaged a C.E. of 125 feet. He was made lead bombardier.[5]

Turning at the IP, Stan was still sweating. He was so focused on trying to find the elusive target through the smokescreen that he didn't even notice the Flak exploding around him. "Mickey," the radar system designed to see through the smoke, was out. It had literally gone up in smoke, catching fire before they reached the IP. It was now up to Stan.[6]

"I've got a longin' way down in my heart, for that old gang that has drifted apart," he sang softly to himself as he peered through the Sperry eyepiece. "Where in the hell are you?" he mumbled as *Mickey* approached what he knew must be the target area. That just wouldn't be good enough. *"They were the best pals that I ever had, I never thought that I'd want them*

---

5. Correll, John T. "Daylight Precision Bombing." *Air & Space Forces Magazine.* October 2008, vol. 91, no.10.

6. AFHRA folder GP-449-SU-OP-S, 19 July 1944. Mission 99. Ship #20 Interrogation Report.

so bad." Time was running out. "I sure could use Bob's help right about now," he thought.[7]

Slowly, like the sun beginning to break through a gloomy afternoon rainstorm, the target, composed of three large rectangular shops with a railroad siding spur, miraculously appeared through the smoke. Swinging the plane over, putting the middle shop in his bombsight optics, he toggled the bombs while keeping the crosshairs on the shop during the 40-second bomb run. The rest of the Group followed Stan's lead.

That afternoon's reconnaissance flight photos revealed that "the three large workshops were seen either being hit or receiving severe blast dama ge."[8] The interrogation report of ship #34, *Hoppy*, said it best: bombing results were "perfect, best yet."[9]

Grottaglie, 719th Squadron Parking Area, July 22, 1944, 10:12 hrs.

BIRD HAD NEVER GOTTEN so much attention. Maybe not since

---

7. *That Old Gang of Mine.* Henderson, Ray; Rose, Billy; and Dixon, Mort. Irving Berlin Inc., 1923.

8. AFHRA folder GP-449-SU-OP-S, 19 July 1944. Mission 99. Narrative Report Number 99.

9. The bombing of the Dornier-Werke aircraft factory, like the bombing of most munitions/armament factories, needed to be accurate to minimize the slaughter of the innocent. At least 2,000 forced laborers from France, Italy, and other European countries, as well as prisoners from the nearby Dachau concentration camp, worked at Dornier and were housed adjacent to the factory complex. Not that the crews, or perhaps Air Force Command knew, or cared. This was war and there was going to be "collateral damage." See: https://departure-neuaubing.nsdoku.de/en/projekte/mind-the-memor y-gap%20%20%20%20 for a provocative, well-done video.

she had first met her boys way back in February. Back there in California, another lifetime ago. She was loving it. She had noticed *Jimmy* driving past her from the direction of headquarters when he suddenly did a U-turn, drove up next to her, and came to a quick stop. That's when she caught sight of her boys, at least the six enlisted ones, disgorging out the back and sauntering up to her.

"Hey corporal, mind taking a picture of all of us?" Cecil yelled to the driver, holding out his Argus C3 "Brick" camera.

Crowding in front of *Bird's* nose art, Cecil Yeates, Joseph Windham, Bill Blankenship, Joseph Fox, Charley Debord, and James Reed posed with cheesy grins. They were on their way home.

One by one, they all affectionately patted her on the nose, on her bomb-straddling Kiwi bird caricature, anywhere. Some, like Cecil, just stood and stared at a particular gun position, in his case the front turret. With an expressionless, vacant look on his face, his eyes slowly welled up with tears of conflicting emotions. A quick honk of *Jimmy's* horn shook him out of his reverie. With a quick wipe of his sleeve across his face, Cecil joined the rest of the gang in the back of the truck. They had a Naples-bound plane to catch.

"Sure was good of the guys to see me off," *Bird* mistakenly thought, as a test flight crew pulled up in *Toledo*.

"Hey there, *Bird*," *Toledo* said with true sincerity in his voice for once. He knew how long *Bird* had been waiting for this day. Thirteen days to be exact. Chief Clarence Lambertz and his crew had worked miracles. Removing and installing three new engines in two days, patching the numerous large holes and tears in her skin, and repairing flight controls to make her airworthy had been no small task.[10]

"Well, hey there, *Toledo,*" *Bird* enthusiastically replied. Not even *Toledo*'s presence could get her down today. "I tell you what, I feel like a new girl. I do. I sure wish they would have painted those bright aluminum patches, though. I look like a patch quilt," *Bird* lamented as she glanced down her fuselage and across her wings, noticing the hundreds of riveted, gleaming bright patches contrasted against her olive drab skin.

"Oh, *Bird,* consider those well-deserved war trophies. You look great," *Toledo* countered, as his driver started him up to prudently move him out of the way as *Bird*'s number three began its slow start-up churn.

With all four engines now warmed and idling at their prescribed 1,000 rpm, *Bird* was relishing in the vibrations coursing through her entire airframe. With an increase in her number four engine and the release of her parking brakes, she made a slow turn toward the taxiway.

"Hey, wait a minute. Something isn't right," she exclaimed, though no one paid her any mind. The further they proceeded down the taxiway the more anxious she got. While the hands gripping her yokes didn't feel quite as confident as Pop's and Harry's, it was the inattention of the engineer that had *Bird* concerned. For he was in his station fiddling with the complicated fuel valves instead of where he should have been.

While the tricycle landing gear arrangement of a B-24 afforded the pilots a better view of the runway as compared to the nose-high "tail dragging" arrangement of most other planes, there were still plenty of blind spots for the pilot to contend with. Hence, on takeoff, the engineer should

---

10. Downey, Richard F. Letter to William G. Stanley. November 19, 1986. Author's collection. Richard Downey was the 449th Bomb Group Association secretary. In this letter, he relayed detailed information he had received from Clarence Lambertz concerning *Worrybird*'s repairs and subsequent taxiing accident.

have been halfway out of the top escape hatch directing taxiing movements for him.

"Bill would have been staring ahead, yelling directions down to Pop before the brakes were even released," Bird scoffed, amazed at the lackadaisical attitude of this crew.

Summer is the driest season of the year for southern Italy, receiving less than half an inch of rain in a typical July. They had surpassed that average the day before, leaving the grounds, taxiway, and runway muddy, with many hidden water-filled holes on the side. The slick, muddy ground looked featureless as the pilot continued taxiing, not noticing *Bird*'s right wheel slowly veering off the taxiway.

She sensed her right-wing dip violently before the sickening, tearing of metal was heard, then felt. It was beyond anything she had ever experienced. Worse than Flak fragments ripping through her or 20mm shells exploding inside of her after piercing her thin skin. No, this was excruciating, as her right landing gear sheared and went clear through her wing, penetrating a fuel cell along the way. It was equivalent to a compound fracture of a human's tibia.

The damage done to *Bird* might well have been beyond the capabilities of even Sergeant Lambertz and his crew. If even possible, it would take weeks to make her airworthy again.

RETURNING FROM ANY MISSION always felt good, a wash of relief flowing over you, but returning from a Ploesti mission was different. All of one's senses and emotions were magnified. Standing on the flight deck behind Captain Charles Harton, who was piloting *Miss Bad Penny*, Stan felt buoyant, having completed his 47th mission. Hopefully it would be his last to Ploesti. Three to go, but who's counting? Harton lined up the runway and extended full flaps, slowing *Penny* appreciably.

Stan had witnessed many gut-wrenching sights, either approaching the airfield or while feathering out a landing. From burning, crumpled hulks that could not quite make it the last few hundred yards, to a plane's gears collapsing, sending them careening off the runway. But the sight that greeted him as they touched down opposite the 719th parking area was a sucker punch to the gut, totally unexpected. The wing-down attitude of a ship on the taxiway caught his eye. Before the sight disappeared, he caught the tangle of metal protruding from its starboard wing's upper surface. At the final second, the last view he had was of the tail section where the number three was prominently displayed. There was only one number three: "*Worrybird*," Stan breathlessly whispered.[11]

23,500 feet over Toulon, France, August 6, 1944, 13:21 hrs.

WAITING. NEITHER OF THEM were good at it. While Stan had completed missions number 48 and 49 on "easy" milk runs to Albania and Hungary soon after his last Ploesti mission, he had hit the mission doldrums. It seemed no one needed a bombardier, and he was without a crew.

For *Bird*, it was a time of watching everyone else going on missions, being attended to, being involved. She just sat with scaffolding surrounding her right wing, which was propped up with tall jackstands. At least they had determined that she was indeed worth fixing. After all, she did have three new engines in her.

Finally, Stan noticed his name listed on the pinned-up mission orders as nose gunner in *Hot To Go*, flying lead on tomorrow's mission. Relief and chilling anxiety coursed through his body at the same time, colliding in confusion. Later, putting pencil to paper in his diary, he was better able to convey his thoughts before the mission than if he had confessed to Pop, Bob, or Harry, who were busy reading or writing their own thoughts at

---

11. Stanley, William G. WWII oral remembrances with family.

the moment. Besides, you just didn't do that—"spill your guts" of your demons.

...I'm really sweating brother...This will be my 50th.

I certainly will be sweating this one. It will be a relief when it's all over. A person can't realize what a strain it is unless they go through it themselves. You're always on edge. You imagine things. Those imaginations lapse over into your dreams. Flak is horrible to experience. In a dream, it's hell.[12]

Flying in the nose turret of the lead ship in the high "C" element, Stan had an expansive view of the thirty-six ships about to release their ninety-ton version of hell onto the German submarine pens and docks of Toulon harbor. Eleven of his fellow squadron's ships were with him, including Liddycoat's old ship, *Skipper*, which was being piloted by Harry, his first time flying in the left driver's seat.

They had caught the Germans with their pants down. Smoke generators were just now being activated in an attempt to mask themselves. Too late. Stan watched with complete satisfaction as 360 bombs made their arching four-and-a-half-mile trip to the surprised naval force currently building up steam to try to get the hell out of harm's way. Too late.

"We plastered them good, Crisman!" Stan yelled down to *Hot To Go's* bombardier, Lt. Harry Crisman. Hundreds of "Old Faithful" geysers erupted in the harbor, along with flames and smoke as the subs, destroyers, and tankers were hit. As the planes turned at the rally, at least one tanker and two destroyers were seen on fire and listing precariously.

---

12. Stanley, William G. Personal WWII Diary: July 30, 31, 1944 entry. Author's collection. Stan was scheduled to fly on the next day's August 1st mission to Ploesti to finish his 50-mission tour. They were getting ready to taxi out to the runway when red flares were shot, indicating the mission was off. I'm positive his pre-mission sentiments were the same for August 5th, the evening before his actual final mission.

Then pilot Lt. Shelby McArthur feathered the number three engine. It was a long four-hour trip home on three engines. Plus they had their worse nemesis to contend with: weather. While the Group was busy bombing, large cumulonimbus clouds had begun bellowing upward behind them, and they were between the returning Group and home. Towering above the now limited *Hot To Go*'s maximum ceiling altitude, Lt. McArthur went through them instead.

"God help us," Stan prayed. These weren't Flak-caused shock waves jarring them, but nature's own version, bouncing them around like a bird's feather in a tempest. It reminded Stan of what they had gone through in Florida.

Finally, flying on fumes, *Hot To Go*'s wheels touched Grottaglie's runway, and Stan let out a sigh of relief as they taxied into a parking space between the rebuilt, ready-to-fly *Bird* and the just-having-returned *Skipper*.

Walking on air, Stan met Harry as he painfully lowered himself out of *Skipper*'s bomb bay. It had been a rough, eight-hour-long mission for a pilot's leg muscles. Harry enthusiastically pumped Stan's hand, congratulating him on the completion of his 50th, while Stan led Harry over to *Bird*, handing him his own Argus C3. While he had completed his 50th in *Hot To Go,* somehow it just wouldn't be right not to have his picture taken in front of *Bird,* forever thought of as his plane.

Writing that night, Stan tried to put into words what he was feeling:

How does it feel to be done? Really, I can't tell just yet. I still expect to fly, to face the flak. It is a definite relief. I really didn't expect to finish. There were just too many fellas going down. I've really wondered just why certain fellas are lost and others not. I'll never understand it. Vic [Victor Jensen, 719th co-pilot] *and I went to church and sang in the choir. That makes four Sundays in a row. Really a crude affair. Sit on bomb cases and the organ is really a sad instrument. Really wheezes around. Chaplain isn't too hot either. All I can say is, I'm thankful.*[13]

"Stan" in front of Worrybird's nose art following his 50th and final mission. 6 August, 1944. [Author's collection]

13. Stanley, William G. Personal WWII Diary: August 6, 1944 entry. Author's collection.

22

TOGETHER AGAIN?

THIS WAS A DAY for which *Bird* and *Skipper* had been waiting a long time—to be flying together again. Even in the predawn darkness they could sense each other's infectious grins.

"You stay tucked up close on my wing, *Skipper*," *Bird* instructed as her new crew arrived and made their way to their appropriate stations. She was a new ship to them, too. Time to get familiar.

"Don't you worry there, girl. I'll be as close to you as a tick on a hound dog," *Skipper* replied. "Oh, how I've missed her," he thought, gazing affectionately at *Bird* as *Jimmy*'s headlights flashed across her ridiculous nose art. He wouldn't have traded it for world peace.

They would need to stick close together for safety. They had just learned from *Jimmy* that their target was an oil refinery well into Slovakia, almost to the Polish border. This would be their furthest mission yet. They'd be over enemy territory for over 500 miles. "And get this," *Jimmy* blurted, sounding almost as braggartly as *Toledo*. "Some fool of a brass hat decided our Wing doesn't need escorts!" Close together indeed.

Lined up on the taxiway like lemmings, with their engines idling, the old familiar pre-mission nerves circulated through *Bird*. But she knew that once her pilot revved up her engines and released her brakes, beginning the race down the runway, her nerves would evaporate like West Texas rain in the sand, as *Skipper* would say. But not today.

Red flares suddenly arced across the sky, squashing everyone's mission expectations. For some it was a relief. It was, after all, going to be a rough one. Others were disappointed, for it would have been their 50th and final mission. *Bird* and *Skipper* were with the latter, they wanted to fly together that badly.

But there was always tomorrow.

Grottaglie Outdoor Theater, August 10, 1944, 22:00 hrs.

"I'M SURE YOU GUYS are tired of looking at this ugly mug. So how 'bout I bring out a pretty lady? Would you like that?" Jack Haley asked the now-boisterous crowd. That line never failed to bring out the primal instincts of a thousand sex-starved, twenty-year-old boys-turned-men.

"Geez. You'd think you haven't seen one in a while," Jack said, breaking out in a wide, expansive grin. "Without further ado, Mary Brian! Give her a hand" was barely heard over the whistles, cheering, and cat calls.

"Wow, these boys mean business, Jack," Mary said, strutting across the stage and grabbing the microphone. "They're a rough bunch. Don't let those swanky uniforms deceive you." She eyed the men, some in their "pinks and greens," others at least wearing ties. No overalls, flight suits, or even Eisenhower jackets here. Not for a USO stage show.[1]

"You better watch it, Jack. I bet if you were in your Tin Man costume, they'd be up here with tin snips cutting out patches for their planes," she quipped.

Jack was about to respond with a quip of his own when suddenly the stage, the faces in the audience, and the entire theatre were bathed in a quick flash of bright yellow light fading to orange. Then the rolling, deep concussion swept over everyone. Those in the crowd knew what had just happened. They had heard it many times before. A plane had just crashed and exploded on approach, attempting to land in the dark.[2]

For the past twelve nights, the Group had been practicing night take-offs and aerial rendezvous and landings, just like the British RAF. Something special was looming. With the recent increased bombing of gun positions and harbors on the southern French coast, the answer was obvious to everyone: a second invasion of France was approaching. It was just a question of exactly when.

Two hours earlier, Lt. Cruiser Crossley and a skeleton crew of four others had climbed into *Skipper* to get in some more of the required night flight training. All of the ships had been through it. Even *Bird*. The recent cancelled missions meant more time for training.

---

1. 449th Bomb Group Association. *Tucson to Grottaglie*, p. 111. 1985. Overhead theater photographs of 449ers waiting for performances of "*Rhapsody in Blue*" and comedian Joe. E. Brown, show all men, officers and enlisted alike, dressed in uniform coats and ties.

2. Jack Haley of *Wizard of Oz* fame, Mary Brian, Frances Faye, Betty Yeaton, and Judy Manners gave 50 USO performances over seven weeks across the Italian front. Their Grottaglie appearance was the evening of August 13th. The movie, *See Here, Private Hargrove*, was actually being shown in the theater when *Skipper* crashed, lighting up the screen.

"Sure wish we'd get this over with. I've flown blind once before and I didn't like it," *Bird* said, watching flight engineer Sergeant Louis San Antonio hand turn *Skipper*'s number three propeller. She was scheduled for flying blind tomorrow evening; therefore, she was just a spectator tonight.

"Oh, it's not too bad," replied *Skipper* as Lt. Bernie Gray settled himself into the right co-pilot's seat and began his engine-starting sequence. "Just have to trust the instruments, that's all."

After engine warm-up, Crossley released the parking brakes and *Skipper* began his turn onto the taxiway. "I'll see you in a bit, kid. Remember, this is just routine."

A sudden chill surged through *Bird*'s five miles of wiring, her nervous system. She had heard those words before, in another lifetime. In Tucson, the Rincon Mountains, and Pensacola. Scenes of routine death. "*Skipper! Skipper!*" she yelled to warn him. But it was too late. His wheels were just now leaving the ground.

Flying over Grottaglie, Skipper marveled at the simple beauty of the town's nightlights which reminded him of a swarm of late evening fireflies. He wished *Worrybird* was beside him to enjoy the moment. Even in the pitch-black darkness, he knew he would have been able to sense her presence, their thoughts and dependence tethered together as one. It was rare indeed when they both could enjoy the actual freedom of virgin flight such as this.

Mesmerized by the solitude of the night and the constant droning of his engines, it wasn't until Lt. Gray pulled back his throttles and lowered his flaps and Lt. Crossley turned his yoke and applied right rudder to initiate a banking turn for the landing approach, that *Skipper* knew he was in deep trouble. It happened so suddenly, for he had been complacent. While Lt. Crossley had to simultaneously rely upon five different dimly lit instruments to gauge his banked, night-time approach, the impending disaster was inherent to *Skipper*. Instinctively he knew that without quick action by the pilots they all were going to die.

"Lieutenant! Look at my air speed and bank indicators. Give me some throttle for God's sake!" *Skipper's* pleas came too late. He stalled and his right-wing tip cut a furrow into the ground.[3] In the fleeting few seconds it took for his nose to ram into the soft earth, catapulting him into a fuselage crushing cartwheel, *Skipper's* brief six-month life flashed before his eyes as his fuel tanks exploded. His birth, the ecstasy of his first winged flight, the camaraderie of fellow planes, the feeling of sorrow upon the loss of those same planes ... the destruction he himself had unleashed. As the final blast of fiery hot metal fragments severed his vital wiring and hydraulic lines, his voice feathered into a whisper. *Skipper's* last vision and conscious thought was of the one who meant more than anyone or anything left in the war-torn world: "*Worrybird.*"

When the flash of light, followed shortly by the deep, thunderous rumble reached her, *Bird* instantly knew her soulmate was lost. It was as if a glass fuse had blown, abruptly cutting off the constant presence of *Skipper,* intertwined with her own consciousness. She could have sworn she felt *Skipper's* actual presence as a soft, southern breeze cooled her still warm sunbaked skin.

Over the next month, *Bird's* life, and her family, totally unraveled. The day after *Skipper's* death, another plane, *Brass Monkey*, was lost during night training. Even when Harry climbed into her pilot's seat three days later for a mission to take out large German coastal guns, she couldn't appreciate his comforting, familiar hands on her yoke.

<u>Grottaglie Airfield Taxiway, August 15, 1944, 02:30 hrs.</u>

---

3. Blomgren, Norman E. The War Diary of Capt. Norman E. Blomgren: August 10, 1944 entry; Simmons, Robert M. Diary: April 3, 1944 to August 29, 1944. August 10, 1944 entry. Author's collection.

THE MOONLESS SKIES were ridiculously dark at 02:30 as *Bird*, idling on the taxiway, passed the time observing the shimmering overhead star constellations as she waited for her turn to take off. There were twenty-four planes of the Group in front of her. Her belly was full of 100-pound fragmentation bombs to drop on German coastal troop and gun emplacements precisely one hour before the U.S. Army's VI Corps was to land on the beaches of southern France.

Bird's night vision was suddenly extinguished as the sky was once again grotesquely lit by the ignition of not only 2,700 gallons of high-test gasoline, but the discharge of 4,500 rounds of ammunition and the detonation of 4,000 pounds of bombs. *Bucket of Bolts #2*, being flown by Lt. James G. Allen and Lt. Leo A. Betzen, had failed to climb enough to avoid the invisible power lines at the south end of the runway. The feeble light of the just now rising crescent moon had not been enough to illuminate the deadly braided filaments. Further take-offs were delayed twenty minutes to let the explosions subside, yet everyone still had to fly over the conflagration fifty feet below them where the released souls of eleven crew members were being transformed into stardust.

Over the next week, *Bird* would lose three more of her close-knit, olive-drab family. *Patches* would crash land on the island of Corsica trying to get home, while *Sweet Mother* and *Lonesome* were flown off by skeletal crews, never to be seen again. *Toledo* spouted the gossip that you didn't want to be flown off like that. It meant only one thing for the war-weary olive drab planes: salvage.

Even when she bombed Ploesti for the last time on August 18th, *Bird* couldn't join in on the Group's celebration of the enemy oil center's final demise. Neither could she join in on Pop, Stan, Bob, and Harry's muted celebration. It had been Harry's 50th and final mission. For *Bird* had made a friend the day before. Something she swore she wouldn't do.

On the previous evening, eying last week's virgin newcomer parked next to her, *Bird* saw condensation dripping from its flaps. "Boy, this ship is as nervous as a teenager on their first date," she thought. Noticing the freshly painted #15 combat number painted on its tail, she realized it was the replacement for *Patches*. Sighing heavily and going against her rule of not making the acquaintance of any newcomers, she struck up a conversation. She thought she owed it to *Patches*.

"Hey there, kid," *Bird* said, trying to get *#15's* attention. "I noticed the serial number on your tail. You from Dallas?" she queried, noticing the number 2-78604. All 2-78XXX ships were from Dallas.

"Y-y-y-yes," *#15* replied. Having arrived at the Group six days prior, its new crew hadn't decided on a name yet.[4]

"Well so am I, though I predate you by quite a bit," *Bird* replied, eying the gleaming bright aluminum of the newcomer's "J" model skin. *Bird* was a "G." They had stopped making them not long after *Bird* rolled off the line. "First mission tomorrow?"

"C-c-can you tell?"

"Ha. Pretty obvious. I noticed Lt. Watson and his crew go into my old crew's tent. With them on board, you'll have nothing to worry about. They have almost 50 missions under their belts, so they know what they're doing. And you just tuck in next to your wingman. You'll be fine," *Bird* advised, exuding confidence for the newcomer's sake.

"Yeah, they are my crew. They received a bunch of care boxes from home and they said they were going over to 'Pop's' tent to share and have a few beers. Was he part of your old crew?"[5]

"Yep, my pilot," *Bird* said, a surge of nostalgia coursing through her. She could imagine the good times they were having now.

"Hey, I tell you what. I can't keep calling you 'hey kid' or 'hey neighbor.' Mind if I give you a name like an old friend of mine did for me?"

---

4. AFHRA. Maxwell AFB. Reel ACR-68. Aircraft Record Card 42-78604.

5. Simmons, Robert M. Diary, April 3, 1944 to August 29, 1944. August 17, 1944 entry. Author's collection.

"Not at all," replied the newcomer, who didn't stutter for once.

Eying the silver-bodied beaut up and down its fuselage, *Bird* stopped at its tail and noticed its combat number, fifteen. "*Keen-say.* That's what I'll call you. Sure heard plenty of Spanish back home, didn't we?"

A slight grin broke out under *Keen-say's* nose and the condensation stopped dripping.

As it turned out, *Keen-say* was to be *Bird's* wingman on the mission, flying off her left wing. A good place to be over Ploesti. However, providence intervened, and *Bird* couldn't stay to protect him. She had to return early after her number four engine caught fire soon after the next morning's takeoff.[6]

Keen-say had been left dangling by himself, feeling vulnerable in the back of their six-plane box. Sliding over into *Bird's* vacant spot, *Keen-say* felt better. He was now sandwiched between *The Buzzer* and *#31*, another new unnamed arrival that had come off the Dallas line the same day as himself. It was old home week.[7]

Seven hours later, *Keen-say* was in trouble. All returning planes circled while twenty-one-year-old Lt. Henry Watson attempted to land. Over Ploesti, Flak had taken out his ailerons and the rear left vertical stabilizer was actually gone. The only way Lt. Watson could control flight direction was by precariously alternating engine rpms. But one mile from base the number three engine quit. Only the gunners sitting against the bomb bay bulkhead survived the inevitable crash.

Later that evening, staring at the empty space occupied just that morning by *Keen-say, Bird* realized the explosion she had heard earlier had been the demise of her new friend and possible protégé. Being a brand new ship obviously didn't offer protection against Ploesti Flak.

---

6. AFHRA folder GP-449-SU-OP-S, 18 August 1944. Mission 116 Formation Position Map.

7. AFHRA. Maxwell AFB. Reel ACR-68. Aircraft Record Card 42-78596.

Bird felt a new emotion, one she hadn't yet experienced, or at least had chosen to ignore. Guilt. More precisely, survivor's guilt. If she hadn't returned early, she'd be the heap of smoldering, molten aluminum north of the runway, and *Keen-say* would be silently sitting in his spot thanking his lucky stars, or God, or whatever he believed in, that he hadn't been in *Bird*'s flight position. That Flak shell had been intended for her. It had been her turn, yet she had hoodwinked fate once again.

Even the return of Lieutenant Charles Lynch from his Rumanian imprisonment didn't cheer her. He had taxied her over to the squadron area the day she first arrived, introduced her to *Hoosier,* and was captured the next day after *Hoosier* disappeared into the Danube. Too many memories. And no sooner had she greeted him back than she lost Stan, Bob, and Harry a few days later. Only Pop was staying behind for now since he had things to do before he left for home.

A Group stand down had been declared, otherwise she would have missed them entirely. She had observed *Toledo* packed with men approaching her early one morning, burning more oil than gasoline, based on the black-blue smoke trail she was leaving. Then she noticed who it was—her boys!

Pop, Stan, Bob, and Harry untangled themselves, walked up to *Bird,* began to pat her affectionately, and then took pictures of themselves in front of her, reminiscent of the way her enlisted boys had done over a month earlier. Boys she hadn't seen since. It then slowly dawned on her that they weren't there to take her up as they had done so many times before. No, they were there to say goodbye! This was affirmed when they soon got back in *Toledo* and drove over to *Salty Dog,* got in, and eventually took off on their last flight together, in the direction of Naples.

Over the next five weeks, *Bird* would fly on twenty-four missions piloted by twelve different pilots. "I swear I'm being passed around like some cheap whore," she thought, as yet another new pilot came to check her out before that morning's mission. She had never felt so alone. She was now the oldest ship in the squadron after *The Buzzer* had been sent to headquarters, relegated to transport duties. They had emasculated him by planking over his bomb bay, pulling his guns, and installing, of all things, seats. Humiliating is what it was. Besides *Nancy Jane #2*, who had arrived a few weeks after her, *Bird* was the only other olive drab plane left out of the now twenty-member-strong squadron.

Occasionally, Pop would walk by and glance in her direction, as if to make sure she was still around. Soon, very soon, she would get her wish. She would be flown by Pop one last time.

23

DEATH

GROTTAGLIE, 719TH SQUADRON PARKING AREA, SEPTEMBER 19, 1944, 14:00

*B*IRD FELT THE ALL TOO familiar tickling under her nose. It was a sensation she had felt many times before, seventy-three times to be exact. With a slow downstroke of the thin brush, glistening with bright yellow paint, Sgt. Lambertz was about to put the finishing touches on his work when the approaching whine of a Jeep engine stopped him in mid-stroke.

The approaching Jeep also caught *Bird's* attention for a couple reasons. First, it wasn't *Toledo*, but a new Jeep calling himself *Chester*, after Ford's Pennsylvania plant where he had been built. Secondly, the driver was none other than Pop, and it was apparent that he was coming to see her. It had been a long time.

"Afternoon, Lieutenant. Or should I say Captain?" Lambertz said with a knowing grin, holding the paint brush in his dangling arm.

"Now don't jinx it. My papers only went in a little over a week ago, Sergeant," Pop replied, looking at Lambertz's recent artwork.

"Anything I can help you with, sir?" Lambertz asked, noticing Pop's intense stare and mouth slightly agape, as if he was about to say something.

Deciding not to reveal what he was really thinking, Pop started *Chester* back up. "Oh, nothing, Sergeant. Just finish what you're doing. She deserves that at least." And with that, the clutch was popped, sending a small rooster tail in the air as Pop quickly drove away.

Lambertz shrugged his shoulders, not quite understanding Pop's obscure meaning, and went back to finishing up the final details needed to complete his project.

Stepping off the ladder a minute later and taking a few steps back, Master Sergeant Clarence Lambertz, the only crew chief *Bird* had ever known, admired the work he had begun over five and a half months ago. The seventy-four yellow bomb icons and single swastika adorning her nose represented more than missions and the confirmed downing of a German fighter.

To him and his maintenance crew, those icons represented an ungodly number of man-hours, some of them in horrendous, exposed conditions, in order to keep *Bird* flying. Up in the air to face danger all over again. Clarence shook his head and glanced over at *Nancy Jane #2*, the only other olive-drab in a sea of gleaming aluminum, and wondered how long she could keep it up.

Bird was thinking the same thing. She was getting tired. Even her "new" engines, which now had almost 200 hours on them, were getting close to overhaul time. Her bones hurt.

But seeing Pop again had made her feel youthful, spirited, up to the task. If only she had her old crew back, she'd be up for another 50 missions, she told herself. But that was not going to happen. They had left her, gone home, never to return. For another thing, the Group had started a plane "pool," where squadron pilots and their crews were assigned planes before a mission, whichever six to ten planes were up to the challenge that morning. The intimate camaraderie between a plane and its crew was gone.

Ramsey, Aldrich, Bache, Nelson, Witt, Waller, Kilpatrick, and now, for this morning's mission to Kraljevo, Yugoslavia, Mugler. All of them were just names. Names of pilots who in the past month had flown her just once. It was tough feeling part of a team when there was no consistency, no feeling of ownership. Besides, it seemed that bad things happened to her when piloted by one of those single-flight pilots.

It had been Lt. Krawiec piloting her over Ploesti when she was ripped to shreds, eventually leading her to be passed around like a cheap party favor. This also led to the boys not finishing up their missions with her, cruelly not giving her a chance to really shine for them one last time.

It had been Lt. Rogers piloting her over Bologna, Italy, when four hung-up 500-pound bombs eventually decided to drop, landing squarely on an unsuspecting Italian farmhouse two miles outside of Bolagnina.[1] That one got to her. She wasn't sure why because she knew, she had seen, the damage she was capable of delivering. She typically justified the devastation because it was to Hitler's war machine. It had to be stopped, no matter what. That was her whole purpose in life. But that farmhouse, those inside eating their noontime dinner before they went back out into the fields, they were innocent. She was glad that Stan hadn't been the bombardier. That would have added yet another chapter to his litany of expanding nightmares.

There had been one pilot, though, who had piloted her nine times during that period of time: Lt. Harry Mahoney. She had almost gotten used to the feel of his hands. Almost. She still yearned and prayed for the feel of Pop's hands on her yoke and controls just once more. She'd give anything for that.

---

1. AFHRA folder GP-449-SU-OP-S, 5 June 1944. Mission 74. Ship #3 Interrogation Report.

<u>Grottaglie, 719th Squadron Parking Area, September 20, 1944, 08:00 hrs.</u>

BIRD HAD JUST WATCHED seven of her squadron mates successfully take off for a mission to bomb a German airfield outside of Bratislava, Slovakia, when she noticed *Chester* coming her way loaded with passengers. While she didn't recognize the two riding in the back, she certainly knew the one riding shotgun: Pop. And not only that, he was wearing his flight suit and cap. Could it be? When they got out and Pop opened her bomb bay doors for entering, she knew her prayers had been answered. Maybe there was something to this religion stuff after all.

"Hey there, *Chester*. See who's back to take me up again? My first pilot. My only pilot, if you ask me," *Bird* said with conviction. "I just knew he hadn't forgotten me." She was relishing the moment with his familiar touch, his voice, his presence of command. She didn't recognize the feel of the co-pilot or of the engineer's hands on her fuel valves, however. Not that that was unusual lately. Not with the constant changing of her flight crews. It was a shame the rest of the gang wasn't here, she thought, as she noticed Stan's empty bombardier station and all the vacant gun positions. "Funny, there's no one at Bob's navigation table checking the charts." That made her perplexed as to just what sort of flight this was going to be.

"Hey there, *Bird*," *Chester* replied, breaking her contemplation. He knew where *Bird* was heading. Just like the cantankerous *Toledo*, he too listened to the verbal exchanges of his fares. But unlike *Toledo*, he exercised discretion as to when, where, and to whom he would regurgitate the scuttlebutt. This was not one of those cases. *Bird* deserved that at least.

Once her wheels left the ground, she noticed that Pop wasn't letting her gain much altitude. Cruising at only a few thousand feet, at a heading slightly west of due north, *Bird* realized where she was probably heading. She'd been there many months before. Gioia. The boys had taken her up there to have some new radio equipment installed back in early May.

Chuckling, she recalled the flight with delight. For it hadn't been Harry occupying the co-pilot's seat, but Stan. His hands. That's the thing she mostly remembered. Big, calloused, farming hands, not yet softened by a year and a half of college, were gripping her yoke as he took over control from Pop. Good memories.

"That's what Pop's doing. He's bringing me to Gioia to be upgraded. Or heck, maybe even a big overhaul like they did to *Skipper*," she convinced herself. But a slight trepidation coursed through her frame when she remembered *Toledo*'s warning about being taken up by a skeleton crew. "You'll never return. You're heading to be scrapped," is what he had warned. "Well, they showed you, *Toledo*," *Bird* thought. "Took you away never to return. Replaced by *Chester*. Much more of an agreeable fellow, I must admit," she averred, though with an odd tinge of desire to hear *Toledo*'s incessant blathering once more. "Boy, I'm getting too sentimental here," she said as Pop lined her up for a landing.

The view of the parking areas adjacent to numerous hastily built hangars is what caught *Bird*'s eyes. 283 planes in various degrees of repair or disrepair lined the field, filled the parking areas, or were unceremoniously dumped to the side along fences. B-24s, B-17s, C-47s, and a few fighter planes filled out the rolls.[2]

Trepidation returned once again when Pop taxied her over to a large group of planes and cut her engines. Even after the co-pilot and engineer left the flight deck, Pop remained sitting, kneading his hands on her yoke. A new emotion emanated from Pop's seat. One she hadn't felt before. There had always been the feeling of the strain and stress of command, of being responsible for his crew's life. Of downright fear when enemy aircraft pressed the attack or when flying into an opaque wall of Flak. And

---

2. AFHRA folder GP-AD-41-HI. 1 September 1944. Unit History, September 1944. For the month of September, 1944, 49 B-24s and 202 B-17s were received for repair or salvage at Gioia.

when flying through nature's wrath or trying to land without some of her engines or controls. It was rare indeed that she had felt his elation from the pure joy of flying, and never when he was on a mission.

But this. This emotion was of sorrow and sadness, combined with a trace of guilt. But imprinted on it all was a sense of, well, thankfulness. Thankful of what? Of whom? Then she realized, "Of me?"

He was glad he had done this. Flown her on her last "mission." When he had heard yesterday that the *Worrybird* had been declared "war weary" and was to be flown to the Gioia depot, he made it abundantly clear to everyone that he would be the one who flew her, and absolutely no one else. Pop slowly lifted himself out of his seat and made his way out of the bomb bay. Walking to the waiting Jeep, he turned around, looked at her one last time, and whispered, *"At least one thing is comforting; the Krauts couldn't knock you out of the blue sky."*[3]

Watching Pop drive away sent mission-like shivers through her. The surrounding planes were of no comfort, for they had no souls. There was no greeting, no interplane conversation or camaraderie filling the air. This reminded her of the lifeless airplane "flotsam" she had flown over when landing at El Aouina Field, Tunisia, so long ago.

It was deathly quiet, and within those macabre surroundings, her imagination began to overwhelm her, just like when she was in the middle of a mission. "I've got to get a hold of myself here," she told herself. "At least until Pop comes back for me."

She then did what one of her boys did to soothe his nerves, his fear. *Bird* began to sing like Stan had done so many times before:

---

3. Blomgren, Norman E. The War Diary of Capt. Norman E. Blomgren: September 19, 1944 entry. Author's collection. This sentiment was actually written the evening before, when told of her "war weary" status. Pop's September 20th diary entry was *"Sure hated to say so long to that ship."*

"Off we go into the wild blue yonder, climbing high
into the sun,

Here they come zooming to meet our thunder
At'em boys, giv'er the gun

Down we dive spouting our flames from under

Off with one hell-uv-a roar

We live in fame or go down in flame

Nothing'll stop the Army Air Corps!"

EPILOGUE

Worrybird

POP NEVER DID come back for her. *Worrybird* was officially condemned after the salvaging of all her useful parts on February 4, 1945, exactly one year to the day from her acceptance into the Army Air Corps. Some birthday present.[1]

She was in the minority. Of the North American Aviation, Dallas-built B-24s that were sent to the 15th Air Force, 71% were lost. They never made it back to base following a mission, or were lost in the many accidents, such as what happened to *Skipper,* or they never survived the transatlantic trip

---

1. Email correspondence from Air Force Historical Research Agency researcher. *Worrybird*'s aircraft record card was missing from the microfilm file records. The AFHRA was able to discern her final salvage date from other archival holdings. See Historical Research Frustration Addendum.

in the first place. The other 29%, like *Worrybird*, were eventually salvaged, after giving their "last full measure" to the war effort.[2]

Bird's replacement, whose first mission was three days after her departure, lasted only three weeks. Known as *Spirit of Plainfield, NJ*, it was shot down over Vienna, Austria on October 17th. Its replacement, the fourth 449th B-24 to carry the #3 combat number, *Collapsible Susie*, was taxied over an abandoned latrine area. Its left landing gear collapsed, sending it through her wing and damaging the wing's two engines. Crew Chief Clarence Lambertz wasn't there to repair her. She was soon salvaged. It was rough bearing the combat number three on your rudders.

The worst, most gut-wrenching accident to occur, perhaps in the entire 15th Air Force, happened to *The Buzzer* during the cloudy, snowy midafternoon of December 9, 1944. Relegated to ferry service, *The Buzzer's* flight crew of five were transporting eleven 719th Squadron airmen, seven of whom had finished their fifty missions, to Naples for either R&R or a boat trip home. They never arrived, having slammed into a 5,000-foot mountain peak outside the Italian village of Oliveto Citra. Having completed fifty missions, including harrowing experiences to Ploesti, Munich, and Vienna, only to meet their fate against a snow-covered mountain peak on their home journey's first leg, was a grotesque, inexplicable example of just how unfair life can be. One that could test your faith. Over 2,700 years ago, the Prophet Isaiah preached that "...*peoples shall beat their swords into plowshares, and their spears into pruning hooks.*"

---

2. AFHRA. Maxwell AFB. Reel ACR-68. Aircraft Record Cards 42-78070 to 42-78692. The last ship sent overseas, 42-78692, named *Ramp Tramp* by his 464th Bomb Group crew, was lost over Neuberg, Germany on March 21, 1945.

A farmer outside of Oliveto Citra took that passage to heart when he beat *Buzzer*'s salvaged bomb bay doors into his chicken coop's roof structure.[3]

By late July 1944, B-24s produced at the Dallas plant were being sent to storage, deemed "excess." The Arsenal of Democracy was outproducing the demand from the machinations of war. All B-24 factories were told to cease production, save Ford's massive Willow Run plant in Ypsilanti, Michigan. A completed B-24 was, after all, rolling off the assembly line at the incredible rate of one every hour. Thank you, Edsel Ford.

Of the 18,483 B-24s built during the war, only thirteen are surviving today. Of those, only two are airworthy, and they are indeed flying: *Diamond Lil'*, owned by the Consolidated Air Force, and *Witchcraft*, owned by the Collings Foundation.

Even though the B-24 Liberator was the most produced military aircraft for the United States Armed Forces, few people remember it. Asked what was a famous WWII bomber, most military aviation enthusiasts will respond by naming the B-17 Flying Fortress, or possibly the B-29 Superfortress. B-24 enthusiasts in turn will ascribe the discrepancy, somewhat tongue-in-cheek, to the fact that the B-17 had an eleventh crew member that the B-24 did not have. That was a "public relations officer." Recently there was a cable network program on a channel that purports to be all about "history." A clip was shown of Ford's massive Willow Run B-24 factory, with B-24s as far as the eye could see. They described them as B-52s. Wrong plane, wrong war. B-24s just get no respect.

With recent loss-of-life crashes of a number of WWII aircraft, including two B-17s, it is only a matter of time before all WWII warbirds are permanently grounded. It will be a sad day for military aviation history when their engines go silent. Never to be heard again. Just as the voices of the airmen who flew them slowly fade into the dust of memory.

---

3. 449th Bomb Group Association. *Maximum Effort: A History of the 449th Bomb Group, World War II. Book IV*, pp. 250–251. 2000.

Back Yard Of Stanley Home, Wheaton, Illinois, Summer 1972

"MAKE SURE TO MIX in the aggregate that's settled to the bottom," my father, known to his crew mates as "Stan," instructed me as I pushed and pulled the concrete mix, almost unsettling the wheelbarrow. Scraping the mixture against the steel sides with the hoe drowned out all other sounds, just me against the concrete. So I did not notice what had suddenly caught Dad's attention. Not until I saw him standing off to the side with arms akimbo, staring intently toward the western horizon did I stop my mixing and listen.

The cloudless, blue sky was featureless except for a few jet contrails heading to and from O'Hare Airport. Something had caught Dad's interest enough for him to abandon his opportunity to educate me in the finer art of concrete-mixing. Unusual for him, as he was a driven, focused individual when a task was at hand. To me, the only thing out of the ordinary was the sound of an airplane engine; no, multiple engines, somewhere below the trees.

Then it appeared. At first just a flickering of motion between the tree branches. Suddenly there it was, almost an apparition, something out of time and place, a B-24 in flight at just a few thousand feet of altitude, backdropped against jet-engined contrails of modern, trans-ocean aircraft. As I watched it transect the western sky, it slowly dawned on my slow, dimwitted teenage mind that even after twenty-eight years, my dad recognized the sound of those four Pratt and Whitney engines, knowing what was approaching before it was even visible.

He just stood and stared, following the Liberator's flight until it disappeared over the roofs of nearby homes. He never said a word and I could tell he was deep in thought, in remembrance. I decided not to break that train of memory and remained quiet, standing motionless as the simple, unique sound of a B-24's droning engines transported my father back to 1944. At least those memories caused him to smile.

Worrybird as she would have appeared with her final paint scheme on September 20, 1944, on her way to the Gioia Depot, though the bottom ball turret would have been winched up into her fuselage. Tail markings were changed August 8, 1944. [Courtesy of Jason Stanley]

William G. "Stan" Stanley – *Worrybird* bombardier

May 11, 1945

PUSHING HIS AIRCRAFT'S THROTTLE to its stop while simulta-neously applying hard right and back-stick pressure along with hard right rudder, Stan attempted to execute a high-g roll. He was desperate. His pursuer had a potential gun solution on him, as he had been complacent. Complacency in a dogfight is one sure way to get killed. His attacker must have been complacent also, for he overshot Stan. Stopping his plane's climbing roll and sending it into a dive, Stan successfully positioned him-self behind his attacker, who was now the hunted.

Skimming fifty feet above the alien marsh and swamp terrain, Stan centered his opponent's cockpit in his gunsights. There was no need for a deflection shot. Pulling the imaginary gun trigger on his control stick, Stan visualized the machine-gun bullets ripping a stitch down the length of his roommate's plane's fuselage. Pulling up next to his "kill," Stan mimicked with hand gestures that he was low on fuel and they needed to return to base.

The Army Air Corps was in a quandary in the waning months of the war in Europe. What were they going to do with thousands of battle-hardened, trained flight officers who had completed their allotted missions? It was obvious: train them to be fighter pilots for the planned invasion of Japan. The Army wasn't done with them yet.

Stan learned to fly in the Stearman PT-13 bi-plane, stationed at Carlstrom Field outside of Arcadia, Florida. He always considered this time one of the best of his life, weeks of "dogfighting" with his roommate over the Florida Everglades. His dream of flying had finally come true, so many years after that frosty Christmas night of 1933.

Graduating from primary training a week after Germany surrendered, he was then sent to Maxwell Field in Montgomery, Alabama for basic flight training. Here he learned how to fly a "real airplane," to put it in his words. The AT-6 "Texan" had been built by North American Aviation in a building next to where *Worrybird* had been built. After graduation, he was sent to Selma to begin advanced flight training on August 6th, the day the *Enola Gay* dropped an atomic bomb on Hiroshima. He only got to solo in his invasion-designated aircraft, the huge P-47 Thunderbolt fighter-bomber, for one hour before they stopped the training. There was not going to be an invasion. The war was over, and his time as a citizen soldier was history. Now what?

Back home in Kansas, Stan was also back to being "Bill." He went searching for answers. He first sought advice from who else? His father.

A hard-working farmer, a lover of the land, my grandfather's advice to my dad was, *"Bill, my philosophy has always been that it doesn't matter what*

I am, or what I do; a farmer, or a politician, or a musician, as long as when I leave this earth, the world will be a better place because I have been here."[4]

In October of '45, Bill visited his music professor, Dr. Levi Dees at Southwestern College, located in Winfield, Kansas. He had attended for three semesters before the war intervened. While he loved working the dirt, he knew he didn't want to be a farmer. The world of science and engineering always intrigued his inquisitive mind. He ultimately decided to return to school with the help of the GI Bill. Besides, there was that auburn- haired, pig-tailed beauty of a music major sitting in Dr. Dees's outer office who he'd like to get to know better.

Bill married Cloyce Belle Brown of Halstead, Kansas the following August, and they soon started a family while he completed his schooling at Southwestern College. He graduated with a Bachelor of Science degree in Physics, and furthered his education at Kansas State College of Agriculture and Applied Science with a Doctorate in Chemistry. Then it was time to find a job.

The young family that now included two children had scraped by on the $75 a month GI Bill. The offer to be a research chemist for Standard Oil of Indiana seemed like a Godsend. However, it wasn't so simple for a man with high morals and a strong conscience. War memories intervened in his thought process.

He had to square the incongruity of working for a company that, just a few years earlier, he had been doing his best to bomb out of existence at Ploesti. Heady stuff.

He evidently quelled his concerns, for he ultimately had a thirty-three-year career with Standard Oil. He spent his time in the laboratory challenging his inquisitive mind devising refinery process improvements, developing new plastics, to probably his most gratifying personal achievement, creating the rocket fuel for NASA's Mercury space program.

---

4. Stanley, William G. *Remembrances from the Past.* 2005. Author's collection.

3,000 Feet Above Atlanta, May 23, 2005, 11:00 hrs.

"DO YOU WANT to take the stick, Mr. Stanley?" asked the pilot, now wondering if that was the prudent thing to do, giving controls of a Waco WWII bi-plane trainer over to an eighty-two-year-old. "Well, sure! It's just a matter of remembering your training, that's all," Bill said as he put his hands on the stick and settled his feet on the rudder pedals.

He then showed the "youngster" that he still had what it takes. For the next thirty minutes, Dad put the aging Waco through its paces. Performing turns, rolls, stalls, and loops, the experience brought him back to those wondrous, easygoing times when he was young, flying carefree over the Florida Everglades. *It was just like riding a bike.*

My father was the last of *Worrybird*'s "band of brothers" to leave us. Dying peacefully in his sleep, William G. Stanley, 95, flew his last mission on 8 June 2019. At least it wasn't Ploesti.

To view a 2008 Library of Congress, Veterans History Project interview of "Stan," scan the QR code or follow the web link: https://www.loc.gov/resource/afc2001001.72949.mv0001001/

Norman "Pop" E. Blomgren – *Worrybird* pilot

Written by his son, Norman Burton

Pop with a pensive look on his face lying on his bunk. After a mission?
[Author's Collection]

NORMAN E. BLOMGREN was born on December 9, 1917 in McHenry, Illinois, the second son of a solidly middle-class Swedish store owner named Lewis Blomgren and his Swedish wife, Teckla. Norm and his brother, Lewis, Jr., grew up in a lakefront house on the Pistakee Bay, an idyllic setting for two young boys. They sailed boats, fished, and later raced hydrofoils, an early indication of Norm's love of fast machines. After high school he found himself working at Montgomery Ward and Company, but the war was soon to change his life completely.

Selected for pilot training in the Army Air Force, he completed his training and was assigned to fly B-24's for the 15th Air Force, 449th Bomb Group, 719th Bomb Squadron based at a bombed-out airbase near Grottaglie, Italy. He gained the nickname "Pop" because he was 27 years old in a world of 20-year-old men.

After surviving 50 combat missions over southern Europe, he returned home to Pistakee Bay where he met and married Shirley Covalt, an attractive, headstrong woman from a relatively wealthy family. Her nickname was "Sassy" and she lived up to that moniker throughout their tempestuous marriage. He demonstrably loved Shirley till the day he died.

After the war, while everyone else was returning to civilian life, he chose to make the Air Force his career. This decision was guided by a simple truth: he loved to fly airplanes and he liked the Air Force life. The first post-war posting for the newly married couple was the Panama Canal Zone. He dragged his new bride away from her familiar world to a place she could never have imagined. It turned out to be an exciting place to live, and she made the adjustment quickly. While in the Canal Zone they became fluent in Spanish, had a great time driving their Jeep and exploring the beaches, and Shirley gave birth to their first child, Barbara Ann.

Their next transfer came in 1949, back to the USA to a truly unique installation, Hamilton AFB. It was the same base where, five years earlier, Norm and his crew had picked up *Worrybird*. Just north of San Francisco on the Bay, the entire base was white Spanish stucco and red tile roofs. The surrounding area was one of God's gifts to humanity, with giant Redwood forests, beautiful beaches, and snow skiing all within a short drive. They made great use of the nature around them by constantly exploring. Norm fell in love with the area and always dreamed of coming back to live there. At this point two good things happened. Norm was promoted to Major, and he got his dream job, instructor pilot in his beloved P-51D Mustangs. Fast machines. Though I should have said three good things happened; I was born at the base hospital in 1951.

The Air Force was soon to shake up the family again in 1953 with a transfer to Asuncion, Paraguay. Asuncion is situated deep in the jungle at the headwaters of the Parana River, dead center in South America.

Needless to say, the little rich girl from McHenry, Illinois was pretty sure she wasn't going to like this transfer... she was wrong.

In Paraguay the American Military lived like royalty ... which was right up Shirley's alley. We had a small mansion, maids, a cook, and a 1953 Chevy, highly prized in South America. As kids, my sister and I grew up chattering in Spanish and playing in the jungles. Norm and Shirley lived like a 1940s' Bogart and Bacall movie, cigarette in the right hand and martini glass in the left. The American Military community loved to throw parties outdoors in the beautiful surroundings: jungle patios, pet monkeys, and war stories. As for "Pop," the MAAG, (Military Air Assistance Group) worked as "USAF Ambassadors" to the South American air forces. They were given one "Super Goony," a C-47 with the big Pratt and Whitney supercharged engines to make it over the Andes. I think they wore that plane out traveling to Santiago, Rio de Janeiro, Lima, Buenos Aires, and La Paz. Dad, as always, had one hand on the yoke and the other on a camera pointed out the window.

Then in the late 1950s, the papers came in and pulled us out of our little paradise, back to a modest life of middle-class Americans in Georgia, at Tinker AFB. Norm got the chance to pick up his jet rating there. Faster machines.

Thankfully, we were soon transferred to Langley AFB, Virginia. This was a nice transfer for all of us. As for the kids, we lived on the same street as original Mercury astronauts and played with their kids. Langley was HQ for NASA at the time.

This was a big career move for Norm: he got a promotion to Lt. Colonel and was given the task of putting together the first squadron of KB-50s. What's a KB-50? The Air Force was developing the new art of air refueling, and the biggest plane in the inventory to lift fuel into the air was the B-29 Superfortress bomber. They filled the bomb bays with gas tanks and strung three hoses with funnel-like hook-ups for fighters to fuel up. The B-29 at full throttle flew right at the stall speed for most of the fighters of the day, making the hook-up a tough proposition. I believe Dad was instrumental in the idea to sling two jet engines on the wings, and the KB-50 was born. They had "4 turning and 2 burning."

The story of Norman Blomgren almost ended here. One day on the ramp during the engine run-up, a fire broke out in the fuselage of his fully fueled KB-50. He rang the fire bell and waited for everyone to get out. When the plane was clear his exit was in flames and he barely managed to jump through one of the small windows in the cockpit, where he sprained an ankle and crawled away before the whole thing blew up in spectacular fashion. I saw the smoke from our front yard and had no idea it was my dad's plane.

Fortunately, the story continues. One average day in 1960 Dad came home with papers... a transfer to Santo Domingo, Dominican Republic. We grabbed the World Atlas and looked it up... the Caribbean, next to Cuba. A couple of weeks later we were there.

Shirley was once again in heaven. We had our mansion back, and this one was bigger, with two maids, a cook and a houseboy named Francisco. We had another C-47 at the disposal of the military families. This plane was our "station wagon" to fly to Puerto Rico for groceries and for the other needs of the American military community. I was a teenager in braces, and that bought me a ticket on the flight every month to see the orthodontist. Dad, much to the distress of his copilot, would put me in the left seat and let me fly most of the trip. I got a lot of hours but he never signed my logbook.

Then one day in 1962 Norm came home with papers again ... Alamogordo, New Mexico. Back to the World Atlas... this one was in the middle of nowhere. We kids were not looking forward to this transfer. Alamogordo is where they set off the first atomic bomb and we were pretty sure it was going to be a barren wasteland. To our surprise the place really was the "Land of Enchantment."

This posting was to be our longest, and Norm's last before retiring in 1970. We spent most of the summer weekends camping and water skiing on a huge New Mexico lake. Shirley was absent for these trips as she could not seem to get the hang of camping, no surprise.

It was during this time that Norm did something that was nothing short of amazing: he got his college degree! He had always felt that he missed having a degree, and took advantage of an Air Force program to get one from the University of Nebraska. I think the only disappointment in Dad's Air Force life was never making "Full Bird Colonel" before taking full retirement in the spring of 1970.

But his life was not over at 53 years old; he and Shirley were looking for a new one. They just didn't know where they were going to find it. That's when they came up with a brilliant plan: they bought a travel trailer and connected it to Shirley's Cadillac and pointed it West. The idea was to try out places to live and look for a job along the way. It was one of the best summers of our lives as we pulled our "house" through all the little camper parks throughout the Western states. The battle was between Shirley, who had become an avid "desert rat," and Norm, who was trying to point them back to California. In a compromise that I never understood, they wound up in south Texas.

Norm got a job as the manager of the Harlingen Country Club, which wound up being a sweet deal for the two of them, as they could now live on the golf course, and Dad could walk the half block to the clubhouse.

But Shirley was endlessly trying to move them back to the desert, and in 1975 her efforts paid off. The couple left Harlingen to move to Scottsdale, Arizona. This proved to be short-lived as Norm tried his hand at a vending machine business and was bored to death without a "real job." In 1976 he was interviewing for club manager positions again and was surprised by a job offer from Preston Trail Country Club in Dallas, Texas. So again they moved, purchased a new house, and set up a new life in Dallas.

"Pop" was a lucky man throughout his life. He got himself and the crew of the *Worrybird* through 50 missions, won a lot of poker games, and generally got a lot of breaks in his life. But his luck ran out in 1978 when a pain on the right side of his back turned out to be liver cancer.

The doctors gave him three months; he cheated them and lived nine. On his deathbed in the hospital the cancer had spread to his brain and he was delirious toward the last. I can tell you, though, that his heart was always in an airplane, perhaps the *Worrybird*, because in his final delirium he was asking, "Did you check the cockpit?" He died on Flag Day, June 14, 1979.

We moved him to the Holloman AFB Chapel for the service. The Chaplain called him "One of the heroes of the raids over Ploesti." Upon our exit, a formation of F-15s thundered overhead in the "missing man formation." He was buried with a 21-gun salute at the National Cemetery in El Paso, TX.

Prologue

IT HAS BEEN SAID that a son tries to surpass his father's achievements. I'm afraid I don't stand a chance of being able to do that. What always struck me about the man was how gentle and kind he was. I think this story tells it all:

In New Mexico, the highway to White Sands ran right on the other side of our backyard fence. One day when I was about 13 years old a car broke down on the other side of the fence. It was a scene out of *The Grapes of Wrath* with a skinny young man, his skinny wife with a baby in her arms, and their broken-down old car. My dad grabbed me and we drove out the base gate and back up to where they broke down. He spent his Saturday afternoon driving the 16 miles back to Alamogordo for parts and driving back, and then fixing this family's car. When it was running again, he reached in his wallet and handed the young man a $50 bill. They just got in their car and drove off without thanking him. But Dad didn't care. It wasn't about getting thanks. It was about helping someone who needed help. He did it all on autopilot.

What a guy!

Harry N. Bursten – *Worrybird* co-pilot

Information supplied by Stanley Bursten, Harry's son

Harry taking a self-portrait with his Argus C-3. The camera was later stolen while he was visiting Rome. [Author's Collection]

AS WITH MOST RETURNING WWII veterans, Harry did not talk much about his wartime experiences. It was time to move on with his life. First on the agenda was getting married, as most men did upon returning home. Gertrude Carr became his bride in their hometown of Kansas City, Missouri in July of 1945. Within a few years they found themselves living in Denver, Colorado, where Harry supported his growing family as a wholesale furniture salesman.

Soon two of his older brothers offered him a position in their small chain of Kansas City grocery stores called Justrite. So back home they went: Harry, Gertrude, and their three young sons. Harry worked his way up, eventually becoming the manager of their largest store. Later, as his brothers got out of the business, Harry bought their equity. Eventually he was able to expand to four store locations, situated in each quadrant of the city.

One of his career highlights was being selected to be part of a twenty-six-member food industry delegation arranged by the United States Cultural Visitation Exchange Program in 1964. Visiting England, Belgium, Sweden, Germany, Poland, Hungary, and Russia, they met governmental officials and exchanged ideas with European food wholesalers and retailers. One of the highlights of the visit was to tour Russia's Gosudarstvenny Universalny Magazin, or GUM, which translates to "State Department Store." Situated in the middle of Moscow's Red Square, it was, and is, a beautiful monument of architecture. However, based on the photographs taken by Harry, while quite large, it wasn't modern or sophisticated when compared to its Western counterparts. Perhaps being under forty-seven years of Communism had something to do with that.

Harry retired in 1989 after competition from a large grocery chain put him out of business. He died at the age of 78 on April 21, 1999.

Robert M. Simmons – *Worrybird* navigator

Written by Barbara Simmons, Bob's daughter

Bob was always studying. Not sure how he could concentrate with the "nose art" on his wall though. [Author's Collection]

MY DAD, ROBERT "BOB" SIMMONS, began his government service as a civilian at Olmstead Air Field in Middletown, Pennsylvania in 1940. He registered for the national military draft in late 1940 and was inducted into the Army on June 19, 1941. He was assigned to Camp Lee, Virginia for basic training as a medical soldier. In September 1941 Dad reported to Langley Field, Virginia to take a three-day written test for cadet training. He returned to Camp Lee, completed basic, and was assigned as a clerk at a hospital at New Orleans Airfield as a Private.

When war was declared, Dad was assigned as one of five enlisted personnel to the 2nd Reconnaissance Squadron at what would later become Edwards AFB in California, where they flew submarine patrols. In the spring of 1942 he was promoted to Pfc. In the summer, with the encouragement of his Medical Officer, he applied for Officer Cadet School. He was accepted, and Aviation Cadet Simmons reported to Nashville, Tennessee on October 7, 1942, and was sent to preflight school. He was unable to master the landing techniques so he could not become a pilot. He requested another chance to undergo aviation training, and was assigned to Santa Anna on March 20, 1943, where he began his training. Upon its completion he was assigned to aircraft gunnery school in Las Vegas, Nevada on June 10, 1943. He then entered Navigational Training at Mather Airfield, California on August 1, 1943. The school moved to Ellington Field, Texas in October 1943, and Dad graduated as a 2nd Lt. on December 4. On the 16th he reported to Mountain Home, Idaho, and his journey with the 719th Bomber Squadron began.

When his missions were completed, Dad returned to his hometown, Marietta, Pennsylvania, on September 28, 1944. He married my mother Betty just ten days later, on October 7, and reported to Miami Beach shortly thereafter. He was given a physical, and after three weeks of daily exams and normal EKGs, after showing signs of a heart problem, the doctor finally found what he was looking for and Dad was medically discharged on December 26, 1944 due to atrial fibrillation.

They moved back to Pennsylvania where Dad continued his civil service career with the Department of the Air Force at Olmstead Air Force Base, and raised my brother and I in Hummelstown, Pennsylvania. When Olmstead closed in 1966 we moved to Okinawa, then still under U.S. jurisdiction. He returned to Tinker AFB, Oklahoma in 1971 and retired in 1976 after thirty-five years of service. He and mother spent their retirement years in Tucson, Arizona enjoying traveling and life in general.

Dad never spoke much about his time in the service, but he did keep a diary of some of his experiences, particularly the time with his crew overseas. He decided to convert his writings to print in 1995 and gave me a copy. That was the first time he had ever shared anything with me.

Dad died of congestive heart failure on April 4, 2004 at the age of 84.

The rest of the crew of the *Worrybird*

The whole gang together for one of their egg fries? Looks like they've already been in the Seagram's. [Author's Collection]

THE ENLISTED MEN of the *Worrybird* were no different than the rest of the 16.5 million men and women who served in the war—they just wanted to get back to life. Get back to normal by melding unceremoniously back into society.

Cecil Yeates, Joseph Windham, William Blankenship, Joseph Fox, Charley Debord, James Reed, and later-joining gunners Mark Turkiewicz of Hamtramck, Michigan and Peter Abromovich of Barnesboro, Pennsylvania all did so, with some taking advantage of the GI Bill to either start or complete their education. One became a high school teacher and a newspaper printer; one a computer technician; two became auto mechanics; while one picked up where he had left off and finished an almost forty-year railroad career, while another capped over fifty years in the Pennsylvania coal mines.

These men became part of the post-war middle class, the backbone that powered the United States' engine of prosperity that transformed us into the world's leading economic power and foremost bastion of democracy. They were members of the "Greatest Generation" that Tom Brokaw so eloquently labeled.

Some joined veteran groups such as the VFW or the American Legion, to enjoy the camaraderie or to take advantage of listening and talking with others who had similar, wartime endeavors. Most, however, went on quietly with life, rarely, or possibly never discussing their experiences. Their trials and tribulations were forever locked away, unless revealed much later in life, either in the spoken, or in this case written, word.

I certainly do not intend to belittle their contributions to the success of the *Worrybird,* and their efforts in keeping her and the entire crew safe during those harrowing missions by writing so little about them. I truly wish I knew more about their post-war lives. Perhaps someone will enlighten me of their further endeavors.

While scrutinizing more recent photographs of some of these men, with the imprint of time staining their once youthful faces, I look at the eyes. As is said, the eyes are windows into the soul. And I see that, in their youth, their hearts were touched with fire.

High Flight

Oh, I have slipped the surly bonds of earth and danced the skies on laugh-
ter-silvered wings,
Sunward I've climbed, and joined the tumbling mirth of sun split clouds
And done a hundred things you have not dreamed of – wheeled and soared
and swung
High in the sunlit silence. Hov'ring there,
I've chased the shouting wind along, and flung my eager craft through footless
halls of air
Up, up the long, delirious, burning blue, I've topped the windswept heights
with easy grace
Where never lark, or even eagle flew.
And while with silent, lifting mind, I've trod the high untrespassed sanctity
of space,
Put out my hand, and touched the face of God [5]

---

5. *High Flight* was written by Pilot Officer John Gillespie Magee, Jr., a Spitfire pilot for the Royal Canadian Air Force. He was killed over the skies of England in December 1941, three months after composing *High Flight*. It was recited at both Norman Blomgren's and my father's celebration of life services.

ADDENDUM

HISTORICAL RESEARCH FRUSTRATION

THE STILLNESS FOUND WITHIN the Air Force Historical Research Agency's reading room library was almost stifling. The only sound was the soft clacking of laptop keys from the lone occupant: me. I was anxious, my pulse quickening, as my fingers pressed the final key, prompting the much-anticipated file to open. I had just slid in a DVD-R which contained a file holding the Individual Aircraft Record Cards of all B-24s made at North American Aviation's Dallas, Texas plant. They were essentially their individual "birth" certificates as well as permanent records. Finally, I would be able to read a condensed, though cryptically abbreviated, life narrative of my father's plane. I could possibly answer some of my early nagging questions pertaining to *Worrybird*'s life, such as when was she "born," what were her cross-country stopovers enroute to Morrison Field, West Palm Beach, Florida, and perhaps most mystifying of all: what was the date of her final demise and where?

Quickly scanning to within ten planes of *Worrybird*'s 42-78173 serial number, I began to slow down to savor, to relish in the anticipation of the moment. My throat was becoming parched. I stopped breathing:

- XX170

- XX171

- XX172, here it comes...

- XX174. What the.....???

Frantically scrolling the mouse wheel back and forth, sending air-craft cards streaming across the screen like an old silent movie, I slowly, mournfully, came to the realization that *Worrybird*'s card was MIA. An audible "What the Fuuuu....!" embarrassingly escaped my lips, a murmur that would have made librarian Marion Paroo blush, and *Skipper* proud. Fortunately, I was still alone.

Out of the 750 North American Aviation, Dallas B-24 record cards, only one was missing. How could I have been so lucky? I should have immediately gone out and bought a lottery ticket.

I am used to the frustration of missing records when it comes to re-searching and exploring the brittle historical records of my other historical passion, the American Civil War. But that's understandable. After all, that was 160 years ago, and many records were burned (especially Confederate), lost, or never recorded for posterity. But World War II? That was just yesterday in the historical scheme of our nation's young history.

It wasn't until further examination of the preceding card, *Skipper*'s 42-78172, that I "found" *Worrybird*'s. The bottom few millimeters of *Worrybird*'s card was there, peeking out from behind, as if to taunt me. Apparently, the microfilming technician had not noticed *Worrybird*'s card "piggybacked" to the flipside of *Skipper*'s card. Alas, once microfilmed, the original record cards were disposed of. Sigh.

The only solace I have is knowing that, as in life, *Worrybird* and *Skipper* will be bonded together, to perpetually trod the high, untrespassed sanc-tity of time. My sincere apologies to John Gillespie Magee, Jr. for altering one of the last lines of his poem, *High Flight*. It just seemed so appropriate.

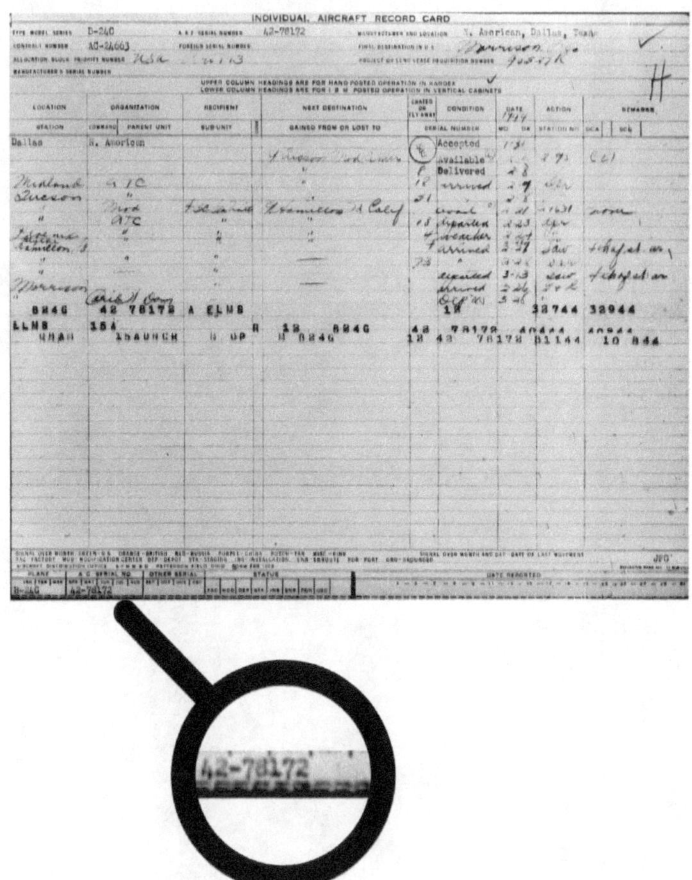

Skipper's 42-78172 Aircraft Record Card. The bottom set of base "perforations" is in actuality the base of Worrybird's 42-78173, its elusive ARC peeking out from behind. In the other 748 cards, the base is composed of a single set of perforations. [AFHRA Aircraft Record Card 42-78172]

AFTERWORD

U pon completion of this book, the realization of just how ordinary these citizen solders turned sky warriors were finally dawned on me. Ordinary people in extraordinary times. Of course, this was not limited to those solely overseas in combat. They could not have accomplished what they had without the support of the 135 million men, women, and children back on the home front. Whether they were men welding steel sheets onto the hull of a Liberty ship, women riveting aluminum sheets into nascent military aircraft, or children being the foot soldiers of the scrap metal, paper, and rubber drives, the United States homefront was in the war too. It had become all so personal with so many families contributing a son, father, or husband to the war. No one was untouched. Everyone made sacrifices. Some small, some the ultimate, but all contributed to the final victory on VJ-Day.

When my dad arrived home in September of 1945, he noticed two things missing from the farmhouse. The hickory post that had held the family's large cast iron farm bell was standing bare, denuded of his grandfather's bell. He also noticed a vacant shelf in the barrister bookcase which previously had held books and papers of special interest, including his great grandfather's copy of the *Personal Memoirs of U.S. Grant*. Private James K. Stanley had fought under then-Major General Grant and had spent his remaining years on the Stanley farm. Both items had been given up, respectively, to the metal and scrap paper drives. Small, but oh so personal sacrifices, gladly made, if they in any way helped bring their two oldest sons safely home. These seemingly insignificant contributions multiplied by 135 million citizens equated to victory.

Another aspect of *Worrybird*'s life story didn't come to mind until I was writing the Epilogue. This had to do with the significance of what her pilot, Lieutenant Norman "Pop" Blomgren, had accomplished by flying the *Worrybird* to Gioia on her last "mission." The odds were far against it from ever happening. Not all pilots kept the plane that they had flown over from the United States once they landed in their combat theater. Fewer pilots still survived their mission allotment with that same plane. After all, the vast majority of planes were lost in combat or accidents. Only a handful of pilots would have still been in theater when their plane, if it had survived, was sent to be scrapped. But Pop did more than that. He actually flew his plane on its fateful last mission to the scrapyard. Few, if any other pilots, did what Pop had done. From the very beginning to the bitter end, Pop had been there for *Worrybird*.

Was it worth it? My father pondered and wrangled with the answer to that question many times in his post-war life. Was the Army Air Corps' involvement in the Combined Bomber Offensive worth the incredible amount of time, money, and manpower spent delivering over 1.5 million tons of bombs to Germany's war machine? Much post-war scholarship has been written purporting that it was not. Those authors theorize that the effort would have been better spent strengthening Army ground troops, building greater numbers of tanks, artillery, ships, armaments, and a larger Air Corps fighter fleet with the ability to neutralize the Luftwaffe sooner. Post-war statistics do provide some cover for such a possibility. However, Mark Twain's attributed adage, "There are three kinds of lies: lies, damned lies, and statistics," may apply to this kind of Monday morning quarterbacking.

Who would know better about the consequences of the massive Allied bombing campaign than Germany's High Command? From General

Adolf Galland, the Luftwaffe's Chief of Fighters: "In my opinion it was the Allied bombing of our oil industries that had the greatest effect on the German war potential." Field Marshal Albert Kesselring, Germany's last Commander-in-Chief in the West, stated: "Dive-bombing and terror attacks on civilians, combined with the heavy bombing, proved our undoing. Allied air power was the greatest single factor for the German defeat." And from Dr. Hjaimar Schacht, Nazi Germany's Finance Minister: "Germany lost the war the day it started. Your bombers destroyed German production, and Allied production made the defeat of Germany certain."[1]

The *Worrybird* and her crew had been but a small cog in the United States' Arsenal of Democracy that delivered a death blow to Adolf Hitler's dream of a world-domineering Third Reich. Could the war in Europe have been defeated solely by the Army Air Corps? Certainly not. Could it have been won without them? Absolutely not. A reminiscence of freedom won that the world cannot forget.

---

1. Tillman, Barrett. *Forgotten Fifteenth*, p. 258. Washington, D.C.: Regnery History, 2014; *Maximum Effort, Book IV*. 449th Bomb Group Association. pp. 252–253. Panama City, FL: Norfield Publishing, 2000.

ACKNOWLEDGEMENTS

This book journey would not even have begun if not for the crew of the *Worrybird*, especially those who decided to put their thoughts on paper: William Stanley, Norman Blomgren, and Robert Simmons. To complete the story, a heartfelt thank you is given to Norman Burton, Stanley Bursten, and Barbara Simmons, who not only gave me valuable insights not found in their fathers' diaries, but also correspondence and documentation of their WWII experiences which neither I, nor my dad, possessed.

My immense gratification is given to the past and present members of the 449th Bomb Group Association. Without their diligence at preserving the history, stories, and photographs of the 449th, my story would not be anywhere near as complete. Please visit their website for stories and photographs of other crews and their aircraft. https://449th.com/

Without the help and diligence of the staff at the Air Force Historical Research Agency, I would have been completely lost amongst the over 100,000,000 pages of Air Force history. A special thanks to Tammy Horton and Archangelo DiFante, who sleuthed *Worrybird*'s ultimate fate.

I am indebted to Ken Murphy, Philip Stanley, and Jason Stanley for their initial critique of this manuscript. Their observations and suggestions were essential to the success of the completed project. Jason deserves additional gratitude for his artistic talents in creating the cover art along with numerous images throughout the book.

And last, but certainly not least, I am indebted to my wife Jane, for her love and support through our many years together. Additionally, as my first reader, she definitely did not spare the red ink during her many editing passes. It was wise of me to listen, and to heed her suggestions.